"Then you do care for me?"

Damaris prodded.

Gavin frowned down at her. "How could you believe otherwise? Every time we're together, I end up kissing you. At the Maidens, I almost did a great deal more."

His words and the pain behind them gave Damaris a warm feeling in her middle. "You were tempted?"

"Tempted? I was almost undone!" He turned back to the sea. "Any woman would know that. You taunt me."

"No, I wouldn't do that. I have so little experience with men. I thought you simply didn't care for me."

Gavin turned and pulled her into his embrace. "No woman is that innocent. You all seem born with the knowledge of how to drive a man insane. And you are better at it than most."

Dear Reader,

Although summer is drawing to a close, Harlequin Historical continues to provide the best historical romance has to offer.

This month, reacquaint yourself with bestselling author Willo Davis Roberts in the reissue of her epic saga, *To Share a Dream*. Three sisters flee England to find a new life in the colonies, but Massachusetts is not at all what they expect.

Healer Damaris Fleetwood battles for possession of her home in *Thornbeck*, a medieval romance by Lynda Trent. But when the Queen sends aid in the form of Sir Gavin Rutledge, can love yet win the day?

Author Susan Amarillas premiered in March Madness 1993 with *Snow Angel*. Her latest release, *Silver and Steel*, centers on Mary Clancy, who is convinced that the railroad is the answer to Rainbow Gulch's prayers, though attorney Alexandre Moreau is prepared to fight her every step of the way.

Popular historical author Ann Lynn makes her Harlequin Historical debut with *Beautiful Dreamer*. In this heartwarming tale, ex-Confederate soldier Connor O'Malley finds new purpose in life at Lindy Falen's dilapidated ranch, as well as a secret the beautiful Lindy is determined to hide.

We hope you enjoy these selections. Look for Harlequin Historicals next month when Claire Delacroix takes us once again to the pageantry of the Middle Ages and Merline Lovelace pens her third book in the *Destiny's Women* trilogy. Join us for all four exciting titles!

Sincerely,

Tracy Farrell
Senior Editor
Harlequin Historicals

Please address questions and book requests to:
Harlequin Reader Service
U.S.: 3010 Walden Ave., P.O. Box 1325, Buffalo, NY 14269
Canadian: P.O. Box 609, Fort Erie, Ont. L2A 5X3

LYNDA TRENT

Thornbeck

Harlequin Books

TORONTO • NEW YORK • LONDON
AMSTERDAM • PARIS • SYDNEY • HAMBURG
STOCKHOLM • ATHENS • TOKYO • MILAN
MADRID • WARSAW • BUDAPEST • AUCKLAND

ISBN 0-373-28832-8

THORNBECK

Copyright © 1994 by Dan & Lynda Trent.

Printed in U.S.A.

LYNDA TRENT

started writing romances at the insistence of a friend, but it was her husband who provided moral support whenever her resolve flagged. Now husband and wife are both full-time writers of contemporary and historical novels, and despite the ups and downs of this demanding career, they love every—well, *almost* every—minute of it. The author is always glad to hear from her readers.

**To Paul and Anita Story,
who know the path to the Maidens**

Prologue

"Can ye not push harder, my lady?" Meg asked uncertainly. "Don't give up yet."

Matilda lifted her head from the pillow in an effort to comply with her lady-in-waiting's wishes. The sound of an animal crying out in pain reverberated off the stone walls, and then she realized the scream had come from her. Exhausted, she fell back on the bed.

The room was hot even though it was still early spring. The midwife, who firmly believed that mothers in labor and newborn babes profited from warmth, had ordered several braziers of coals brought into the lying-in chamber. At the moment, Matilda could scarcely breathe the heavy air and wished in vain for the strength to order the coals taken away.

Meg, who had been Matilda's constant companion for years, seemed to know her mistress's thoughts. "We can't open a window, my lady. There's a storm brewing. Can ye not hear the thunder?"

Matilda listened and did indeed hear a distant growl.

It reminded her of the day she had come to Thornbeck as Owen Fleetwood's bride almost ten years ago. She hadn't known him, as their marriage had been arranged by their parents, but she had been well pleased, indeed. Owen was near her own age, gentle and handsome. From the first moment he had seen her, his eyes had held a softness for her. She had loved him almost with the first words they had exchanged. And despite his having been born the younger of two sons, Owen was to inherit the stronghold of Thornbeck.

Years earlier, when their king, Henry, the eighth of that name, had divorced Catherine of Aragon and married his leman, Anne Boleyn, the elder of the Fleetwood brothers had incurred first his family's, then his sovereign's wrath. William had claimed that King Henry had no valid reason, son or no son, to divorce his wife, the queen, and had been so vocal with his opinions that word traveled the length of England and seared royal ears. King Henry, never a man of great forbearance, had ordered that William be arrested for treason.

William and Owen's father was loyal to the crown to his last breath, and he agreed with King Henry that William had gone too far. William was, however, his son. By the time Henry's men had reached Thornbeck's almost inaccessible island, William had been warned and had sought and received asylum in Scotland. As a gesture of the senior Fleetwood's continued loyalty to the king, he disowned William and designated Owen as heir apparent to the family's castle and island.

Although Thornbeck was far removed from London, it was a valuable property. Situated just north of Holy Island in the North Sea, it lay almost on the border between Scotland and England. Whichever country held the island stronghold had a strategic launching spot from which to wage war on the other. For several generations the Fleetwood family had maintained and defended the fortress for the British crown, and as a reward for their service, King Henry had recently bestowed a barony on the family.

When Owen's father had realized he was about to die, he arranged for Matilda to become Owen's wife. A few months later, Owen stepped into the rank of baron. Matilda's life with Owen had been tranquil and happy. She knew of almost no wife who loved her husband as she loved Owen. But their happiness had been marred by the fact she had been unable to give Owen a son.

Matilda had been fertile, bearing a child almost every year, most of which were sons, but none of the babes had survived more than a few weeks. Matilda, like Owen, had been heartbroken over the row of tiny graves beneath the chapel floor in the tower. By the time she had quickened with the child she was now struggling to birth, Owen had given up hope that an heir would ever come.

Another muscle spasm racked Matilda, and she tightened her grip on the rope of sheeting the midwife had given her to pull on. A sharp pain tore through her.

"I see its head!" the midwife shouted. Her relief was obvious even to Matilda. "Push, my lady!"

Matilda tried again. Meg put her small hand on Matilda's swollen belly and tried to help her expel the child.

"I have her!" the midwife cried out. "It's a girl, my lady! A fair daughter!"

When Matilda heard the baby cry, she closed her eyes in silent thanksgiving that it was finally over. This birth had been so much harder than any of the others. Would she be able to live through another? "A girl," she whispered hoarsely.

"A beautiful girl," Meg amended. "Listen to her cry!"

Matilda could hear all the women who were attending her laughing with relief, and this told her more than anything else how near she had come to dying. But everyone knew a daughter, however much she might be loved, couldn't inherit a castle or anything else. Owen had needed a son.

Meg leaned closer to Matilda. "Next time, my lady. A son next time." Commiseration softened her voice.

Matilda opened her eyes. Meg had been not only a companion to her, but a confidante all the years she had lived at Thornbeck. "Next time?" she whispered, her voice breaking.

Meg looked away. "God be willing."

"I'll not survive another like this," Matilda said as the midwife finished her chore. "I marvel that I live still."

"Aye, my lady. I feared for you."

Matilda tried to smile as she patted Meg's hand. "Dear Meg. You never speak me false." She rolled her head on the pillow to see where the other ladies were cleaning the baby and wrapping her in a small blanket. "May I see her?"

"Of course." Edith, the eldest of her women, brought the babe to her. "Here she is. See how beautiful she is?"

Matilda pulled a corner of the blanket aside to see a tiny infant blinking at the light from the candles. She was red like all newborns, but already her skin was paling. Her hair was a dark red like Matilda's own and lay close to her well-shaped head.

"What name will you give her?" Edith asked. Edith was a decayed gentlewoman and a distant relative of Owen. The look she bestowed on the baby showed a pride of kinship.

Matilda thought for a minute. They hadn't discussed names, she and Owen, not this time. Although neither she nor Owen had said it, neither wanted to choose a name for a baby that might never draw a breath of air.

"You have to name her," Meg said anxiously. Meg was superstitious and had often told Matilda about how the fairies could steal away an unnamed child before its baptism. "The chaplain is waiting in the chapel," she added.

"Good. I want her baptized as soon as possible." This was an irregularity. Most babies were taken to church when they were older. The chaplain was waiting because it was unlikely that the baby would live long enough to follow custom. "Damaris," Matilda whispered. "I want to call her Damaris." There was no need to consult with Owen. He would allow her to name the baby whatever she pleased, especially as it was a girl.

"Damaris," Meg said with a smile. "Such a pretty name. She'll grow strong, God willing."

Edith took the baby away to show her to Owen and to take her to the chapel. Matilda closed her eyes as the women finished cleaning her and the room, and one by one they left, all but Meg.

"My lady?" Meg said uncertainly.

"I'm fine. It's just that I'm tired." Matilda tried to smile but she was almost numb with exhaustion.

Meg turned to go but Matilda said, "Meg, wait. Bring me the copper bowl." Her eyes met Meg's. "I have to know."

Meg hesitated as if she wanted to refuse. She alone knew Matilda possessed the second sight. Meg was fascinated by the gift, but also frightened of it.

"Please, Meg. I can't get the basin for myself," she said, her voice filled with pleading. "Are you so afraid of what I'll see?"

"Of course not, my lady," Meg lied. Dutifully she went to the water pitcher on the oak chest and poured some water into the copper bowl that had been hanging next to the chest on the wall. She brought it carefully to Matilda.

Painfully Matilda pushed herself up high enough to gaze into the water. She forced her thoughts to be still, and in a few moments, wavering pictures began to form in the water, seen only by her. After studying what she saw there for a while, she closed her eyes and lay back on the pillow, her face as pale as the sheet beneath her.

Meg glanced into the bowl, though she knew she wouldn't see anything. She watched as a tear slowly slid down Matilda's cheek. "Is it bad, my lady?" she asked.

"It's not unexpected."

Meg looked at the door. It was closed and no one could overhear them. She leaned nearer Matilda. "We could take her to the Priestess," she whispered.

Matilda opened her eyes and faint hope sprang to them. "Take the babe to the Whispering Maidens?"

"I've seen it work before. We have only to pass the babe through the hole. Do you remember when my cousin Matthew's daughter had her second baby? The one that couldn't breathe well?"

Matilda nodded silently.

"His ma took him to the Whispering Maidens and passed him through the hole, and he's grown to be a strapping lad! It's not done often, but it could help the wee bairn."

Matilda nodded again, her eyes on Meg's face. "It seems so far to the Maidens. It's storming out."

"The storm hasn't broken yet. It's still building over the sea. I could help you down the stairs."

Determination fed by fervent hope began growing within Matilda. "I want to do this. Let me rest a bit. As soon as they return with the child from chapel, bring her in here and dismiss the rest of my ladies."

"Aye, my lady."

Distant thunder growled again. As Meg had said, the storm was still offshore, but it was building, and like all such storms it would move inland. Could she reach the circle of standing stones and get back to the castle before it hit? Could she even get out of bed and down the stairs?

Matilda closed her eyes. She had to sleep for as long as she was able in order to build her strength. She didn't dare think about what Owen would say. He had no patience with the superstitions of the peasants on his island. To him, the stones were no more than that. Just stones. To Matilda and Meg they were much more.

As a girl, Matilda had lived near a circle not unlike the Whispering Maidens. Her stones were rumored to have been an army of men who had plotted against some ancient king and who had been turned to stone for their treason. As a child, she had played there often and before long she had discovered she knew things other children did not, that she could foresee events that had yet to come to pass. Because Matilda had been a sensible girl, she had kept this strange gift a secret from almost everyone.

Again she thought of the image her copper bowl had shown her: a row of tiny stones in the chapel floor, each marked with the name of a tiny infant—except for the last stone, which had been marked with her own name, as well as that of tiny Damaris. Matilda didn't fear death, but she didn't welcome it, either. What would Owen do without her or a child to love? Her heart felt as if it were breaking. A few minutes later, sleep thankfully brought surcease from her pain and worry.

When Meg came into the room, barely an hour later and with the baby in the crook of her arm, Matilda awoke easily and pretended to feel stronger than she actually did. Hiding her struggle against aching muscles and persistent pain, she got out of bed and took the baby from Meg and looked for a long time into the tiny face. Damaris gazed back, seeming for all the world to be able to focus her eyes as well as if she were a much older child.

"The storm won't hold off much longer," Meg said. "Maybe I was wrong to suggest this. Lord Fleetwood will half kill me if aught happens to either you or the babe! Lie back down, my lady. There will be time in a day or two to take the bairn to the Priestess."

Matilda shook her head. "Get my cloak, Meg. If it rains before we return, it will keep the babe dry."

They slipped out of the bedchamber into the hall and Meg paused to listen. "Come, my lady. No one's about."

To minimize the chance that they might be seen, they went down the back stairs, which were normally used only by the servants. Here the steps had been fashioned using the archaic technique of carving them out of the tower wall itself, and they were precarious in the extreme. Matilda refused to consider what would happen to her and Damaris if she slipped or if she was unable to make the trek to the stones and back without mishap. The memory of the picture of her and Damaris's burial stone in the water of the copper bowl kept her going.

Miraculously they were able to slip out of the castle unseen. Keeping her voice to a whisper, Meg marveled over their cleverness all the way across the green and up the hill they had to mount to reach the stones.

As Matilda forced her feet to climb the formidable grade, she gazed across the roiling sea to the angry mountain of clouds. Once the storm arrived, it would be a terrible one, indeed. Lightning flashed within the smudgy black clouds and the sea tossed fitfully beneath. She tried to walk faster, but she could barely stay erect at all.

With each step, the hill seemed steeper than it actually was. Matilda remembered all the times she had run effortlessly up the slope and wished for that strength now that she needed it so badly. "If I can't make it," she said to Meg, "Promise me you'll take the babe on up and pass her through the Priestess."

"I can't," Meg protested. "If I could have done this alone, I'd never have let you risk yourself in coming out! It will take both of us, one to hand the baby through one side, the other to receive her."

"I know. It's just that I'm getting so tired."

"It's not much farther now. See? There's the avenue ahead."

Matilda saw they were indeed nearing the double row of smaller standing stones that marked a path for the last hundred yards or so. Ahead she could see the stones, dim and

ghostly in the fading, eerie light, and she could almost believe they were moving ever so slightly.

The early spring grass was soft under her feet and
thousands of wildflowers were already dotting the undula-
tions of the hill. Matilda tried to focus on these familiar details instead of the pain in her body and the increasing
fierceness of the approaching storm. Due to the strain, her
head was starting to swim, and she had to blink to keep the
stones in sight.

"We're here, my lady. Hurry as much as you can." Meg
reached for her hand and led her onto level ground, and as
they passed the flat altar stone, Matilda realized she was in
the circle already.

She had no memory of entering it. All around her the
stones stood like sentinels. Beyond, she could see the sea and
taste the salt on her lips. The light was failing, but she knew
it wasn't evening as yet.

Matilda reached out and touched the Priestess stone. It
was taller than the others and slightly bluish in cast. In its
center was a hole. Whether the hole had been formed naturally by wind and water or by the artifice of man, Matilda
had no idea. All the other stones were solid. She pressed her
palm against the stone's cold surface. As happened so often, she felt a tingling course up her hand and arm and into
her body. It gave her strength.

Taking the baby from Meg, Matilda lifted her face to the
sky. "I ask that this babe be given the strength of the
Priestess! That she fare well and live long! That her life be
one suitable to a child of the Priestess!" She hesitated. In
order to ask such a boon, a price must be paid. "I ask that
I be taken in her place! That my life be forfeit for hers if
such must be!"

"My lady!" Meg gasped in shock. "You mustn't!"

Matilda ignored her. She knew what she had seen. If she
could cheat the heavens out of this one tender life, what did
she have to lose? What mother could do less? "Hear me, O
Spirits." She lifted the baby and passed her into the smooth
opening in the center of the rock as Meg moved to the opposite side. Meg's warm hands touched hers and she took
the baby from her mistress and carried her through.

Matilda leaned against the stone, relief flooding through her. "Thank you," she whispered so softly that no one but the stone could hear her.

Meg ran around from the back of the rock and settled the baby into her arms. Damaris looked about with interest. All the red had left her little face and her eyes were on the storm clouds.

"My! It's like she can already see," Meg exclaimed. "Look at her, my lady!"

Matilda touched Damaris's cool cheek. "Take good care of her, Meg. See that she remembers me."

"My lady, don't talk so! Quick! Say a prayer!"

Automatically Matilda bowed her head, but her silent prayer was for Damaris, not herself. She didn't think her own fate could be altered, but that of her child would be if she had any means to accomplish it.

They had almost reached the castle when Owen and a number of his men came running out in search of them. His face was drawn and pale with worry and fear. "Matilda!" he shouted as he closed the distance between them and embraced her. "What have you done?"

She managed to smile up at him, even though his face seemed dim and vague. "I had to take our daughter to the Priestess. It was the only way."

Owen glared at Meg. "You'll pack your things and go! Now! If harm comes to my lady and the babe—"

"No, no, Owen," Matilda said quickly. "It wasn't Meg's fault. I forced her to go. I couldn't put the babe through the hole alone. I had to have help." Her voice trailed off as the dimness closed in. She couldn't tell if she said more or not. She wanted to let Owen know that she had done it for him, so he wouldn't be alone after she was gone. She wanted to say she loved him and would miss him wherever she went.

Owen lifted his wife into his arms and carried her into the castle. Meg hurried along behind them, holding the baby close as the first drops of rain spattered around them. No sooner had they reached the safety of the castle than the storm broke in all its fury.

Meg had never seen such a storm. It seemed as if the stone walls of the castle itself would tumble down in the onslaught of wind and lightning and thunder. She could hear the shrieks of the more timid maids as they cowered from the storm. She looked down at the baby girl.

Damaris lay quietly, her gaze taking in the castle and the storm outside. As Meg carried her up the fine new staircase that rose from the screens passage, Damaris closed her eyes, sighed and fell asleep. Meg was almost as much in awe of the baby as she was of her mistress.

During the next week, under the watchful eyes of Owen and his staff of servants, both Matilda and the baby seemed to grow stronger. Owen began to hope that this time there would be no reason to pull up a paving stone in the chapel. Even the physician seemed pleased with the progress of mother and child.

Then Matilda began to weaken. It was almost imperceptible at first, no more than a tiring glance and a languid gesture. Then he realized that Matilda was losing ground as quickly as Damaris was gaining in strength.

Owen was in the great hall when Meg came to fetch him. He didn't have to ask what she wanted. Her dark eyes were sad and a tear was on her cheek. Taking the steps two at a time, Owen ran up the stairs and into the chamber he shared with Matilda.

She lay in their bed, the baby in her arms. Owen's gait faltered as he neared the tall bed. Matilda's skin was as luminescent and pale as that of the saints pictured in the chapel. Her eyes were like jewels in her thin face. A faint smile parted her lips. "I've asked Meg to care for Damaris. I don't want her sent away from the island for any of our cousins on the mainland to raise. She belongs here."

"Don't talk like that," he protested, fear knotting his stomach.

"Owen, there has to be truth between us now. I can't stay. Not even for the two of you." She looked down at the baby. "She will be company for you. Love her for my sake." Her eyes implored him to understand.

Owen nodded. He had known other men who had rejected their babies after their beloved wives died in childbed. Tears stung his eyes and for the first time in his life he didn't care that he cried. He reached out and brushed a strand of red brown hair away from Matilda's face. "I've always loved you," he said, not caring that all her women were in the room and would hear the endearment.

Matilda smiled at him. "As I've loved you." She handed him the baby and lay back on the pillow as if the effort had exhausted her.

That night, while Owen sat by her bed and the ladies and the chaplain murmured prayers, Matilda slipped away in her sleep. Her lips were still slightly curved as if she were having a pleasant dream, but they lost what little color they had retained. Owen sat in silence, holding her hand and wondering what he would do without her. Son or no son, he knew he would never marry again. Not after having loved and lost his beloved Matilda.

At last he did all he could. He leaned nearer to her and whispered, "I'll keep Damaris safe here at Thornbeck. When she's of an age to marry, I'll see to it that she has a good and gentle husband who will treat her kindly. After that is done, I'll come to you."

Owen didn't have any claim to second sight, but he knew in his heart that Matilda heard him and was pleased.

Chapter One

The North Sea off the coast of England
1565

Damaris strolled down the double avenue of standing stones, her violet eyes on the larger stones ahead. In the twenty years since her mother's death, Damaris had become a beautiful woman, but she was still unbetrothed.

The sea wind tugged at her hair, so she removed her bongrace to let the wind lift her waves of bright auburn. Damaris loved the island and Thornbeck, but most of all she loved the Whispering Maidens.

Meg had nurtured her and raised her and had been a mother to her. Edith Fleetwood had taught her all the things a lady ought to know, pulling memories from the days when she was the daughter of a fine castle on the mainland, before her branch of the family fell into decay from several early deaths, unwise marriages and too many extravagances. Meg had given Damaris more.

From Meg she had learned of the unusual circumstances surrounding her birth. Meg had gone with Matilda to the standing stones and had received Damaris as she was passed through. To Damaris this meant she had three mothers: Matilda, Meg and the Priestess. She loved them all.

Of course, she had no memory of Matilda. But Damaris knew what her mother had looked like. She had often studied the miniature portrait of her mother that her father always wore on a gold chain next to his doublet, and in the long gallery in the castle hung a larger painting of her, as well. The resemblance between Matilda and Damaris was remarkable. They both had the same unusual shade of red hair, the same translucent skin and the same knowing expression that made the superstitious villagers whisper among themselves that both mother and daughter talked to the fairies. Only their eyes were different.

While Matilda's had been blue, Damaris's were violet. No one else on the island had violet eyes and that also stirred the villagers to gossip. If they hadn't all loved the lady of the castle, they would have feared her and called her a witch. But they knew Damaris loved them and cared for them when they were brought low by illness or poverty and they responded with strong loyalty to her.

Meg hadn't volunteered everything she knew about Matilda. She hadn't, for instance, told Damaris about the strange and mystifying pictures Matilda had been able to see in her copper bowl. One day Meg had found Damaris with the bowl, and when she asked the girl what she was doing, Damaris explained that she was looking at the pictures in the water and then held the bowl toward Meg as if she assumed that everyone could see them.

From that day on, Meg had noticed a certain fey quality in Damaris. She had cautioned the girl to be careful who knew of her gift, and Damaris had promised, obeying Meg not out of any sort of fear of her newly discovered talent, but rather because she loved and respected Meg. She didn't see how anyone could fear so unique a talent, let alone harm her for possessing it, but nevertheless, she kept it quiet as she'd been told. Damaris rarely left her island and always felt perfectly safe there.

She entered the stone circle and paused to look around. The lush, verdant grasses within the circle waved in the breeze and thousands of wildflowers spangled the area with color. Yellow-eyed daisies lay like snow amid the white and red tufts of clover and yellow meadow buttercups. The smaller, less showy blooms of the lady's slippers attracted flocks of blue butterflies. Golden honeybees hummed over the nodding clover and birds circled lazily overhead.

Damaris spread her arms and rotated in a circle as if she would embrace all the stones. She knew each one intimately. Close to the center of the circle lay a flat rectangular altar, which was presided over by a bluish stone with a circle in its middle. Damaris walked quietly to the Priestess and paused for a moment before touching it. As always when she touched the stone, she felt a tingle run up her arm and an accompanying sense of elation.

She sat on the altar and gazed at the tall, blue stone. What or who had carved the precise circle, and how had they, assuming it was made by man, known to carve it? Had the knowledge come to someone in a dream the way knowledge sometimes came to her? What had his neighbors thought when he started carving the circle? Damaris knew she would never know the answers to her questions, but this didn't diminish her wonderment. She loved mysteries and gladly accepted them into her life.

By that same token, who had erected the stones and why had they brought them here to this hill? None of the stones were like any others found naturally on the island and the Priestess was unlike any she had seen anywhere. She had no way of knowing how much the stones weighed, but common sense told her they would be extremely difficult to move.

She could see why the villagers chose to believe the mystical story that the stones had been once a group of girls who danced in defiance of heaven and were petrified for their insolence. It not only explained the stone circle, but served as a handy threat for their misbehaving children. Damaris knew the stones didn't really move in the moonlight when a wild wind blew in from the sea, as legend suggested, but she could see how someone living in the village below the hill could believe it. Even to her eyes, the stones sometimes seemed to shimmer and shift under such conditions.

It was true, on the other hand, that no one knew for certain how many stones surrounded the Priestess. Damaris had tried to count them on many occasions and could never arrive at the same answer twice. It was part of their mystery.

She lay back on the altar stone and her flame bright hair spread about her like a cloak. Above her the sky was brilliant blue with peaceful white clouds. It was the most perfect of days. Or it would have been if her father hadn't broached the subject of her marriage again.

A frown puckered Damaris's brow. She didn't want to marry; not because she disliked men or feared a wife's duties, for she had no prudish qualities at all, but if she married, her husband would own Thornbeck and the island and her, as well. Damaris preferred to remain free.

The subject of marriage had come up time and again for years. She knew her father was concerned about her future, and even Meg, who wasn't married, either, said Damaris was foolish to turn down every man her father suggested. Owen had lived a half century already; no man lived forever. If he died, when he died, what would become of Damaris?

Damaris was tired of the question. She had argued for years that if she had been a son, no one would be so anxious to see her wed. Besides, her father was in good health despite his years, and she would have ample time to marry after his health started to fail. Neither Owen nor Meg agreed with her, so she had come to the stone circle where she could be alone with her rebellion.

She ran her hands down her flat stomach. She was already twenty. By the time her mother had been as old, she had borne and buried several children. This worried Damaris. Would she, like her mother, be unable to bear strong children? Meg had told her often that only the intervention of the Priestess had preserved her health. Damaris didn't doubt this at all. She had too often felt the surge of power that flowed from the stone through anyone who touched it. Not that many dared.

She rolled to her stomach and watched as a rabbit hopped into the circle. He saw her and paused before coming closer. Damaris smiled as she studied him. Animals were never afraid of her, not even wild ones. She wondered if this one would come close enough for her to pet him. He sat up on his haunches and began to nibble at the red clover.

This was another reason she didn't want to marry. Everyone, Edith especially, had told her that a wife and mother had to stay in the castle and tend to running it smoothly. She wouldn't have time to go to the Maidens and pass hours in peaceful contemplation. Damaris knew she would never agree to such restrictions on her life, so why marry in the first place?

She was a reasonable person, despite how often she might argue against her father's logic. She knew the castle and island belonged to her father and that she, as a woman, could never inherit it. If he died without a son-in-law to rule in his stead, the island would go to a distant male relative on the mainland or revert to Queen Elizabeth. Either way, Damaris would likely not be allowed to remain.

On the other hand, if she married, her husband might move her to holdings on the mainland anyway, and she couldn't imagine herself living anywhere but at Thornbeck. She was as much a part of the island as were the Whispering Maidens. Neither her father nor Meg knew she secretly worried about leaving the place she loved so dearly.

In the castle on the taller hill, Owen was in his closet writing a letter. From time to time he lifted his head to gaze unseeingly at one of the maps hanging on the wall or one of the pictures of his favorite dogs or horses. This was a difficult letter and he wasn't enjoying its composition.

Whether Damaris wished it or not, he had to find her a husband. To let a maid determine her fate was not to be considered. She had no way of knowing what was best for her.

As he recalled his last promise to Matilda, he held her miniature portrait out from his body in order to see it more clearly. His eyesight had been faltering lately, and he could no longer see her face in sharp detail. "I'll find Damaris a husband if it's the last thing I do," he vowed. "I promised you that I'd do it and by God's bones, I will!"

At the time he had made the promise, Owen hadn't expected the tiny baby to grow up with such a stubborn streak. Damaris was more willful than any maid he had ever seen.

He considered that to be his own fault. He had loved her too well to discipline her as harshly as some of his friends might have if she were their daughter. He had rather enjoyed seeing such fire and determination in so small a child. If she had been a son, what pride that stubbornness would have engendered in him! Since they seldom left the island, and since Damaris could be biddable when she chose, her independence hadn't mattered so much.

But now she was determined not to wed! Such a move was unthinkable! Didn't she know he wouldn't live forever? Since the destruction of the nunneries, she wouldn't even be able to fall back on a life among the nuns—which might be just as well, for Damaris was singularly unsuited for such a life. They had no close kin, and Owen wasn't that fond of the few cousins that he knew. None of them would allow Damaris to stay on the island, nor would they allow her such freedom of speech and action. No, he had to see her safely wed.

During his last visit to court, Owen had met the family of his old friend Edwin Rutledge. Edwin's youngest son, Gavin, was unmarried, and Owen had liked the young man on sight. He was handsome, which he knew would appeal to Damaris, and he was even-tempered and intelligent, which appealed to Owen. Gavin was Edwin's favorite, but he stood to inherit nothing at his father's death. It was unlikely all his older brothers would die before his father, and even if they did, several already had sons to inherit the Rutledge fortune. Edwin would almost certainly welcome the proposal that Gavin be betrothed to the only child of the wealthy Fleetwood family.

Owen lifted his head and gazed at the far wall. Although there was no window in this room, he could picture the island in his mind's eye as if there were. He loved this place. He had been born here as had his father and many generations before him. Thornbeck was as much a part of him as was Damaris. That Matilda had also loved it had been a bonus he hadn't expected. Would Gavin or any other man love it as well?

Strategically, the island was important and whoever ruled here would have to be strong enough to preserve the island from marauding Scots. There had been no serious assault made on the island in the past two years, but Owen remembered many battles over the years. Thornbeck was solidly built and could withstand most enemy forces. Her master, however, would have to be versed in warfare if the castle was to remain that way. Gavin fit that description perfectly.

When Owen had first seen him, Gavin had been working out in the tiltyard. His seat on his charger and his dexterousness with the lance had been impressive. Later Owen had talked with the man and had found him to be sound in his knowledge of castle defense, as well.

He went back to the letter he was composing. Edwin had been his friend for so many years. The alliance would be a good one. Had Owen known Edwin still had an unmarried son, he would have pursued the matter earlier.

Owen tried not to think what Damaris would say about this. She would most certainly not be pleased. Owen had no intention of telling her until the matter was sealed.

Edwin received Owen's letter and read it with growing interest. He had almost forgotten his old friend had a daughter, but vaguely recalled from the time he had seen her with her father at court that she had been a slim girl, a bit on the tall side, with masses of reddish brown hair and eyes of a strange color. Edwin had assumed she would have been married long ago and his curiosity was piqued.

He reread the letter. There was no mention of Damaris being a widow. Why hadn't she married earlier? Was she mean tempered or undesirable in some other way? Twenty was old for a maid to remain at home.

Edwin remembered the times he had visited at Thornbeck. The last visit had been many years before, when Matilda was still alive. She had been like a jewel in the rugged castle, and Edwin had spent more than one night envying Owen his bedmate. Had Damaris grown into such a beauty as her mother had been? Edwin was somewhat disappointed that Owen had sent no likeness of her with the letter, but in retrospect he decided it was just as well, for he had known of many portraits that bore little resemblance to the young ladies they were meant to represent. She had been a pretty child, and Edwin thought it most likely that she would still be attractive, if not beautiful.

Then there was the matter of babies, of sons to inherit the Fleetwood fortune. Matilda had borne only one child who had lived. Owen had once said that Matilda's parents had sired only two children, both daughters, who had survived past infancy, and Matilda's sister had also died in childbed. Would Gavin be able to beget a line of sons to follow him if he were married to Damaris?

Edwin loved his youngest son more than all the others and wanted him to be well settled. His only hope for fortune was to marry it. Damaris would bring him that fortune. Not many fathers would be willing to marry their daughters to a younger son if they could choose one with an inheritance. Why was Owen willing?

Edwin put down the letter and went to the window that overlooked the gardens. A group of women below were walking on the path among the flowers, and even from this distance he could hear snatches of their laughter. One of them carried a lap dog, and one of the others held a flower she had picked in passing. Edwin enjoyed court life. Did Gavin?

He had known for months that Gavin had taken a mistress, a woman by the name of Claudia Godwin. The only problem was that Claudia was married to Percy Godwin, a man with a quick temper. Percy had been away from court for the past season and Claudia had amused herself with Gavin. It could never come to more than that, nor did Edwin wish that it could. If Claudia wouldn't be faithful to one husband, she wouldn't be loyal to another in his place. Faithfulness wasn't in her makeup. Getting Gavin away from court before the Godwins were reunited or before Claudia found herself with a by-blow child might be a wise move.

It occurred to Edwin that he should discuss the matter with Gavin, but he wasn't of that inclination. In his experience, a young man with a pretty mistress wasn't likely to be eager to discuss marriage to a woman he had never seen. Edwin could hardly blame a man for that. He had had a mistress or two in his time, and he knew the power they could wield. But on the other hand, he knew Gavin was levelheaded and capable of seeing the advantage of marrying the daughter of a rich man with no heir.

Continuing to think this thing through, he realized the proposition was not without potential problems. Because of the island's importance, Gavin wouldn't be able to leave it unprotected and return to court with or without his bride, as most men could. Marrying Damaris would also mean marrying Thornbeck. And with Edwin's joints so indisposed to travel, he couldn't easily go to Thornbeck to visit, so he might never see his favorite son again.

Edwin knew this would take a great deal of consideration.

Gavin Rutledge reined in his large gray stallion and the horse tossed his head in objection. Gavin knew that when the scent of battle was in his mount's nostrils, the animal hated to give up the fight, even if it was only mock jousting. "Hold, Robert," he called to the man on the other side of the tiltyard.

Robert Grainger pulled his horse around and cantered back to Gavin. "Tired so soon?" he asked with a laugh.

Gavin grinned and shook his head. In the afternoon sun his hair was golden in sharp contrast to his deeply tanned skin. "I promised Claudia I'd meet her in the rose garden. She's likely already there."

As they rode toward the stables, Robert said, "I don't know why she puts up with your habit of keeping her waiting like this. And you'll go to her smelling of horse sweat!"

"Claudia likes the smell of battle almost as well as does Woden." He patted his horse's hard-muscled neck. "As for keeping her waiting, she likes that, as well."

Robert snorted in disbelief. "What woman cares for that?"

"One who is married to another man and who enjoys the dangers as much as the pleasures. As long as she's waiting in the rose garden, there's a chance someone will happen along and ask her why she's there. If it's a close friend or someone who knows Sir Percy, she'll have to give up the wait and walk a bit with them. Before she can manage to return to the trysting place, I may have come and gone. Believe me, Claudia loves the intrigue."

"You have the best luck of anyone I know. Sir Percy has challenged men for much less than you've accomplished with his lady."

"I know, but Sir Percy isn't here and Claudia is. If she's willing to take the chance, I'll not pull a prudish face and say nay."

Robert looked at him closely. "Are you in love with her?"

"Of course not."

"She's a pretty woman and popular around court."

"She's also no more inclined to monogamy than the cats outside the kitchen door. Claudia isn't the one for me."

"Then who is?"

Gavin became serious for a moment. "I'm not sure. When I meet her, I'll know. Until then, I plan to enjoy myself."

At the stable they dismounted. Two young boys ran up to hold the horses while Robert and Gavin loosened the saddles. Gavin handed his saddle to one of the boys and took Woden's reins. He always curried his horses himself, especially Woden. He didn't want his war-horse to hurt one of the boys and Woden could be mean tempered.

His other horse, a gelding named Merlin, whickered softly as Gavin approached and thrust his brown head over the top rail of his stall to be petted. Gavin obliged, keeping Woden's teeth out of reach of the other animal. The two horses got along reasonably well, but Woden was unpredictable, as were most stallions, and he was jealous of Gavin's affection for Merlin.

As Gavin brushed the tall gray animal, working the tangles out of his white mane, Woden rolled his eyes but suffered Gavin's touch. Gavin was almost the only person Woden would allow near him.

When the animal had been fed, Gavin waved goodbye to Robert and left the stables. He paused at the pump out front to sluice water over his hands and arms and splash his face clean. The young boy posted by the pump handed him a square of linen for use as a towel and Gavin thanked him. When he was dry, he went to the rose garden.

Claudia was there, tapping her foot impatiently and pacing a few steps, then turning and pacing back. Gavin glanced around to be sure they were alone. Privacy was a rare commodity at court.

"What has kept you?" she demanded as he drew near.

"I told you I would be in the tiltyard this afternoon."

She wrinkled her nose. "I can tell." She didn't, however, look displeased.

"Would you have me lie around court all day and become soft and weak?" He grinned because he knew the answer.

"Not ever, Sir Gavin."

"Have you waited long?"

"Yes, I have. Everyone I know has walked by at least twice."

"You shouldn't have waited."

Claudia stepped closer and would have kissed him if Gavin had bent to her. He didn't. She frowned petulantly. "You act as if you're not glad to see me."

"No, I act like a prudent man who would like to keep his hide intact. Sir Percy also has friends at court. You don't want word to reach him of our intimacy, do you?"

Claudia tossed her head and her pink bongrace floated over her shoulder. "I care not about Percy. He's an animal. I would rather have you."

Gavin made no comment.

"I've thought much about it of late. I could claim consanguinity with Percy and have our marriage annulled. Then we could wed." She smiled up at him. "You know Percy and I are distant cousins. Just because the fact was overlooked in order to marry me to him in the first place, it need not be overlooked forever." She put her hands on Gavin's chest.

He covered her hands with his and gently removed them. "Don't play at leaving your husband, my lady. Such was never in our bargain."

"Then let's change it. I adore you and would be your wife. Don't you love me, Gavin?"

"No. I've told you before that I don't. I'm fond of you, but I've never led you to believe that I love you."

Claudia pouted and became less pretty. "You're just teasing me. You know you love me. We've been lovers for months."

"Has it been that long?" He thought back and realized she was right. "Then your husband will return to court soon."

"He wrote that he's coming back in a week." Claudia made a face. "I detest him. You know I do."

"Yes, but many husbands and wives have no fondness for each other. He's not cruel to you."

"I think it's cruel that he wants to be around me at all! He knows I dislike him." She tried again to maneuver Gavin into an embrace by stepping close to him and looking up, her blue eyes wide and innocent. "I'd much rather have you, and I intend to tell him so."

Gavin put his hands on her shoulders and moved back a step. "No, Claudia, you won't."

"Why not?" Her lower lip protruded.

"Because if you do, he'll beat you and challenge me, and I'll have to kill him."

Claudia's eyes opened wider. "You'd do that?"

"To protect myself? Yes." Gavin wasn't violent by nature, but he was trained in warfare and knew he wouldn't shrink from the challenge. "Sir Percy wouldn't stop at less than death for one of us, and I don't propose to die for you or anyone."

"Not even for me?"

He laughed. "First you want me as a husband, now you want me dead. No, Claudia, I won't die for you any more than I'll marry you."

She hit him on the ribs. "You're cruel, Gavin. Cruel and selfish."

Gavin didn't stop laughing. "The past few months have been pleasurable. Too bad they have to end."

"Why do they? Just because Percy is returning to court?"

"Of course. It's one thing to have a liaison with a lonely woman and another altogether to cuckold a fellow knight under the same roof."

"That makes no sense at all!"

"Then believe it's because I don't love you and all affairs must eventually come to an end. This one has lasted several weeks longer than your others, but now it has to be over. You'll have an entire week to miss Sir Percy and become eager for his homecoming."

"It's just like you to throw those other men up to me." Claudia crossed her rounded arms over her chest and frowned at him. "You know they meant nothing to me."

"And neither do I," he said gently. "That's how it's always been between us. You've played at love, I have not, but we both know it's only a pretense."

Claudia sighed. "You'll not come to my rooms tonight? It's truly over?"

"Yes." He bent and placed a kiss on her forehead. "Be well, Claudia."

"I will be," she retorted. "But I won't be lonely!" She flounced off in search of other game.

Gavin watched her and felt a pang of remorse. He didn't dislike Claudia for all her unfaithfulness, and it was true that she detested her husband. Unfortunately, that was the way of life.

He went into the palace and up the staircase to the floor where he and his father had their apartments. As he was about to go in his own door, Edwin stepped out into the corridor and motioned to him. Gavin joined him in his sitting room.

"I've had a letter that will interest you," Edwin said after they had exchanged pleasantries. "It's from my old friend, Owen, Lord Fleetwood."

Gavin tried to recall the man who fit that name but shook his head. "I don't remember anyone of that name."

"You've met him but he rarely comes to court. I expect that like me, his bones ache too much these days to allow him to travel easily."

Gavin picked an apple from a bowl of fruit on a nearby table and, after rubbing it on the sleeve of his doublet, he took a bite. "What is it about his letter that will interest me?" He smiled at his father. They were friends, as well as parent and son.

"Lord Fleetwood has a marriageable daughter. He's proposing a match between the two of you."

Gavin stopped eating the apple in mid-bite. "A daughter?"

"Her name is Damaris, and I believe she's about twenty."

"Twenty? And unmarried?" Gavin was becoming uneasy and his green eyes narrowed. "For what reason?"

"He doesn't say. You should also know that Owen is a wealthy man and, as his son-in-law, you'd be his heir. There is only the one child, you see. They live on an island in the North Sea not far north of Holy Island."

"That's near the Scots border."

"Yes, it's strategically placed. Whoever is left in charge of the island must be loyal to our queen, and no one could have doubts of you on that score."

Gavin went to the window and tossed out the remainder of the apple. "Are you saying that you want me to marry this woman? Sight unseen?"

"It's how I married your mother and that worked out rather well," Edwin reminded him. "You have to marry sometime, Gavin. This will make you wealthy in your own right. Unless I miss my guess, Queen Elizabeth will also bestow the barony on you."

Gavin nodded but said nothing as his thoughts were whirling in an effort to find a way to refuse without hurting his father's feelings. "If I were to go so far away, you'd be here alone. My brothers and sisters seldom come to court. You'd detest having to leave here and live with them as you grow older. You've said so yourself."

"I have a few good years in me yet, my boy."

Gavin looked at his father. Edwin had aged markedly in the past few years. Although he still stood as tall as Gavin, his frame was frail now and his hands trembled when he was tired.

"I know you had hoped to marry for love," Edwin said gently. "I understand that. All people wish this were so. But someday you'll be as old as I am. Without wealth to fall back on, you'll become one of the queen's pensioners and how will you like a life like that? Living only to repeat endless prayers for her well-being and for the bowls of porridge they'll dole out. Or you'll have to go to one of your brothers or nephews and live on their charity. You'd hate that."

Gavin nodded. He and most of his brothers were close, but there could be only one head of an estate and he wasn't at all sure he could stand to live under the rule of any of them—not when he was so accustomed to being his own master. "As you said about yourself, I've a good many years left. I'm not yet thirty."

Edwin smiled sadly. "I can remember when I could have said that. I thought old age was something that would never visit itself upon me. But it has. It creeps up before you see it coming. I don't want to go to my grave worrying about your welfare. You've always been my favorite son. You know that. It would please and relieve me if you'd marry this girl."

"At twenty she's hardly a girl," Gavin retorted. "I'd like to know something about her. What does she look like?"

"I've not seen her for years. As a child she had dark hair with a great deal of red in it and large eyes of an odd color. Her mother was a beauty and I recall thinking the girl had taken her looks from that side of the family. I expect the girl has grown to be like her mother."

"Then why hasn't she married?"

"My friend doesn't say. Perhaps it's because Thornbeck is so isolated. Perhaps Owen has been reluctant to part with her. Her mother died soon after she was born and Damaris has been lady of the castle."

"Damaris?" Gavin said. "It's a pretty name."

"Then you'll consider it?"

"You could order me to marry her and I'd obey."

"I know. But I prefer for you to be happy and I know you'd never be if I have to order you to do this thing."

Gavin sat silently as he thought. After a while, he said, "You may tell Lord Fleetwood that I will marry his daughter. But," he added quickly, "I want to see her portrait first!"

Edwin looked relieved. "I'll tell him."

Chapter Two

Damaris looked up from the tapestry she was sewing. "Hello, Papa. I thought you had gone down to the village."

Owen sat on the stool nearest Damaris. He had a forced smile and a wary look in his eye. "I have good news. See? A letter arrived today from my old friend, Edwin Rutledge."

Damaris glanced at the letter. They rarely received mail and a letter was an event. "Have I ever met him?"

"Yes, of course. You saw him when you were last at court."

Damaris laughed indulgently. "Papa, I was only a child. Not even twelve years old. How could I remember just one of many?" Her eyes softened as she recalled that time. "It was so marvelous! All those people and such fine clothes and tapestries worked with gold and silver! I remember the singers and jugglers. And at the banquet we were served a marzipan globe filled with live pigeons tinted pink!"

"You did love it, didn't you?" Owen was watching her closely.

"As a diversion, yes. I wouldn't want to live there, of course. I'd probably go mad with all those people about continuously. I was glad to return to our Thornbeck." She reached over and patted his hand. "What does the letter say?"

Owen looked uncomfortable. "It seems Edwin still has a marriageable son. A young man named Gavin. I remember him quite well as a boy. He had an almost regal bearing and his hair could have passed for gold. I saw him again a few months ago when I was at court. You'd have met him, too, if you hadn't been so determined to stay on the island."

"A marriageable son?" Damaris's fingers stilled on the tapestry.

"Edwin and I believe the two of you would make a brilliant match."

Damaris turned away. "We've been over all this before, Papa. I don't want to marry."

"You must," he said bluntly. "Gavin would be an excellent husband for you. I know the family well and they're congenial and well-bred. Gavin is the youngest son and wouldn't, of course, bring an inheritance to the union, but I believe this match will be an excellent one for you."

"A younger son?" Damaris felt her anger building. "Your friend wrote you and proposed that I be wed to a man who will inherit no title or holdings?"

"You won't require any. As your husband, Gavin will inherit all I possess, and I feel certain that our good queen will extend to him the barony I received for our family's loyalty and defense of this island, as well."

Damaris stabbed her needle into the tapestry. "I won't marry him. I don't even know him!"

"I've been too lenient with you. Lady Edith has often told me so and I should have listened. I want you to marry this lad."

"No! I'm not leaving my island. Why do you insist on getting rid of me?"

"I'm not. Gavin would come here. This island must be held for England. While you may go on occasional journeys, you'll be here most of the time. How many daughters may stay in their own houses when they wed?"

"Regardless of that, I'm not marrying this Gavin or anyone else. How can I? He will only be interested in my inheritance, not me for myself. I don't remember him at all, if indeed I ever met him! Papa, how could you?" Her eyes filled with tears. "I don't want to leave you or to bring some husband to our island. For all we know, he may be mean natured or given to drunkenness, whatever the rest of his family may be like."

"I'm telling you I renewed our acquaintance when I was last at court. You'll have to take my word that he's a good match for you. It wouldn't be proper for me to ask him to come here so you may look him over like a horse offered for sale at the fair. Edwin has frequently told me that Gavin is his favorite son. He wouldn't feel that way toward him if he were mean tempered or given to excess drink."

"Papa, mightn't your old friend only be saying that in order to marry his son to the riches of Thornbeck? Men do lie. Especially men at court. I've heard you say so yourself."

Owen sighed and gave her a long look. "What will become of you when I'm gone?"

"Faith! I'll worry about it then." She sensed he was about to give in to her, so she smiled at him and reached over to pat his hand. "You're still young."

"No, Damaris, I'm not."

She looked away, because she knew this was true and she hated knowing it. "Many men live to be much older than fifty-eight." She glanced sharply back at him. "You're feeling well, aren't you?"

"Of course."

"Then we'll have no more talk about this. Why borrow trouble, Papa?"

"I'd like to see a grandson before I go."

"And I'll give you one. I just don't want to be married now." She smiled at him coaxingly. "Come now. Let's walk down to the village. It's too beautiful a day for us to stay inside."

"You go. I have to write Edwin."

She held her breath. If her father insisted that she marry this stranger, she would have no real say in the matter. "What will you say to him, Papa?"

"What else? I'll tell him that the match is not to be." He sighed again and rested his palms on his knees. "I hope you don't come to regret your procrastination, Damaris. And also that I don't live to regret giving in to so many of your whims."

"Neither of us will have regrets, Papa." She stood and came to place a kiss on the top of his head, then turned and walked lightly out of the room.

Owen felt a strong foreboding, but he had given her his word. Reluctantly he went to his closet to write his friend with the bad news. As he passed the portrait of Matilda over the fireplace he shook his head. He doubted Matilda would have fared any better with their daughter. Damaris was uncommonly stubborn.

"He has refused?" Gavin asked in confusion. "I thought the marriage was his idea."

"I don't understand it, either," Edwin confessed. "He doesn't explain it, only expresses his regrets that our families won't be joined in marriage." He turned the paper over as if the answer might be written on the reverse. "It's a puzzle."

"If you ask me, the daughter is no prize and he had a stroke of conscience at the last minute. After all, if you're such good friends, he *would* waver at tricking you into marrying your son to a maid that's not all she should be."

"If that were true, Owen would never have suggested the marriage in the first place. Now that you mention it, I suppose it is odd that the prospective bride's father opened negotiations. It's usually the father of the groom that suggests the marriage. Because of our friendship, I thought nothing of it. After all, how could I know she was available if Owen hadn't told me?"

"I'd say we're fortunate to be out of the agreement."

Edwin still looked puzzled, but he nodded. "I suppose we must view it that way."

Gavin tried not to let his wounded pride show. Could it not have been that Damaris and her father decided at the last minute that a younger son wouldn't be a good enough match for the daughter of a baron and the heir of a fortune? He forgot his own relief at being free of the match in his surprise over being spurned. Now he wondered more than ever what Damaris was like and whether he would have cared for her as a bride.

* * *

A sour mist hung about the foot of the Scottish castle and drifted into the small, untidy courtyard. On the battlements a man stood, his feet braced well apart, his hands clenched behind his back. He was frowning as he looked out over the land in the direction of the sea, as if he were disappointed that Craigmore was too distant from the sea for even a glimpse of the water.

A younger, broader man joined him and waited for his master to recognize him.

"Yes?" William Fleetwood said brusquely.

James McIntyre stepped forward and handed him a roll of paper. "This is a list of the supplies we'll need."

William unrolled the paper and read it. "See to it."

"Aye, Sir William. And when will we leave the castle?"

William turned back to stare out over the land. "In two days we'll be under a dark moon. If we go to the sea tomorrow, we'll be ready to attack under the most favorable of conditions." He glared up at the leaden sky. "If the rain holds off, that is." He hated this dreary corner of Scotland and frequently wished he had settled elsewhere.

"I'll tell the men." James was William's second-in-command and loyal to his master beyond question.

William looked at the younger man. At times he wondered if James was loyal out of respect for him, or if it was simply a family habit for the McIntyres to be loyal to the masters of Craigmore Castle. James's father had been the steward here when William arrived thirty-two years ago and James had been no more than a baby. Now he was a man in the late prime of his life and William had yet to succeed in taking Thornbeck Castle.

"What say you?" William queried. "Will we succeed this time?"

James was silent for a moment. He was a dour man and not given to idle talk. "Aye. We can do it."

"Why do you say so?"

"My men are ready. The signs are right. This morning I saw a hen put flight to a rooster. Last night toward the stroke of twelve, I awoke and looked out to see strange lights in the sky."

William studied the man. He was superstitious, as was almost everyone else, and he put great stock in signs and portents. "See that the men hear of these signs."

James nodded and turned to go. William looked back in the direction of the sea. In his mind he could see Thornbeck as clearly as he had as a boy. He had grown to manhood within its lichen-covered walls and had thought to rule there as a man. It had been his right to do so.

After all these years William still felt cheated out of his inheritance and title. He had been knighted for his allegiance to Scotland by Mary of Guise, but given no rank of peerage. Now the older Mary was dead and her daughter, Mary of Scotland, was queen. In the four years since she had returned to Scotland from France, Mary had completely charmed William, as she had so many of her male subjects. If he presented her with Thornbeck, he thought she might grant him a rank, as well as title to the castle that was his by birthright.

William mentally compared Thornbeck with Craigmore and became more determined than ever to win it. Craigmore was situated beside a fen and was frequently surrounded by a yellowish fog that smelled of putrid gases. Such a fog was even now wrapped around Craigmore's protecting wall and lay in the streets of the mean town that served the castle.

William was accustomed to the dampness. Having lived on Thornbeck's island throughout his youth and at Craigmore most of the years since his hasty departure from his childhood home, he took little notice of the pervading moisture that caused tapestries to rot prematurely and rushes to go sour long before spring. Nor did he object to the vile odors that rose from the filthy streets of the village and the lower floors of his castle. He was accustomed to them, too, though that had taken some time for adjustment after having breathed the clean sea breeze at Thornbeck.

He looked up at the sky and hoped his astronomer had judged the date correctly. The man had assured William that the stars were now in favor of him accomplishing some great task. To William's mind there was no task greater than taking Thornbeck away from his brother.

He had never liked Owen. As boys, William had been the risk taker, Owen the student. William had loved learning to wield a sword, whereas Owen had detested it. Owen had mastered the necessary battle skills, but he had never found a glory in them the way William had. This had been unfortunate in his parents' eyes, because Owen, as the younger son, would be expected to live by his sword in service of the crown.

In a gentler time, Owen could have entered a monastery and continued his love of learning, but when King Henry had dissolved the religious houses, that option was no longer open to him. William's place in the sun had been short-lived, however, because his outspoken manner had brought him to grief.

William had never known how word of his discontent with the crown managed to reach the king in faraway London, but the message from London with the news that William was wanted for questioning in regards to treason left no doubt that it had. Luckily for William, the message arrived before the king's men, and his father had been too softhearted to allow him to come to harm. He had been allowed to flee to safety in Scotland with several days to spare.

He struck the palm of his hand on the battlements' rough stone. After King Henry died, William had tried to return to Thornbeck but entrance had been denied him. His own father had called down from the walls that William was no longer his son and heir. That Owen would take his place. In that instant Owen had become his enemy and William had sworn to see him defeated.

In the intervening years, William had tried on several occasions to take the castle. He knew its weak points and strengths as no one else could. He even drew a detailed plan of the castle from his memory and pored over it for hours at a time, trying to see some way to breach its walls or to tunnel through the solid rock on which it was built.

Owen had surprised William by becoming skilled at defending the castle. His strengths lay in his mind, not in his sword, and in his role as leader, Owen excelled. He seemed to know exactly where William would strike and with what forces. At times it was almost as if someone in the castle were able to see William's intentions as soon as they formed in his mind. Because of this, William had become superstitious about attacking the castle and now called on the services of astrologers and seers to give him the most propitious date. All of them had agreed on the date two days in the future.

William clenched his jaw as he looked over the land that was now so familiar to him. He would have Thornbeck this time! Already he could imagine Queen Mary bestowing rank on him, as well as riches. The island's strategic position all but guaranteed it.

True, at the time, Mary wasn't speaking of war with England and was calling Queen Elizabeth her cousin and friend, but William knew war was inevitable. The two countries had never liked each other and had never been truly at peace. Even now raiders from both sides crossed the border constantly, stealing cattle along with whatever wealth could be found and generally causing trouble. Only a woman would think such a peace would be possible or even desirable.

William glanced around uneasily, his near-treasonous thought unspoken but not necessarily unheard. One couldn't be too careful these days and he cautioned himself to curtail such notions, even within the confines of his mind. Mary was a woman, young and beautiful, but she had a half brother and many other men to lead her. She would be a good queen. He had to believe so.

When she had arrived to occupy the throne, there had been some grumbling that she had been in France practically all her life and her ways were French, not Scottish. At first William had thought it might have been better for the throne to go to the old king's bastard son, a man strong enough to wage war successfully, but then he had met Mary and from that moment on he had been her loyal subject.

William had never married and had no intention of ever doing so. In his opinion, women weakened a man, and too much association with them would bring about a downfall. But Queen Mary had a sweet smile and beautiful hands with long, delicate fingers. She was tall, but she was also graceful, and was romantically lovely. It pleased something deep inside of him to think he could do her this service. It was as close to love as William had ever come in his life.

He gazed toward the North Sea, planning every move of the battle: where they would set up camp on the shore, where they would land on Thornbeck's island, where they would strike the castle. Every step had to be executed perfectly. Each man had to be employed with precision. William was well past his prime and this could be his last chance. He intended for this campaign to succeed.

The boats skimmed silently through the inky water. Thick clouds hid the stars, and even if there had been a moon, its light would not have penetrated them. The men signaled from boat to boat when necessary by using hooded lanterns turned carefully away from the island they approached.

"It'll soon be rainin'," the harsh voice of an oarsman muttered.

"So much the better," William Fleetwood answered, narrowing his eyes and peering into the darkness. His astrologer had said tonight would be the perfect night to take Thornbeck. So far the man had been right, but the unanticipated total darkness and rumble of the approaching storm were unsettling to William because he and his men were in such small boats. Fortunately, the wind always associated with such storms had not yet picked up and the sea was relatively calm. All ten boats were likely to make the crossing without mishap.

It had been decided between William and his next in command that ships with their tall white sails would be too easily seen. Part of Thornbeck's impregnability lay in the fact that invaders could be spotted long before they were within arrow range of the castle.

The first spatters of rain struck William's face. He grinned. He hadn't tried to take the castle for well over two years and fully expected his brother's men would have relaxed their vigilance long before this. Rain would probably send those on watch scurrying into the turret doorways for protection where they would be even less likely to spot the invasion of small boats.

The island loomed closer, a black hulk against the ebony sky. William sniffed the air and recognized the fishy smell of the rocks at the base of the castle. Soon he could hear the rhythmic slap of the waves against the stones. And still no alarm had been raised.

William led the other boats around the cliffs to a narrow beach between the castle and the village. The slope of the beach here was so shallow that two hundred yards off the shore was a submerged sandbar that even at high tide under a full moon was too close to the surface for a ship to sail over. For that reason, his father had considered the sandbar a natural defense against invaders landing there, and as far back as William could remember, little if any attention had been paid to guarding this approach to the island. He felt sure his brother saw it the same way—so much so that he was gambling on it.

Down the beach to his right, he could see a few yellow squares of lamplight shining through the windows of the villagers' homes, but for the most part, the village was dark, and the fishermen and their families were likely fast asleep. Oil for the lamps was dear and was reserved for the hours before daybreak when the fishermen arose and prepared themselves and their nets for the day's work to come. No one in the village was likely to notice the invasion of William's army of men.

They skimmed their shallow draft boats across the sandbar, beached them above the high tide watermark and swarmed over the tumbled boulders and up the hill toward the castle, following William's lead. As William drew closer to the stone fortress, he spotted a lone sentry on the wall, but the man was looking out to sea, not down at the green. William notched an arrow into his bow and prepared to shoot. If the man remained unaware of their presence, there was no need to kill him, thus drawing attention to themselves. With a nod of his head, William signaled his men to proceed to the base of the castle. The guard saw nothing, so William quivered his arrow and caught up with his men.

Finding the castle's great gates closed for the night, just as he had expected them to be, William quietly made his way to the tradesman's gate. Prepared to break the door down if necessary, he pushed against it first, and a broad grin crossed his craggy features as the door swung open easily. This had been the part of his plan of which he was the least sure—and again it had gone his way. It would seem the two years he had spent gathering more men had also allowed time for his brother to become lax.

Staying in the deepest of shadows, William and four of his men slipped into the castle and started up the wooden stairs in the tower that flanked the main gate. One of them tripped and fell in the darkness, but the noise he made was covered by a crack of thunder. William took this as another good omen and urged them on.

Three men were in the room at the top of the tower, talking casually as each looked out to the sea in the distance. Before any of them realized what was happening, William's men slipped up behind them and stabbed them to death. After giving their leader a few seconds to run down the steps, William's men heaved against the wheel that controlled the portcullis and the barrier began to rise. William encountered opposition from only one of Thornbeck's men, also caught off guard, and swiftly dispatched him with his sword. As he reached the main gate and threw open the bolt, he heard the first shouts of alarm, but the warnings came too late. In seconds, William's invaders were through the gate and into the courtyard. William put an arrow to his bow and silenced the guard on the wall who was still shouting in vain.

Following his lead, twenty of William's best men swarmed up the steps to the main entrance to the castle and hacked at the defenders as they appeared. William was jubilant as he rushed into the great hall. They were inside Thornbeck, and it was as good as his own!

As the melodic notes of a lute drifted soothingly across the chamber, Damaris drew her needle through the tapestry in her lap and knotted the silk thread so she could begin another color. Owen was all but dozing by the fire, his eyelids growing heavy. Their men and ladies attending them were engaged in sewing or quiet conversations. Nothing about the evening was unusual.

Damaris smiled across at Meg, who was working on the other side of the tapestry. "This will be lovely in the hall."

"Aye. The old one is falling apart."

"Sometimes I wonder about the Fleetwoods who lived before us. Do you?"

"Nay, my lady. I have enough to do in keeping up with the current ones." Meg smiled to soften the meaning behind her words.

"I think of them often," Edith said from her place nearer the fire. Her eyesight had failed to the point where needlework was impossible for her. "I recall having seen that tapestry in my youth. It was fine. Truly fine. Now the colors seem so blurred. Perhaps it's due to the dampness of the walls. Thornbeck is so damp!"

"The colors have faded. The new one will be much nicer." Damaris was too kind to tell the aging woman that the problem was with Edith's failing vision, not the cloth.

Owen roused and said, "You should be making that tapestry for your own hall, not mine."

"Papa, don't start that again. I don't want to marry a man I've never seen. Besides, you told me you had written to Sir Edwin and refused his son."

"And so I did." Owen sounded tired.

Meg lifted her head. "Did you hear something?"

Damaris paused to listen. "I'm not sure." She looked at the dog that lay on the floor. He had lifted his head and was watching the door.

"It was the wind," Owen said complacently. "No doubt a rain is blowing in."

"It wasn't the sort of sound that wind makes," Damaris said with a small frown. "There. I heard it again."

Owen lifted himself from his chair and went to the door. He opened it and stepped out. Faint sounds could be heard from below. Two of his men joined him. "What can be making that noise?" Owen asked. "Go and see." One of the men left the doorway and started down the hall.

Damaris started another stitch but she was listening carefully. Something about the sounds didn't seem right. No servants would dare get into a fight within the castle, however much reason they felt they might have, but the sounds seemed to be that of a scuffle.

Suddenly the man at the top of the stairs began to yell something, but his words abruptly ended and the only other sound to be heard was the thumping of his body as it fell down the stairs. Moments later the other man standing with Owen shouted and staggered back, an arrow embedded in his chest.

For a stunned moment Damaris and her ladies sat frozen. Then the ladies started screaming and leaping to their feet. The other men in the room ran to the door and one pulled Owen back inside. Moving instinctively, Owen shoved the bar into place to secure the door.

"Papa! What is it?"

"Men are in the castle! There's fighting below!"

Damaris still couldn't comprehend. "Our men? Fighting?"

"No! We've been invaded!" His face was grayish and pale. "Quick! Damaris, take the women out the back way and run to your chamber. Bolt your door and don't open it for anyone!" He ran to Damaris and pushed her toward the opposite door that led to another corridor.

Damaris herded her charges out of the room as the splintering of wood sounded behind them. Fearfully she looked back as the door gave way and several men lunged into the room. The older of the men struck at her father.

"William!" Owen shouted in dismay.

The man, a darker and angrier replica of her father drew his teeth back in a snarl. "Thornbeck is mine!" he growled as he lifted his sword.

Owen grabbed the dagger at his belt, but it was no match against his brother's weapon of war. With one blow of his sword, William struck Owen, and as Owen fell to the floor, blood rushed from his neck. Damaris saw there was nothing she could to do save him. She turned and ran after her ladies.

As she made her way through the relative darkness of the back corridor, she could hear the clash of metal against metal and the shouts of fighting men, but she felt curiously detached. All she could see was her father falling to the floor, mortally wounded. Ahead was the door to her chamber. "Hurry!" she shouted at the women. "Get inside!"

She grabbed one of the younger maids who had fallen and dragged the girl to safety. She and Meg slammed the door and Meg shot the bolt through the metal braces. This was the older part of the castle and all the doors could be barricaded. Damaris ran through the chamber where her ladies slept, the one where Meg slept and her own bedroom, securing each as she went. As she bolted the door that led to a closet and beyond that into a corridor, she heard the angry shouts of men. Someone threw his weight against the door, but it held firm.

Her women crowded about her, crying and wailing and thoroughly frightened. "What happened?" Kate, the youngest, kept asking over and over.

"Thornbeck has been taken!" Damaris's eyes met Meg's. The unthinkable had happened.

"Who can it be? Scots?" Meg asked, her hands trembling visibly as she tried to comfort Kate with hugs and pats.

"Aye." Damaris had never seen a likeness of her uncle, but the family resemblance to her father had been unmistakable.

"Don't fear, my lady. Your father and his men will soon send them packing," Meg said.

Damaris couldn't answer. She couldn't tell them her father and their master already lay dead on the floor of the chamber they had just left. She tried to tell herself she was wrong. After all, she had never seen a mortal wound before and even small wounds could bleed profusely for a while. But even as she tried to hold on to the thread of hope, she knew her father was gone.

During the relative quiet that followed, the ladies huddled together in a corner, but Damaris couldn't be still. She paced the chambers, checking the security of first one lock, then another. At each door she paused to sniff at the cracks in the wood. If the marauders set the castle on fire, she had to somehow get her ladies out and to another, safer place.

After what seemed to be forever, there was a pounding at one of the doors. The women screamed and Damaris motioned for them to be quiet as she reluctantly approached it.

"I know you're in there," a gruff voice said. "Open this door at once."

"I'll do nothing of the kind," Damaris retorted. "My ladies are in here and I'll not see them harmed." Behind her she could hear them crying and praying brokenly.

"No harm will come to you or to them."

"I have no reason to believe you. Who are you?"

"I'm your uncle, William Fleetwood. Thornbeck is mine now and you must come out eventually or starve."

Damaris paused. What he said was true. She went to the door, despite the protests of her women, and drew back the bolt. The door burst open and several men stepped into the room.

Damaris faced them squarely, hoping her fear didn't show. "I'm Damaris Fleetwood. What have you done with my father?"

William looked her over before he spoke. "Owen is dead," he said with no effort to soften the words.

"I know that. I saw him fall under your sword. I asked where he is."

Grudging respect flickered in William's eyes. "I'll have him taken to the hall and laid there with the others."

Damaris refused to let her voice quaver. "He must be buried with due respect in the chapel."

"You're in no position to command anything. However, he's my brother and I'll give him this." William nodded to one of his men. "See that it's done."

"And my people?" she asked.

"I've not counted the dead and wounded. They're still being gathered." He added, "You're overly calm for a maid. Don't you fear what may befall you?" He gave her a mirthless grin.

Her ladies began sobbing and praying fearfully aloud. Damaris met his eyes. "No, I don't. As your niece by blood, I ask sanctuary for my ladies and myself. On your honor as a knight, you cannot refuse me." She hoped the Scottish code of honor was the same as her father's.

William looked as if he were considering this, then said, "Very well. I grant you sanctuary. And sanctuary for your ladies, as well. But you should keep to this chamber this night or I can't vouch for my men."

From below, Damaris could hear screams and her blood ran cold. "And for the other women in the castle?"

William smiled cruelly. "Don't ask too much, my lady, or you'll lose what ground you've gained. My men have been at battle. I'll not stop them from taking whatever booty they claim."

She wanted to put her hands over her ears to muffle the sounds of women's screams from below, but wouldn't give William the satisfaction. She hoped her ladies' sobs and prayers prevented them from knowing what was happening in other parts of the castle.

William made her a half bow. "Until later then."

Damaris closed the door behind him and when she heard their footsteps fading away, she again bolted it.

Meg rushed to her. "My lady! What are we to do?"

"We're to wait. Whatever you do, Meg, don't open any of our outside doors or allow any of the others to do so. They must stay bolted until I tell you differently."

Meg nodded, her eyes large and fearful.

Damaris went to the ladies and tried to soothe them, but she had little luck. Their families were in the castle or on the island and there was no assurance that they weren't all being raped or slaughtered.

The night was long and the candles had guttered and gone out long before dawn light touched the windows. Damaris hadn't slept at all, but most of her ladies had collapsed with fright and weariness.

She stood, gazing out at the broad expanse of sea and wondering what on earth she was going to do.

At midmorning the following day, Damaris, followed closely by her ladies, left the sanctuary of her chambers to venture downstairs. None of them spoke as they went down the corridor and past the door that led to the chamber where Owen had died. At the head of the stairs Damaris paused.

"We could go back, my lady," Meg whispered. "No one has seen us yet."

"There's nothing to eat in the chamber," Damaris said. "We can't stay there forever."

She lifted her chin and started down the stairs, her ladies close behind her. She couldn't help but notice that the wooden stair treads beneath her feet were randomly stained dark red from the blood shed in the battle. Hoping she wasn't drawing attention to the ghastly evidence, Damaris stepped around the stains and held her skirts away even though she knew the wood was no longer wet.

As soon as she reached the lower floor, a group of men reeking from their plundering of Thornbeck's wine cellar stopped them. Damaris stared them down. "Where is my uncle, Sir William Fleetwood?"

"In the hall there," one of the men said.

Damaris led the way to the hall and stepped past the screens passage. She almost didn't recognize the chamber as the one she had known all her life. Dead and wounded men were lying on the tables where Damaris was accustomed to eating dinner. Others lay on the rushes, some crumpled with obvious disregard. The straw was splotched with crimson and the stench threatened to overpower her. At the far end of the room she saw her uncle William seated at an empty table with several of his men. Squaring her shoulders so she would appear confident and mask her fear, she headed in his direction.

As they passed between the tables, several of her ladies exclaimed and began to moan, apparently recognizing faces of friends and relatives who had not been as fortunate as they. Young Kate gave a startled sob and moved as if to bolt from the room, but one of the older ladies restrained her and whispered something to her, no doubt reminding her that what safety she might be afforded by being attached to Damaris would be lost once she separated herself from the group.

As the ladies approached, William and the other men looked up, but no one spoke.

Damaris drew to a stop only a few feet away from William, her arms relaxed in front of her and her hands lightly clasped together. Looking down on him, she boldly asked, "When is my father to be properly buried?"

As casually as if he were asked such a question every day, William said, "As a man of my word, we were waiting for you before beginning."

She let herself glance about the room, keeping her face a careful mask. "And these others?"

"My men are digging a pit outside the castle walls for the dead. The wounded will be allowed to go to their homes in the village after they have sworn loyalty to me. Those who refuse will be killed."

The cold, calculating manner in which he had spoken of taking even more lives gripped her heart with fear, and for a moment Damaris couldn't speak. Somehow maintaining her composure, she said, "I will meet you in the chapel," then she turned and walked away.

As she passed a group of Thornbeck's wounded men, one caught her skirt. "We tried, my lady. I'm sorry."

Damaris knelt beside him. "You're not to blame. We were taken off guard. Listen carefully to me. Swear loyalty to Sir William. Do whatever you must to save your life. Tell all the others to do the same."

A man beside him whispered, "Never! I'll die before I swear loyalty to a Scotsman!"

"That's exactly what will happen if you don't. I need you alive. Not dead."

The man ducked his head but nodded.

To the first man, Damaris whispered, "Have an able man meet me at sundown in the kitchen garden." From the corner of her eye she saw William and his men approaching, so she touched the heads of the wounded men and said aloud, "I thank you for all you've done to keep Thornbeck safe and I blame you not. Sir William is master here now. I bear you no ill will."

As quickly as she could without being obvious, Damaris hurried herself and her ladies-in-waiting from the room and into the entry. For a moment she thought she was going to be sick, but stifled the gag reflex. So many were dead! Even more were wounded! She hadn't expected the toll to be so heavy. Thornbeck's carpenters always kept a few coffins on hand for unexpected deaths, but they would be busy day and night for weeks trying to meet this need. Then she remembered William had said a pit was being dug. The men who had fought so valiantly defending Thornbeck weren't to have coffins at all.

Keeping her head high, she went to the chapel. Her father's body was there, as her uncle had said it would be, and she was relieved to see it had been placed in a coffin. Steeling herself against the emotions that would reveal her vulnerability, she went to the coffin and looked in at him. He looked as peacefully at rest as if he were sleeping. Thankfully, someone had wiped the blood from his neck and face and had draped a cloth over his clothes to hide the stains.

"They might at least have let us prepare him!" Meg said. "'Tis barbaric to lay him to rest in the clothes in which he died."

"Apparently that's an apt description of my uncle." Damaris wanted to touch her father, but Edith caught her hand.

"Don't, my lady. It's best not to touch him."

Damaris understood. This gray skin wouldn't feel like the father she had known and loved. She led her ladies to the pew they normally occupied for regular chapel services.

Several of William's men came forward, fitted the lid on the coffin and hammered it in place. Damaris didn't so much as flinch.

Once the reverberation of the hammering stopped, the chaplain came into the chapel, his face filled with fright. Respectfully, he nodded to Damaris, and she nodded in return. She thanked God that the chaplain's life had been spared and hoped he would be allowed to conduct at least a brief service for the mass grave outside, as well.

Noisily, William came down the aisle and sat in the pew opposite Damaris. He glanced at the coffin, then turned to look at her and proceeded to watch her during the entirety of the short service. Damaris stayed in the chapel until the stone slab covering her father's final resting place had been removed from the floor and his coffin lowered into the grave. Her eyes were painfully dry, and although she no longer was trying to hold back her emotions, she was unable to cry and feared that she would choke on her feelings instead. Her grief was too deep for expression.

With a harsh scraping noise, the stone was levered back into place and dropped with an echoing thud. Edith and Damaris's other ladies were crying, but Meg was as dry-eyed as her mistress.

Damaris looked over at William, who was still staring in her direction. Fueled by righteous anger, she said, "My ladies and I want food brought to my chambers. I don't trust your men."

William looked as if he were about to refuse, but he nodded. "I'll give you three days' grace for mourning. After that, you'll be expected to take your meals in the hall."

She wasn't sure she would ever be able to eat in that room again, but she nodded. With her ladies behind her, she went silently back to her chamber.

That same evening, when the shadows started to lengthen, Damaris had Kate bring her the gown Kate had worn when she first came to live in the castle. It was plain and not unlike those worn by the village women. Although it was short on Damaris, it would serve the purpose.

"What are you about to do?" Meg asked for the hundredth time. "Why would you want to wear such a gown?"

"I don't want to draw attention to myself." She turned to let Kate and Lettice, another of the younger women, lace her into the bodice.

"You're not leaving the chamber!" Meg exclaimed, staring in disbelief at her.

"Of course I am. You heard me tell that man to send someone to meet me in the kitchen garden."

"You'll have him take you to the mainland?" Edith asked. "But where will you go then?"

"I'm going nowhere. I wouldn't abandon you and I couldn't hope to take you across the water in such a boat as I have in mind."

"Then what are you going to do?"

"Don't worry. I'll be careful."

She let herself out and waited until she heard the bolt slide into place, securing the door behind her. Her ladies would be safe until she could return.

With the household routine disrupted by the invasion, the evening's rush torches had not been ensconced along the corridor to take the place of the rapidly failing daylight. For a moment Damaris stood still, allowing her eyes to adjust to the growing darkness, then she moved as quickly and silently as she could toward the back stairs that were used only by the servants. There, the steps were all but invisible in the inky blackness and every footfall was risky, but she didn't mind. A light could give her away, and that would be a much greater risk. For a few seconds she paused on the ground floor landing, keeping to the shadows while she assessed whether the way was clear. From the boisterous singing and stamping of feet coming from the great hall, she assumed that William's men were already well into their cups and likely not paying close attention to anything other than the ale and wine. Bending low, she darted across the landing and headed down the short flight that led to the kitchens.

Nearing the kitchen door, she heard a voice and shrank back into the shadows. Whoever it was must have turned into the kitchen, and she breathed a sigh of relief. It was probably only one of her servants, and even though she knew they were all loyal to her, she didn't want anyone knowing that she was no longer in her chamber.

Fleet as a deer, she shot past the kitchen doorway and skittered down another flight of steps into the blackness below. She knew by memory she was in the buttery, and the cold, clammy air that enveloped her was reassuring. Even with her eyes adjusting, she could see nothing beyond her nose. Feeling her way along, she found the butts of wine she knew to be nearest the outside door and prayed no one had locked it. She gave the door a shove, and when it gave under her hand, she let out her pent up breath.

Early night had fallen, but there was enough light from the windows of the kitchen for her to make her way quickly to the walled kitchen garden. She let herself in through the side gate and looked around. "Are you here?" she whispered.

"Here, my lady."

A boy who lacked manhood by several summers moved in the deep shadows to show his position and Damaris went to him. She recognized him as one of the Hobson family. She knew him to be one of Meg's cousins and to be dependable, as well as brave. "I'm glad it's you, Gil." she said in relief.

"What will you have me do?" he whispered.

"I want you to find a boat and row to the mainland for help."

"I cannot, my lady. All the village boats have been taken. So have the castle's, I'm certain."

"There's a boat Sir William's men may not have found yet. Do you remember Old Jack Farley?"

The boy nodded. "He's the crazed old man that lives in the cliff beneath the Maidens' hill."

"He has a fishing boat. It's small and old, but it's seaworthy. Don't tell him, just take it. I'll buy him another when this is all over. As addled as his brains are, he might tell the wrong person you took it."

"Aye, my lady."

Damaris pulled a ring from her finger and put it in Gil's hand. "By whatever means you can, make your way to the court in London and give this ring to the queen."

"To court?" he gasped. "To the queen?"

"She has to be told that Thornbeck has been taken. The crest on my ring will prove to her that you speak the truth. Tell her all you know and she'll send men to take back the island." Damaris glanced over her shoulder. "Here are some coins, as well. There aren't many, but it's all I could put my hands upon. Use them to buy a horse and food when you reach shore. Go now, before I'm missed."

He slipped the ring and coins into a pouch that hung from his rope belt and hesitated. "My cousin, Meg," he ventured. "Is she . . . unharmed?"

"Aye, Gil. She's quite safe. All my ladies have been spared. I'll get word to your mother so she won't worry about you."

He smiled and nodded. "Goodbye, my lady."

"Fare well, Gil, and be careful."

She waited until he faded into the darkness beyond the gate, then retraced her steps.

The stairs were easier to climb on the return trip, but she was fearful her absence had already been noticed. When she reached the upper corridor, she was about to run down it when she heard voices. She froze into the shadows, her gown blending with the darkness, and turned toward the wall so her pale skin wouldn't give her away.

The men were drunk and were staggering as they approached. For a terrible moment she thought they had seen her, then realized they were only bragging about their conquests the evening before. Her stomach churned as they described in lurid detail the direction their pleasures had taken.

The slamming of a door told her they had gone into the chamber across from the one where her younger maids slept. Damaris waited for a moment, then hurried down the hall as fast as she could. She heard the door opening again and dodged into a corner, but no one came out and soon the door was shut again.

She went to her chamber and rapped lightly on the door. "Meg, let me in," she whispered.

The bolt was drawn and she pressed through the crack in the door. All her ladies crowded around her. "I'm all right. I've sent Gil for help."

"He's a good lad," Meg said in a worried voice. "If any can reach London, he can."

Damaris blew out the candle nearest the window to darken the room and looked out into the night. At first she could see nothing, then she made out the shape of a small boat rowing away from the island. The boy's body was silhouetted against the sea as he pulled on the oars. For a minute she thought he was escaping undetected. Then a cry went up from the battlements. Arrows whistled through the air and she saw tiny plumes of water spring up as they landed around the boat.

Damaris leaned against the window, her heart racing. Would he make it? In the dark she could no longer be certain that she saw him sitting erect in the boat. Was he hurt or killed? Slowly the boat drifted on the tide toward the mainland.

Damaris stepped away from the window.

"What is it, my lady?" Meg asked. "Could you see him?"

"Aye." She didn't want to worry Meg if Gil was unharmed. If ill had befallen him, they would know soon enough. "We've done all we can. Now we must wait." She prayed the boy had escaped unharmed and that he had only been lying low and riding the tide out of the range of the arrows. Otherwise, they were trapped on the island with William and his men and with no means of rescue.

Chapter Three

Gavin had been restless of late, with no idea as to what was troubling him. He had never before had difficulty sleeping, but now he was beset by nightmares and sleepless nights. Claudia, who continued to seek out Gavin for conversation, attributed his uneasiness to the fact that her husband was again at court, but since Gavin had ended his relationship with Claudia, he had no interest in Sir Percy's whereabouts.

"I've never seen you so short of temper," Robert Grainger said as they cantered their horses through the parkland toward Windsor Palace. "Are you ailing?"

"No." Gavin frowned at the palace. "I feel as well as always. You know I never sicken."

"Then what's troubling you? For the past two days you've all but taken my head off whenever I've tried to talk to you. It's not Claudia, is it? You've not gone and fallen in love with her."

"No, of course not. In truth, I find her pursuit of me trying. I wish Sir Percy were keeping a closer eye on her."

"They say she's started to bestow her favors on Sir Hugh Fraser."

"He's welcome to them. She dislikes her husband and I believe the feeling is mutual. Soon Sir Percy will journey back to his estates and his mistress and Claudia will be happy again."

"If it's not Claudia, then what is it?" Robert pursued.

Gavin reined in his horse and looked around. The park was as it always had been. Beyond the trees he could see the open green and, past that, the pale gray of the palace. "I don't know. I can't explain it. It's as if something is wrong, but I don't know what it can be. It's the way a man feels before a battle, when he knows the enemy is out there waiting for him, but they've not yet set eyes upon each other."

"You think the French or Spanish plan to attack England?"

"No. I don't know what to think." Gavin tried to laugh it off. "Perhaps I'm growing as wearisome as an old maid, with staying so long at court. I need fiercer play than Claudia offered."

"We could go boar hunting on my father's estates in Northumberland. We've not been there in nearly a year. I'm sure the queen would grant us leave to go."

"Perhaps so." Gavin gazed back toward the palace. A rider was coming their way. He narrowed his eyes as the man approached.

"Pardon, Sir Gavin, Sir Robert," the rider said as he drew up his horse. "The queen has sent for you."

"The queen?"

"She said for me to bring you to her as soon as I could find you."

Gavin exchanged a look with Robert. "Let's go."

Elizabeth was in her presence chamber. Kneeling in front of her was a towheaded boy dressed in peasant clothes. Gavin bowed to his sovereign, then looked at the boy.

"Tell him what you told me," the queen commanded.

The boy scrambled to his feet. "Sir, I'm Gil Hobson, of Thornbeck. The castle has been taken by Scotsmen and I've come to beg assistance."

"Thornbeck?" Gavin said. Wasn't that the name of the castle belonging to the Fleetwood family that he was recently expected to marry into?

"Aye. It's been taken by Sir William Fleetwood of Scotland." The boy's eyes were large and fearful. He seemed to be as frightened of the opulent room and glittering people as he was of the marauding Scots. "He's killed our Lord Fleetwood and many of our men at the castle. Our lady of the castle is held prisoner, along with her ladies."

Gavin looked around and saw his father was there. Edwin's face was drawn and sad. He was still adjusting to the news of his old friend's murder. "Have the ladies been harmed?"

"No, sir. Not the ones living in the castle. Not when I last saw them. Our lady said she's keeping her attendants close by her for their protection."

Gavin wasn't too sure what to make of this. He looked at Robert, then at their queen. "Your highness, I ask that I be allowed to go to Thornbeck with my men to take it back for England."

"That's why I sent for you." Queen Elizabeth's voice was calm and strong, but he could hear the checked anger beneath it. "Thornbeck is too important an island for me to allow it to remain in Scottish hands. You're to take it back and remain there until I decide who will be given the island and castle." She glanced at Edwin, her black eyes as sharp as arrow tips. "You father tells me Owen, Lord Fleetwood, died without heirs."

"There's a daughter," Gavin said.

"I'll find a man to marry her. A man strong enough to entrust with the castle and island. In the meantime, you'll remain there and keep it safe for England."

Gavin bowed. "You may depend on me, madam."

Elizabeth gestured. "Mistress Woodard, take the boy and find him something to eat. He looks half-exhausted." A woman motioned for Gil to follow her. He bowed awkwardly and left with her. To Gavin, Elizabeth said, "The boy is familiar with Thornbeck castle. He can tell you the best way to breach it." She held out a small ring with the insignia of a griffin. "Return this ring to the lady of the castle."

He took the ring and bowed as she waved a dismissal at him.

In the corridor, Robert caught up with him. "Is this, then, the battle you foresaw? I never knew you to have the sight." His words were only half-joking.

"Nor do I have. Call it instead a premonition." Gavin grinned and his strong white teeth gleamed. "So it seems I'm to journey to Thornbeck after all."

"But on a more dangerous mission."

"Maybe. You heard the lad say the lady of the castle keeps her women close to her and that she is their protector. In faith, this griffin on the ring may be her likeness for all we know!" The ring lay small in his palm. The lady who had worn it had slender fingers.

Robert laughed. "If such be so, you've done well to avoid her snare."

"At least we'll have something more interesting to do than to ride after our hawks or to hunt boars. I'd rather do battle with Scots any day."

"As would I."

Gavin parted from his friend and went to his chamber to ready himself for their departure.

As he was instructing his manservant what to pack, Edwin came in. "So. You're to meet her after all."

"Father, I'm sorry for your friend. And I'm sorry you had to hear his fate so abruptly."

Edwin made a dismissing gesture. "I fear more for his daughter. Scots are barbarians."

"This particular Scot bears her family name."

"Yes. William Fleetwood. The castle would have been his, but he was a traitor to King Henry and had to flee to Scotland long before you were born. Owen often told me of his brother's attempts to take the castle." Edwin became thoughtful. "I was never able to picture Owen as a fighter. He was gentle and a scholar. The castle must be a stronghold indeed."

"If it is, it could be difficult to regain it." Gavin shook his head as his valet began packing a finely embroidered doublet in Gavin's traveler's bag. "Bring those when you come, George," he said. "I need only what I'll wear in battle at first." To his father he added, "But I'll have an advantage. There are people inside the castle that will want my men inside. We'll gain access."

"Be careful, son." Edwin put his hand on Gavin's arm, his eyes filled with worry.

"I will, Papa." Gavin smiled at him fondly.

"I would that you had been betrothed to Damaris Fleet-wood. Then this might not have happened, and Owen might still be alive."

"My betrothal wouldn't have stopped the Scots. How could they even have known of it?"

"True, but then you'd have Thornbeck and its wealth. Now they'll go, along with the lady, to some other man."

"That suits me well. I do admit, though, to a certain curiosity. What sort of lady is able to safeguard her ladies against warriors? She sounds like a dragon."

"I know nothing of her temperament," Edwin admitted. "Now it matters not what the lady is like. You're not to have her."

"Let's hope the queen finds her a suitable husband quickly. I don't think I'd like to be fastened away on an island with a dragon, whether it's to be mine or not." He laughed softly. "As soon as I may, I'll write to you and tell you I'm safe and that you're fortunate not to have this lady for a daughter. You'll see. All will be well."

"Godspeed, son. I'll worry about Owen's daughter until I hear from you that all is well."

"I must go to ready my men. I'll see you at the table tonight." Gavin left Edwin to finish overseeing the packing. For so many men to travel so far required planning. Fortunately the court moved fairly often and the men were accustomed to it, as were their servants. Within days of Gavin's men arriving at Thornbeck, the bedding, clothing and servants would arrive on the slower wagons. Gavin hoped by then to be in command of the castle.

Gavin found Robert with most of the other men in the room that served as a barracks for the unmarried knights with no household staff. They were all talking eagerly and none seemed reluctant to go.

"I've sent a boy for the weapons we'll need," Godfrey Hammett said. He was Gavin's third-in-command and was a fierce warrior despite his prematurely graying hair. "The wagons are already being packed." He pulled forward the boy Gavin had seen in the presence chamber. "Young man, tell us about the castle."

Gil looked from one to the other. He seemed more than a little afraid and determined to hide it. "Thornbeck sits on an island in the North Sea, just north of Holy Island."

"What of its docks? What defenses has it?" Gavin asked.

"There are places to dock boats such as the ones we use for fishing all around the island. The most direct approach will take you directly under the old wing of the castle. On that side, the cliffs lead from the sea straight up to the castle."

"That doesn't sound like the best place to land."

"No, but it's the last direction they would expect attack from."

Gavin gave him a look of approval. "Then there's a way to go up the cliffs?"

"Aye. I've climbed them many times. If you know where to step it's not so difficult."

"What of the other landing places?" Robert asked.

"The best place is at the village, but you'd easily be seen there and word would reach the castle of your rescue effort before you could cross the green."

"That wouldn't do." Gavin took out his knife and knelt to draw on the floor. "Show me where the castle and village lie."

Gil awkwardly drew an outline of the island. "The castle is here, on the side nearest the mainland. The village is below it and to the southwest. Up here are the Whispering Maidens."

"Who?" Gavin asked.

"It's a magical stone circle. Cliffs lie below them. That's where I escaped. I stole Old Jack Farley's boat and rowed for the mainland."

"We'll see that it's returned," Gavin said with a grin. "Your thievery was necessary."

Gil bent back over the crude sketch. "The way up the cliff is here. It twists and turns back upon itself until you reach the top."

Godfrey frowned. "If we're seen, the Scots will be able to pick us off one by one."

"It would be hard to see into these clefts from the castle wall," Gil said. "We could go across at night."

"Once we're at the top, how do we enter the castle?" Robert leaned forward to study the drawing.

"There's the hard part," Gil admitted. "A path leads to the main gates, but they're sure to be barred. There's a small gate here—" he pointed "—that leads into the kitchen gardens, but anyone on the wall might see you."

"We could use explosives," Godfrey said.

"Or we could tunnel under the wall," Robert added.

"Thornbeck sits on solid rock," Gil said, his eyes wide. "No one could tunnel under it."

"Explosives would bring down the wall," Gavin said, "but then the castle would be indefensible for us. We have to leave the walls intact."

"There's another way. It will take longer to enter the castle, but there's less chance the Scots will be alerted." Gil pointed back at the cliffs. "There's an entrance here from the sea. It leads into the room where the castle fishing boats are kept, but it has a lead door that's certain to be locked. We might be able to signal someone to open it from inside. There's no other entrance to the castle, at least not that I've ever heard of."

"You're a good man, young Gil. I couldn't have asked for a better guide."

The boy flushed and grinned as he ducked his head.

"When we get there, we'll manage to breach the walls somehow," Gavin said with confidence. "Finish preparing for the journey, men, and get plenty of rest tonight. We'll be on our way before dawn light."

Robert and Godfrey exchanged grins of expectation. "We'll all be ready."

Damaris sat silently in the chapel, gazing at the stone that covered the grave of her father. Her mother lay beside him and a stone effigy of her topped her grave. In time Damaris intended to commission a similar one for her father. She had no intention of allowing the castle to remain in William's hands.

William and his men had left her women undisturbed and the castle had settled into an uneasy calm. Damaris didn't trust any of the invaders, however, and kept her ladies in her chambers whenever possible. She had seen the lecherous grins on some of the men's faces at meals, and she didn't want to take any chances. As William's niece, she was somewhat safer, especially if she was in the chapel. The Scots were too superstitious to attack anyone here. In the past few days Damaris had come here often.

Again her mind went back to the night she had sent young Gil Hobson for help. He was so young! Had he been able to reach shore safely? No one claimed to have seen him fall into the water, though she had heard William's men discussing his escape. Most of them were of the opinion that he was merely a frightened youth who had decided to head for the mainland while he could. She was glad to let everyone think so.

If Gil had reached land, had he been able to find London? Most of England lay between the capital city and her island. Gil had never been off the island in his life. Had he been able to buy a horse with the few coins she had given him?

She wished a dozen times she had sent someone older and that she had been able to give him adequate money to aid his journey. He had been gone two weeks already. What if help never came?

Damaris rubbed her eyes wearily. She was tired to the bone from pretending to be brave. Her ladies needed to see her strength, but there were times when she simply wanted to curl up and cry. She missed her father terribly and had no one she could confide in. Meg would have listened, but Meg was afraid, as was everyone else. Damaris had no one to lean upon but herself.

"Papa," she whispered toward the cold stone at her feet, "you were right. I should have let you betroth me to someone. Anyone!" Tears stung her eyes and she had to blink them away. "I won't give up! Gil will reach court and bring men back. I have to believe that. It's been two weeks, but he may have had to walk most of the way. Or he may have gotten lost. But he will eventually find London, and the queen will send men to regain control the castle."

She put out her hand and touched the damp stones of the chapel wall. This, the oldest part of the castle, dated back to when the motte and bailey castle had been dismantled and a stone one erected in its place. This chapel, according to her family legend, had been the first of the new buildings. Now it was so ancient the stones seemed to have grown into their present shape, rather than having been man-made.

Damaris stood and left the chapel. She couldn't stay inside another minute. A glance out the nearest window told her it was still early. Her ladies wouldn't miss her if she was gone a little longer.

She walked briskly along the short corridor to the old steps that led down into the ground floor. There was a door there that was rarely used as it was dangerously near the edge of the cliff. She wasn't sure why it had been put there in the first place. The castle children had been positive it was used as an execution place and that all sorts of traitors and murders had been shoved out the door and over the edge of the cliff to their deaths. As a child she had believed the tale; as an adult she could see many reasons why it was unlikely to have been true.

Damaris stepped out of the castle and walked along the narrow rock ledge. Beneath her, she could see the waves breaking on the black, wet rocks. Birds swooped and called but she paid them no attention. They nested in the cliffs and had fished these waters for as long as there had been cliffs and birds.

She kept close to the castle so no one could see her until she was all the way around to where the land was covered by downy grass. There she stepped onto a path that led up and away from the castle. Ahead of her were the Maidens, who were always waiting for her.

The path circled around the stones then back down the hill. At the closest proximity to the stones, she left the path and crossed the blowing grasses. Soon she was flanked by the first of the ancient stones. Her pace increased.

As usual, there was a strong wind on the unprotected hill and it tugged at her bound hair, trying to pull it free. Damaris ignored it. She couldn't take the time to recomb it before returning to the castle and didn't want to raise attention to herself by arriving with it flowing down her back.

As was her custom, she paused before stepping into the circle. The green, with its myriad flowers, undulated in the wind, and the stones seemed to utter soft sighs as the wind blew past. This was a sound Damaris was long accustomed to, and one that prompted the villagers to say the stones spoke at times.

Reverently she entered the circle and walked to the very middle. Slowly she turned around full circle, looking for a moment at each individual stone and recognizing it and loving it. For the first time since the invasion, she felt safe and at peace.

Slowly she went to the Priestess and put both her palms on the bluish stone. Strength surged up her hands and arms. Damaris closed her eyes and let her body relax. She was safe here. She always had been.

Her mind began to drift and pictures started forming behind her eyelids. Patiently Damaris let the pictures become clearer and then the meaning behind the vision came to her. A tall woman with hair the same color as hers was smiling at her, though the standing stones behind her seemed to be different from the ones surrounding Damaris. Her lips never moved, but Damaris heard her say, "Be brave. Follow your destiny."

As quickly as the picture had come, it started to fade, and Damaris tried to hold on to it. "I don't understand," she said aloud. "What do you mean?"

The smile on the image's lips grew sad as if she wanted to say more but was unable to do so. "Your destiny," she whispered without speaking.

"What *is* my destiny?" Damaris asked. "What am I supposed to do?"

"When the time comes, you'll know," the woman whispered, then vanished.

Damaris opened her eyes and glanced around. She was still alone, of course. She had seen this woman before under like circumstances. Her messages were always this obscure and Damaris often wondered why that was. If someone, presumably her mother, was trying to give her a message, why not just come right out and say what she meant and be done with it?

She sighed and sat on the altar stone. The pictures she saw in the copper bowl were often as vague, and they didn't have the added advantage of being audible. The woman wanted her to follow her destiny—whatever that might be. Did anyone have the option not to follow it, Damaris wondered fretfully. Could destiny be averted? Apparently so, since the woman told her to follow it.

She looked back at the castle. It seemed to shimmer in the sunlight, as if silver were threaded among the stones. On the highest parapet a flag bearing the crest of Scotland, not England, fluttered in the breeze. It hurt Damaris's eyes to see it. She could see men pacing atop the battlements, gazing out to sea and passing the time of day. She doubted that they would notice her unless the color of her gown and kirtle drew their attention. The Maidens didn't beckon most people the way they did her.

Damaris let her gaze wander out to sea. She could see the mainland far in the distance to the west. To the south she imagined she could make out the landmass of Holy Island, but she had never been sure that wasn't a trick of her mind.

Occasionally, after a particularly fierce storm, she had walked on the beach nearest Holy Island and found some of the small pebbles with holes through them, known as St. Cuthbert's beads. These were believed to protect the wearer against drowning. They were prized among the fishermen in the village and, as St. Cuthbert was the patron saint of Thornbeck and its island, most of the men and boys wore at least one of those beads around their necks. She wondered if Gil Hobson had been wearing one that day she sent him off alone.

It bothered her that she had sent the boy on such a mission. What if he had died as a result? Damaris felt responsible for the people on her island and had always acted in their best interest.

Resolutely she rose and left the circle. Not bothering to go down the stone-marked path, she cut across the fields as she had as a girl, straight toward the village.

She knew which cottage belonged to the Hobsons, as she knew which family lived in every cottage or croft on the island. She went to the Hobsons' door and it was opened immediately by a woman not much older than herself, but who was already worn with work and childbearing. "Hello, Bess. May I talk to you?"

Bess Hobson looked surprised at the visit but nodded and stepped aside. "Of course, my lady."

Damaris went into the cottage and looked around. The room was small but Bess kept it clean. A small child played on the dirt floor, two others sat at the table, frankly staring at her.

"Have ye heard from our Gil?" Bess asked breathlessly. She clutched her soiled apron and kneaded it in her worry.

"Nay, Bess. Not yet." Damaris wished she weren't seeing the pain in Bess's eyes. "I've come to see if all is well with you. Have the Scots harmed you or yours?"

"Nay. They come marching down the road betimes, but they don't stay. They just go to their boats and do their business and leave again." She motioned for her children to move away from the table so Damaris had a place to sit. Once Damaris was seated, Bess sat opposite her, not taking her eyes off her mistress.

Damaris smiled at her. "Meg is well. She would have sent you a greeting if she had known I was coming to the village."

Bess nodded and almost allowed herself to smile. "I'll tell her mother. She worries so, you know."

Damaris nodded. "Do you have enough to eat?"

"Aye. The Scots have started letting our men fish again. I guess they finally realized we can't live on seawater and air." Her voice was sharp in her dislike of the invaders. "You'd think anybody would know a fisherman has to go out in a boat if they're to live."

"I'm sure they were afraid the men would try to head for the mainland and get help."

"And some likely would, if it wasn't for leaving their families behind. The Scots told us they'd kill any family that was left."

"Just do as they tell you. Keep yourselves safe." Damaris reached down to touch the fair hair of the youngest child, who was staring at her with innocent, round blue eyes. "She looks like you." The child smiled up at her.

"That's my youngest. She don't talk yet." Bess leaned toward the child. "Can you bob a curtsy to our lady?"

The child laughed, turned and ran across the room to her brother and sister.

"Don't mind her," Bess said quickly. "She's no more than a baby."

"I know. I was thinking how good it must be to have little children about."

Bess looked at her as if she thought Damaris had lost her mind. "I never thought of it before. When you're married, the bairns just come, bidden or not."

"Yes." Damaris stood and went back to the door. "I'll let you know as soon as I have word about Gil."

Bess curtsied. "Thank you, my lady."

As Damaris was leaving, she saw Bess's husband, Wat, coming toward the cottage. He didn't look glad to see her. "Good day, Wat," she said when he was near.

"Is there word of my lad?" he demanded.

"Not yet."

"If he's dead, I'm out a fisherman," Wat said. He had been drinking even though it was early in the day, and he was known to be a mean drunk. "He was just getting old enough to bring in a catch and pull his own weight."

"I pray he's safe." She met his eyes and waited until Wat dropped his glare. "Good day to you, Wat," she said with studied composure. She had never cared for the man and couldn't see for the life of her why Bess, so gentle and pretty in her youth, had married him.

Wat watched her go and spat on the ground where she had stood. One of his cronies was passing by and he came to Wat. "Is there news of young Gil?"

"No, and I'm doubting there ever will be! He's gone. Drowned in the sea for no reason at all."

The other man scratched his head. "He was sent for help."

Wat made a growling sound. "Use your noggin, Ben. What difference does it make to us if the gentry in the castle is English or Scots? All we do is fish and drink and die. My life's no different. Neither is yours."

Ben shook his head. "I doubt the Scots will look after us so well as the lady and her father did. None of us have ever gone hungry. Not even that winter all the fish seemed to have left the sea. The castle kept us fed and clothed. When a man is lost at sea, they see to it the widow isn't turned out."

"And what help is that? If she's a widow, she ought to give over her house to a working man. I'd see all the widows herded together and done away with if it was up to me." Wat watched Damaris go up the road toward the castle. "I seen her in the Maidens not an hour ago."

Ben followed his gaze. "I see her there often."

"She's a witch, if you ask me. Her father might have been a decent sort, but she's a witch like her mother was before her."

"I can't remember her mother and neither can you."

"No, but my old mam can. She said they look so alike that it's downright peculiar. That it's like seeing Lady Matilda alive and walking again."

Ben crossed himself for protection. "That can't be. Not really."

"I've heard it all my life and so have you. Have you ever looked at the color of her eyes? They're the color of the sea just before a killing gale cuts loose!"

"I've noticed that." Ben moved uneasily and glanced after Damaris again.

"She's always up there in the Maidens. That's not a place for a man, let alone a woman. And lady of the castle or not, that's all she is—a maid! We'd not let our womenfolk go up there to them rocks!"

"My womenfolk wouldn't go if you dragged 'em."

"That's just my point. It ain't natural for her to be like that. She's a witch, I tell you."

"Don't say such in front of my woman," Ben said with a half laugh. "She sets a store by our lady. She says we'd have lost our second boy to the fever if the castle physician hadn't come to look at him."

"You let your woman take too many liberties. You ought to keep her in line the way I do my Bess." Wat wiped at his nose with his sleeve and glared after Damaris. "The boy might not have fallen sick in the first place if she hadn't cast those peculiar eyes in his direction.''

Ben shook his head doubtfully. "I always reckoned it was that fishhook he stepped on. It festered and went bad. You know how that can affect a lad.''

Wat was still staring after Damaris. "No good will come of her. Mark you my words! We've got Scots commanding the island and a witch woman in the castle. One of 'em has got to go!''

Ben shifted his weight. "I don't reckon how either one is going to leave. Not unless her uncle finds a man and marries her off.''

"Scotland still has convents. He can send her to one of 'em. Best be rid of her any way he can!''

Ben crossed himself again. "Mayhap. Mayhap.''

Wat sighed and turned toward his house. "Are you going to the tavern later?''

"Most likely.''

"I'll see you there.'' He saw no reason to stay at home when he could be anywhere else at all. Bess was home to look after the young ones and that was a woman's duty. A man's was to provide food and shelter. As long as they had a cottage and he was a skilled fisherman, Wat saw no reason to give Bess companionship, as well. He went into his cottage to see if she had his meal ready.

Chapter Four

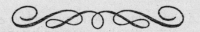

"So you'll be leaving, Uncle?" Damaris said, her eyes cool and distant. "After so long an absence from Thornbeck, I assumed you'd tarry longer." With her fork she pushed the food about on her trencher. After seeing the tables here in the hall used for the dead and wounded after the siege, she could hardly bear to eat off them.

William looked with distaste on his niece. She epitomized everything he disliked in women. "I'm going to court. Queen Mary must be told of my conquest. No doubt I'll return a lord."

Damaris shrugged. "Who will be in command while you're gone?"

With the knife he was using to spear his food, William gestured down the table at the swarthy man who often accompanied him around the castle. "Sir James there. You'll do as he says."

Damaris was careful to keep her face expressionless. She had noticed that James was too fond of the women in her castle. Without William in command, she and her ladies might not be as safe.

William seemed to divine her thoughts. "I've noticed him watching those two young maids of yours. I'd keep them close if you want them to remain maids." He gave her an evil grin.

Damaris glanced at Kate and Lettice, who were seated nearby. Neither were much older than fifteen, if that old. A man like James McIntyre wouldn't be stopped by the fact that the girls were little more than children.

A server brought by a platter of canolyne and presented it to Damaris, but she shook her head. Three weeks had passed since Gil had escaped from Thornbeck seeking help. Would he ever return? "When will we be honored by your absence, Uncle?" She never missed an opportunity to remind him of their kinship. This was all that had kept her and her ladies safe.

"I leave on the tide in about an hour."

"You'll travel most of the way in the dark, then. How appropriate." She took a tansy cake from the next server's platter and bit into it.

"Guard your tongue, my lady. I'm your only protector."

"Then a poor one you be, for you've killed my father, allowed your men to rape the women of my castle and village, and have killed many of my serving men who meant only to defend their home."

"You do push me too far." He threw down his fork and shoved away from the table.

At once James McIntyre's black eyes met Damaris's. She looked away, but not before a shiver started in her middle. James had seen William's anger with her. Was her position weaker for her mistake? She pretended to be interested in the food on her trencher.

Edith nudged Damaris's knee. "That man over there, the one who looks like a devil. He's watching you with such a leer!"

Damaris turned so that her bongrace hid her lips from the man's view. "As soon as we can, leave the table and go directly to my chambers. Sir William is leaving on the hour for the mainland and that man-devil is to be left in charge."

"Say it's not so!"

"It is. Don't look at him! Don't do anything to draw attention to yourself. Tell Meg what I said. It's also important to keep a close watch on Kate and Lettice. They mustn't leave us for a moment."

Edith's wrinkled face looked shocked but she nodded. She turned and leaned toward Meg to pass the message on.

As soon as the chaplain said the final grace, Damaris and her ladies rose and left the table. She felt as if dozens of pairs of eyes were boring into her back, but she didn't allow her steps to be hurried.

There were always more men at Thornbeck than women, for the simple reason that many of the men-at-arms couldn't afford a wife. Now there were virtually no women in the castle at all except for the serving wenches, her ladies and herself. The widows of the men who had been killed had been sent to live in the village and most of the wives had gone with them. The others kept to their rooms.

As they went down the corridor, Damaris caught one of the wenches by the arm and said in a low voice, "Have food brought to my chambers until Sir William returns. Tell the other women that they are to go to the village at night and not stay in the castle. Do you understand me?"

The woman nodded and swallowed. "Aye, my lady."

Damaris and the others went to the adjoining suite of rooms and locked the doors behind them. Only now did she feel safe. She went to the window and stared out at the sea. In an hour's time, she saw a ship carrying several men set sail for the mainland of Scotland. Her only protection, as meager as it was, had left the castle.

After three days of being cooped up in her chamber, Damaris was as eager as her women to be outside, but she didn't dare allow them out of her sight. The nights were worse. Her ladies slept, but Damaris was restless and couldn't stop pacing. Late one night she could stand the confinement no longer and decided to slip out onto the battlements and get some air. She felt sure that at this hour, no one was likely to be about.

She wrapped a dark cloak around her demure black nightgown and left through the door in her inner chamber. She paused in the corridor to be sure there were no sounds to indicate anyone else was awake. The silent castle seemed immense in the darkness.

Feeling her way up the servants' stairs to the upper floor, Damaris found the wooden door that led onto the parapet walkway. She opened it and stepped out onto the hourds. The wooden beams were even beneath her feet. To her left lay the outside crenellated wall and to her right a smaller parapet that overlooked the bailey far below.

Damaris looked around cautiously. As weeks had gone by without incident, William had become lax about setting guards. Now that he was no longer in the castle, the parapet was deserted. She walked slowly along, breathing the clean, salty air and enjoying the freedom of being outside again.

Beneath her she could hear the rhythm of the sea as it lapped at the rocks, and as she looked out, the undulating face of the sea far below was illumined by a three-quarter moon. Damaris leaned closer. What was that on the water?

She strained for a better look, wishing the moon were brighter. Were those small ships? If so, they were not under sail. But as she listened, she could hear the faint sound of oars dipping rhythmically into and out of the water. They were closer to the castle than she first thought and not ships at all, but fishing boats. And so many of them! Her heart leaped into her throat. An arrival from Scotland wouldn't be coming from that direction. They could only be Englishmen.

As she watched, she saw a faint light from the lead boat. It flickered once, then longer, then another short beam. She had seen signals like this all her life. It was the sign the fishermen used to gain entry to the castle through the water gate. Damaris gathered up her skirts and ran for the door.

She hadn't been to the water gate in years, though she and the other children in the castle had occasionally gone there to hide from tutors and parents. As she raced down the several flights of stairs, lower into the rock that supported Thornbeck, the steps grew progressively wet and slick. She could smell the fishy aroma of the boats as she drew near the level of the sea.

When she reached the boat room, she risked lighting a rush with the flint that was kept beside it. Its flaring yellow light showed her the rows of fishing boats tied in preparation for the next day's work. Piles of net and floats lay in the boats and in heaps on the stone floor. Damaris picked her way over them and went to the iron wheel set into the wall beside the iron-barred gate.

She tugged on the wheel and thought for a minute she wouldn't be strong enough to turn it, then it grudgingly shifted under her hands. Damaris pulled as hard as she could, and her efforts were rewarded by the metal latticework in the gate beginning to inch upward. By the time it cleared the water a few feet, her back and arms ached.

A silent boat glided into the dock. Damaris wrapped her cloak tighter as she saw the strangers' faces. At the prow was a giant of a man with hair as golden as sunlight. His green eyes met hers as the man beside him leaped onto the rock ledge to secure the boat to the dock. Damaris felt her heart racing and her mouth was dry. The clothing the men wore wasn't telling, and until one of them spoke, she wouldn't know for certain if they were English or Scots.

"My lady!" a familiar voice called out.

She looked into the rear of the boat and recognized Gil Hobson's eager face. "Gil! You've come back!"

The boy jumped onto the ledge beside her and knelt to kiss her hand. Damaris rested her palm on his head for a moment. "I'm rare glad to see you, Gil!"

Following the lead of the blond man, the others leaped out of the boat and established a guarded perimeter around the room. The leader looked about for a moment, checking the security preparations, then came to her. Gil stood and grinned up at him. "My lady, this is Sir Gavin Rutledge. He's been sent by the queen. I saw her myself! I even talked to her!"

Damaris gave the boy a quick smile, but her attention riveted back to Gavin. "Sir Gavin?" she asked. The name was familiar.

Gil said, "This is our lady of the castle, Damaris Fleetwood."

Gavin raked her from head to foot with his forest green eyes, as if he were sizing her up, and Damaris pulled the wrapper she had thrown on over her nightgown closer beneath her chin.

"We might have met under more pleasant circumstances," he said wryly.

She remembered suddenly where she had heard his name. This was the man her father had wanted to betroth her to! Her mouth dropped open.

"Young Gil says he knows little of the castle on the inside. Where are the Scotsmen lodged?"

Damaris wished she were fully clothed and her hair properly confined instead of hanging down to her hips. She didn't want to appear vulnerable to this man or his followers. She had seen what the Scots did when they took the castle, and although these were Englishmen, they were strangers and not to be trusted. More of the boats were crowding into the room, all of them filled with fierce, silent men. Finding her voice, she answered, "Up these stairs and down the corridor. You'll soon find yourselves in the entry by the screens passage. The men are lodged in the hall and also up the staircase on the first floor. No doubt they'll find you as soon as alarm is raised."

"And you, my lady? Where are you lodged?"

Damaris lifted her chin in defiance. "That need not trouble you."

Gavin gave her a peculiar look for a moment, then a faint smile lit the corners of his eyes, though it never reached his lips. "I want to know so you may be kept from the fighting."

She blushed with embarrassment and averted his eyes as she said, "My ladies and I are in the west wing, in the round tower there."

"Is there a bolt on your door? If so, secure it and don't come out until I tell you it's safe."

"And will we be safe from you?" she demanded. "I've seen one band of warriors attacking the women of my castle. Are yours any better?"

"If not, you're in most grave danger where you stand," he pointed out. "Your hair is loose and your cloak doesn't completely hide the fact you're in your night rail. Go to your chamber and stay there."

Damaris glanced at the growing number of men who were climbing out of the other boats that had followed the lead boat into the dock and she backed away. "St. Cuthbert be with you," she said as she made a hasty retreat. She could have sworn she heard him laughing while she scurried up the stone stairs.

She ran to the round tower and climbed the older, seldom-used steps. Below, she could hear the sounds of men shouting and the clash of arms. Already it was starting!

She dashed into her chamber and slammed the door, throwing the bolt into place. Meg cried out from the next room and hurried in, her hair braided and hanging over the shoulder of her gown.

"My lady! You've not been out!"

"Aye, and it's good that I was. Our rescuers have arrived. Young Gil was with them and he's well."

Meg listened at the door. "I hear fighting!"

The other women were awake now and were hurrying into the room. "What's happening?" Lettice asked as she gripped Kate's arm in fear. "What do I hear?"

"The castle is being taken back." Damaris smiled at them all. "Quickly! Get dressed."

As they ran to obey, Damaris pulled off the cloak and hung it on a peg. She opened the trunk at the foot of her bed and removed her black gown and replaced it with a white chemise that fit from her neck to her feet, with sleeves that gathered at her wrists. Damaris caught one end of the gathering string in her teeth and managed to tie it before Meg returned. Meg had pulled a kirtle over her own nightgown and was pushing the gown's sleeves out of sight.

"Here. Hold out your arms." Meg quickly tied the other sleeve and dashed to the small closet room in the wall to fetch a kirtle for Damaris.

Damaris went to her mirror and began brushing her hair. The battle might last for hours, but she didn't want to be caught in a disheveled state again.

Meg returned with a dark blue kirtle and helped Damaris pull it on. As she laced it down the back, she said, "I ought to scold you for wandering about the castle dressed in your night rail! What were you thinking of?"

"I couldn't stay in this room another minute. I had to get some fresh air. I was careful that no one saw me. If I hadn't been on the parapet, I don't know how the men would ever have entered the castle. Gil apparently took the risk of us-

ing the fisherman's signal in hopes someone from Thornbeck would see it and respond. I almost couldn't get the gate
open." Her words were tumbling over each other in her excitement.

"You took a terrible chance! What made you think the
queen's men would be more trustworthy than Sir William's? You should have gone to alert one of the castle men
you know you can trust and come straight back to your
chamber."

"There wasn't time! I had to get down there before they
went away again." Damaris started pulling tufts of chemise
through the slashings in the sleeve of her kirtle. "I hope Gil
will be safe. Do you think he went home rather than join in
the fighting?"

"Knowing Gil, he'll be in the thick of it." Meg went back
into the small room and returned with a beautiful bur-
gundy gown. "Put this on."

"They'll be victorious. I know it! Thornbeck will be mine
again!" Damaris was all but gloating as she slipped her arms
into the loose sleeves of the gown. She fastened the clasp at
her waist.

"Sit down so I can have a go at your hair," Meg instructed, then called over her shoulder, "Kate? What's
keeping you girls? Must I do her hair myself?"

Damaris could hardly sit still. "If only they had come
three days earlier. They could have captured Sir William, as
well. Wouldn't that have been a nice gift for our queen?"

"Be still, my lady. Kate!"

The girl hurried into the room, her own clothing unlaced. She took the brush from Meg. Lettice followed her
and laced Kate's kirtle while Kate combed their mistress's
hair.

Damaris tapped her foot impatiently. "I wish I could slip
out and watch the battle. I'd stay out of the way."

"You'll do no such thing, my lady." Meg went back into
the small room and returned with a gold tissue French hood
and a frilled cap. "You could be hurt or killed."

Kate braided Damaris's hair in a thick plait, then coiled
it into a net. Lettice took the cap from Meg and put it on
Damaris's head, then covered all but the lace with the

French hood. Meg gave her a gold tissue bongrace to fasten to the back of the hood. It was a flattering style for Damaris and accented the graceful curve of her slender neck and her high cheekbones.

"There." Meg looked at her in satisfaction. "Now you look the part of the lady of the castle." She frowned at the girls. "Finish dressing and comb your hair. Where is Edith?"

Damaris went to the window and pulled aside the drapery that kept out the night drafts. "It's almost dawn. I must have slept longer last night than I realized."

Lettice was at the door, her cheek pressed against the wood. "I don't hear anything. Can the fighting be over?"

Damaris joined her. "I'll see." She pulled back the bolt and opened the door. Over Meg's protests, she went out into the corridor. She could hear shouting voices below, and the fighting seemed to be continuing. Pale morning light had driven the darkness from the corridor and she had no trouble finding the top of the main staircase. Holding her skirts close about her, Damaris crept partway down the stairs.

She had never expected to see so many bodies, and the sounds of battle reverberating off the stone walls were deafening. Men lunged against men, and with apparent ease they swung overhead massive battle swords that she would have had difficulty lifting off the ground. Blades clashed against chain mail and body armor. There were shrieks of agonizing pain and sickening thuds as William's men fell mortally wounded.

Her eyes found the tallest man in the room and she couldn't look away. He was slashing with sword in one hand and dagger in the other. His golden hair was tousled in his lunges and thrusts, his eyes intent with blood lust. As she watched, he hacked three men to their deaths and a fourth tried to flee, but in vain.

As if they realized at once that their cause was hopeless, William's men tried to run out of the castle. Gavin's men blocked the way. Those who continued to fight were dispatched by red-flashing swords. The others huddled together like a pack of frightened rabbits.

Damaris had been holding her breath. She made a small movement and Gavin's attention locked on her. She backed up a step without thinking. He looked half-wild. A superficial cut on his cheek and another on his sword arm were still bleeding, but he seemed unaware of any injury. His eyes riveted on her and she froze, not daring to move.

Then he blinked as if he suddenly realized who she was. He made a curt gesture to his men and they began rounding up the enemy survivors.

"I see you've followed my orders and stayed safely in your chamber," he called up to her.

She tried not to flinch at the anger behind his sarcasm. "So I did . . . for the most part."

A growl rumbled from deep in his chest and he strode away to see about his own casualties. As he passed one of his men, he said something Damaris couldn't hear and jerked his head in her direction. The other man looked up and saw her. Gavin went outside.

The tall man with graying hair to whom Gavin had spoken came to her and gave her a half bow. "I was about to come in search of you. I'm Sir Godfrey Hammett," he added. "Where can we imprison the Scotsmen?"

Damaris nodded toward the smaller stairs at the end of the passage. Her heart was still hammering wildly. "There's a lower room down there that was made to hold prisoners. It will keep them quite secure."

Godfrey signaled to his men-at-arms and they started moving the Scotsmen toward the dungeon.

Damaris watched as the men who had been killed were being carried out of the castle, and the wounded were taken to an inner room to be cared for. The rustle of skirts behind her told her Meg and the other women were there.

There was a loud noise from the passage and the tall blond man came back into view, shoving three men in front of him. He pushed them into the knot of prisoners and went to her. His eyes never leaving hers, he made a bow. "My lady, the castle is secure."

"Thank you, sir knight."

"Sir Gavin," he corrected.

She had remembered his name perfectly. Had he yet realized who she was? "You and your men are welcome in my castle. I hope you'll not be leaving too soon. When Sir William learns what has happened, there may be more trouble."

"We'll not be leaving for days, possibly weeks."

"No?"

"Queen Elizabeth has ordered me to stay here until the proper bridegroom may be found and sent here to wed you. She doesn't intend to allow Thornbeck to fall into enemy hands again."

"I beg your pardon? Bridegroom, did you say? I'm not betrothed."

He smiled as if he were taking a perverse pleasure in giving her the news. "That matters not. The queen will choose you a husband among the peerage."

Damaris felt her anger rising. "I'll not have a bridegroom chosen for me. If I wouldn't allow my own father to do so, I'll not welcome a complete stranger any more willingly." She realized her mistake. "You'll tell the queen I thank her for her intervention, but a marriage won't be necessary." It wouldn't do to anger her sovereign.

"You misunderstand my words. Your permission isn't required. A husband will be forthcoming." He seemed to be enjoying this.

Although she was tall, he towered over her. She glared up at him. "Are you slow of wit? I said I'll not have one!"

"Thornbeck is no longer a possession of your family. It's now a ward of the crown until a husband can be sent and the wedding performed. That's why I'm to be in charge of the castle."

"I'm quite capable of defending my own castle!"

"Forgive me if I'm mistaken, but you appear to me to be a woman, not a warrior."

"My father taught me all he knew of defense. I can command my men as well as any man."

"You'll forgive me again, but your father lost both the castle and his life. That sounds as if he wasn't the most brilliant of strategists."

Damaris drew back as if she had been struck. "You dare to speak ill of my father to me?" she exclaimed.

"I'm a warrior, not a puling fop to mince pretty words. I speak my mind."

"You're a knight," she snapped. "Is chivalry dead?"

"Some would say so. At any rate, I'm in command of this castle until my replacement comes." His insolent eyes pored over her. "Where may my men be bedded down? We've traveled hard to get here and haven't slept all night."

"You may do as Sir William's men did and take the chambers on the first floor. Just see to it that no one comes near my chambers in the west wing. I'd not have my women set upon."

"They'll be safe enough." Gavin glanced at the women and nodded to them. "My men aren't beasts."

Gil ran up to them, his eyes sparkling with excitement. "My lady. Sir Gavin. Is it over? Is the castle ours again?"

"Aye, lad. You've served your queen well."

Gil fished around in the leather pouch at his belt and fetched Damaris's ring. "Here 'tis, my lady. Safely back to you."

Damaris took the ring and pulled a garnet ring set with small diamonds from her finger. "Here's your reward, Gil."

The boy stared at it. "For me, my lady?"

She smiled at him. "For your future. You may decide not to live as a fisherman. This is your way to a better life."

To the boy, Gavin said, "Mayhap you'd like to try your lot with me. I was about your age when I was sent to be trained in the ways of knighthood. I have no page to serve me."

Gil stared up at him. "You'd have me?"

He reached out his hand and ruffled the boy's hair. "I'd have you and gladly."

"But first you should go to the village and tell your mother you're alive and well," Damaris said. "She's worried about you day and night."

"Pa won't take kindly to me becoming a knight's page," Gil said, ducking his head. "He's set on me being a fisherman."

"These are decisions a man must make," Gavin told him. "You have to follow the path your stars have mapped out for you."

Damaris's attention snapped to Gavin. That was almost what the tall woman had told her during her last visit to the Maidens. Why was she hearing these words coming from this man's lips? Was this a sign?

Gil trotted off and Gavin turned back to her. "Why do you stare so, my lady?"

She looked away in confusion. "I didn't mean to." Did he know who she was? Nothing in his manner or speech indicated that her name meant anything to him. Was she perhaps confused as to his own identity? Could there be two Gavin Rutledges?

"Come walk with me. You may show me which rooms my men may use."

Damaris went with him to the stairs, her ladies close behind. "Do you have any idea who the queen will send to Thornbeck?" She hadn't wanted to ask him, but she needed to know as much as possible about her future.

"No, she doesn't confide in me."

"Can you hazard a guess?" she asked rather tartly. "Surely she won't choose some man who's a stranger to court."

"It's possible. On the other hand, there are a number of unmarried men at Windsor. I assume she will bestow a barony on the man, whoever he is."

"You mean he's to be a man from below my station?" This could open the field widely. Any man at all might be chosen.

"Or he could be the younger son of a baron," Gavin said evenly. "He might be below your station in rank, but not in birth."

Damaris looked back at her ladies. "Leave us, please."

"But my lady—" Meg protested.

"Go, Meg. I'll be back to my chambers soon."

When the women went away, she turned back to Gavin. "I must ask your pardon, it seems. I didn't know if you were aware of the match my father and yours proposed."

"And which was dissolved before it had a chance at life."

"I had no reason to believe my father would be dead in a matter of days! I thought I'd have years before I would need a protector."

Gavin looked at her with interest. "So you're the one who decided against the marriage? And your father allowed you to choose?"

"My father loved me," she retorted.

"Had he loved you more wisely he would have seen to your future safety."

"He thought I was as safe at Thornbeck as a person could be anywhere, and he didn't know you. Not really. How was he to determine if you'd make me happy?"

Gavin stopped walking and pulled her around to face him. "I could have not only made you happy, I could have kept you safe." His large hands held her firmly but not painfully. "I have no doubts at all on either count."

Damaris gazed up into his eyes and saw he was both hurt and angry. "Then you wanted the marriage?" she whispered. "You never met me!"

"No! I didn't want it." He glared down at her as if he weren't too sure what to do with her. "I told my father so but he was so certain the match would be a good one, I agreed."

"You were only after my wealth and Thornbeck," she threw at him.

"Aye, my lady. I was. I'm a younger son. I have no inheritance of my own, and I'm smart enough to know I won't be able to swing a sword or wield an ax to my queen's honor forever. I have no desire to become an almsman and follow her from hall to chapel telling my beads! What man wouldn't rather have a barony of his own and a castle to defend?" The words were bitten off short in his anger. "Aye, I'd even take a castle beset by Scots and embedded in the North Sea. I was even willing to take a woman to wife who was well past marriageable age, and not ask too many questions. That's how eager I was."

Damaris flinched back from him but he didn't release her. "Can you not see how that wouldn't make me feel any the safer? A man that eager for money and holdings might treat me cruelly and hate me, and I'd have no one to champion me. How could I risk that?"

He pulled her body tight against his. Damaris could barely breathe, but not because his grip on her was too firm. "I've never been cruel to a woman or an animal in my life."

"How was I to know that?" she demanded, determined not to show him how his closeness was affecting her.

"You could have trusted our fathers! That's the way it's done!"

"And how many happy marriages have you seen?" she retorted. "I may live an isolated life here at Thornbeck, but we're not hermits here. I've seen many married couples, and I've yet to see a happy one."

"Nor would ours have been. You have too great a temper." He released her so suddenly, she fell against him.

Damaris pushed him away and glared. "I've no temper at all! Not to speak of! You're enough to try the patience of St. Cuthbert himself! Or any other saint, most likely! You say you're not cruel, but you've pulled and hauled at me and likely have bruised my arms. Is this a way to treat a lady?"

He grinned at her. "No, this is." He pulled her to him again before she knew what he was doing. His fingers caught the hair at the back of her neck and he tilted her face up for his kiss. His lips claimed hers, and though she struggled, he didn't free her.

As his hot lips moved over hers, Damaris found her body turning traitor. Her movements became more languid until her shoves at him were but caresses and her blows an embrace.

When he at last lifted his head and gazed into her eyes, Damaris was more frightened by herself than him. Her lips felt dewy and were slightly open as if she wanted him to kiss her again, and she found her arms were around him.

Her cheeks reddened as she turned away. She was about to run from him when he said, "Don't go, my lady."

She didn't dare look back at him for she was too embarrassed over her reaction to his kiss, but she stopped and listened.

"Again I must ask your pardon." His voice sounded strained as if the kiss had affected him, too. "I had no right to touch you and certainly I had no right to kiss you. I was angry with you for refusing me without knowing any more about me than my name. That didn't give me the right to do what I just did.''

Damaris didn't dare risk speaking. She was too near tears. Instead she nodded and hurried away. When she was out of sight, she stopped and put her fingers to her lips. She could still feel the imprint of his kiss on every nerve in her body. Would her ladies be able to tell what had happened by looking at her? Damaris had never been kissed before, and she was shaken to her soul.

Gavin stood in the corridor and watched her until she was gone from his sight. His body ached, and it had nothing to do with the battle he had just waged. He hadn't intended to pull her into his embrace, and once there, he hadn't intended to kiss her. He had never in his life kissed a woman who wasn't willing. He glared around the empty corridor, looking for an enemy on which to take out his anger. No woman had ever made him unaccountable for his actions.

He looked back the way she had gone. He certainly hadn't expected the dragon daughter to be so beautiful or so full of fire in such an enticing way. Again he cursed the fate that kept him from being her betrothed.

Outside the castle, a man lurked in the paling shadows. James McIntyre had escaped from the fighting, and from the sound of things, he knew his men had lost. James had no martyr instincts so he ran from the castle and toward the village.

Rounding a bend in the road along the sea, he found a man standing beside a boat. Before the man knew what was happening, James pushed him roughly aside and jumped in. Ignoring the man's protests, he pushed the boat away from the dock and fitted the oars into the locks. As he headed for Scotland, he wondered what he could tell Sir William that would save his own skin. His master would be extremely displeased, and James dreaded the message he must give.

As he rowed, he tried to invent a tale that would put himself in the best light. Somehow he would help Sir William find a way to retake Thornbeck and get back into his good graces. James rowed harder.

Chapter Five

Now that Thornbeck was no longer under enemy control, Damaris chose to avail herself of the freedom to visit the Maidens again without fearing for her or her ladies' safety. Standing amid the stones the following afternoon, she pulled the hat and netting from her head and shook her hair loose in the breeze. The sun was warm on her shoulders and her hair glistened with red highlights.

Slowly she strolled around the circle, touching each familiar stone and humming a song her father's minstrels had played so prettily. Now that William was vanquished, the musicians were willing to play again, and she was looking forward to it.

She was also looking forward to rendering William helpless once and for all. That morning she had discussed this with the Priestess stone and had heard the tall woman speaking of vengeance and destiny. She hadn't a single doubt that Gavin was here in order to fulfill his destiny of putting an end to William.

A rabbit hopped into the circle and Damaris wondered if this was the same animal she had seen here before. She knelt on the ground and held out a piece of clover toward the rabbit. It hopped nearer, its nose and ears twitching nervously.

"Peace, rabbit," she said softly. "I mean you no harm."

As if it understood her, the rabbit came closer. After a moment's hesitation, it took the clover from Damaris.

"Do you have a nest near here?" Damaris asked gently. "You must take care that the village dogs don't find you."

She picked another red clover and presented it to the rabbit. "At least you picked the safest place on the island to have your family. No one ever comes here."

The rabbit stiffened, then bolted.

Damaris looked up to see Gavin striding into the circle. She got to her feet.

"Who were you talking to?" he asked as he looked around. "I see no one."

"It doesn't matter. What are you doing here?"

"I saw this odd arrangement of stones from the castle and thought I'd take a closer look."

"No one comes here, not even my ladies or the children from the village."

Gavin looked around. "I've seen such stones before, but never in so awesome a setting."

"You should be up here when a storm blows in from the sea."

"It would be too fierce here for a woman at such a time," he said confidently.

"Not for me. I was born here during such a storm." She saw the disbelief in his eyes but didn't elaborate.

"During our very brief courtship, my father told me that your mother died soon after you were born. I'm sorry. This island must have been lonely indeed for a maid such as yourself to have no mother to talk with."

She smiled mischievously. "Why do you assume that I no longer talk with her?"

He lifted a curious eyebrow but let that pass. "I can see the mainland from here."

"Aye. On clear days you can even see Holy Island. But on foggy days Thornbeck's island disappears."

"That's not possible."

"Are you so sure? I can no longer see Holy Island or the mainland. Who's to say they aren't still there but I can't see them because my own island has vanished?" She was enjoying her verbal sparring with him.

"Islands don't vanish. You're only seeing a fog bank."

"Nevertheless, the island is impossible to see. When you return from Scotland, I'll come up here and light a signal fire if the weather is bad. Perhaps it will guide you back safely.''

''Scotland? I have no intention to go to Scotland.''

''Of course you do. How else will you bring my uncle to justice?'' She smiled at him as if he were a willful boy. ''I'm sure some of his men in the dungeon could be bribed to tell where to find his castle.''

''My orders are to stay here at Thornbeck until someone arrives to relieve me. If I were to go into Scotland after your uncle, I'd find myself in trouble with our own queen, as well as the Scottish one.''

Damaris's smile vanished. ''But he killed my father! And caused the death of many of the men of my castle! Surely you don't intend to allow this to go unpunished!''

''That's not my decision. I'm the queen's man and I obey her orders.''

''But the Priestess said that his death would be avenged!''

''What priestess? I've seen none but a chaplain on this island.''

She went to the tall stone and touched it with reverence. ''This is the Priestess.''

Gavin looked from her to the stone and back again. ''You talk to stones as well as to yourself? And they answer?''

''Don't look at me like that.'' Damaris lifted her chin defiantly. ''She puts pictures in my mind and they come true.''

With an inquisitive gleam in his eye, he stepped closer to her. ''That's not possible.''

''No? Touch her.''

He shrugged and casually extended his hand, placing his large palm on the stone's surface. Suddenly he jerked his hand away.

''There? You see?''

As Gavin circled the stone, his brow was deeply furrowed and his lips were pressed tightly together. For a long while, he studied it carefully as if he suspected she had tricked him somehow.

''Everyone feels that tingling when they touch her. Of course almost no one dares try.'' She sat on the altar and watched his perusal of the stone.

"Why does it do that?" he asked without taking his eyes off the stone.

"I'm not sure why, but I believe these stones to be magical."

"Pah!" he snorted, turning his attention back to Damaris.

"You don't believe me? Touch her again, then."

Gavin stepped closer to Damaris instead. "Stones have no life, and I don't believe in magic." He sat beside her and looked into her eyes. "At least I don't believe in magical stones. My father also said you had eyes of a strange color. It's true."

She met his gaze. "Perhaps I have a bit of the stones' magic."

The wind caught her hair and floated it across her back like a cape. Gavin put out his hand to capture it. The curls waved about his hand like a skein of silk. She saw a small muscle tighten in his jaw.

"You have remarkable hair. Most women don't allow it to fall loose like this."

"I'm not like most women." With him so close, she was losing her composure. She liked it better when he was distant and she could tease him with her games. She tried to move away.

He caught her hand. "Stay."

His fingers seemed to burn her flesh in the most enticing way. Damaris knew she should pull free and put him in his place, but she couldn't seem to speak.

"I didn't come up here only to see the stones. I also saw you walking alone among them and wanted to talk to you."

"For what reason?" Why did his nearness make her heart beat faster?

"It's rare for two people to be able to speak alone in a castle. There are always people about."

"Then one wonders how there can be so many liaisons between men and women."

Gavin smiled. "You surprise me again. I'd have thought you had no knowledge of such things."

"As I pointed out to you before, Thornbeck is isolated but it's not a convent. We have our share of lovers' trysts.

Papa's guests often had intrigues of their own. I observed and I learned what they were about. Did you think such things only happened at court?''

"Forgive me. I didn't mean to imply that Thornbeck isn't a hive of clandestine meetings and speculations.''

"Sarcasm is wasted on me." Damaris looked away and studied the colors of the sea. "I'm a simple woman, given to simple pursuits.''

"There are many ways I'd describe you, but simple isn't one of them," he said wryly. "You may not frequent court, but there are as many sides to you as to the sea.''

Damaris smiled. She rather liked that comparison. "Perhaps you aren't so unlikable after all.''

"A pity you didn't consider that a month ago. We could have been betrothed, and you'd not be about to wed to a stranger.''

Her smiled faded. "I suppose I could agree to marry you. After all, we've met now, and I don't find you unappealing.''

To her surprise, he laughed. "My lady, you amaze me. You seem determined to shape your own future. I'm no longer in the bidding for your hand.''

"You dislike me, then?" Pain shot through her.

"No, but the queen isn't considering me. She sees me only as one of her knights, a man who has nothing to bring to this marriage but himself. Because your father was a baron, she will choose among the peerage for you.''

"Then why did you say what you did before about her choosing a younger son—such as yourself?''

"I was trying to tell you that I recognized your name and that of Thornbeck and that I wasn't so dull witted as not to know that I once had a chance at being master here.''

"And the kiss?''

"That was only because I wanted to kiss you.''

Damaris stared at him. "You think you can take such liberties with me when you know there can be nothing between us? You've insulted me!''

"You didn't find it insulting at the time. I was under the impression that you thoroughly enjoyed it.''

Damaris stood and stalked away several paces. With her back to him, she said, "Leave me. I don't care to talk to you any longer."

When he spoke she was startled to find him so close to her. "I didn't mean to anger you," he said sincerely.

"No?"

"I didn't mean to anger you quite so much," he amended. "I do admit to baiting you."

She turned to him. "I don't understand you."

"You should. I'm playing your own game."

Damaris studied him. "What game is that?"

"That of confusion, my lady. You play it better than most."

"You're confusing indeed, sir knight. You come all the way from London to protect my castle, then you refuse to pursue the man who will threaten it again. You say you're here to protect me, but you refuse to do that which will leave me in safety."

"Thornbeck is a strategic island. If your uncle weren't trying to capture it, some other man would be. That's the price for living here. That's why the man who rules here is given a barony."

"Doesn't it matter to you that my father lies unavenged in his grave? How can you, as a knight, allow this to be?"

"It does matter to me. Not only because he was murdered in his own castle by a traitor, but because he was my father's friend and because he was your father. Do you think I can shrug at a woman left unprotected on a speck of land in the North Sea, scarcely a stone's throw from Scotland? I have sensibilities, my lady. But I also have a brain. There's nothing I can do to render this island forever safe. My task is to follow the orders of my queen and to do her bidding."

"Fortunately for my father, he had me and not a son!" she retorted. "My loyalty is deeper than that and I will see him avenged!"

"I hope so," Gavin said. "But I'll not be the avenger. Not unless your uncle tries again to take the island while I'm here. If he does, I'll gladly fight him for you."

The wind tossed Damaris's hair over her shoulder and she thrust it back from her face. "I can't wait for fate to mete out his punishment." She turned and walked away. How was it he managed to anger her so easily? It was well, she thought, that he wouldn't be her husband. She tried not to think who might be.

Gavin watched her go, her red hair whipping about her in the wind. What made her so different from other women? Was it her spirit or her unusual way of thinking that he found so appealing? She wasn't at all like Claudia or any of the other women he had been attracted to in the past. A wise man would be glad he hadn't found himself betrothed to her. But Gavin was no longer glad at all.

He slowly walked back to the tallest stone, the one she had called the Priestess. He had felt something strange when he touched it and wasn't too eager to try it again, but he was unwilling to let a rock frighten him.

Cautiously he reached out his hand and touched its cold surface. The wind sighed through the hole beside his head. As before, a tingling sensation ran up his arm, but he kept his hand on the stone. There could be no trick. He was alone in the circle.

Slowly Gavin backed away. There was something about these stones that made him uneasy. Rocks were only rocks and he didn't believe in magic, but he couldn't discount the way he was feeling.

He looked in Damaris's direction. She was halfway to the castle now, her hair still blowing loose about her. Obviously she wasn't fearful about being here alone. He went to the lane to watch her. She was beautiful and willful and he wanted her more than he had ever wanted a woman in his life.

Gavin gazed around the stones. Did they somehow have something to do with his wanting her? Could they influence him in that way? Everyone knew standing stones had a power of sorts, call it what one might. Why else would he want a woman he couldn't have and who had already refused his hand in marriage? This, like Damaris, was a mystery.

* * *

Damaris was still angry when she reached the castle. She paused long enough to put her hair back into the net and to set her cap and hood in place. Then she went to the chapel.

She sat on her pew and looked at her father's grave. "He wouldn't have done for me at all, Papa," she fumed. "He won't avenge your death unless the queen specifically bids him do it. Thornbeck is miles from London. Who would know if he went into Scotland or not? How would the queen ever find out? But he refuses anyway."

She stood and paced to the communion rail and back to her pew. "There's only one way. I'll do it for you."

That made her feel better. "Yes. I should have thought of it before. I'm your only child. It's only right that your vengeance should come through me. Sir William won't expect a woman to take him to task. I'll have surprise on my side."

She frowned. "But how do I find him? I've never been in Scotland. I know the name of his castle, but not how to find it." She thought for a minute. "How would a man discover William's whereabouts? He would go in pursuit and ask. That must be the answer. I can do that."

She gazed down at the tombstone. "I swear it, Papa. I'll find my uncle and I'll make him pay for your death."

Footsteps behind her drew her attention, and she turned to see Meg coming into the chapel.

"There you are, my lady! I've searched the entire castle. I should have known I'd find you here." Meg came to her and looked down at the stones. When she spoke, her voice was soft. "He was a fine man, your father. As was his lady wife. There have been so many times I've wished you could have known her."

"Aye." Damaris said quickly, "Meg, I know what I must do. I have to avenge my father's death."

"In what way?" Meg asked in alarm. "You can't mean he's coming back here! There's not to be another battle!"

"Calm yourself. No, I have no word of Sir William's return."

Meg relaxed perceptibly. "You frightened me for a moment. You mean you'll avenge Lord Fleetwood by praying for him. You gave me a turn."

Damaris shook her head. "I'm going to Scotland and find Sir William myself."

Meg stared at her. "That's not possible. Not for a woman alone."

"Joan of Arc was a woman alone. She went to war."

"She's said to have been a saint! You have no men-at-arms, no army!" Meg touched Damaris's cheek. "You aren't running a fever and talking out of your head, are you?"

"I'm perfectly well. Don't you see, Meg? Sir William would never suspect me."

"No! I could never allow you to do such a thing!"

Damaris frowned. "I'm not a child. I don't see how you can stop me. I must go now. I have much to think about."

Meg waited until her mistress was gone, then ran in search of Gavin. He was nowhere to be found within the castle walls, but on the advice of one of his men, she headed up the lane toward the standing stones and found him coming out of the circle. She ran up to him and crossed herself as she glanced at the stones.

"Is aught the matter?" he asked. "You look upset."

"And that I am. My mistress says she's going to avenge Lord Fleetwood herself!"

Gavin laughed. "She was exaggerating. She's only angry because I can't leave Thornbeck unguarded and go after him."

"No, no. I've seen her this determined before. She really means to do it!"

"Meg—you are the one called Meg, aren't you?—she can't possibly go after Sir William. None of my men would even consider going with her against my orders. Nor, do I wager, are the men of Thornbeck so foolhardy."

Meg wasn't convinced. "You don't know her like I do, Sir Gavin. When she gets her mind set, there's not much that can dissuade her. She's even speaking of Joan of Arc."

"I'll have a talk with her if it will put your mind at ease."

Meg breathed a sigh of relief. "She's most likely in the solar. She always likes to go there when she wants to think."

Gavin got instructions from Meg on how to find the chamber and left her. To think Damaris or any woman would seriously consider such an undertaking was ludicrous.

As Meg had suggested, he found Damaris in the solar with the rest of her women. His eyes met hers. To the others he said, "Leave us, please." The women hurried out.

"I hadn't expected the honor of your company again so soon," Damaris said coolly.

"Nor had I. Meg has told me what you said about your uncle."

Damaris frowned. "Meg sometimes talks overmuch."

"Don't scold her. She's only worried about you. Surely you weren't serious about going to Scotland." He smiled and waited for her to laugh at the absurdity.

"Perhaps."

He frowned. "You can't. No men will go with you. I'll give orders to that effect."

"I don't care. I can find the castle alone."

"My lady, use your head. You can't even get from here to Scotland unaided."

"No? I'd not be so sure." She continued to sew on the tapestry in her lap as calmly as if they were discussing the weather.

"I refuse to let you."

She looked up in surprise. "I wasn't aware that you had any control over me. Why do you consider that you do?"

"I'm in command here."

"Must I remind you that I'm not one of your men?"

Gavin strode closer. Her sewing continued unabated. "I forbid you to leave this island."

"Very well," she said mildly. "I won't."

"I don't believe you!"

She smiled at the tapestry and said, "As you please, sir knight."

"You know my name. Why do you refuse to use it?"

"I wasn't aware that I was required to do so. Is that another of your commands?"

"God's bones, but you're infuriating! You're not to leave the island!"

"I've agreed not to. Do you like this tapestry? It's to hang in the hall behind the dais. I've decided that's the best place for it. It depicts one of my ancestors battling a sea serpent. See?'' She held the cloth toward him.

''I care not for the design of tapestries. Tell me Meg was wrong and that you have no intention of doing anything foolish.''

Her eyes met his with feigned innocence. ''I never do foolish things. My way may not be exactly like those of others, but I'm not a foolish woman.''

''You're also not to do anything that I would think fits that qualification, either!''

''How am I to judge what you might think?'' Her words were now coming with barbs. ''I'm only a woman on a speck of land in the North Sea. I couldn't hope to know or interpret the mind of a great knight from London.''

''Stop it, Damaris!'' He glared down at her, not realizing he had used her name as familiarly as if they were betrothed.

She threw the tapestry from her and stood to face him. ''Don't push your authority too far, sir knight! I am of your rank and I'll not stand for it!''

''You're a woman! As such I have the necessity of seeing to your welfare!''

''I relieve you of your necessity! Take your men and go! I can defend Thornbeck myself. And I can also prevent this proposed husband from taking my island! I'm not some weak and pliable woman to be pushed here or there at anyone's whim! I'll thank you to remember that!''

''The queen of England is hardly just 'anyone,' '' he told her angrily. ''You'd do well to remember that.''

''Leave my presence,'' she snapped. ''I may not be able to oust you from my castle, but I need not suffer you in my solar!''

''Gladly, my lady. And I thank the stars constantly that I was saved from the curse of being betrothed to you! If ever there was an unbiddable woman, it's you!''

''Thank you, sir knight! I consider myself fortunate as well!''

Gavin strode from the room before he could say more. How could she get under his skin so easily? He had never passed so many angry words with a woman in his life! Not even his sisters could drive him to such distraction.

He took pleasure in slamming the door of the solar behind him. It sounded like an explosion as it reverberated along the stone corridor. Damaris's ladies came hurrying from a room down the way and dashed past him as if they thought he would do them harm. This did nothing to assuage his temper.

Robert was walking on the ramparts when Gavin found him. "I curse the day I came to this piece of rock!" he growled in greeting.

"I gather you've been talking to the lady of the castle again."

"In faith, she's enough to try the patience of a saint!"

"And we both know you're far from saintly." Robert grinned at his friend. "What has she said to you to cause such a humor?"

"You'd not believe it. She intends to go to Scotland and do away with her uncle bare-handed!"

"That's impossible," Robert said. "She was baiting you."

"No, I got it from one of her ladies. When I confronted Damaris with it, she didn't even deny it!"

Robert glanced at him. "You're on a first-name basis with the lady?"

"No, of course not. Why would you think that? I can barely stand to speak to her! She refuses to call me anything but 'sir knight.' Have you ever heard of anything so ridiculous?"

"Never." Robert turned away but Gavin saw his smile.

"Go ahead and laugh. You don't have to deal with her. What will I do if she takes it into her head to go to Scotland?"

"That's easy enough to prevent. Simply command your men and those of Thornbeck not to take her. You'll be obeyed. For all her strange ways, I doubt that she can walk there across the water."

"What strange ways are you talking about?"

"Haven't you heard? The people from the village and those here at the castle consider her to be something of a healer."

"She knows herbs and potions? Most women do." Gavin shrugged the information away.

"No, it's apparently more than that."

"I don't believe in such nonsense. There's no such thing as a healer in the way you mean."

"Maybe, maybe not. You should ask the people who have known her all her life. They say differently."

"She's a maiden. Nothing else!"

"As you say. And so being, she can't go to Scotland and rid herself of her uncle. So there's no need for you to worry about it."

"I'm not worried! I'm angry!"

"That's useless, too. In a few short weeks the queen will send her a husband and men to hold this castle. We may leave and return to court and never see the lady or Thornbeck again."

Gavin struck at the parapet with the flat of his hand. "I wish it were that simple. In faith, Robin, she bewitches me!"

"Oh?"

"Every time I'm near her, I want to take her into my arms. Why does she affect me that way when the rest of the time I want to throw her into the sea?"

"I have no idea. She doesn't have that effect on me."

"No? Then how do you see her?"

"I see her as a beautiful and desirable woman, but not as a maddening one. I can understand the urge to embrace her, but I had never thought of throwing her into the sea."

"You're making light of me. I should have known you'd take that attitude."

"I'm rather enjoying it, too. It's not often I see you at a loss. It's refreshing."

"I'm at no loss!" Gavin glared around him. "Now there's talk of her being as magic as her circle of stones. Impossible, I say!"

"You've been up to the stones?" Robert looked back at the hill and its mysterious circle. "I've heard that everyone else avoids them."

"They are rocks. Nothing more and nothing less. Go see for yourself." He looked down at the hand that had touched the Priestess. "Nothing else is possible."

"I agree. Why do you sound so angry about that?"

Gavin rested his palms on the parapet. "I think I've taken leave of my senses since coming to this cursed place. While I was there, I almost believed what she was saying about the stones. I guess you find that humorous as well."

"No."

"When I arrived there, she was talking to someone. I saw no one, but when she moved, a wild hare bounded off into the grasses. She must have been talking to it and it had come up to her hand! A wild rabbit! And she has a way of talking in circles and riddles that's most confusing."

"I'd say you can hold your own in that respect."

Gavin shook his head. "She confuses me, Robin. I know not what to make of her."

"Make nothing. She's only a pretty lady who will soon wed another. I'd say the less you think of her, the better off you'll be."

"You're right. I'll put her from my mind." Gavin glared out to sea and wondered how he was to accomplish this.

Chapter Six

"Hello, my lady," a deep voice said.

Damaris's eyes popped open and she wheeled around to see Gavin standing a short distance from her beside one of the upright stones. In a heartbeat, the soft sounds of the nearby sea and the scents of warm grasses and wildflowers she'd been enjoying were forgotten. Without waiting for further invitation, he moved toward her. "What are you doing here?" she demanded.

"I came to look around. I've been here several times since we last spoke here."

"You have? Alone?" This amazed her.

"I find it peaceful and strangely compelling."

Damaris reached behind her to coil her hair back into its netting. Gently he caught her hands and took them away from her hair. "Leave it. I like to see it flowing loose." He touched a strand and let it glide through his fingers. "You have marvelous hair, my lady. It's a pity to confine it."

She pulled away and pretended to be angry in order to cover her feelings, but left her hair free. His touch had sent the most wonderful sensations coursing through her. "If you've somewhere else to be, I'll not keep you, sir knight."

"What did you mean about being born here? Wasn't your mother confined to her rooms in expectation of your birth?"

"Of course." Damaris walked to the next stone and ran her hand caressingly over its surface, enjoying its cool and slightly irregular texture.

"Then why did you say you had been born in this circle? Did I misunderstand you? I've puzzled over it many times."

She was quiet for a moment. "My mother and my father were married many years and had no child to inherit Thornbeck after them. I'm told this was the only sadness between them. Many children were conceived, but even of the ones that had been born, none had lived."

Gavin waited, his eyes following her.

"Then I was born. Meg was there and she tells me it was a most difficult labor. My mother almost died several times. When at last I was delivered, Mother knew she would never survive another birthing. Meg said she and my father were happy to have brought me alive into the world, but neither expected me to live any longer than the others had."

Gavin kept pace with her as she made her way to the stones nearest the tall one by the altar.

"My mother had the sight. Meg tells me she was uncanny in her ability to foresee the future. It frightened Meg so she tried to discourage my mother, but on this day, Mother asked Meg to bring her the copper bowl she used for seeing." Damaris went to the Priestess and gazed up at it. "When Meg did as she was bidden, my mother saw the chapel and a row of graves, one of them being her own—and mine."

Gavin was watching her closely, careful not to miss a word. From the expression on his face, she couldn't tell if he was believing her or not.

"Mother couldn't allow that to happen. She knew she would die, but she couldn't bear that my father would be left alone. So she and Meg brought me up here." Damaris touched the Priestess. "She stood here, where I am now and Meg stood where you are. Then she passed me through this hole and Meg received me." She turned her gaze on Gavin. "Therefore I'm born not only to my parents, but to Meg and the Priestess, as well." She waited for his deprecation of the story.

"I see."

"No derision, sir knight? You amaze me."

"Your words seem to be true."

"I've told you what happened. I lived and grew strong. Mother weakened and died. Papa thought she would have lived if Meg hadn't put the idea into her head to take me to the Maidens, but Meg said she could tell Mother wouldn't have lived, even if she had stayed in bed. Meg is no midwife, but she has a way with herbal medicine and I believe her words."

"Did your father blame you for the death of his lady wife? I've heard of men who felt this way under similar circumstances."

"No. Papa loved me from the very start. I look like the portraits of my mother, and I'm sure this made it seem she was still around, in a way. No, Papa never blamed me for anything."

"Then you having reached your age without marrying wasn't because he ignored you." Gavin seemed to be thinking aloud.

"I'm only twenty," she retorted. "I have years left to bear children. He didn't betroth me to anyone, because I wished it to be this way."

"I'd not have said you're a woman who dislikes men."

"Nor am I. But I love my freedom more."

Gavin watched her silently for a time. "With the right husband, you'd have been allowed your freedom."

"Would I, sir knight? That's not been my observation of married couples. The women seem always to be with child. They grow weak and wane long before their bodies refuse to conceive yet another. Almost invariably they die before their husbands. I didn't wish that for myself. I believe Papa also understood this and that's why he didn't insist that I accept a husband. He wanted to save me an early death such as my mother suffered."

"He must have loved you more than was wise."

"What do you mean by that?" she demanded.

"He also saved you from knowing a man's love. Many women would risk anything to be with the man they love. Childbearing has always been dangerous, but I know many women who dare it gladly because they love their children and their husbands as well."

She looked at him curiously. "You know women who are in love with their husbands?"

"Of course. They are too few, but I've seen great love between couples. My own parents were like this. When my mother died of a fever a few years back, my father was inconsolable. We thought we would lose him as well from grief. Without her, his health has failed and he's becoming an old man before his time."

Damaris was enthralled. "Did they know each other before their marriage? Did their parents allow them to marry who they pleased?"

"No, they never met before they were betrothed. My mother came from near Dufton in the Eden Valley, my father from London. By the time their first child was born, they were deeply in love."

"In faith, they were more lucky than the usual couple. I know of no couple who love each other and several that cannot abide the persons they were forced to marry."

"My parents were born to parents who loved them and who wanted their happiness. Their union wasn't planned to unite fortunes or land, but to cement relations between two families that were already compatible. Their fathers were friends, just as ours were."

Damaris turned away and Gavin wondered what she was thinking. "We might have been as lucky as my parents, had fate been kinder."

"Had I been more biddable, you mean," she retorted.

Gavin watched the breeze toying with her hair and yearned to do the same. The sun touched the slender column of her neck and he wondered what her skin would taste like. To think like that was not only foolish but dangerous. The queen herself was finding a husband for this woman. In the seven years Elizabeth had ruled, she hadn't seemed as mercurial as her father and sister before her, but it was never safe to meddle with royal decisions.

"Yes. If you had done your father's bidding, you would be safely married now and your uncle might never have dared attack Thornbeck."

"And how would he know of my marriage?" she countered. "We have no contact with him. For all my uncle knew, I was married ten times over and had a royal champion for my husband."

Gavin wondered if she knew he, himself, was considered at court to be in that class. Had her father known that when he proposed the match? Apparently he hadn't told Damaris a great deal about the family he expected her to marry into. "It's a great pity I didn't journey to Thornbeck when the match was first proposed."

She turned to face him. "Why didn't you?"

He shook his head. "At the time I was no more eager for it than you were. I had never seen Thornbeck." He paused. "I had never seen you."

"Papa sent no likeness of me?"

"I assume he would have done so in his next letter. But by then you had refused me." His eyes met hers squarely. She looked so alone; he longed to take her in his arms and safeguard her against life's storms. Then she half turned her head and he saw a strength in the line of her jaw and the tilt of her chin. She might look tender and vulnerable, but there was iron in her. "What a match we would have made," he said softly.

She looked back at him, her eyes the same hue as the sea. "What a shame you weren't stronger of heart. You might have come anyway." She went to the flat stone and sat on it, spreading her gown wide about her. "Were you in love with someone at court?"

"No. Why do you ask?"

"In one of my dreams, I saw you with a woman. She had pale hair, a cleft in her chin, and a small scar on her hand."

He stared at her as if he'd been struck. "I know such a woman. You say you dreamed of her?"

"Aye. I saw her beside you, then I saw a smaller, darker man come to her and take her away. You saw me, but there was a deep chasm between us."

"What happened then?"

"We were preparing to jump across that chasm when I awoke." She tilted her head to one side. "Do you understand this dream?"

"The woman you describe is named Claudia and she's married to a man who's small and dark. I'd say the meaning of the chasm is obvious."

"Yes. That's what I thought, as well. I just didn't understand the meaning of the other couple. She was looking at you as if she weren't married to another man."

Gavin frowned. "They aren't happily married," he said brusquely.

"But you don't love her?"

"You speak freely for a maid." He frowned at her and she shrugged. Before she turned her face away, he saw her smile but the faint smile was touched with sadness. "When did you have this dream?"

"The night after Papa first told me he wanted me to consider having you for a husband."

"How could you know what I looked like? We had never met."

"I thought you were the dark man and that the dream was telling me you were in love with the blond woman."

"And you based your refusal of me on the false interpretation of a dream?" He stared at her in disbelief. "This is what comes of letting a maid chart her own future!"

"I'm not usually wrong!" she snapped. "How was I to know you were the other man?"

"The fact that I was trying to come to you could have been a clue. You refused me on the weight of a dream?"

"Not entirely. I would have refused you anyway."

Gavin frowned at her. "You can be the most maddening of women."

"I didn't want to have to compete with another woman nor have a chasm separate me from the man I was to marry."

Gavin stepped nearer her. "I could have built a bridge across the chasm. You should have given me a chance."

Damaris looked up at him and the unhappiness he saw in her eyes pierced his heart with pain. "I know that now," she said.

Against his will, hope leaped within him, but he had to deny it. "It's too late now," he said to bring his thoughts back into line. "By this time, your husband-to-be may already be on his way. Queen Elizabeth was eager to see you wed as soon as possible."

Damaris looked down and for the first time he saw her true vulnerability. With her head bowed low, she said, "I don't want to marry this stranger. The idea frightens me."

He reached out and touched her cheek. Her skin was warm from the sun and as soft as the down on a peach. "You have no choice this time. To refuse him would be to disobey the queen and that would be foolhardy if not dangerous."

"I know that!" she snapped. She jerked her head up and anger blazed in her eyes. "At times it's difficult to be a woman!" The animosity in her voice surprised him.

"I'd not have you be anything else," he said with a sad smile.

"What if this stranger is cruel to me? What if we hate each other? I'll have no redress. None at all."

He knew this was true, and the idea of a man trying to tame her wildness was unthinkable. Damaris would never be a docile woman as some men demanded; he couldn't imagine her being submissive. In some marriages this would make her life difficult, perhaps even precarious. "I can't answer about that. I have no idea who the queen will choose."

"Her primary thought will be to find a man strong enough to hold Thornbeck, not a man who will be good to me." Damaris's eyes misted, but she fought to hold back tears. Until now Gavin hadn't realized she was actually afraid of what her fate might be. "Once we're married, I'll belong to him just as Thornbeck will."

"You're borrowing trouble. It's also possible that you'll love him on sight." The words brought him a pain he didn't want to analyze.

A tear rolled down her cheek and Damaris brushed it away. "I don't want to be owned by anyone!"

Gavin had never thought of all this from a woman's perspective. He had always believed he would marry someday and that he would be the undisputed head of the family. If he chose to continue to live at court, he could do so, with or without his wife. He had assumed that this was the way of the world and that no one ever really questioned it, especially not a woman. Now he saw it in a very different light. A husband could do anything to his wife short of murder her and no one would intervene.

Without knowing he was going to do it, he reached out for Damaris and drew her to her feet and into his embrace. She came willingly.

She fit into his arms as if she had been made to his measure. She was tall for a woman, but he was overly tall himself. The top of her head nestled beneath his chin and her hair smelled of flowers and sunshine. Gavin closed his eyes and let himself enjoy the rare moment.

Damaris raised her head to look into his eyes, but he couldn't read her expression. What was she feeling, this beguiling woman who could be earthy and defiant one moment and as fey as the fairies the next? She was a mystery he wanted to spend the rest of his life trying to solve.

"I don't often make a mistake," she said. "I may always regret this one." She closed her eyes and stood on tiptoes to kiss him.

Gavin wasn't sure if she meant the kiss was a mistake, or having refused his hand in marriage. It didn't matter. All that existed was Damaris in his arms. He kissed her gently at first. Her breath was sweet in his mouth and her body molded perfectly against his. Then he kissed her again and felt her lips part beneath his.

A thrumming began in his blood, and Gavin found himself trembling in his effort to restrain himself from taking her. His kisses became more fierce and demanding and she returned them with a matching passion. He knew what he was doing was wrong, but he made no effort to stop himself. This could be the only moment they had. He didn't want to waste an instant of it with ill-placed logic.

Her arms were about him and her hands ran up his back. He pulled her closer and only stopped kissing her so he could gather her up into his arms. For a moment he gazed into her eyes, darker now with her desire, then he laid her onto the soft grasses between the altar stone and the Priestess, where they would be shielded from the view of the castle and village. Her hair spread out beneath her and he wrapped a skein of it around his hand as his pulses raced. She reached up and touched his face gently, as if she were feeling the same emotions as himself.

"Gavin?" she asked in a whisper.

"You've finally said my name," he said, tracing his finger down the curve of her cheek. "I like the way it sounds in your mouth."

"We can't do this," she whispered, but she didn't release him and her fingers laced in his hair.

"I know that." He kissed the warm curve of her throat where her pulse beat as erratically as his own.

She made no false protests that someone could see them or that he was frightening her with his passion, as some of the women at court did in order to make a man seduce them. Gavin instinctively knew she would never resort to a ploy such as that or any other. He lifted his head to gaze into her eyes. "You bewitch me," he said. "And I fall under your spell too gladly."

"In faith, I seem to be under a spell of my own." Her voice was softer than he had ever heard it. There was wonder in her words. "I know not what comes over me when you're near. At times I want to kiss you and at others I want to strike you."

"Neither reaction is prudent," he advised as he put a kiss on the warm skin beneath her ear.

"Yet you make no haste to release me."

"Do you wish to be released?" he asked as his hand circled her waist and trailed up her body to cup her breast. Beneath the layers of cloth he felt her, full and yielding. He yearned, he ached, to touch that flesh with his own.

In answer, she kissed him again, drawing his face down to hers and meeting him halfway. Her lips were warm and succulent and he felt he could become lost in her loving. Reluctantly he drew back.

She felt the distance as keenly as he did. He could see it in her troubled eyes.

"We can't continue," he said.

"I know."

He sat up and ran his fingers shakily through his hair. She lay where she had been, but she no longer touched him.

"God's bones, but you make me forget myself!" He looked back at her. Her hair was spread fanlike behind her head and her face was pale. He was reminded of a beautiful painting he had once seen, and for a moment it was hard to believe she was as mortal as himself.

"I never kissed a man before you came to Thornbeck," she surprised him by saying. "Do I do it incorrectly?"

He half laughed. "You do it all too well. But you shouldn't do it with me. You should save your kisses for your husband. And everything else as well."

"And if I don't love the man?"

"You can't know that!" He spoke sharply in his effort to maintain distance from her and resist the urge to lie beside her again. "For all you know, you're on the brink of one of the greatest loves man has ever known."

She sat up and her eyes were earnest. "You feel that as well? As if something important were about to happen?"

She was too close. He could see each separate eyelash, the amethyst flecks in her violet eyes, the way her hair grew to a peak along her forehead. For a moment time stopped spinning and he was lost. "Damaris," he murmured.

They swayed toward each other and her lips parted expectantly. He caught himself a hair's breadth away.

In desperation, he scrambled to his feet and stared down at her. "I can't have you!" he rasped. "You tempt me overmuch!"

Hurt flickered in her eyes and he knew she misunderstood him. But it was better that way. She mustn't have any hope of loving him. Gavin stopped speaking and held his breath. Love? Was that what he was fighting so hard against?

She averted her face and he suspected she was crying. He forced himself to back away. He couldn't love this woman. He couldn't allow himself to feel anything for her. He was here as her protector and he was on the verge of becoming her seducer. How could he live with himself after that? But how could he live without her?

"I'm sorry," he said, and his voice sounded ragged. He backed away. "Will you be all right?"

She nodded without looking at him or speaking.

Damaris heard him leave and dared lift her eyes to follow him. What had happened to her? She had never forgotten herself like this, nor had she ever felt an emotion such as he engendered in her. She could still taste his kisses, and her body ached for him to hold her again. Only her pride kept her from calling out to him. He hadn't felt this. If he had, he wouldn't have been able to leave her.

Damaris lay back down in the grass and let the hurt flow through her. Was she falling in love with him? Had it already happened? She didn't know. She had seen so few people outside of Thornbeck's own that she had never had the usual bouts of first love and infatuation. Certainly none of her father's friends or their sons had stirred her like this on any of their visits. What she felt for Gavin was so deep she felt her world was rocking beneath her and would never again be steady.

Without looking, she knew he was gone from her sight. It was as if she had some part of him in her soul or of herself in his. She could tell when he was near without having to set eyes on him or hear his voice. He had kissed her, laid her in the grass and left her. Damaris felt his rejection as keenly as if a knife had been plunged deep into her bosom. If he had been trying to wound her for her refusal of his proposed betrothal, the wound had been too severe.

The better part of half an hour passed before she sat up and looked out to sea. She couldn't allow herself to love him, and she would do whatever was necessary to stop. She needed something else to occupy her mind. That would do it. She had once heard Edith giving Lettice much the same advice when she had become infatuated with one of the guardsmen. Love could be averted with action. In Lettice's case, embroidery work had sufficed. Damaris would need something more compelling.

Her uncle. If she were avenging her father's death, she wouldn't have time to think about loving Gavin. Carefully she put aside all her personal worries and longings and started planning how she was to reach Scotland and find Craigmore Castle.

* * *

Two evenings later, Damaris waited until her ladies were asleep, then dressed in a gown she had bought that afternoon in the village. It was a plain brown dress such as the wives of the fishermen wore. She wanted to draw no attention to herself. In this dress she reasoned that she could pass unmolested through the Scottish countryside until she reached Craigmore. She put her hair out of sight under a simple linen hood and tied a purse at her waist. She would need money on her venture.

Being as quiet as possible, she let herself out of the door that led from her chamber directly to the corridor. Silently she hurried down the stairs and out of the castle. She was afraid, so she didn't allow herself to think. When Thornbeck loomed large and dark behind her, she slowed her gait and walked purposefully to the village.

The fishermen were all asleep and the boats were unguarded. Damaris hadn't rowed a boat since she was a child, but she was certain she remembered how it was done. She untied a boat, climbed in and cast away from the dock.

It took her a while to get used to the rhythm, and the oars were hard to pull, but she was able to get the boat pointed in the right direction. Soon her arms were aching and her back felt as if it were on fire, but she didn't stop. She had come too far to turn back now. Already the kitchen staff would be awaking and starting the day's baking and the fishermen would be going to the docks.

An hour later she saw the first lights on the shore of Scotland.

Chapter Seven

Meg ran down the stairs and, still holding her skirts disgracefully high, she raced into the hall. Gavin and his men looked up at her entrance. "Sir Gavin!" she called as soon as she saw him. "Sir Gavin!" She arrived breathless at his side.

"What is it, Meg?"

"My lady is gone!"

"What do you mean 'gone'?" he asked, trying to overcome his sense of foreboding.

"She's gone! She's left the castle!"

Robert glanced at Gavin in amusement. "Doesn't she usually come and go as she pleases?"

Meg shot him an angry look. "She left in the night. I've looked everywhere. I even went onto the parapet and looked at the Maidens. She's not on the island!"

"How could she leave it? Surely she's only gone to the village," Gavin reasoned.

"My lady has no reason to go to the village so early. We didn't help her dress or comb her hair or even see her since we awoke. I tell you, she's gone!"

Robert said, "That's not possible. No man would take a woman alone off the island, especially not the lady of the castle, and leave her unprotected. You have to be wrong."

"You don't know my lady," Meg snapped. "If she gets something in her mind, it's nigh impossible to oust it again."

"What was in her mind, Meg?" Gavin asked.

"Last night when we were readying her for bed, she asked how far I reckoned it was to the Scottish mainland and how long it had taken Sir William's men to row here. They didn't use their sails, you see, but came the other way so as not to be seen so easily. I told her I had no idea. I certainly never asked them.''

Gavin watched her closely.

''Then she asked if I had ever heard where Craigmore Castle is located. Again I told her I had no idea. It could be on the moon for all I know, I told her. Now she's gone!''

Robert laughed. ''You don't think she's gone to Craigmore? That's not possible. What reason could she possibly have to even want to risk the journey? She hates her uncle.''

Gavin felt his heavy dread solidify. ''I'll have my men search the island.''

Meg looked relieved. ''You'll not stop until you find her, Sir Gavin?''

''Of course not.'' He stood away from the table and strode out. Unlike Robert, he thought there was an excellent chance that Damaris had at least attempted to reach Craigmore. She had told him it was her intention. Why hadn't he watched her more carefully? Concern knotted in his stomach.

Gavin went to the village with several of his men and soon discovered unrest among the fishermen. One of them, a man the others addressed as Wat, was waving his arms angrily in the air.

''My boat has been stolen,'' he said as soon as he saw Gavin and his men. ''I came to the dock and it was gone!''

''Could it have come untied and drifted away?'' Gavin asked.

Wat gave him a condescending glare. ''I've been tying me boat up since I was a lad, and I've never lost a one. A fisherman that don't know how to tie a simple knot ain't worth the air he breathes.''

Gavin looked out to sea, but the boat was obviously not in sight. ''Did anyone see a stranger on the docks?''

''What do ye take us for? If we'd seen a stranger, we'd have run to the castle. This is an island. We get no strangers here. I know every man on this island and so do all the rest of us." Wat glared at his fellow fishermen. "How am I to bring in a catch without a boat? What of my family?"

"You won't go hungry. Thornbeck looks after its own."

"Someone stole my boat," Wat grumbled again. "If I knew the sod who did it, I'd break his neck!"

Gavin ignored him and looked across the water to where the faint shoreline of Scotland could be seen in the mist from the sea. To his men, Gavin said, "Come back to the castle. We have much to discuss."

They gathered in the closet that had been Owen's office. Gavin pointed to the map on the wall. "Craigmore Castle is here, according to this map. We may thank Lord Fleetwood for his affinity for details and records. It's not so far from the coast and we'll have to go through no large towns."

Robert spoke up. "You can't mean we're to go to Scotland? What of our orders?"

"Our orders were to safeguard the lady of Thornbeck, as well as the island. The lady has gone into danger and we have to bring her back to safety."

Robert and Godfrey exchanged a look. "A man rowed her over? What of him?"

"I think we'll find she rowed herself," Gavin said dryly. "You forget she grew up on this island, and Meg says she once knew how to row a small boat, as did all the children of Thornbeck."

"A girl was taught to row?" Godfrey looked amazed.

"Lord Fleetwood was an unusual man." Gavin wished he could show the man just what his permissiveness had wrought. "If a man had gone with her, he would have taken his own boat, not Wat Hobson's."

"That stands to reason," Robert agreed reluctantly.

"I expect to find she took no one with her on this excursion."

"But what possible reason could she have for going to Craigmore?" Robert reasoned.

"Vengeance. She wanted to deal with Sir William for the death of her father."

The men all glanced at each other. None of them had ever heard of a woman doing such a thing. Gavin wished he had been more alert to the danger that she would carry out her threat. Why had he thought he could keep her on the island simply by forbidding her to leave?

Robert studied the map. "Could she reach shore, do you think? Tides can be tricky, even for a man."

Gavin was silent for a moment. "I have to believe that she reached shore without mishap."

Godfrey pointed to the place marked on the map. "If she reached shore, she would have to go in this direction to reach the castle. It's not so far."

"Memorize the map. We may have to find the castle in the dark." He looked around the room. "Robert, you'll come with me. And you and you. Godfrey, I'll leave Thornbeck in your hands."

Godfrey nodded. He was quite capable of keeping it safe.

Gavin frowned at the map. "We have to be careful where we land. It can't be obvious that we've come from Thornbeck or we'll never reach the castle."

Robert pointed to the border. "We could dock here and cross by land. It's a bit farther, but we could go this route by day and not have to wait until night to make landing."

Gavin nodded. "I've thought the same thing. We can take a larger boat that way and have our horses. Their speed will make up the difference of what we could travel by the shorter distance on foot. Prepare to leave. We don't dare wait any longer."

As they went to do his bidding, Gavin stared at the map. Who would ever have thought a woman would try such a preposterous plan? Who but Damaris would have been able to get away with it? As angry as he was with her, he had to admire her.

Damaris reached the shore without too much difficulty and docked on a beach some distance from where the boats belonging to the local villagers were tethered. She managed to pull the boat a little way onto the shore and tied it to a fallen log, but she wasn't at all sure it would still be there when she returned. The marks on the shore told her she hadn't arrived at high tide. The boat could float away, assuming no one stole it before the tide came in. She couldn't worry about that, however. She had to do what she had come to do, then find a way to return to Thornbeck.

She was exhausted after the long trip at the oars, but she didn't dare take the time to rest. Already she would be missed and Sir Gavin would surely figure out where she had gone. It wasn't likely Sir Gavin, himself, would come after her, as he had told her he would not violate the queen's orders by leaving Thornbeck until his replacement arrived, but he might send some of his men in his place. With no time to waste, she resolutely went to the village and soon found the livery stable.

"I'd like to buy a horse," she told the man.

He gave her a long look. "I've not seen you about before."

"My family and I are new here. We've come from Aberdeen."

"Have you now? I hadn't heard of it. Are you at the old McBane place?"

"Aye," she said with a winning smile. "That would be us."

He looked at the horses that were in the pen. "I could let you have that roan. She's a bit long in the tooth, but she's gentle for a lady."

"I like the looks of her. What will you take?"

After haggling with the man for a moment, so she wouldn't appear too eager and arouse his suspicion, they agreed on a price. As soon as the man had the horse saddled, Damaris rode out of the village. It had been so simple, she thought. Why had Gavin made it seem so impossible? No one expected a woman to travel alone and therefore assumed that she had to be exactly who she claimed to be.

She took the road out of town that followed the coast, since that seemed to be the direction most people were taking. She had no idea where Craigmore was located and didn't dare ask in the village. A strange woman recently moved to the area wouldn't need to know such a thing.

She rode for several hours before stopping in front of a lone house set back from the road. A woman was working in the yard alone and it looked like a safe place to make an inquiry. Damaris rode up to her. "Good day. Can you tell me where to find Craigmore?"

The woman stopped hoeing the weeds in her tiny flower garden and gave Damaris a measuring look. "I never heard of it."

"You must have. There's a castle there."

The woman went back to work. "There ain't no castle about here."

Damaris hadn't expected this. She was accustomed to her island, where all the people knew everything about everyone. Perhaps, she reasoned, she hadn't gone far enough.

Gavin and his three men arrived on the mainland and set out for the border. With every minute that passed, Gavin became more worried. They hadn't seen a drifting boat on the journey over, but that didn't reassure him. The sea was vast and it could have drifted anywhere, had Damaris fallen overboard and drowned. The thought left him cold inside.

Robert had been his friend for so long, he knew what Gavin was thinking. "We'll find her," he said confidently.

"Will we? And what then? She may be at Craigmore by now. She'll certainly be there before we are. She had a head start."

"But she's on foot and we aren't. A woman traveling alone will have to take care not to be seen, whereas we look like men on our way to market."

Gavin glanced down at his clothing. He wore plain leather leggings and his doublet covered the leather body armor that would protect him from weapons. His cloak was plainly woven and untrimmed. No one looking at him would take him to be anything but a man out with companions on a summer's day.

In order to be less conspicuous, they had left their valuable war-horses at Thornbeck and had brought animals from the castle's stable. Gavin regretted not having Woden under him. The horse was trained to fight, as well as to carry Gavin into the thick of battle. But horses such as Woden were uncommon and would have drawn attention.

Robert shifted uncomfortably in his saddle. "Gavin, would you remind me again why we had to take these horses instead of our own? This nag has no comfortable gait at all.''

"I was just thinking the same thing about this one. And you don't need reminding that even our saddle horses are all of such good stock that they would be as noticeable as our war-horses. Besides, you know we may have to leave these behind in order to escape.''

"I almost hope we are forced to leave this one in Scotland. The Scots deserve it.''

Gavin smiled. The other two men were solemn and rarely spoke. He had chosen them for their fearlessness, not their company. Will Kerwin and Henry Laibrook had been with him in many campaigns, and he knew them to be loyal and brave warriors.

The sun was high in the sky by the time they crossed the Scots border, and to conserve time, Gavin decided they should eat in the saddle as they traveled. Gavin cut a bite of roasted boar and ate it from the end of his knife while he planned what they would do when they reached the castle. Gaining entrance would be difficult. Once in, however, they could find a way out. Castles were meant to be impervious from the outside, not the inside.

"Do you think there's a chance she hasn't reached the castle yet?'' he asked Robert.

"I don't see how. Going by boat, she would have headed for the nearest shore and that's just below Craigmore. Even on foot and staying out of sight, she would be able to reach it in a few hours.''

"She'll have no trouble getting in. All she will have to do is present herself.'' Gavin rolled the remaining dried meat back into the cloth and put it in the pouch that was tied to his saddle. He knew he should eat, but he had no appetite for food.

"What do you suppose she will do then?''

"I have no idea. Surely she must realize that if she openly attacks Sir William, she will be set upon by all his retainers. She's no fool. I'd say she'll wait until night and go after him when everyone is asleep.''

"Knife him, you mean?" Robert thought for a moment. "A knife isn't a woman's weapon. No, I think she'll poison him."

Gavin wasn't so sure. "Where is she to obtain this poison? Perhaps she'll try to push him off the ramparts."

"She's not strong enough to outwrestle a man."

Gavin swore under his breath. "I wish I could see into her mind. What could she plan to do?"

Damaris was becoming alarmed. She had ridden for hours and still no one had heard of Craigmore. The only explanation was that she had taken the wrong road from the village. At a gallop, she rode back and started again.

It would be dark soon and she had no place to spend the night. To sleep in the open would be dangerous for a woman alone and Damaris had never in her life slept without a castle's stout walls to protect her.

She considered asking directions again, but none of the villagers seemed particularly friendly, and she didn't want to draw attention to herself. At last she found a group of children and went to them. "Can you tell me the way to Craigmore Castle?" she asked.

The children looked at her, then at each other. One said, "I believe it's that way."

Damaris thanked them and headed down the road he had indicated. She had no idea if the boy was correct. The road seemed small and too seldom traveled to lead to the area's castle. Perhaps, she told herself, the castle bought goods from another village and had little commerce with this one.

The setting sun was soon in her eyes, and with her horse tiring, she knew she would have to stop before long. For the past hour or so she had seen not one woman, and she had not dared ask any of the men she passed for directions. They all looked unfriendly and stared at her with looks that were unsettling. With no recourse but to pretend that she knew where she was and where she was heading, she kept riding on.

As dusk settled about the countryside, she had to stop. The horse was walking slower and slower and she hadn't the heart to urge it to move faster. She had no idea where she was and she didn't want to harm the animal by pressing it to a faster pace.

She had passed several crossroads and, each time, she had taken the larger road, reasoning that a castle's traffic would keep the road open. None of the roads were well kept. Tall bushes grew right up to their edges and at times she wasn't sure she was still on a road and not following some path made by farmers passing from one holding to another.

Thoughts of highwaymen raced through her head every time the wind rustled the bushes. Thieves and murderers could be lurking in every dark arm of woodland or behind every outcrop of stone. Damaris wasn't nervous by nature, but she felt exhausted from being constantly on her guard.

She guided the horse off the road and stopped next to a stream. She hadn't seen anyone in over an hour, so this seemed to be as safe a place as any.

When Damaris dismounted and her feet touched the ground, pain shot through her legs. She wasn't accustomed to spending hours on horseback, and she hurt all over. The horse lowered its nose and drank noisily from the stream while Damaris looked around. There was no place to fence the animal, of course, nor did she have a rope to tie him. For that matter, she wasn't entirely certain she could saddle him again. She studied the leather thongs and belts that held the saddle on, and even though it seemed that it would be difficult to get them all back together correctly, she decided to remove the saddle anyway. If the horse wasn't rested, he would be of no use to her the next day.

She left the bridle in place and tied the reins to a tree, then put the saddle on the ground to use as a pillow. She lay down and covered herself with the horse's blanket. Never had she been so miserable.

Her thoughts traveled to Thornbeck. By now Meg and the other ladies would have finished dinner and would be in the parlor. They would be sewing or playing games and listening to the musicians and gossiping, filling the time before bed as they always had. Or would they? Without her presence, would the routine be unaltered? She didn't like to think of Meg and the others worrying about her.

A night bird called from far off in the woods and Damaris looked in the direction the sound had come from. Were there wolves in these woods? Bears?

Above all she missed Gavin. This surprised her a bit. After all, he hadn't been a part of her life for long. She found herself remembering the way sunlight touched gold in his hair and how his voice sounded. Was he worried, too?

He would certainly be angry. She had disobeyed his orders, and she wasn't sure what she could expect from him on her return. If he no longer spoke to her or sought her out, would her love for him eventually die? She didn't think so.

The bird called again and this time it seemed to be just above her head. Damaris looked up but could see only a canopy of leaves between her and the stars. Now that the sun was down, the forest seemed incredibly dark and not nearly as silent as she wished. There seemed to be something moving beneath every bush and in every tree. Even the stream seemed to be gurgling louder. There were sounds she had never heard in her chambers at Thornbeck or in her rare excursions with her father to the mainland.

She could see the bulk of her horse in the darkness. He was docile and seemed to think nothing of being tied to a bush all night. He stood with his head drooping and one back leg propped on the tip of a hoof in relaxation. She wondered what she would find to feed him in the morning. Or what she would eat, for that matter.

She hadn't thought to bring food, and while she had bought bread and cheese from a peasant woman at noon, that was long since eaten. There had been no reason to save it since she had been positive she would be at Craigmore before dark.

A twig snapped in the woods behind her, causing her to jump. She wished she had Gavin beside her. If he were there, she knew she wouldn't be afraid of the thousand sounds and the darkness that wasn't bounded by any walls or roof. But Gavin was miles away at Thornbeck.

She closed her eyes and allowed herself to think about him. The way his lips had claimed hers and how perfectly their bodies had fit together. She would have given herself to him that last day at the Maidens. Damaris had wanted him to continue kissing her and touching her and driving her almost to distraction. She still didn't understand why he had pulled away.

Was it that he didn't desire her? Even with her lack of experience, that seemed unlikely. He had been too passionate in his kisses. She had felt him trembling from the effort to hold himself in check.

Gavin was a knight and the queen's trusted man. Was it really because he wanted to leave her untouched for her future husband? Damaris's emotions toward this were at odds. On one hand, it was the chivalrous thing to do. A knight was sworn to uphold a lady's honor. She had read in one of the old books at Thornbeck that knights were at one time encouraged to keep themselves pure of thought and deed, but she wasn't sure that was still a rule. She had heard of too many liaisons at the castle to believe that.

On the other hand, she regretted that Gavin had left her, whatever his reason might have been. She had no desire to keep herself for some man that she had never heard of and that she almost certainly wouldn't love. If she could give herself to Gavin, wouldn't that be better so she would have something special of him to remember on the long nights after he was gone from Thornbeck forever? If she had one day of loving, wouldn't that help sustain her in the years without him?

A tear beaded in her eye and traveled down her cheek. She loved Gavin and missed him terribly. Even though she hadn't known him that long, how could she bear to live without him? Her world had begun to circle him and she knew that no matter how far he might travel, he would never leave her heart. What was he thinking about her? Was he on the parapet and gazing out to sea in hopes of catching some glimpse of her? Or was he in his chamber and remembering their kisses and burning for her as she was for him?

Despite her longings and fears, exhaustion claimed her and soon she drifted into sleep.

Gavin couldn't rest. He and his men had stopped for the night in a secluded glen. Their horses were tied and he could hear the deep breathing and occasional snores of the others as they slept. He lay awake, staring up at the leaves above him and wondering if Damaris was safe.

He didn't know for certain that she had even reached the shore. If she had, he couldn't be positive she hadn't been waylaid by the first man who realized her clothing wasn't that of a village woman. Damaris's silks and velvets and brocades would be like a banner in a village or countryside where people had to weave the cloth for whatever clothing they wore. How could she hope to pass unnoticed?

Even if she had somehow escaped attention, had she been able to find the castle? He thought she must know its location or she wouldn't have set out on this journey in the first place, but he knew what roads were like away from the larger towns and it was easy to lose the way, even if one was accustomed to traveling.

If she had found the castle, had her uncle imprisoned her on sight? That seemed likely. After all, he knew she hated him. He wouldn't be so foolish as to believe she had only dropped by to pay a call. William would also expect that someone had traveled with her, and he would be on guard for the arrival of Gavin and his men, for by now word had surely reached him of Gavin's successful taking of Thornbeck.

He had to find some way of getting into the castle unnoticed. Who had access to it? The people who lived there, naturally. He couldn't hope to pass as one of them. Castles were too intimate. Four strange men would be seen right away.

Peddlers had access, tinkers, minstrels, jugglers. Gavin could sing but he doubted any of his men could, so they couldn't get in under the guise of musicians. Nor could they juggle or tumble or do any of the tricks that would win them access as performers. They had no skills as tinkers, either, and everyone knew tinkers traveled alone.

The best bet was to buy a peddler's wares and hope no one asked why it took four of them to push a cart and sell ribbons and laces and nosegays. Would that work? All women loved to rummage through a peddler's goods and there were certain to be women in the castle. Once inside the gates,

Gavin and the others could find a place to hide until nightfall. Then they could search for Damaris.

Where would Sir William put her? Gavin had seen enough dungeons to be half-sick at the idea of her locked away in such a place. Would the man be chivalrous enough to give her lodging in a bedchamber? Could Gavin find her and get her out again without alerting the men-at-arms?

He groaned at the seemingly impossible problem. Why had she done such a foolish thing? He had known many women, but he had never known one who would set out on such a dangerous mission. Women were supposed to gentle, retiring creatures who were content to sit at home and sew fine seams and discuss recipes and home remedies with other women. They were supposed to be sweet and demure and occasionally exciting. But they weren't supposed to be warriors bent on vengeance.

Damaris was such a contradiction. At times she was soft and her smiles were gentle and wistful. Sometimes he wasn't altogether positive she was flesh and blood, when he saw her in the grasses, for instance, surrounded by her Maidens and talking to a wild rabbit that was totally unafraid of her.

Then again she was so real, she could shake the foundations of his world. She could tempt him as no other woman ever had. He had had his share of dalliances and more, but he had never been loved by one of them, and he had never been tempted to dally in such a way as to incur royal wrath. His queen wouldn't be pleased at all to know he had kissed Damaris in the cool grasses on the Maidens' hill, or that she had returned his kisses with such fervor.

He ached at the thought of how she had felt in his arms. He hadn't been exaggerating when he told her she had bewitched him. Nothing else could explain his lack of restraint where she was concerned. Lack of restraint? No, rather he had been stronger than he had thought possible. Otherwise she would have been his in every way before they left the stone circle.

Gavin recalled the way Damaris's lavender eyes had darkened as she lay beneath him, and his body responded as eagerly as if she were lying beside him at that very moment. He shifted on the hard ground and wished he wasn't so moved by her. He had always prided himself on being master of his body, but she had put an end to that.

How could he bear to leave her, assuming he was able to return her safely to Thornbeck? Soon a retinue from London would arrive there, her future husband among them. Even now the man could be on his way. Gavin wasn't at all certain he could hand her over to him. Especially if the man didn't seem kind or fond of her. Would it be any easier if the man loved her? Gavin didn't think he could give her up at all. Yet he had no choice.

Robert moved and Gavin found his friend was awake. Robert glanced around to see if a noise had startled them both. "Are you having trouble sleeping?" he whispered in order not to rouse the other two.

Gavin nodded his head. "I find I can't stop thinking long enough to sleep."

Robert sat up and rubbed his eyes. "I'll keep you company."

"No, you need your rest. One fool in this company is enough."

"Which is it, worry over her safety or over how to breach the castle?"

Gavin smiled. "You know me too well, Robin."

"After all these years, who could know you better?"

"I suppose I'm worried about all of it." Gavin sat up and leaned his forearms on his crossed legs. "We've never had to solve such a tangle. I've thought we could get into the gates if we passed as peddlers."

Robert considered the idea for a minute. "That might work. Or beggars. Maybe two of each."

"Yes."

"And what about the fair lady?"

Gavin knew he could trust Robert with any thought. "At times I think I may have had the misfortune to have fallen in love with her."

"Oh? And at others?"

"At others I'm sure of it."

Robert was silent for a long time. "I was afraid that was the truth of it."

Gavin lay down. "We have to sleep. We can't find her and get her to safety unless we're at our best."

He heard Robert lie back down but he didn't look his way. Despite his words to the contrary, he wasn't so sure he could sleep. All he could think of was Damaris and whether or not he would ever see her again.

Chapter Eight

Saddling the horse wasn't as difficult as Damaris had feared it might be. She remembered where the various leather straps attached, and the animal cooperated by standing quietly while she tightened the band that secured the saddle. Damaris led him to a rock and used it as a mounting block to get into the saddle.

She made her way back to the road, and after a few minutes she came upon a farmhouse. To the woman who was scrubbing the steps out front, she said, "Pardon, but might I buy food for myself and my horse?"

The woman looked at her cautiously but nodded. "I have some bread and a bit of meat from last night. The beast is welcome to a bucket of oats."

Damaris felt as if she hadn't eaten in days. As soon as she fed the horse, she sat on the steps with the woman and ate the bread and meat.

"Ye aren't from around here," the woman accurately observed.

"Nay. I became lost while out riding. I had to sleep in the woods there." She nodded in the direction she had come from.

The woman made a disgusted sound. "Ye're lucky to still have ye purse and animal, then. That stand of trees is the hideout of Black Toby."

"Who?"

"He's a highwayman hereabouts. Ye've never heard of him?"

"As you said, I'm not from here." She took a tankard of ale from the woman to wash down the dry bread and over-cooked meat. "I'm trying to find Craigmore Castle," she added with little expectation of an informed response.

"It's half a day's ride from here."

Damaris looked at her hopefully. "You know where it is?"

"I ought to. My own son Harry lives there." The woman's pride in the connection was clear.

"Please, can you tell me how to find it?"

The woman nodded. "When ye leave, go down the road you turned from to get to this house. Take it to the south until you come to the third crossroads. Turn west. That will take you straight to it."

Damaris was so grateful she gave the woman a gold angel in exchange for the food and directions. The woman stared at the coin as if she had never seen one in her life. From the looks of the farm, Damaris thought perhaps she hadn't. As soon as she mounted her horse, she was on her way.

Gavin and his men reached Craigmore Castle before noon. Without being obvious in their interest, they studied the castle from a distance. Finally he said to Robert, "Do you see a way in?"

Robert shook his head. "We'll have to gain entrance by trickery. See? There are guards on the towers and along the parapets. The gates are sure to be watched."

"Is Sir William in such ill favor here that he has to post guards during the day against his own village?" Gavin wondered aloud.

"So it would seem."

As they skirted the perimeter of the castle, Gavin studied it with an experienced eye. It was strong and solid. The stones were stained dark from the dampness of the nearby fen and streaks of fungus were prevalent along most of the walls. A fetid yellowish mist floated on the fen's stagnant water.

"It doesn't strike me as a propitious place to build a castle," Robert observed. "The sickness must stay here year-round."

Gavin automatically touched the cross he wore beneath his doublet. "Let's hope we're out of here before it finds us." He had seen whole armies laid waste by sickness. It was more to be feared than weapons because it came without warning and couldn't be fought against with any hope of winning.

"The castle is being closely watched," Gavin agreed when they were back around to the front. "Let's ride away before we draw attention to ourselves."

Unlike Thornbeck, Craigmore's village squatted directly against its walls. The remains of an older wall was visible around most of the town, but it had fallen long ago into disrepair. Even casual observation showed that many of its stones had been taken for use, plugging holes in the streets or supporting walls of the cottages. The streets were winding and dirty, the people inclined to be silent and sullen.

Gavin bought a bundle of rags from a vendor and gave them to Will Kerwin and Henry Laibrook. "Here, men. You've just become beggars. You haven't the gift of gab it takes to be peddlers."

The men took the clothing without comment.

"You can change clothes in the woods there. Meet us at the town well when you're done. Take our horses and tie them with your own."

Gavin and Robert went in search of a peddler. They found a costermonger pushing a cart of laces and ribbons and other gadgets that would appeal to women. The shriveled old man was more than happy to part with his cart and goods for the amount Gavin offered him.

Soon Gavin and Robert were strolling along the cobbled streets in the direction of the well. Two beggars sidled closer to them as they paused, pretending to be getting a drink from the common dipper.

"Have you seen any man that might be Sir William?" Gavin whispered.

Kerwin shook his head. "We've seen no one that could be the master of a castle. Some of the people have stared at us,

though. The village is too small for four strangers to pass
unremarked.''

"Aye." Gavin glanced around. "Then let's try our luck
at the castle. If we're separated, we'll meet in the woods."

Laibrook spoke up. "I've tied the horses in high brush
beside a rock outcropping. I think no one will discover them
there." He nodded toward the woods. "Head for that large
oak and veer south."

Gavin nodded. With a motion to Robert, they strolled
toward the castle, calling out their wares the way the costermonger had done. They didn't dare hurry or be too direct. Their safety lay in appearing to be nothing else but men
who had things to sell and all day in which to sell them.

One of the village women stopped them before they
reached the gate. "What ribbons have you?"

Gavin pulled some from the cart. "Fine ones, good wife.
Here's a pink that would grace any bonnet." From the corner of his eye he saw a woman coming up the road to the
castle on horseback. A closer look showed her to be Damaris. "Take the ribbon, with my good cheer," he said
hastily.

The woman stammered in her surprise. "I cannot! Are
they not for sale?"

"Aye." His eyes met Robert's and he motioned with his
chin.

Robert followed his gaze and he moved away hurriedly to
intercept Damaris before she could reach the castle.

"How much then?" the woman was asking. "I'm not
made of money, but I need not take charity from a peddler!"

"I meant no offense." Gavin watched as Robert tried to
hail Damaris. She never glanced in his direction. Laibrook
also saw her and waved his arms to attract her attention.
Damaris rode on.

"A penny," Gavin said, not paying any attention to the
sale at all. Damaris was almost to the gate.

"A penny? First you try to give them to me, and now you
seem to think they're made of gold. Too much."

"A farthing then." He saw Robert break into a run and
actually shout her name. Damaris neither saw nor heard

him. She rode up to the gate and Robert looked back at Gavin in dismay.

"Very well. A farthing. For all the pink." She held out a coin.

"Take it." Gavin thrust it at her and pushed the cart away before she could ask to see more.

Robert looked as if he could hardly contain himself. "I couldn't stop her! She rode past before I could get her attention!"

"I saw." He glanced at the two beggars who seemed to be engaged in the same conversation. "Come on. Maybe we can still catch her attention."

Damaris rode to the guard at the gate and said, "My name is Damaris Fleetwood. I'm here to see my uncle, Sir William."

Surprise flickered in the man's eyes, but he nodded. He motioned for his assistant to come closer. "Take her to Sir William. She says she's his niece." This man also seemed surprised.

Damaris rode into the courtyard and looked around. It was smaller and dirtier by far than Thornbeck's court. As was the custom here, as well, a number of small shops ringed the inner walls and she could hear the clang of a blacksmith working. Two maids went by arm in arm, their giggles seeming out of character with the dour castle. She dismounted and gave her horse's reins to a stable boy.

"This way, my lady," the man sent to escort her said.

She followed him up the steps to the castle's main door. Because it was summer, the doors were open and several children and dogs dashed out as she tried to enter.

Her guide told the steward that she had come to see Sir William. "She says she's his niece," he added almost in a whisper.

Damaris was beginning to wonder at the manners of the castle's staff. They were certain to wonder at her arrival, but her people at Thornbeck would have been more circumspect. So far she had seen nothing about Craigmore to recommend it.

Sir William came striding to meet her. His amazement was obvious. "What are you doing here?"

Damaris managed a convincing smile. "I've come to visit, Uncle. I had some of your men bring me. They've already gone back to Thornbeck."

"Some of my men brought you?" Disbelief was strong in his voice.

"Aye. You're not to be angry with them. I insisted." She looked around. "So this is Craigmore."

William watched her closely. She apparently wasn't aware that James McIntyre had escaped the battle and had come to Craigmore with the news that the castle had been overtaken by the English. He looked past her head into the courtyard. Nothing seemed to be at odds. "Go into the parlor," he said. "That woman over there will show you the way. I'll have some claret brought in."

Damaris smiled and did as he bid.

William's smile disappeared as he crossed the courtyard to where his men were guarding the gate. "Who was with the lady?" he demanded.

"No, one, Sir William. She rode in alone."

"That's not possible! She can't have come alone."

"I saw no one," the guard insisted. His fellow guardsman nodded in agreement. "No one at all."

William glared at the crowd just outside the gates. "Be on guard, and tell the others on the wall, as well. Something is wrong here." For a minute he studied the activity of the village but nothing seemed out of the ordinary. In his experience, the village was like a flock of geese. If anything upset their daily habits, they squawked and complained loudly. After a moment he turned and went back to the castle.

Sir James McIntyre met him at the door. "I hear your niece has arrived. What can this mean?"

"I know not. Go to the men on the towers and tell them to be especially alert. I have no idea why the English would send her here if they plan to attack Craigmore. She would be in grave danger. But what else could have brought her here?"

Sir James shook his head. "I can't guess."

"From her words, she doesn't know that you were able to escape with news of the English retaking Thornbeck. I want you to stay out of her sight. Whatever she's up to, I want us to have the element of surprise in our favor."

"I'll do as you say." Sir James gave a half bow and left.

William was thoughtful as he returned to Damaris. "I've told the groom to put your horse in the stable and feed him."

Damaris gave him a smile. "Thank you, Sir William. He's a poor specimen of a horse, but he can't help that."

"You say some of my men accompanied you here?" he said. "I find it odd that they didn't come into the castle before leaving to return to Thornbeck."

She shrugged. "They were afraid of your wrath. After all, you told them to stay on the island. It's all my fault that they didn't follow your orders. You're not to be angry with them."

"Why did you want to come to Craigmore?"

"I wanted to see where you live. After all, now that Scotsmen have taken Thornbeck, it's a Scottish castle. I'm curious about my new country."

"You're taking this awfully well. Especially since you were so upset when I saw you last."

"I'm a reasonable woman," she said easily. "I changed my mind. All women do from time to time." She smiled again. This was amazingly easy. "Naturally I was angry and upset over my castle being taken. But that was a month ago. I've had time to adjust."

"And what of your father's death?"

Damaris paused in order to keep her voice steady when she answered. "I still grieve my father. He was a kind and peaceable man and I loved him."

"I'd not believe you if you said otherwise." William poured claret for himself and offered to refill her goblet.

She shook her head. She didn't want the wine to muddle her reasoning. "He was your younger brother. Surely you must feel something, too."

"I feel surprisingly little remorse. Probably no more than Owen did in depriving me of my birthright."

Damaris refused to be baited, though his words made anger boil in her. "This is good claret. I hope you decide to stock some like it at Thornbeck."

"You intend to return there, then?"

"Of course," she said in some surprise. "It's my home."

"I hope you now regard Craigmore as your home, as well."

"Gallantly put, Uncle." She sipped her wine and looked around the room. There were tapestries on the wall, but they were old and not as well worked as the ones at Thornbeck. Even though it was still summer, the rushes on the floor were already soured. A damp cold seemed to radiate from the stone walls. She would be glad to leave this place.

William lifted a bell that sat on a shelf near the door and rang it. In moments a woman servant came into the room. "We have a guest, Mable. Ready the chamber in the water tower."

Mable stared openly at Damaris. "Should I tell the cook?"

"No, there's only one extra mouth. Our usual fare will suffice."

Mable stopped staring long enough to bob a curtsy, then left. As she closed the door, she cast a glance back at Damaris.

William smiled. "We see few guests at Craigmore," he said in explanation. "You have to excuse my people's rudeness."

"I did notice they were staring at me. I'd have thought that guests would be frequent here on the mainland. We entertain even at Thornbeck."

"I have no lady of the castle," he said smoothly. "A bachelor is more likely to visit than to receive."

She supposed that could be true. She had no experience to the contrary. "Craigmore is lovely," she lied. "I had no idea it was so old."

"It's not, really. It's the fen. It tends to add age to everything." William sounded as if he weren't particularly fond of his castle.

"Thornbeck is surrounded by water and it's not a problem."

"There's a vast difference between a storm-swept island and an inland fen," he replied dryly. "After you've been here a while, you'll see what I mean."

She laughed. "I doubt I'll be here long. In faith, I'm already homesick for my island."

"You mean *my* island."

She made herself smile. "A mere slip of the tongue." She stood and went to the narrow window. Through the arrow slit window she could see almost nothing except the village just beyond the wall and a narrow slice of courtyard below. "Do you have many men here?"

"Now why would a pretty maid like you want to know the answer to a question like that?"

"I have no reason other than curiosity." She touched the stone sill and found it was slightly damp. "You say I'm to sleep in the water tower? Is that beside the fen?"

"Just over it."

"How nice." She barely managed to keep the sarcasm from showing in her voice. "It seems I shall become acquainted with the fen after all. And do you sleep in that tower, as well?"

"No, I'm in the east one." He paused. "Why would you want to know that?"

Damaris laughed. "You amaze me, Uncle. Don't you ever engage in polite conversation here at Craigmore? I'm only getting to know you and your castle. What do you think I intend to do? Take it single-handedly from the inside?"

He laughed, too. "Of course not. That would be ridiculous. As for my number of men, I have enough and more to defend it. There are a number of villages in the vicinity that owe fealty to Craigmore. I'll be able to hold both my castles quite securely."

"Good." Damaris walked to the next window and looked out. The view was almost the same. In the courtyard she saw two dirty beggars sitting in the shade of the wall, bowls in their hands. A couple of peddlers were bringing a cart into the enclosure. "Tell me of Queen Mary," she said to pass the time.

"What would you have me say? She's our queen."

"I know that. As an English subject, I must have heard false words about her. I'm her subject now and I'd rather know the truth."

William looked uncertainly at her, and she smiled to put him at ease. "I've seen her myself. She's tall for a woman, about your height, I'd say. Her hair has a bit of red in it, too. Her face is nothing like yours and her hands are exceptionally beautiful."

"You've seen her?" Damaris was genuinely interested. "I've never seen Queen Elizabeth. When I was a girl, we went to court, my father and I, and I saw the young king, Edward. He was dressed in the most beautiful clothing, but he was sickly. I remember hearing him cough and it sounded as if he would come apart with the effort."

"Our queen is in perfect health," William reassured her. "I wager she'll give Scotland strong sons to rule after her."

"God be willing," Damaris said automatically. She came away from the window and sat back on the stool near her uncle. "Tell me of Scotland."

As she listened, she tried to think just how to best kill William. It had seemed so simple when she was in Thornbeck. She had planned to go to him in his sleep and stab him. She wore a dagger under her skirt that she had brought for that purpose. Now that she was here, however, it was a different matter.

Damaris had never considered killing anyone before. William was alive and strong in spite of his advancing years. She found she had qualms about ending a person's life. Would God and the saints understand? Until now she had never considered that it could be wrong to kill the man who had murdered her father before her own eyes.

How hard would she have to strike him, assuming she could do so at all? Where should she aim? Now that she was sitting in front of him, engaging in an idle conversation, she couldn't imagine slipping into his chamber at night and stabbing a knife into him. Had she made a terrible error in coming here?

Anxiety churned in her middle. She felt sick when she contemplated what she had to do.

"Are you feeling ill?" William asked. "You seem pale all of a sudden."

"I'm tired, I suppose," she admitted. "If it wouldn't be rude of me, might I be shown to my room? I'd like to rest."

"Of course." William again rang the bell. When Mable entered, he said, "Show my niece to her chamber."

"Aye, Sir William." Mable hesitated, then added, "She had no trunks to take up or anything."

He gave Damaris a measuring look. "You brought no luggage? No change of clothes or linens?"

"I've traveled so rarely," she said quickly. "I didn't know what to pack and had no one to advise me."

"Use Craigmore's linens to prepare her room," William told Mable. "And find clothing for her to wear."

"Aye." Mable didn't look too pleased at being given this task.

Damaris followed her out of the parlor. She tried to memorize all the turns and twists the corridors and stairs made in order to be able to find her way back out of the castle once the deed was done. She would have to do so without anyone seeing her.

As she entered the water tower, she noticed a flight of steps that led downward. "What's down there, Mable?"

"Naught but the buttery, my lady. You're in the older part of the castle where the men were once lodged."

"I see." That suited her perfectly. All buteries had outer doors in order for the huge butts of wine to be brought into the castle.

"I've heard it's haunted," the older woman said matter-of-factly. "I've never seen aught myself."

Damaris's steps flagged. She could well imagine a ghost in this castle and the thought wasn't pleasant. "Are there women in the castle who might be assigned to me during my visit here? I'm not skilled at dressing my hair."

Mable laughed roughly. "You'll find no lady's maids here. The guardsmen and all have wives, true enough, but none that could dress hair." She laughed again at the thought. "I'd say you'll have to learn to do for yourself, like the rest of us, and put it up however you can."

Damaris was silent. She didn't need help in her toiletries as much as she desired company. But having someone around would hinder her going to Sir William when she got up her courage to do him in. "Are you saying I'll be all alone in this tower?"

"That's it exactly. No one else will stay in it." Mable laughed again as if she were enjoying Damaris's discomfort.

"How welcoming Craigmore is to guests. I marvel that a constant stream aren't knocking at the gate, eager to sample such unique hospitality."

Mable looked back at her, trying to decide if Damaris had meant those words as insults. Sarcasm was clearly lost on her.

The chamber proved to be directly over the fen. Damaris could see its noxious yellow mist as soon as she looked out the window. The aroma of the stagnant water and rotting vegetation had arrived in the chamber before her. "Are there tapestries to hang over the windows?"

"No, my lady."

"Find some," Damaris said tartly. She might have to spend some hours in this dismal place, but there was no reason to breathe in its fumes, as well. "And I want candles. Not rushes, but candles. Maybe they will drive the smell from the room."

Mable looked as if this were going too far but she didn't refuse.

While Mable made the bed, Damaris looked around the room. There was no antechamber for ladies' maids and no small room to hang clothing in. The walls were bare except for one thready painted cloth that seemed to be rotting where it hung. No rushes were on the floor and the wood was rough and uneven. It seemed the perfect place for a ghost to inhabit. She tried not to think of that.

Mable finished tucking the linen onto the bed and started for the door. Damaris reminded her again about the tapestries and candles, then allowed her to leave.

The castle was completely silent when Mable's footsteps died away. Damaris had rarely been alone in her life, and she found it unsettling. Why had William seen fit to put her in a tower so far removed from the rest of the castle? Did he suspect something?

Damaris went to the door and pulled on it. To her relief, it was not locked. She told herself that she was letting her nerves play tricks on her. William had no cause to be suspicious, let alone to lock her in.

The silence told her something else. Craigmore wasn't a large castle. It was considerably smaller than Thornbeck and her castle was full of people. That meant he had a smaller contingent of men here than he would have led her to believe. Not that it mattered. She had no men to attack it and no reason to want to take it. It was good to know, however, that the men still imprisoned at Thornbeck accounted for most of the fighting men who made their home in the castle. That could mean some degree of safety for Thornbeck in the immediate future. As for those men imprisoned in Thornbeck's dungeon, Damaris assumed that Queen Elizabeth would send orders as to what to do with them.

She went to the high bed and poked experimentally at the mattress. The rustle told her it was stuffed with husks, not goose down. She reassured herself that she wouldn't be sleeping on it anyway. If she couldn't bring herself to do what she came to do, she would slip away in the night and somehow return to Thornbeck. She didn't want to stay in this place a minute longer than was necessary.

After Mable returned with tapestries and a few candles, Damaris supervised hanging the cloth over the windows, then allowed Mable to leave.

As soon as the maid was gone, Damaris went out into the corridor. She had to learn her way around the castle while it was daylight if she was to find the east wing in the dark. She tried to remember what the castle had looked like from outside in order to give her a clue as to where the corridors might be.

Fortunately for her, Craigmore was fairly four-square and not extremely complicated. The tower stairs led down into the buttery just as Mable had said. It was a smaller room than the one at Thornbeck, but it was well stocked. Looking at the number of butts of wine, she thought William and his men must enjoy their tankards. On the far wall she saw double doors that led outside.

She crossed the room and went up the short steps and into the kitchen corridor. To her left she could hear the chatter of scullery maids and spit boys. She turned to the right.

When the corridor branched, she found herself near more stairs. She went up and down a long, dark room that seemed to have no purpose at all. At the far end, she found windows and, from the angle of the sun, she deduced that she was in the east end. Not far away she saw a bulge in the outer wall that indicated a tower. It wouldn't be difficult to find William, even in the dark.

Damaris retraced her path and found her way back to her chamber. It wasn't a pleasant place, but it was preferable to spending time with her uncle. Besides, he thought she was resting from her journey. She pulled the steps out from under the bed and climbed up onto the top mattress. It crackled under her weight and husks poked at her through the bedding. Mable hadn't bothered to find blankets or furs to keep out the clammy air. Even though it was the warmest season of the year, the nights were uncomfortably cool on her island and would be here also. She lay down and tried to make her plans.

Despite her discomfort, Damaris dozed and awoke when Mable rapped sharply on her door. "There's dinner in the hall," she abruptly announced.

"Thank you. Will you see that warm covers are brought up?" Damaris slid off the bed and touched her hair to see that it was still properly confined. She knew there was no hope of finding a mirror in this place.

"Aye, your highness. Will there be anything else?" Mable said sarcastically.

"Not for now. If there is, I'll let you know." Damaris whisked past her and out the door. If she had intended to stay here, she would have taken the maid to task or reported her behavior to Sir William. As it was, there was no reason to bother. Damaris intended to be away from this castle in a few hours.

Dinner was disorderly and not a pleasant experience. William had musicians playing, but they were inferior and the noise from the diners often drowned out their efforts. Damaris tried not to look too closely at the food on her trencher. The table beneath it was dirty in the extreme.

More than once men rose to their feet and shouted across the hall at acquaintances or enemies. Once, a wedge of cheese was thrown and hit a man on the shoulder. Damaris pretended not to see. She was feeling more and more uneasy. If William had no more control over his men than this, how safe was she in his castle? Somehow that had never occurred to her.

There was no chaplain to end the meal with a prayer. When William was finished, he simply stood up and left the table. Damaris didn't dare remain behind, nor did she wish to, so she left in his wake. She was relieved when she was able to escape back to the water tower and its ghostly, silent shadows.

Chapter Nine

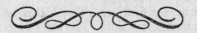

Gavin and Robert smiled at the women in the courtyard and affected a fawning manner to keep anyone from noticing how unlike peddlers they really were. All the time, Gavin's eyes were studying the courtyard, the outbuildings and the keep.

Across the way Kerwin and Laibrook, passing as beggars, held a cracked wooden bowl between them that Kerwin had found somewhere, and were pleading and mumbling for coins from all who came near them. They ventured too near a man-at-arms and from behind, the guard shoved Laibrook out of his way. Gavin froze for a moment. Laibrook had a fierce temper when it was roused and Gavin wasn't sure what his man's instinctive reaction would be to an attack from the rear. Fortunately, Laibrook maintained his composure, and as he slunk away from the man-at-arms, Gavin let himself relax.

The remainder of the day was uneventful; the four continued playing their parts and learning all they could of the castle's routine. As sundown approached, the local tradesmen began making preparations to leave the courtyard and return to their homes. Laibrook and Kerwin were near a shed built onto the inner wall. No one had come or gone from the shed all afternoon. When no one but Gavin was watching, Kerwin opened the door a crack and peered in. He nodded to Laibrook and they slipped inside, unseen by anyone else.

"They've hidden," Gavin whispered to Robert in the pretext of examining a wheel on the cart.

"Do you have a plan?"

Gavin was working the peg out of the wheel's hub. The axle dropped to the cobbled ground. "Our wheel has given up for good this time," he said loud enough for the nearest people to hear.

Robert looked around and pointed to one of the shops along the inner wall. "There's a wheelwright shop. Can we have it repaired, do you think?"

Gavin counted the four pence they had earned that afternoon. "Just barely, I believe." To the women examining their wares he said, "You'll have to pardon us, fair ladies. We have to repair our cart or we're out of business." He smiled and bowed to them. The women wandered away.

Together he and Robert pushed the cart to the shop where they could see a man working on coach wheels. "Can you repair this?" Gavin asked.

The man glanced at the cart. "I only work on the belongings of Craigmore. Fix it yourself."

"We have money," Robert said.

The man looked more interested. "Aye. I can fix it. Not today, though. It will be dark soon and I have enough to do of my own work. Leave it here and I'll try to find time to work on it tomorrow or the next day."

"Thank you," Gavin said as he bobbed a series of bows. "Thank you." He thought it was a pity that the wheelwright would likely never know that his rudeness could have cost him a knife in the ribs if they weren't so dependent on not being caught.

He and Robert left the cart, and without it to draw attention to themselves, were able to slip into the stable. They climbed into the loft, pulled hay over themselves and prepared to wait for the inhabitants of the castle to fall asleep.

Several hours later he nudged Robert and sat up. The stable was dark and silent except for the sounds of the horses shifting occasionally in the stalls below. Robert combed his fingers through his dark hair to remove the hay.

Gavin motioned for him to follow and climbed down the ladder to the ground. He opened the smaller door in the front of the building and slipped out into the courtyard, Robert behind him.

Above the gate he could see a guard walking. Another was leaning on a crenellation and staring out into the night toward the back of the compound. Neither was looking their way. He and Robert kept close to the buildings where the shadows were deepest and hurried to the shed where Kerwin and Laibrook were hiding.

"We thought something had gone wrong," Kerwin said when he recognized Gavin and Robert.

"I wanted everyone to be fast asleep before we go in." In the moonlight he noticed Kerwin and Laibrook had thrown their beggars' rags into a corner and were again dressed in their own clothes. "Let's go."

They circled the courtyard and stopped in the dark shadows at the base of the keep. The main doors were closed as Gavin had expected them to be, but he wouldn't have used them anyway. They were too visible to the guards. He pointed at the parapet and held up two fingers. Kerwin nodded and faded into the night. The other three felt along the wall until they found the kitchen door.

When he tried to open it, the latch rattled and a dog barked softly twice, then stopped. Gavin paused. The dog apparently accepted their presence, because there was no further sound from him. Gavin carefully opened the door and they eased inside.

The kitchen was vast in the darkness. Just barely, he could make out the shapes of several huge pots and the cavernous fireplace where the food that wasn't prepared over the outside fire was cooked. Like ghosts they passed through the room.

A short corridor beyond the kitchen's inside doorway led to the servants' hall, where the men who worked in the kitchen and at the more menial jobs around the castle were sleeping. From the snores, he felt sure that no one was awake. Gavin and his men took their time crossing the room. If they awakened anyone, they were doomed.

When they were in the comparative safety of the corridor opposite from where they had entered, Robert touched Gavin's arm and pointed up. Gavin nodded. He didn't need to know the layout of the castle to know the sleeping quarters would be above the main level.

They found a staircase and started up, but the going was slow as they had to freeze in place for a moment each time one of the stair treads popped or creaked under their weight. At the next floor they paused. Several doors lined the corridor and all were closed. The only light in the corridor came from the guttering, wall-mounted rush torches. Gavin chose a route and the others followed.

The first door they tried opened onto a chamber which was so long that the light from the corridor didn't reach the opposite side. From what little of it Gavin could see, the room appeared to be unused. Gavin was about to withdraw and try another when he saw a flicker of light in the dense blackness at the far end. He waved his men back into positions of hiding in the corridor and crouched into the shadows just inside the doorway and waited to see if they had been found out.

As the light moved closer at an unhurried pace, Gavin concluded that he and his men had not been seen. Gavin drew his dagger and prepared himself for the struggle that would come if this person saw them and tried to sound an alarm to the castle guards. Not until the flickering candlelight was relatively close did Gavin recognize that its bearer was none other than Damaris. He motioned for two of his men to slip inside the room and wait next to him, and whispered his plan to them.

Damaris paced the confines of her chamber in the water tower, terrified of what she was about to do. The wind moaned in the arrow slit windows, and the tapestries Mable had brought to cover them shifted as if someone were hidden behind each of them. Several times Damaris had thought she heard someone in the corridor outside her room, but decided it was her strained imagination.

She was becoming more and more reluctant to go to William's chambers and avenge her father. Now that the time was here, she found she wasn't at all sure she could carry it out. To steel her nerves, she forced herself to remember seeing William murder her father and how the women of Thornbeck had screamed and pleaded to no avail against

William's men. At last her resolve was strengthened to meet the task at hand, and she opened the door to leave the room.

The corridor was completely black. In such darkness, she knew she wouldn't be able to face the frightening stairs and the long room that linked the old section of the castle with the new. It had been bad enough in the daylight. Since there was no sign that this wing of the castle was in use, she reasoned she could carry a candle with her as far as the long room and leave it there until she had done away with William. Then she could use it to light her way to the buttery. After that, she would have to find her way in the dark.

Her mind was on William and the atrocities he had wrought upon Thornbeck as she entered the long room. The flame of her candle lit the floor immediately around her but did nothing to dispel the shadows along the walls. Damaris tried not to think what might be lurking there. Once, she thought she heard the faint sound of a door opening and closing and she paused, her heart beating wildly in her throat.

When no one called out, she assumed she had been mistaken and forced herself to continue her way across the room. She repeated over and over in her mind that ghosts probably didn't exist at all, and if they did, the one she'd heard was resident here was presumed to stay in the tower that Damaris had already left. She wasn't reassured.

Suddenly a large hand closed over her mouth and nose. Damaris tried to scream, but no sound escaped. The man was holding her close, and although she fought wildly, she couldn't break free.

Someone else picked up the candle she had dropped. Miraculously it hadn't gone out. As he held it up and moved closer to Damaris and her captor, she craned her head around to see the face of her assailant. To her surprise, it was Gavin. For a moment she couldn't believe her senses. How could he be here?

He whispered in her ear, "Be still!"

She tried to comply, but she was still shaking violently. When he lowered his hand, she hissed, "You scared me out of my wits!"

"Be silent, or I'll gag you," he said.

Damaris didn't know if he really would, but she did as he said. Now that some of her original fright was gone, she recognized the man holding the candle as Sir Robert Grainger, Gavin's close friend. The other man was familiar, also, but she didn't know his name. They moved back toward a door in the wall.

She put out her hand to stop them. "Sir William sleeps in the tower yonder."

"Then be quiet so that he continues." Gavin drew her toward the door.

"Haven't you come to kill him?" she whispered.

"No, we've come to rescue you."

She pulled away. "I'm not leaving until Sir William is dead!"

Gavin and the others stared at her. Damaris lifted her skirt and pulled the dagger out of the garter she had tied to her leg. She showed it to the men.

"You mean to kill him yourself?" Gavin said in disbelief. "That's where you were going?"

"Of course. We're wasting time. Come on and do it for me."

"No."

"Then wait for me." She tried to pull away, but he held her firmly. "Turn me loose!"

"Keep your voice down! You can't kill him as he sleeps!"

She glared in his direction as the candle went out. "I can hardly do it if he's awake!"

Gavin ended the standoff by putting his hand over her mouth again and pulling her to him. As she struggled, he tightened his hold, so much so that she could barely breathe. She heard the soft click of a door latch and Gavin lifted her into his arms and carried her into the corridor.

She fought against him, trying to tell him she would be quiet if he would give her more air, but he apparently misunderstood her intention. By the time they reached the corridor outside the kitchen, she was dizzy and faint.

Gavin looked up at the empty parapet and motioned with his head for the others to come out. He half dragged her to the small door in the larger outer gate. Another man moved in the shadows and Damaris thought for a terrible moment that they had been discovered.

Robert lifted the heavy beam that secured the door and pushed it open. It creaked on its hinges, but the sound wasn't loud enough to reach past the stones of the keep. Gavin carried her through the door and Robert closed it after them.

When he finally released her, Damaris gasped in air and leaned against him. "You nearly suffocated me!" she said accusingly when she could speak.

"Are you unharmed?" he asked.

"Of course I am! Except for the bruises you've likely put on me!" She jerked away from him.

"Be quiet. The villagers may be light sleepers."

Kerwin whispered to Laibrook, "Remember the man who shoved you? He'll do it no more."

Laibrook grinned and she saw his strong teeth in the moonlight. She didn't ask what Kerwin meant. These were seasoned warriors, and she would have feared them if Gavin hadn't been there. Gavin motioned for the others to follow him, and together they made their way through the silent and dark streets. Occasionally a dog barked but they continued walking.

When they left the streets and headed toward the woods, Damaris said, "We could have killed him! I came all the way to Craigmore, suffered through a meal such as will return in my nightmares for years, and put up with my loathsome uncle for naught! Why didn't you kill him while you had the chance?"

Gavin frowned at her. "You're a bloodthirsty little thing, aren't you? I don't kill sleeping men."

"You could have awakened him, then killed him." She saw no reason to let him know how weak her resolve had become.

"Do you think Sir William would be sleeping alone?" he asked. "Are you so naive as to believe that?"

"He's unmarried!"

The men exchanged chuckles.

"My father slept alone!" she snapped.

"And what of his men? He would have as many men sleeping in his outer chambers as you have women in yours, maybe more. Don't you think he must have wondered at you appearing alone?"

"I told him that his own men accompanied me here, then returned to Thornbeck."

"Damaris, that's not believable."

"But he did believe me!"

Robert grinned. "He must have spent the entire afternoon wondering what was about to happen. No doubt his night is sleepless, as well, waiting for an army to appear and wondering why we would allow you into the castle if we planned to attack it."

Gavin and the others laughed softly.

Damaris frowned. "Are you saying he didn't really believe me?"

"Of course he didn't. No men would have left you at the edge of the village and not gone with you into the castle to see their wives or sweethearts or to get something they left behind when they invaded Thornbeck."

"I didn't think of that."

"It's only a wonder you weren't imprisoned as soon as you arrived. I fully expected to have to break down a door."

"How did you find me?" she asked. "You couldn't have known I would venture into that room."

"I suppose your guardian angel must have whispered it into my ear," Gavin said with another laugh. "Another few minutes and the entire castle would have been alerted." He looked at her curiously. "Tell me true. Did you really intend to kill Sir William yourself?"

"Who else would do it for me?" She glared up at him.

"In faith, you're right," Robert said with a laugh. "She's as bloodthirsty as Boadicea herself!"

Damaris wasn't sure she liked being compared to the female warrior but she ignored him. "I cannot believe you let such a perfect chance be lost!"

"Someday you'll thank me. I just saved your life." Gavin pointed. "I see the horses there."

He mounted and Damaris gasped as Robert put his hands on her waist and tossed her onto the horse's rump. She put her arms around Gavin in order not to fall. The other men swung up onto their horses.

"Look!" Gavin pointed to the castle. Several lights were bobbing along the wall. "The guards have been discovered."

Robert nodded. "We got out just in time."

A horn was sounded and distant shouts could be heard. Lights flickered to life in the windows of the keep. More voices could be heard shouting to one another.

Gavin and the others reined their horses around and kicked them to a gallop. Damaris held tightly to Gavin, pressing her cheek against his back in her effort to stay astride the horse. Without stirrups to balance her, she was in a precarious position.

With so long a head start, Gavin and his men easily lost their pursuers on the maze of roads that surrounded Craigmore. Soon they had let their animals drop back into an easier but steady pace that carried them ever nearer England and safety.

Damaris was in no mood to talk, and she was glad the men were willing to ignore her. By the time they reached the shore, she was more than ready to get off the horse.

Gavin caught her around the waist and lowered her to the ground before he dismounted. Her knees threatened to buckle after the hours of clenching the horse's rounded sides. She ached from head to toe but was determined not to let him know that.

Angrily she stalked away from them and stared out at the sea. Judging by the dark pewter color of the sky, it would be dawn soon. Robert and the two men she didn't know moved farther away and gathered wood to start a signal fire. Gavin came to Damaris's side.

"I still think my plan would have worked," she said defensively.

"Assuming you could have made your way through his guards and that you had found him alone in bed, are you saying you could actually have walked up to a sleeping man and cut his throat?"

Damaris looked away. "It wouldn't have been easy, but I had come too far to leave without killing him."

Gavin put his hands on her arms and turned her to face him. "It's not that easy, killing. Nor is it done quietly. You couldn't have hoped to accomplish it and leave without notice."

"I felt I had to do something!" She looked up at him imploringly. "You know not what a thorn in our side Sir William has been. You weren't in the castle when his men were raping my servant women! I'll never forget their screams for the rest of my life! And I didn't know from one minute to the next if my ladies and I would be next."

"I know it was difficult for you."

"Difficult? Nay, sewing a perfect French knot is difficult. This was devastating! How can I make you understand?"

"I do understand. Do you think I've never seen troops pillage?"

"And you allowed it?" She looked up at him in horror.

"No, I arrived and stopped it." He didn't elaborate as to the occasion.

"At times I feel as if I hardly know you." Damaris wrapped her arms about her waist and hugged herself. "You speak of having seen battles and yet you enter an enemy's castle and leave him unharmed."

"We aren't all as battle-driven as you," he replied with some amusement. "If I ever meet Sir William on the battlefield, I'll kill him properly for you."

Damaris sighed. "I doubt I could have done it, even if I had gained access to him."

"I'm glad to hear that. I prefer softer women."

She looked at him. "I don't believe you prefer me at all."

He looked away from her and gazed out to sea as if that view were less painful. "If I didn't care for you, I wouldn't have risked my best men in rescuing you. I'd have said you were with your uncle and that he was welcome to you."

"Then you do care for me?"

He frowned down at her. "How could you believe otherwise? Every time we're together, I end up kissing you. At the Maidens I almost did a great deal more."

The words he spoke and the pain behind them gave Damaris a warm feeling in her middle. "You were tempted?"

"Tempted? I was almost undone!" He turned back to the sea. "Any woman would know that. You taunt me."

"No, I wouldn't do that. I have so little experience with men. I thought you simply didn't care for me."

Gavin pulled her into his embrace. "No woman is that innocent. You all seem born with the knowledge of how to drive a man insane. You're better at it than most."

She put her hands on the hard wall of his chest. Because he was so tall, she had to tip her head back to see his stormy eyes. "You credit me with more than I'm due. All I did was kiss you." Her eyes met his and she felt herself becoming lost in his gaze. "If only you had come to Thornbeck when Papa was alive," she whispered. "How different it would have been."

"Aye."

He lifted his hand and gently stroked her cheek. His hand felt hard and masculine in contrast to her own.

"It would have been far different. I wouldn't have left without you as my bride."

Damaris stretched to meet him as he bent to kiss her. His lips were demanding, and she could feel the roiling passion behind them. He clasped her to him fiercely. "Are you certain you weren't harmed? That no one touched you?"

She held to him, feeling truly safe for the first time in days. "No. No one came near me."

"When I knew you were gone, I was afraid you had fallen into the sea and drowned," he said as he pulled the hood from her head and rubbed his cheek against her hair. "Then I was more afraid that you were alive and being held captive in Craigmore. I imagined all sorts of atrocities being committed against you."

"You did? I never thought that you would worry."

"Not worry? How can you say such things? I was beside myself with concern! So are Meg and your other ladies."

She looked up at him. "Would you say that your worry is like theirs?"

"It was quite different." He pulled her closer to him and held her snugly against him as if he would never release her again. "Meg and the others love you, but they don't feel what I do for you. Their love is different."

She held her breath. "Are you saying you love me?"

For a long time Gavin didn't answer. "Love is spoken of freely at court. A person may love a friend, a lover or an apple and the depth of emotions hardly vary. I've never told a woman that I love her."

"Never?"

He tipped her chin up so he could look into her eyes. "And now I find that I want to say the words, but I can't."

"Why can't you?" She was trying hard to understand, but he mystified her. "If you love someone, what can be simpler than to tell them?"

"My world isn't that simple. I can't admit love to a woman that the queen of England has decided to marry to another man. It wouldn't be fair to you or to me."

"You may think you're a wise man of the world," she informed him, "but you know nothing about a woman's heart if you'd say such a thing. Do you think that I'll try to bind you to some unspoken promise if you tell me you love me? Do you think I'll refuse to marry this stranger just because I hear those words from your lips?"

"Won't you?"

"I intend to refuse to marry him if you speak them or not."

"Damaris, be reasonable. You'll have no choice. Don't make me insist that you say words that will break my heart."

"I insist on nothing from you. That's what I'm trying to tell you."

He touched her face as if he were memorizing it. "I'll never forget you, Damaris. When my beard grows gray, I'll still remember this summer and how you felt in my arms, and how you offered to defy a queen's orders because you wanted more than we can have."

She reached up and caressed his face. "How do you know it's more than we can have? We haven't tried."

"How can I make you understand? It's too late for us."

"Not if you love me," she insisted. "Not if it's our fate to be together."

He smiled sadly. "You believe in fairy tales. True love doesn't always win out. Not in real life."

"Are you saying I'm your true love?"

He paused. "You'd have me say the words that I know I must never say? Then aye. You're my true love. Can't you feel it when we're together?"

"I love you, too." She felt as if she could float away in his embrace.

He was silent for a long time, just gazing down at her. "I love you, Damaris. God help me, I always will."

Relief flooded through her. "I'll say a special prayer to St. Cuthbert for this miracle."

"Nothing has changed," he reminded her gently. "I feel no differently than I did before I said the words. You must still marry whom the queen pleases. I must still return to court when he arrives."

"No, it's different now. You'll see."

"Damaris, you'll drive me to distraction. Naught has changed. How can I make you see that?"

"It would be better if you had told me at the Maidens," she agreed, "but this will have to suffice."

Robert called to them. "I see a signal in the tower! They will send the boat for us."

Gavin looked at the tiny light flickering in the remote castle. Dawn was breaking and the sea and sky were fast turning a pearly hue. "From here the castle seems to be floating in the water as if it were enchanted," he mused. "It seems to be made of moonbeam and mist rather than stone."

"Thornbeck *is* enchanted," she reassured him. "It's my island." She smiled up at him. "Of all the knights in Christendom, I'd have chosen you."

Gavin sighed and held her close for another long minute. "And I'd have chosen you, God help me."

"I'm sure He will." Damaris confidently rubbed her cheek against his wool doublet. "You'll see."

Chapter Ten

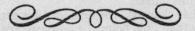

"My lady!" Meg exclaimed as Damaris stepped onto the dock. "You've worried me nigh unto death!"

"I'm sorry, Meg."

Meg hesitated, then asked, "What of Sir William?"

"He still thrives in Craigmore Castle." Damaris couldn't keep the sharpness from her voice, and she cast a telling look at Gavin. "I was 'rescued' before I could give him what he deserves."

"St. Cuthbert be praised," Meg said fervently. "I had nightmares every night you were gone that you'd been hanged or worse." Meg looked at her more closely. "Look how you're dressed! Where did you get such a gown?"

"In the village, and I'll gladly part with it. I've not had it off these past three nights."

"Come to your chamber. I'll have hot water brought up for your bath."

Damaris looked at Gavin and found him watching her with an enigmatic expression. She had heard once that married folk sometimes bathed together, and she wondered what he looked like under his doublet and jerkin. The thought of him naked in her copper tub brought a blush to her cheeks. Gavin smiled as if he had been thinking the same thoughts. "Thank you, Meg," she said hastily. "I'd love a bath."

She followed the woman up the steps. When they were away from the men, Meg said, "You weren't hurt, were you?"

"No. Only frightened. You can't imagine what Craigmore is like. It sits on the edge of a fen, and the smell and dampness is awful! And the castle is filthy, as if it's never turned out for cleaning."

"Likely it's not. It takes a wife to know how to care for a castle." Although Meg had never been married herself, she had a disdain for men who remained single. She caught the sleeve of a passing servant and told her to bring up hot water for a bath.

By the time they had reached the wing that contained Damaris's chambers, Meg was out of breath from the climb up the stairs. "Mercy!" she grumbled as she paused for breath. "These steps get steeper every year."

Damaris had never thought of Meg as aging, but she was almost old enough to be Damaris's mother. They had been friends, as well as companions, for so many years she took Meg's presence for granted.

"Why do you look at me so?" Meg asked suspiciously. "You haven't got more trouble on your mind, have you?"

"No, Meg. I was only thinking that I shouldn't take anything for granted."

"You're thinking again of your father." Meg shook her head. "You'll never find another like him, more's the pity. Pray the good queen sends us another who can hold Thornbeck as well as he did."

Damaris felt guilty for thinking it would be best to find a man who could hold it better. "I pray she sends no man at all," she answered tartly. "I'm not eager to be wed to a stranger."

Meg wisely refrained from responding, but Damaris could see she disagreed by the set of her mouth and the way she looked straight ahead without speaking.

Damaris said, "Would you be glad for such a union, Meg? I'm sure this unknown bridegroom will have single men in his company. I could find you a husband, as well."

Meg frowned at her. "I've got quite enough keeping up with the charges I've got. Lettice and Kate have taken it into their minds to become flirts and, with you gone, they've made eyes at every man who'll look their way."

"I'll have a talk with them."

"And Edith has been sick ever since you left. I believe it's only worry, but she hasn't dressed or come downstairs a single time."

"It's likely because of Sir Gavin's men. You know how she fears strangers and men in particular."

"She has nothing to fear from these. No one has been harmed since they've been here."

Damaris opened the door to her chamber and went in. Her ladies hurried to greet her. She smiled and hugged them as if she had been gone a month instead of only a couple of days.

"We've missed you, my lady," Kate said, a smile lighting her dark eyes.

"So I hear." Damaris looked at Lettice and Kate. She considered them too young to be married. She would have to watch them closely. She smiled at Edith. "I hear you've been ill."

"I'm better now that you're back," Edith said. "'Twas only quacks and poses."

Damaris nodded. Hoarseness and colds were common on the island, even during the summer. "You must take better care of yourself. Let Kate and Lettice go up and down the stairs if you need something from another part of the castle." As Damaris's kinswoman, Edith was above the status of the others.

Lettice's eyes were round. "Did you truly go to Scotland? Alone?"

"Aye." Damaris stood aside as a manservant came into the room to pour the first bucket of water into her copper tub.

"And she'll not do it again," Meg said firmly. "Isn't that right, my lady?"

"No, I'll not do it again." Damaris looked down at her hands. How had she ever thought she could kill a man? "I must have been out of my mind."

"I'm so relieved," Edith said as if she had been holding her breath. She frowned at the tub as the servants filled it. Edith only washed herself with a dampened cloth and was certain that immersing oneself in a bathing tub was bad for the health. "You're so like your mother."

"I am? I hadn't realized she also went to Scotland to try and put an end to Sir William." Damaris knew Edith was referring to her insistence on bathing in a tub and she was too tired to argue about it.

"No, no. Of course not. But she was strong willed and independent for a woman." Edith helped Damaris unlace her dress. "When she first came here, I thought Owen would have his hands full."

"Lady Fleetwood was the most pleasant of women," Meg said firmly.

"Aye," Edith said, undaunted. "But she was independent. You'll grant me that."

Damaris was glad to step free of the coarse kirtle. She started to untie the cord that held her chemise close to her neck. She was used to the good-natured sparring that went on between Meg and Edith and scarcely listened to them.

A woman brought in the kettle of boiling water and poured it into the bathwater to warm it as Damaris pulled the chemise over her head.

"What should I do with these?" Lettice asked as she gathered up the discarded clothing.

"Give them to someone who will use them," Meg said as Damaris stepped into the water. "Our lady won't be needing them again."

Damaris waited until her ladies had gone, leaving only Meg behind with her. Damaris closed her eyes and lay back in the tub. The hot water felt good on her tired body. "I could sleep for a week," she said. "I could lie in this water for days. I've never felt so dirty as I did in Craigmore."

Meg, who didn't share Edith's distrust of being immersed in a bath, handed Damaris the square of soap from the side table. "Wash well, my lady. There's no telling what foul humors you may have been exposed to."

Damaris took the soap and started lathering her arms. Trying to sound casual, she asked, "What did Sir Gavin say when he realized where I had gone?"

"He was beside himself. I was the one who had to take him the news." Meg shook her head as she turned to lay out clean garments for Damaris to put on after her bath. "I've never seen him so angry."

With an effort, Damaris hid her smile. "So he was worried about me, you'd say?"

Meg sat on a stool near the bed and started lacing a blue ribbon through the neck lace of the fresh chemise. "Aye, he was worried! We all were!" She glanced at Damaris. "To watch him, you'd have thought his lady love was endangered. Not just the lady of the castle he's holding for the queen."

Damaris couldn't contain her smile. "I care for him a great deal, Meg."

For a moment Meg didn't answer. "You must be careful, pet. I know you and you're not given to prudence."

"You haven't called me that since I was a little girl."

"Don't change the subject. Sir Gavin's not for you. I've seen other women who were determined to love one man when they must marry another. They were ever unhappy."

Damaris slid lower and wet her hair in the bath. It flowed around her like seaweed. "I know that, Meg. Please don't lecture me today."

Meg leaned nearer. "Someone must. You're alone in the world now, but for Edith, who, if you'll pardon my saying so, is addlepated at times. If I'm not to lecture you, tell me who will?"

"I'm a grown woman. I can make my own decisions."

Meg gave a mirthless laugh. "No woman makes decisions for herself. And your trip to Scotland proves you aren't to be trusted to think clearly. You could have been killed!"

"I wanted to avenge Papa's murder!"

"You're a lass, not a lad. Why can't you grasp this simple truth?"

"I know I'm a woman." Damaris soaped her hair and dipped down to wash as much soap from it as possible.

"So does Sir Gavin and that's why I'm cautioning you."

"He'll not harm me." Damaris pressed the water from her hair and stood up. "I can trust him with my life."

"I know that. How does he feel about you?" Meg picked up the bucket of rinse water and poured it over Damaris's head to remove the rest of the soap.

Damaris gasped at the coldness of the water. As she took a square of linen from Meg and started to dry her body, she said, "He loves me."

For a moment Meg didn't answer. "I had hoped I was wrong."

"No, Meg! I want him to love me. That's how I feel about him."

"I hope you haven't told him!"

"Yes, I have."

Meg dropped the empty bucket with a clatter, disapproval written all over her face.

"Don't look at me that way." Damaris wrapped the towel around her body and picked up another one and began rubbing her hair dry. "I had to tell him."

"No, you didn't. What if he refuses to give you up when your bridegroom arrives?"

"Do you think he might?" Damaris stopped drying and looked at Meg. "That hadn't occurred to me."

"Don't look so pleased. Willing or not, he has to do as he's bid by the queen. You can't be together so it's best that you not wish to be."

Damaris stopped rubbing her hair and sighed. "How do I do that, Meg? I already love him and he loves me. I can't stop the way I'm feeling any more than he can."

"No, but you can pretend to feel otherwise until temptation is out of your range. It would have been better that way. For both of you."

Damaris wasn't convinced. "Have you ever been in love, Meg?"

"No, I'm happy to say," she replied a bit too quickly. "And if I had been, I'd have followed my own advice and ignored it until it was gone."

"Love isn't a fever that passes," Damaris said. "I'll never love another man the way I love Gavin."

Meg came to her and took Damaris's hand the way she had when Damaris was a child and she was trying to impress something upon her. "You must never let another person know how you feel. Sir Gavin is an intelligent man. He'll know to guard his words. What if word of your feel-

ings for Gavin reached the ears of the man who's to be your
husband? That must never happen!''

"Once when I was small, I heard a story in the village
about a girl who was in love with one man, but who was
being forced to marry another. She jumped from the cliffs
below the Maidens.'' Damaris shook her head. ''No, Meg,
don't look at me like that. I'd not do such a thing. But I
know now what drove her to it.''

"I knew the girl," Meg said gruffly. "She was foolish.
She would never have been happy with the lad she fan-
cied.''

"How can you be sure?'' Damaris asked in exasperation. "How can anyone know what's best for another person?''

"You're still young. When you're older, you'll understand.''

Damaris shook her head. "I'll never understand why
Gavin and I can't be wed. Papa chose him for me. Wouldn't
Queen Elizabeth have allowed our marriage?''

"Probably. But it's up to her to pick now, and she'll
choose whichever man she thinks is best suited to the match.
Sir Gavin is a younger son and not as brilliant a match as
you might hope for.'' Meg held the chemise for Damaris to
put it on.

"Perhaps if I write to her—''

"You'll anger her.''

"As much as you may know about other things, I doubt
you know Queen Elizabeth's mind,'' Damaris said tartly.
"It couldn't hurt to let her know my preference.''

"If she thinks you're falling in love with the man she's
placed in control of your castle, she'll likely recall him back
to London and send someone else in his place.''

"But Papa picked him for me!''

"And you refused him.'' Meg pulled the tail of the chemise down over Damaris's hips and started tying the sleeves
close to Damaris's wrists. "Let that be an end to it. He
wasn't a good choice in the first place and that's all there is
to it.''

Damaris wasn't at all convinced. After all, her marriage
to Gavin had practically been her father's last request. As

Meg started to work the tangles from her hair, Damaris wondered if Meg was right. It was possible that such a letter might anger the queen and do more harm than good at this point. And there was still the chance, as small as it was, that the queen might be so busy with state affairs that she would forget to send anyone at all. Damaris decided to bide her time and wait for a while.

"She's enough to drive a man mad," Gavin said as he sluiced the soap and dirt from his body. "Whoever heard of a woman doing the things she does?"

Robert laughed and tossed him a drying cloth. "In faith, you'd have made a good match. She's a far cry from the dragon you thought she'd prove to be."

"Yes. A far cry." Gavin remembered how it felt to hold Damaris in his arms and how her lips had invitingly opened under his. He turned away from his friend and began to dress before his body gave away his thoughts. His valet, George, was laying out a change of clothing on his bed.

"She would have led you a chase," Robert said, oblivious to Gavin's curt answer. "What a pity your father isn't here to see her."

"When do you think the man will arrive from court?" He couldn't bring himself to call the man her bridegroom.

"I can't guess. It shouldn't be much longer, but the queen has more on her mind than this match. The island is strategic, but a Scots army could march over the border at any point, rather than by attacking from the sea. Thornbeck is more important, in my mind, if the enemy comes from Europe. Queen Elizabeth need not spend weeks finding just the right man. I assume she'll discover some man, single or widowed, whom she owes a favor."

Gavin's expression darkened.

"You don't like the truth? Get used to it, my friend. You aren't the first man who's lost a fortune because a marriage contract never came to fruition."

"You believe I'm upset because I want Damaris's dowry? I'm not so crass as that, as you well know."

"Of course I do. And I also know you're too levelheaded to let your body outthink your mind. The lady of this castle isn't fair game."

Gavin made a motion with his hand to send his valet from the room so he could speak freely. He sat on his bed to tie the points that secured his hose to his doublet. "It's no game I'm after, Robin. I've fallen in love with her."

Robert was quiet for a minute. "I was afraid of that. I saw you standing with her while we signaled for the boat to come for us."

"I was hoping you hadn't noticed. There's so little time for us to be alone."

"Then she returns your love?"

"I didn't know that for certain until we were returning to the castle, but yes. She does."

Robert stopped walking about the room and stared at him thoughtfully. "That's too bad."

Gavin pulled on his jerkin and fastened it about his lean waist. "Is it? I can't decide. I know I can't have her and that's enough to drive me to distraction. But love is a pleasant state for the most part. At other times, it's a most exquisite torture." He reached for the gown he wore as an outer layer of clothing. "It's not something I would have chosen, but now that I'm in it, I can't truly say that I wish it otherwise."

Robert tossed Gavin the gold chain he often wore about his neck. "At least the lady need not know."

Gavin didn't answer.

"She doesn't know, does she?"

"Yes, she does. She was the first to speak of it." Gavin smiled at the memory. "She's a most straightforward maiden."

"She told you that she loves you? Before you admitted the same to her?"

"You sound shocked, Robin. Surely you've heard of women taking the lead before." Gavin was amused by the look on Robert's face. "You aren't so innocent as that."

"At court, certainly such things happen. But we aren't at court, and you two haven't the freedom to admit your love to one another."

Gavin turned on him. "What can I do? What can either of us do? We didn't want this to happen! Don't you think I'm heartsick over her future? I can't bear to think of her being unhappy. If I thought she didn't love me, I'd be consoled to think she might be happy, even with another man!"

"It's as bad as that, then?"

Gavin didn't answer for several moments. "Knowing I loved her was bad enough in itself. I hate to think of her being bedded by someone else! Now that I know she loves me, I also know for certain that she'll not willingly accept the husband Queen Elizabeth sends her." His eyes met Robert's. "Do you have any idea what a hell that puts me in?"

"You should leave this place. It's cast a spell on you. I'll remain in charge here. With Godfrey as my second-in-command I can hold Thornbeck as well as you."

"And what reason would I give our queen for disobeying her orders?"

"Tell her you're sick. I'll say you had a fever. It's not so far from a lie. I'll write her myself, if you'd like."

"No, Robin. I'll not do that. God help me, I don't want to be away from Damaris one minute sooner than I must be."

Robert's sympathy shone in his eyes. "You're making a mistake to remain."

Gavin shook his head. "I have to meet her bridegroom. I can't go the rest of my life wondering if he's cruel to her or if he's as repulsive as my imagination will paint him. Mayhap it will ease my mind if I meet him and find he's likable."

"And if he's cruel and repulsive after all?"

Gavin was quiet for a long time. "I'll decide then what to do." He didn't need to tell Robert that he would never leave Damaris with a man like that. Not even if it meant incurring the wrath of Queen Elizabeth or living in exile from England. After all the years they had been friends, Robert already knew Gavin wouldn't be capable of that.

Gavin put on a smile. "Come, Robin. Don't look so glum. Let's go down to the hall and see if the musicians are practicing." An hour or so of music would prevent him from having to make conversation. Gavin wasn't up to conversation at the moment.

Wanting to be alone with her thoughts, Damaris went to the chapel and sat in her family pew. She had told her women that she wanted to be alone to pray, and she knew they would honor her solitude. In an hour or so she would have to go with the others to the hall for dinner and pretend that her heart wasn't breaking over her love for Gavin, but for now she could be alone.

She sat still while she contemplated the graves beneath the flooring. "I failed, Papa. Sir William is still alive and well." She knew he must know that already, but it helped her to say it. She had no doubts that he would forgive her for not being able to accomplish something so difficult. "Perhaps it was a foolish thing to try, but I couldn't sit by and not make the attempt."

She looked at the newly carved stone. Next to the aged marks on the graves of her mother and the babies, the letters seemed raw and too bright. She had intended to have his effigy carved into the stone to match the style of her mother's, but the only man on the island who was capable of doing the work had been killed in the fighting when Gavin and his men took the castle from the Scots.

"So much has happened in such a short time, Papa." How could she tell him about Gavin?

She heard the sound of the chapel door opening and she closed her eyes. Why would one of her ladies bother her in the chapel? But the footsteps that followed didn't sound like those of a woman.

When she looked back, she saw Gavin coming down the aisle. He was halfway to the altar before he saw her. At once he stopped and their eyes met and held. Rays from the stained-glass window played in the gold of his hair and put red and blue and yellow lights on his skin and clothing. "Hello," she said at last. "I didn't expect to see you here."

"I can leave. I have no business here. I only wanted to be alone with my thoughts." This chapel was a private one used by the family in residence at the castle and their retainers. It was presided over by the castle chaplain. The other, much larger church on the island was located in the village and was used by the rest of the castle staff and the villagers. It was headed by the vicar who lived in the village, and it was this church that Gavin and his men attended.

"You may stay if you like."

With an easy stride, Gavin walked to the front and sat beside her. "We must talk."

"I know."

He looked at her. "Perhaps this isn't the best place for us to meet."

She looked around. "I'd say it's the best place of all. It will help us be discreet."

"Do you regret telling me of your love? I had just rescued you. Perhaps what you really felt was gratitude. Maybe 'love' was too strong a word to describe what you were feeling."

"Do you want me to recant what I said to you on the shore? Will that make it easier for you?"

He shook his head. "Nothing is going to be easy for me for a long while. Or for you, either."

"I meant it when I said I love you. It wasn't gratitude. If you recall, I didn't want to be rescued."

"Robert thinks I should leave Thornbeck."

"And will you?" She held her breath as she waited for his reply.

"I told him no. Since then, I've been thinking. Staying will make it easier for me. What will help you? If you tell me to go, I will. I can make some excuse to the queen."

"I don't want you to go. Not ever. Maybe the queen will be so busy with state affairs she won't remember to send a man here. We could be forgotten for years."

"That won't happen. You know it won't."

She looked away. "I know. But I had hoped it might."

Gavin took her hand and held it tenderly. "So small a hand," he said as if to himself. "It's so delicately made for it to have been able to turn my world upside down." He folded his fingers over it. "I spoke the truth when I said I love you. Never doubt that."

"I never will. I've never meant anything more than my words of love to you." She looked at the cross that hung above the altar and at the familiar windows of brilliant color and intricate design. "If I had my way, we would be married here in the chapel. It could be done very quietly. No one need know but the chaplain and one witness."

"If I could do that, I would. Nothing would give me greater pleasure than to be your husband." He smiled tenderly at her, his voice so soft no eavesdropper could have heard either side of the conversation. "I'll never marry since I can't have you."

She smiled sadly. "How easy it is to say that now, when we're both hurting. But the years will be long, and eventually you'll see another woman who will move you the way I do and you'll find you love her, perhaps as much as you love me."

He shook his head. "That's not true. Can't you feel it? Our love is greater than that."

"Perhaps it sounds foolish, but if I can't have you, and you seem positive that I can't, I want you to find happiness elsewhere."

"I just said the same about you to Robert." Gavin's mouth twisted in a wry smile. "We seem to be in a dilemma of fate's making."

"Aye." She gazed at the brilliant colors reflected on his cheeks. He was exactly the way she had always pictured the perfect knight—tall, handsome, strong but gentle in his love. She touched the back of his hand where several pale scars were interlaced on his skin. "You bear the marks of battle."

He glanced at his hand. "I feel as if another one is raging in my head. I can't go away from you and I can't stay."

Damaris couldn't bear to linger on the thought of him leaving. "When I was a girl, Papa read to me from a book about a court filled with knights and ladies that had the most interesting adventures. The men fought dragons and giants and all sorts of enemies. The ladies languished for love and sometimes died of broken hearts."

"Broken hearts are rarely a cause of death. Otherwise there would be no one left at court."

"So cynical," she teased. "Next you'll be telling me you don't believe in dragons."

He laughed. "I'd not destroy all your fantasies at one time."

"In this book the knights were all so wonderful. They were all pure of heart and had golden hair. They looked exactly like you."

"My heart is anything but pure."

"If it wasn't, you'd have no qualms about us."

"Need I remind you where we are?" he asked with a smile. "Don't tempt me."

"I didn't mean it to be tempting. I was only pointing out a fact. As a girl I was positive my knight would come riding up some day on a great white charger and we'd have interesting adventures all the rest of our lives, just like the people in Papa's book."

"My charger is gray."

"It's close enough."

"And I slipped in at night through the water gate."

"That's only a small detail. Your hair is golden and you're sufficiently tall and more than handsome enough to qualify. And best of all, you're gentle in your love."

"How can you say that? We've spent half our time arguing. I'd have said I irritate you more than people you've known all your life."

"That's true. You do." She smiled at him. "That's how I can love you so much. We're a great deal alike, you and I."

"You're a strange one, my lady." His voice was deep and caressing. She knew if they weren't in the chapel he would take her in his arms and kiss her. His eyes looked as if he were considering it anyway. "It's no wonder I love you. I always knew I wouldn't fall in love the conventional way. Of all my brothers and sisters, I was always the one who was different."

"If you weren't, we wouldn't be suited."

"Damaris," he said gently, "I want you to be happy."

"There's only one way either of us can be. Shall I go find the chaplain and tell him he's to perform a small ceremony?"

For a long time he was quiet. "No. We can't."

She sighed. "I know. You're still more conventional than I would have you be."

He squeezed her hand to show her he understood and wished it could be otherwise. She pressed his in return. Together they went out of the chapel and down the corridor that led to the hall and the dozens of people that always gathered there for the evening meal.

Chapter Eleven

Gavin went up to the parapet and walked along the hourds as he gazed out to sea. The morning's mist had risen and he was glad to see there were no boats approaching. To a guard standing at his post, he asked, "How does it go?"

"No boats, Sir Gavin. All is still."

"It may not stay that way. Watch closely and if you see anything at all, come tell me."

"Aye." The man turned his attention back toward the sea.

Gavin looked around at the other men spaced at intervals along the parapet. He had doubled the guard in the hours since he'd returned to Thornbeck. A battle was coming. He could feel it in his nerves.

A flash of brighter color drew his attention and he turned to see Damaris coming toward him. Predictably, her ladies, who had been following a few steps behind her, had stopped near the tower door through which Damaris had come. In Gavin's experience, few ladies ventured voluntarily onto the parapets, for there was always the risk of wind catching their full skirts and toppling them over the side and into the courtyard. Damaris seemed to have no such fear. She came toward him as confidently as if she were in the hall.

"Good morning," he said as he went to meet her. "This is the last place I expected to see you."

She smiled. "I come here often. It's one of the places my women don't follow me." She rested her hands on the crenel and stared out to sea. "I don't see anything. Why have you doubled the watch?"

"Sir William will come. He's lost Thornbeck and we've invaded his castle. He won't let that go unnoticed. You forget my men had to dispatch his guards."

"Thornbeck is safe from Sir William. He caught Papa unprepared or he never could have taken it in the first place."

"It doesn't do to underestimate the enemy. And no castle is impregnable. I expect an attack." He noticed how the sun touched her skin and made it glow. A tiny pulse beat in the warm hollow of her neck and he longed to kiss it.

"I trust you to keep me and my castle safe." Her eyes met his and he was again struck by their mysterious color.

"I intend to keep you quite safe." If it hadn't been for the presence of his men and her women standing nearby, he would have taken her into his arms. His body ached to hold her. Realizing that he needed to steer his thoughts back to a safer route, he said, "If the castle is taken, you and your women are to go into the keep and bolt the door. Don't open it for anyone but Robert, Godfrey or myself. Will you do that?"

"If necessary." She looked away from the sea and toward the round tower that was a focal point of the courtyard and a fortress within itself. "Never in my lifetime have we had to seek refuge there. We've never been so threatened."

"I have servants cleaning it and stocking it with food. Even if the outer walls are breached, you can last in the keep for as long as necessary." He hoped that was true. Sir William and his men would probably be unable to break into the keep, but they would have an unlimited supply of food. Whoever was in the keep could last only as long as the store of food did. "Robert checked the well in the keep's dungeon and found the water is still fresh."

"We've always had good water here."

He turned to find she was looking at him, not the castle. Her eyes were filled with concern, but he sensed it was for him and not for herself. "I'll be safe," he told her.

"You can promise me that?"

Gavin reached out and touched her cheek. Damaris leaned her face against his hand in a caress. "I'll take care. I can promise no more," he said softly.

"I couldn't bear it if aught befell you. I love you too much to lose you."

He knew the wind was carrying their words away, but his physical contact with Damaris would not go unnoticed and would arouse the curiosity of their unintentional chaperons. He pulled his hand away from her face and stared out to sea. "I've never known such torment! How can I bear to see you and not touch you? Have you any idea how difficult it is to know you're sleeping just down the corridor from me and that I mustn't come to your room?"

"Aye. It's that difficult for me, too."

He looked at her. How could she know the agony he was feeling when she had never lain with a man? She knew only the pain of a love refused its natural passion. "You mustn't look at me in that way. It's hard enough not to take you in my arms as it is."

"I believe we're taking too much care." Showing no sign of fear of falling, she boldly sat on the crenel notch in the parapet and leaned back on the hewn stone of the merlon. "I would be rash and more satisfied. If we truly have only a few days or weeks together, are we not foolish to spend them apart?"

"You use a man's argument against me," he said with amusement. "That's what I should be saying to you."

"Then why aren't you?"

"Because I was told to guard you and keep you safe. Not to debauch you."

"You would only be loving me."

He gazed into her eyes and felt as if his soul had found its home. "Yes. I would only be loving you. And if I came to you in the night, don't you realize that would make it all the more difficult for me to leave you and for you to go to the husband the queen is sending?"

"Aye. I guessed as much. If we can hold this castle against Sir William, why can't we also hold it against this unwanted bridegroom?"

"You talk foolishness. He's sent by the queen. We can't go against her. That would be tantamount to treason."

Damaris sighed and looked out to sea as if to find an answer there. "What a muddle we're in. Is there no chance of happiness for us?"

Gavin was silent for a while as he thought. "I can see none," he admitted reluctantly. "It tears at my heart to say it, but I can see no possibility of a happy outcome." His torment increased tenfold when he saw her blinking back tears.

"We'll be safe here against Sir William," she said as if she understood the necessity of changing the subject to one less painful. "You'll be able to fend him off."

He followed her lead. "I've sent Robert to the village to gather all the surplus food he can find. If we're involved in a siege, we'll need all the supplies we can muster."

"Fortunately for us this has been a good harvest. The early crops are already in and others may be harvested any day now. We'll have enough food to see us through."

"I've assigned several of my men to guard the keep and to see that you and the women reach it safely if the worst may happen. They'll safeguard you."

"Where will you be?"

"I'll continue to fight."

Their eyes met again. Damaris's were filled with tears that she refused to shed. "You'll not be in the keep with me?"

"It's not possible." His place would be with his men. They would fight more fiercely if they could see him engaged in the battle beside them. If need be, he would also die beside them. He wanted to spare Damaris the worry of knowing this. "All our preparations may be needless. I, too, doubt Sir William can take the castle."

"And the village?"

"It's unprotected. The people will have to come into the castle. I'll be sure they all understand that. Whoever comes in will be as safe as we are."

Damaris nodded, her face pale. "Women aren't cut out for warfare," she said with an attempt at lightness. "I find I do naught but worry since our return. To make matters worse, I think this might not be threatening us if I hadn't gone to Craigmore and aroused my uncle.''

Gavin put his hand on her shoulder and stroked his thumb over the pulse in her throat. Her skin was silky and warm under his hand and his body responded too eagerly. ''He would have come anyway. This isn't your fault.''

She looked away. ''Thank you for telling me that.''

''Take your ladies below,'' he said gently. ''They look near faint from the height.'' He took her hand and helped her to her feet.

She walked a few steps, turned to say more, then joined her women. Her words were unnecessary. Gavin heard her thoughts in his heart.

William paced in his closet, his hands clasped behind his back. ''How could she have disappeared?''

James McIntyre shook his head. ''I know not. Mable swears she saw the lady to the water tower room and was convinced that she was content to stay there. There was no talk of leaving. She says the lady apparently didn't yet realize she was our hostage.''

''Damaris certainly couldn't have overpowered my guards and murdered them in order to get out the gates,'' William stormed. ''Someone else was in here, as well.''

''How can that be? We would have seen them.''

William scowled at his second-in-command. ''She's but a woman! What else can I believe?''

James shifted his weight and crossed himself. ''I've questioned my men. They say they were overcome by supernatural means.''

''Supernatural? What are they talking about?'' William had always been superstitious.

''How else could anyone have crossed the halls where they slept and not have awakened them? Even the dogs weren't heard to bark. If strangers had set foot in the castle, the dogs would have given warning.''

William gnawed at his knuckle. ''There was talk at Thornbeck,'' he said reluctantly. ''Some of the people there thought Damaris is part fairy.''

James again crossed himself quickly. ''Is that possible?''

"I know little of her. But while I was there, I became aware that she frequented the circle of standing stones on a hill near the castle called the Whispering Maidens. She stayed there for great lengths of time."

"I tried to go there once," James said hastily. "I was unable to enter the circle."

"Oh? For what reason?" William had been fearful of trying this himself; legends about the Maidens had kept him away, even when he was a boy.

James lowered his voice. "It was as if I wasn't alone. As if the stones truly were alive!"

"That's ridiculous! They're only rocks tipped up to stand on their ends."

"Call them what you may, I couldn't enter them."

William had heard other men say the same about other circles. It was considered a great mystery. "When I was a boy there, it was well-known that the stones couldn't be counted. No matter how often it was done, the answer was different." He had even tried this for himself, standing safely on the outside of the circle. "It was said this was true because the stones are still alive and shift about when no one is looking."

James's eyes were large and believing. "Yet your niece was able to go there often."

"She has a fey quality about her, don't you think?" William asked uncertainly. "I noticed that on our first meeting. It seems she's thinking things the rest of us aren't."

"Aye. I saw that myself. And there's the color of her eyes. I've never seen a mortal woman with eyes that color. I can believe she's part fairy."

William shook his head and tried to sound confident as he said, "No matter. She's but a woman and we'll deal with her when we take the castle again. This time I won't be so lenient. We'll hang her from the walls as a warning to the others not to rebel against us again."

"We should have done so in the beginning."

"I believe she entranced me into thinking her to be harmless." William fingered his small beard as he thought. "It was passing strange that she came here. Didn't you think so?"

"Aye. More than strange. How did she do it? No woman could travel here alone. None would try. Natural women are all shy and nervous about being alone. They hate it. None of the women in my family leave their houses unaccompanied, not even to go to the market."

"This is true of all the castle women. And how could she have crossed the sea to reach Scotland unaided? She couldn't have rowed herself!"

"Of course not. A woman row a boat? Impossible." James let out a scoffing laugh. "She would be too timid and too weak."

"Then she must have crossed by the same means that allowed her to escape from us." William was careful not to let his underling see his fearfulness. He believed all he was saying.

"The fairies must have brought her and taken her back again!"

"I've never heard of fairies killing guardsmen. Have you?" William glared at his man.

"Never."

"She must have bewitched some man here at Craigmore and forced him to help her escape. The dogs wouldn't bark at someone they knew. He could walk up to the guards without them raising an alarm."

"It seems incredible!"

"Not as incredible as to think armed men from Thornbeck came into our castle while we all slept, somehow found her in that out-of-the-way tower, and carried her to safety. If they could gain entrance so easily, why weren't we all murdered?"

"This is true. Englishmen wouldn't hesitate to kill a sleeping man. What you say about the lady must be true."

"Don't tell the men beneath you what we've concluded. I don't want them to fear hanging her once we take the castle."

James hesitated. "If she has the dark forces on her side, how can we hope to get inside the walls?"

"We did it once and we can do it again. She was there then, too, remember."

"Aye."

"Queen Mary was happy to hear Thornbeck was ours. I don't dare tell her I've lost it again so quickly." William paced to the wall and back. "She would be greatly displeased."

James nodded. He was too wise a man to agree aloud that William had been careless in his defense of the castle. Especially since the castle had been under James's control at the time of its recapture. "The fairies must be guarding Thornbeck as well as its lady."

"Fairies are no match for warfare." William went to his table and spread out the worn map of Thornbeck. "We'll plan carefully and have it back before word reaches court that you lost it."

James heard the reference to his ineptness but let it slide. He bent over the map with William and they began to work out their strategy.

Wat Hobson scowled at his friend Ben. " 'Twill come to disaster, mark my words. Those folk at the castle will be safe enough. It's us that will bear the brunt!"

Ben chewed the end of the twig for a moment before answering. "I heard tell we're all to go to the castle at the first sign of trouble. That we're to be kept safe in its walls."

"Are you daft?" Wat gestured with the palm of his hand as he said, "Where's Scotland from here?"

Ben nodded toward the castle. "You know as well as I do that it lies yonder."

"Aye! Can you see it from here?"

Ben shook his head.

"Nor can any of us! The Scots could be upon us before we knew they were about! If the ones at the castle are preparing for battle, do ye think for a minute that any of them will come to this village and say, 'We'd be much obliged if you'd join us in the castle'? Of course they won't, you great lout!"

Ben looked uncertain. "They've always taken care of us. Didn't a man come from the castle with a boat to replace the one stolen from you?"

"Aye! And I've always been suspicious about that. Why would they care if I starve or not?" Wat cast an angry eye at the cottage behind him. "Likely that was done out of guilt at keeping my oldest son from me."

"I've seen young Gil. He's happy to be in Sir Gavin's service. He even has hopes of becoming a knight someday."

"The lad's head is full of cobwebs. A fine knight he'll be, the son of a fisherman! Where will he find gold to buy a horse, much less mail and weapons? The lad's daft."

"All the same, he looks happy. You know he never had a head for fishing. You've said so yourself."

"Who has a choice about such? We have to do what we're put here to do. Maybe *I* would rather have been a knight, too! But I was born to a fisherman and I've gone out in my boat, rain or shine, freezing or not, and I've brought back a catch most every time. Where would this island be if all our sons went off to be knights? We'd starve, that's what!"

Ben studied the frayed end of the twig before putting it back in his mouth. "You've got another boy nearly old enough to go out to sea. And several more behind him. They'll look after you in your old age."

"Ain't the same. Gil's the oldest. It's his responsibility. My woman is as daft as he is. She's all for him leaving the island with Sir Gavin. I thought she was fonder of Gil than that. She always has tried to spoil him."

"Maybe she sees this as a way for him to make more of himself. You know as well as I do that no man in this village will ever have two coins to rub together."

Wat frowned back at the castle. "Mayhap we would if the castle didn't bleed us dry."

"They buy our catch. I get a fair price from them."

"Why do I talk to the likes of you?"

"I guess it's because we've been friends all our lives." Ben looked as if he were beginning to question that himself. "We're kin."

"The Scots didn't harm us when they were here. I can't see that there's much difference between them and us."

Ben frowned. "Can't you? The Scots are our enemies."

"They're none of mine. Like I always say, I fish and I eat and I sleep. It don't matter none to me who's living in the castle when I'm out in my boat. It don't to you, either."

"Don't talk so. What if somebody heard you?"

Wat spat on the ground. "Let them. I don't care." His eyes lifted to the hill beyond town and the familiar silhouette of the Maidens. He could see someone wearing green and yellow moving among them. "She's up there again. Our lady."

Ben followed his gaze. "Aye. She's there often."

"It ain't natural. Not a bit of it. By the time my Bess was her age, we had a pack of babes. It's not right for a woman to remain single. Unmarried women got no purpose in life."

"She's a pretty one. I thought old Lord Fleetwood would have married her off years ago."

"They're all daft at the castle." Wat watched Damaris walk on the hill. "Even our Meg is like them now."

"I remember her before she went up to live there. She was a pretty girl. A bit outspoken, but smart."

"For all the good that does a woman. They're happier if they know their place and don't try to get above themselves. If Meg hadn't gone to the castle, she'd likely have a family now instead of drying up into an old spinster."

"She's not all that old and she don't look dried-up to me. Sometimes I see her with our lady and the others at market, and to my eyes she's still pretty for all her years."

"No good comes from the castle," Wat insisted. "You mark my words, they'll be the end of us."

Ben chewed on the twig and made no comment.

Damaris left the stone circle and walked down the ridge toward the castle. The sun was moving low in the sky and the vivid colors of the approaching sunset spread across the water and bathed the castle's pale walls with hues of pinks and orange and gold. She loved Thornbeck so fiercely she ached with it.

But she loved Gavin more.

At times it almost frightened her to think how much she loved him. It seemed that having admitted it to him had caused the emotion to burst into life within her. He colored all her thoughts and observations. She could no longer look at a sunset without wishing that he was watching it, too.

She paused and looked back at the Maidens. In the ethereal pink and gold light, they seemed to sway and shift ever so slightly. Even from this distance she could feel their magic touch her.

Damaris closed her eyes and imagined what it would be like if she could return to the castle and be Gavin's wife. A flood of warmth swept through her. There was nothing she wanted more. "Please," she whispered to the Priestess, despite the space between them.

"Damaris? Are you all right?"

She jumped and turned to see Gavin approaching her. "I'm fine. You startled me."

"I thought you saw me coming and were waiting for me."

Damaris looked back at the circle. Had their magic hidden him from her view so they would meet here on the lonely ridge and not closer to the castle? She liked to think so.

He stopped a pace from her. "I saw you from the parapet and thought I'd keep you company since your ladies aren't with you."

She smiled. "They never come with me to the Maidens. You know they don't."

"I've told all in the village that they're to come to the castle in case the Scots reappear. We'll sound horns from the parapets to warn them."

She looked around. "It's so peaceful. I can't imagine a battle here. Perhaps my uncle will leave us alone."

"I would be much amazed if he does." Gavin gazed at the pink and azure sea. "On an evening like this, I can believe in such a miracle."

Damaris took his hand in both of hers. "When I was a girl, I was convinced that the fairies came out to play in the sunsets. I even convinced myself they were just out of sight, hiding behind a clump of daisies or ducking beneath a bush."

"That didn't frighten you?"

"Of course not. I was sure any fairies around here would know I'm also a part of this island and that we might even become friends."

He smiled down at her. "When I was a boy, my sisters were afraid of elves and the like. I used to tease them unmercifully about it. I even stamped out 'fairy rings' in the grasses to frighten them."

Damaris laughed. "I wish I had brothers and sisters. I had the other children in the castle to play with, of course, but it's not the same. They never treated me as an equal."

"It would have been remarkable if they had."

"Because my mother was dead, none of our cousins offered to send their daughters to be nurtured at Thornbeck. It wouldn't have been proper. And because Papa loved peace, none of them sent their sons here, either."

"Nor did your father send you to your cousins on the mainland for the same reason."

"Papa needed me as much as I needed him. I reminded him so much of my mother, he said. Without me, he would have been lonely." She said it simply, stating it as a fact.

"And because of this loneliness, I find you as different from other women as night is from day."

Damaris looked at him curiously. "How am I different?"

"You enjoy being alone and escape from your ladies as often as possible. Most women couldn't or wouldn't even try. You're so independent you risked your life by going after the man that killed your father. Surely no other woman in the world would do that!"

"It was foolish of me. I can see that now." She watched the sun settle into the water where she knew England to be. "At times I wonder what it would have been like to live on the mainland. To be able to get on a horse and simply ride to the next town. How vast the land must seem."

"Your island has sheltered you. If you'd lived on the mainland, you'd have been taught never to ride out alone. You could have become lost or kidnapped by someone. A highwayman might have found you."

Damaris rubbed her arms as if the thought were chilling. "I'd rather stay on my island forever. It's safe here."

Gavin didn't answer. He only looked out to sea toward Scotland.

"But I'd leave my island for you," she said softly.

"You love me that much?"

"I love you more than that. The women in my family are capable of great love." She smiled and glanced back at the darkening Maidens. "My mother left her childbed to take me to the stones just so Papa wouldn't be lonely when she was gone."

"If she had taken better care of herself she might not have forfeited her life."

Damaris shook her head. "Meg has said she knew she was dying. Her only thought was for Papa and for me."

"That's a great love, indeed," he agreed.

"It's the sort of love I feel for you. I'd do whatever was necessary to keep you safe."

Gavin smiled down at her. "Again you speak my words. It's me who is keeping you safe. Not the other way around."

"Perhaps." She nodded toward the stones. "Or perhaps the Maidens are keeping us all."

Gavin shook his head. "I don't believe that. They have a certain awe about them, but they're only stones, after all. They have no powers."

"Whatever you say," she said easily. What he believed in regard to the Maidens wasn't important. She knew better.

As the night grew closer, he put his arm around her waist. "The night is our friend. I'm glad you don't fear it."

"I've never been afraid of the dark. My ladies don't share my confidence, however. I have to go in or they'll worry."

"I know." He didn't move his arm away.

Damaris leaned into his embrace. "What if someone sees us silhouetted against the sky?"

He smiled and his teeth still gleamed white in the failing light. "They will likely think one of the Maidens has taken it upon herself to stroll down to the castle."

"As careful as you are that no one see how we feel toward one another, I marvel that you aren't packing me back to the castle as fast as possible," she said teasingly.

"I'm only human, Damaris. We have so little privacy. Do you want to go inside?"

"No. I want to stay with you forever."

Gavin bent and kissed her with growing passion. Damaris held him and let herself pretend that she would never have to release him. Beneath his clothing she could feel the powerful muscles of his back and shoulders and she felt small by contrast. She threaded her fingers through his thick hair, reveling in the sensation.

She kissed him in return and when, at length, their lips parted, his breath was ragged on her cheek. She could tell what an effort he was making not to lay her down on the grassy ridge and make love to her. She wasn't altogether glad he was so strong in his convictions. Surely, she reasoned, if he would let her give herself to him, the queen might allow them to wed.

Gavin pulled back and rested his forehead on hers. "You leave me weak," he said.

"I'd have said you're the strongest man I've ever known," she replied. "Otherwise we wouldn't go back to the castle all this night."

He gazed down at her, but she could barely make out the lines of his face in the gathering darkness. The rising sliver of moon cast only a hint of silver upon the planes of his face, but his eyes were too dark to read. "If I had my way, I'd love you forever."

"I believe we'll love forever, whether it's forbidden or not," she answered softly.

He held her to him for one last moment. Damaris tried to memorize every taste and scent and nuance of him. Her memories were all that got her through the long nights. Even though they were always apart at those times, they were never so far apart that she couldn't have gone to him if he had allowed it. After a time, they walked back to the castle in total silence, their hearts too full to express their emotions in words.

Chapter Twelve

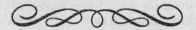

Outside Thornbeck's massive stone walls, a heavy rain was pouring down, and thunder occasionally rolled restlessly across the tossing waves of the surrounding North Sea. But inside, the soft, melodic strains from Thornbeck's musicians drifted down from the alcove in the gallery, soothing the nerves of those who were distressed by such harsh weather. Fires had been lit in all three fireplaces along the corridorlike room to dispel the chill in the air. Damaris and her ladies were passing the day with their needlework and strolls from one end of the room to the other.

When Gavin and several of his men came into the room, Damaris was aware of his presence before she saw him. She lowered her gaze and a smile touched her lips. She enjoyed seeing him go about the castle as if he would stay there forever.

Edith tapped her foot on the floor impatiently. "This day seems more like autumn than summer. Who can remember such a cold day at this time of the year?"

"It's unusual, but the cold has always bothered you more than most." She glanced back at Gavin and wondered if he would come to where she was sitting and talk to her or if he would continue to keep his distance with his men.

The elderly woman nodded. "It's my frailty, I imagine. Papa always said I was the frailest of his children. It's why I never married, you know."

"Yes, I know." Damaris doubted this was the real reason, but at Edith's age, truth was less important than tact.

"I've always thought you took after me a bit, for all you look like your mother."

"I see no resemblance at all," Meg said rather tartly. She had never liked Edith.

"Of course you don't now," Edith said with an equal barb. "However, you would have remarked upon it if you had seen me when I was still young."

Damaris put down her needlework and stood. "I'm going to walk about for a bit." Meg started to lay aside her work, as well, but Damaris said, "You needn't come with me. I'm only going to look at the portraits."

She strolled down the room, pretending to gaze at the likenesses of her ancestors, all the while feeling Gavin's presence with every fiber of her being. He had avoided her the past few days and she knew why. Every time they were together, it became more difficult for them to refrain from kissing and touching, from gazing into each other's eyes as if their souls were merging. Lately she had wanted to do a great deal more than this, and she was sure Gavin was feeling the same frustration.

As she neared the men, she paused to study one of the portraits. It was skillfully done and the old-fashioned clothing in which its subject was attired had always fascinated her as a child. She had never understood why people back then had been content to wear such odd clothing as the cotehardie gowns and hennins with gorgets upon their heads.

Gavin left the others and came to her. She could feel him approaching and her heart quickened.

"Who is she?" he asked, gesturing toward the painting. His tone told her he was no more interested in the painting than she was.

"My grandmother or my great-grandmother on my father's side. I forget which, I'm afraid. They were both dead long before I was born."

"She looks as if she never smiled in her life." He leaned in, feigning a closer examination, and his arm brushed Damaris's shoulder. "She looks a bit like Edith."

"She should. Edith's mother was her sister—or her niece, if she's my great-grandmother. Papa used to be put out with me because I couldn't keep them straight. Of course he knew them when they were alive, so it was easier for him." She began walking again and Gavin stayed with her.

"When I was a child, I tried to imagine all these people living at Thornbeck." She made a sweeping motion with her arm to include all the portraits. "Some of them probably used the chamber where I sleep. Certainly the older ones did. This gallery is rather new, but it encloses a walkway that has been here since this section of the castle was built during the time of Henry V. They all must have exercised here during sunny weather."

"I've missed talking to you these past few days," he said as they paused to look at another painting. He spoke softly so they couldn't be overheard.

"I've missed you, too. Gavin, we can't keep avoiding each other like this. It hurts too badly."

"I know. I've been thinking. It couldn't do any harm for me to write the queen and explain that we've fallen in love and want to be married. If I tell her of our fathers' agreement, that might sway her."

"You were so sure it wouldn't."

"I wasn't as frustrated then." He gave her a smile that made her nerves tingle. "I love you too much now to think clearly. Mayhap the queen will refuse or tell me to leave here before worse is done, but I have to try."

"You'll have to go if she orders it, won't you?"

"Yes, but it's probable that I would have to leave soon anyway. And she might give her permission."

"We should have done this sooner!" Damaris was careful to keep her voice down. They weren't far from the others.

"I thought this couldn't be happening. That my love for you would slacken in time. Instead, it's grown deeper."

"I know. It almost frightens me. If aught were to happen to you, I'm not sure I would continue to live. You say no one really dies of a broken heart, but I'm not so sure. I ache so from love of you, I couldn't bear it if you were gone forever." She looked up at him, her heart in her eyes.

"Don't look at me so, love," he said softly. "I'm finding it difficult enough as it is not to take you in my arms in front of everyone."

Damaris looked away and they proceeded to the next picture. As she pointed out the small dog that lay on the feet of the man in the portrait, she contrived a movement so that she brushed his hand with hers. She heard his sharp intake of breath and would have smiled if she hadn't felt the same jolt.

"You torment me," he accused. "But it's a sweet torment. I'd not have you stop. Ever."

"Nor would I." She took his hand and laced her fingers through his. "I'm tired of pretending, Gavin. We could slip out and perhaps no one would notice us."

"That thought occurred to me, but Meg is glaring at us already."

"Write to the queen. We have to try."

"Yes. I'll do that now and send the letter to the mainland right away." He lifted her hand to his lips and kissed her fingers before departing. It was a gesture any knight might give to a lady, but Damaris knew more than loyalty was pledged.

She watched him leave the gallery. Meg came to her and said in a low voice, "You should take care, my lady. Sir Gavin will soon be gone and many of the people in this room will not. It wouldn't do for anyone to tell your bridegroom that you were overly fond of the man sent here to guard you and the castle."

"I love him, Meg. And he loves me. He's going now to write to the queen for permission to marry me."

Meg stared at her as if she didn't believe her ears. "He's not!"

"The letter will be sent to London straightaway." She clasped her hands tightly together under her chin. "Pray she gives us permission to wed!"

"I'll pray to St. Cuthbert," Meg said. "He's always taken care of those on this island."

Damaris murmured, "Godspeed to that letter. And may it reach the queen when she's feeling romantically predisposed." She knew the next few days would be trying.

* * *

Damaris didn't have to wait long for the queen's reply. Two days later a letter arrived from the queen. She and Gavin managed to slip unnoticed into the solar to read it.

"She can't possibly have received your letter so soon," Damaris said to Gavin as he broke the seal and opened the heavy paper.

He read for a moment, then folded it back. "This isn't in reply to my letter. They must have passed each other on the way. She writes that a groom has been chosen and that he'll be on his way in a matter of days."

Damaris paled and she put her hand on his arm. "No, Gavin! Say it's not so!"

He handed her the letter and she read it for herself. "His name is Neville, Lord Westcott." Her fingers were so numb she almost dropped the paper.

"I know him." Gavin went to the solar window and looked out at the courtyard and keep. "I know him well."

She couldn't find her voice for a minute. "What is he like?"

Again he was quiet. "I think you and I should be married without the queen's permission."

Damaris felt a knot forming in her throat. "Is he so bad you'd risk Queen Elizabeth's displeasure?"

"Lord Westcott is a widower. Twice, in fact. His first wife died in childbirth. His second fell from a parapet. There was some talk that she may have taken her own life."

"She committed suicide?" Damaris gasped. "Rather than live with him? Is he so bad as that?"

Gavin continued to stare out the window. "Lord Westcott is a cold man. I've never seen him in a rage, but neither have I ever known him to speak or act in a kind manner."

Damaris turned away. "What of his appearance?"

"He's not as tall as you are and is thin to the point of gauntness. He had the pox as a boy and his face is scarred. Otherwise he might have been rather good-looking. He has the coldest eyes I've ever seen."

Damaris rubbed her arms. "Why would the queen send such a man for my husband?"

"Lord Westcott is also brilliant at warfare. His men are completely obedient—probably from fear, not loyalty. He has holdings on the Scottish border and is accomplished at repelling raids and quelling uprisings. He seems to know how the Scots think. If only this island were all that's at stake, he would be an excellent man for the job."

"She writes that he will arrive here in a few days."

Gavin didn't answer. Instead, he came to her and pulled her into his loving embrace.

Tears began to rise in Damaris's eyes. "Maybe the queen will reconsider once she receives your letter. She can still change her mind."

"No, love. She won't. It wouldn't be politic to tell Lord Westcott that she's decided to give Thornbeck, its fortune and its lady to a mere knight simply because he has requested it."

"What will we do?" She clung to him. "You won't abandon me to such a man, will you?"

"No. I won't. If it had been some other person, some man I could respect and admire, I would force myself to leave you. Then I could tell myself you'd come to love him in time. No woman would ever grow to love Lord Westcott."

Damaris tried to blink back her tears, but they spilled down her cheeks. She held to Gavin as if she would never let him go.

"We're going to be married."

She looked up at him in surprise. "What?"

"It's the only way. The queen will be angry and Lord Westcott will be furious, but it's the only way to save you from him. Once we're wed and the marriage is consummated, the queen might hesitate to separate us. Marriages can be annulled in only two ways. She can't use consanguinity as a reason because we aren't related even remotely. The other is a previous betrothal, and since I asked her permission to marry you before we learned that Lord Westcott had been chosen, I might have an argument there."

"It's a great risk!"

"Aye. It is. It's possible that even if she allows the marriage to stand, you'll forfeit Thornbeck."

Damaris looked into his eyes. "I'd give up Thornbeck or any castle in order to be your wife."

"Think carefully. I know you love this place."

"I love you more."

Gavin held her close. "The sooner it's done, the better. I don't know if the letter was delayed in getting here. Lord Westcott could arrive sooner than we expect."

She pulled away. "I'll go find the chaplain and have him meet us in the chapel."

"You're sure, Damaris? Once done, it can't be undone."

"You're wasting time. If you want Robert to witness it, go find him. I'll get Meg."

"What of the chaplain? Will he agree to perform the ceremony?"

"I'll find a way to convince him." She wondered what it would be. Father Gregory was a stickler for following conventions.

"I love you."

She smiled at last. "I know. No woman has ever been so loved." She hurried away to find Meg.

Meg and the other ladies were in the ladies' parlor. When she saw Damaris, she said, "Where have you been? We've looked everywhere for you."

Damaris took Meg's hand and to all of them said, "I'm to be married. To Sir Gavin."

"You heard from the queen? I was told Sir Gavin had received a letter bearing the royal seal." Meg's eyes grew large and she hugged Damaris in a motherly fashion. "That's wonderful!"

The other ladies soon recovered from their surprise and began offering their favorable opinions of the match. Gavin was well liked in the castle.

"No, you don't quite understand," Damaris said. "The queen hasn't had time to reply to his letter. She wrote this one beforehand. She says she is sending a man for me to marry. His name is Neville, Lord Westcott."

Meg looked confused. "Then how is it you say you're marrying Sir Gavin?"

"Sir Gavin knows Lord Westcott and says he's a cold and heartless man. We're going to marry before Lord Westcott arrives."

The women stared in stunned silence. Meg finally found her tongue. "You can't do that! She could imprison you for going against her wishes!"

"I know. That's why I don't want all of you to witness it. Meg, I'd have you by me if you're not afraid." She looked at the others. "Edith, your health is already precarious. And Kate and Lettice are so young. I don't want to risk any of you being imprisoned on my account." She looked back at the woman who had been like a mother to her. "If you'd rather not, Meg, I understand."

Meg lifted her chin and said, "You'll not be married without me at your side! The very notion! If you were imprisoned, I'd go with you anyway, and let someone try to stop me!"

Damaris embraced her. "Thank you," she whispered.

"When is the ceremony to be? Will we have time to sew you a new gown and kirtle?"

"No. It's to be as soon as I can locate the chaplain."

"So quickly?"

"We have no idea when Lord Westcott will arrive and then it will be too late. The longer we've lived as husband and wife, the stronger our case will be."

Meg nodded. "Let's get on with it, then. Since the letter only arrived today, we can say you were married before you read it. That might be believed." She straightened Damaris's bongrace and said wistfully, "I had pictured your wedding so differently."

"So had I. This will be much better." Her eyes implored Meg's. "Do you think Father Gregory will agree to perform the ceremony? You know how he is about maintaining traditions. The banns haven't been read even once!"

"Leave it to me. I'll think of something." Meg gave her a reassuring smile.

They hurried out in search of the chaplain. They found Father Gregory in his closet, working on the sermon for the following Sunday. Damaris quickly explained that she and

Gavin wanted to be married and that they wanted the ceremony to be performed right away.

"Today? This is most irregular."

"It's best that it be quickly," Meg said before Damaris could speak. She lowered her eyes modestly to lead the man to think there was a need for haste.

"I see. I see." Father Gregory gave Damaris a disapproving look but he nodded. "Well, my lady, you aren't the first maid to be caught in such a way. Nor, I wager, will you be the last."

Damaris tried to look properly chastised. She would never have thought of leading the chaplain to believe she was with child in order to convince him to go against the usual procedures. "Sir Gavin is to meet us in the chapel."

Father Gregory put down his quill and stood. "Very well, let's go, then."

They walked briskly through the corridors and were soon in the chapel. Gavin and Robert were already there. She could tell from Robert's face that he knew the real reason for their rush.

Father Gregory frowned at Gavin, but he went into the small closet behind the pulpit to get his vestments of office.

"How did you convince him?" Gavin asked. "He looks angry."

"He believes I'm with child."

Gavin looked at her in astonishment. "You didn't tell him that!"

"No, Meg did. I had expected to have to argue him into it. This is better."

When Father Gregory came back into the chapel, they all fell silent. Damaris still held Gavin's hand and she didn't drop it even when the chaplain frowned at her.

He opened the Bible and said in a clear voice, "Dearly beloved, we're gathered here . . ."

In a remarkably short time Father Gregory had performed the betrothal ceremony and the wedding ceremony. Damaris and Gavin were married.

She gazed up at him. It had all happened so quickly she felt as if she were whirling. It was hard to believe Father Gregory's words had made them one. Gavin still looked the same, handsome, tall and as golden as any knight from her father's book of legends. Damaris closed her eyes as he bent to kiss her. The kiss lasted longer than Father Gregory found prudent and he cleared his throat to interrupt it.

Damaris smiled as Gavin straightened. His eyes were as bright as hers felt. Robert was grinning openly.

"We're truly married?" Gavin asked.

"Aye. You're married." Father Gregory frowned at him. "But you're not to think I countenance the reason behind it!"

"No. We understand." Gavin grinned and put his arm protectively around Damaris's waist.

Father Gregory looked as if he wanted to say more but thought better of it. They were, after all, the lord and lady of the castle. He went back to the closet to put away his vestments.

"Will you come to the parlor with me to tell the others?" Meg asked.

"No." Damaris looked up at Gavin with a broad smile. "My husband and I want to be alone."

Robert laughed softly. "I'll come with you, Meg. I can tell we're not needed here."

When they were alone, Damaris took Gavin's hand. "Come with me." She took him out the chapel door and down the corridor that led outside.

"Where are we going? Your chamber is in the opposite direction."

"I know." She led him outside and up the grassy slope toward the Maidens.

He followed her willingly. Damaris said, "I feel I could float upon the air and sing with the birds! Has anyone ever been this happy since the beginning of the world?" She spun around to take in as much of the island as she could encompass.

Gavin pulled her to him and kissed her. "Never. If anyone were happier, he would have died. I'm sure of it."

They ran up the grassy ridge and down the path that led to the stone circle. Damaris didn't stop until she was in front of the Priestess. She pulled her cap and bongrace from her head and shook her hair free. With her eyes shining, she looked up at Gavin. "I, Damaris, take thee, Gavin, to be my husband."

He laughed. "We've already done that."

"Please. For me."

He took both her hands. "I, Gavin, take thee, Damaris, to be my wife. I promise to love you and honor you and to keep you safe for as long as we both shall live." The humor died from his face and he said tenderly, "I promise to love no one save you. To remain beside you, no matter what may befall us. To grow old beside you and to still love you to the depth and breadth of my soul."

Tears of happiness stung Damaris's eyes. "I promise to always love you and to give you honor. I promise to keep you safe as well, to the best of my ability. I want to grow old with you and to give you children who will be your joy and your pride. I promise to do all this out of the love and respect I feel for you and because we've long been married in our hearts."

Gavin drew her close. "I do love you, Damaris."

"And I love you." She leaned up to kiss him. "Now we're twice-over married. No one will dare separate us."

He smiled down at her and there was a bittersweetness in his eyes. "You're as fey as the fairies and as magical. No man has ever had a bride such as you."

She smiled back at him. "I think that's probably true."

He held her close and rested his cheek on the top of her head. A breeze caught her hair and swirled it around them as it billowed her skirts. "I only hope you don't come to regret our hasty actions when the queen learns what we've done."

"I'll never regret it."

"Neither will I." He ran his hands over her, feeling the slenderness of her body and the silk of her hair as it warmed in the sun. "Tonight and every night you'll be mine. I can't believe it. It's like a miracle." He was still haunted by the nightmare of knowing she was to have married Neville Westcott. Gavin had once refused to sell a horse to Lord Westcott because of his known cruelty. As poorly as Westcott treated his animals, what would he have done to Damaris the first time her spirit flared? Gavin held her closer.

"We wasted so much time in arguing when we first met. We could have fallen in love so much sooner!"

He laughed and wrapped her hair around his hand. "It was overly soon as it was, my greedy bride. Had we followed convention when our fathers suggested the match, we would still be waiting several more months yet."

"I've never been fond of convention." She looked up at him with so much love his heart seemed to turn over.

"No, no one could ever accuse you of that."

A mischievous light came into her eyes. "Nor do we have to wait until tonight for us to finish giving ourselves to each other."

"I have no reservations about going to your chambers now," he assured her. "If you recall, I was going there instead of up here."

"I had to come here. It was important."

Gavin looked up at the towering stone. He was sure he would never fully understand the tie Damaris had with this magical ring. "I never thought to marry such a pagan. Will you insist on bringing all our children here and passing them through the stone as you were?"

"Of course." She laughed up at him, as a breeze billowed her hair about her. With a glance back at the castle, she said, "It's a long way to my chambers. I never thought it was before." Her eyes darted up to his in a daring glance. "Fortunately we're quite alone here."

Gavin laced his fingers in her hair. "You are indeed a pagan creature. I never thought to meet a woman who would match me passion for passion."

Damaris kissed him. "You never met a woman who loved you so truly."

"Aye," he said softly. "Love can work miracles."

He kissed her thoroughly as his hands sought her breasts. Women's clothing seemed especially designed to thwart advances. He couldn't tell much about her body beneath all the layers and his imagination made his blood quicken. Damaris was clearly as eager as he was.

He pulled away and said, "No. Not like this. I want our first time to be on a comfortable bed where we have complete privacy and bed curtains to shut out the world."

Her breath was as ragged as his, but she nodded. "If we were in my chamber... our chamber... we could stay there the rest of the day and all night without having to redress and go among people."

He laughed. "You really are decadent!"

"Does it displease you?"

"No. Nor would it any other man to learn his bride is so eager for him. I know of no more auspicious way to begin a marriage."

In the distance he heard a sound and he raised his head to look back toward the castle. He stiffened.

"What is it?" She leaned against him but looked toward the castle. The sound came again. "It's someone blowing a horn on the parapet."

Gavin turned his eyes toward the sea. On the water were ships. Not boats such as the fishermen used, but the sort that could transport fighting men and their weapons. The sails furled against the wind as they sped toward the island. The horn sounded the warning again.

"Scots!" Damaris gasped.

Gavin took her hand and they ran back toward the castle. Already he could see the villagers responding. They were coming as fast as they could, driving their goats, sheep and cattle before them. He could hear their cries and shouts faintly in the distance. A cannon on the parapet roared and he saw a plume of water spurt up just off the starboard bow of the lead ship.

He pushed Damaris toward the castle. "Go inside and find your ladies! Stay with them!"

"I want to help you!"

"You can't. I'm going to help the villagers drive the livestock in. You have to see to the women. Keep them calm and away from the windows."

Damaris nodded and lifted her skirts so she could run toward the castle. Gavin changed direction and headed down the slope toward the village.

He found the villagers almost more confused than their animals. Children were crying and staring about in fright. Elderly men and women were demanding that they be carried faster to safety or that they be taken back to their familiar cottages. Several of the women told him their men were still out in the fishing boats and that they would return to a deserted village, or worse, to a village overrun by Scots.

Gavin reassured as many as possible and goaded the slower ones to a faster pace. The horn still sounding its notes made his blood run faster. How many times had he ridden to battle at such a call to arms?

At last he had all the villagers and livestock in Thornbeck's courtyard. The walled area was spacious, but now it was packed with milling beasts and people. The cacophony of their confusion was deafening. Gavin helped the men lower the first portcullis down the grooves cut into the stone wall. Thornbeck had no barbican for a primary line of defense, but there were two portcullises through which the enemy would have to hack. Behind the second was a wooden wall studded heavily with iron fittings and straps. Thornbeck had a secure defense system.

Gavin shouted orders at his men, and they instantly ran to do his bidding. The cannons were already in place on the walls and he could hear them booming as they tried to sink the ships before they could dock. No army could come up the steep cliffs on the side nearest the mainland so he had grouped his defenses of cannons there. Archers would be more effective against men on foot and his best men were already positioning themselves along the wall that overlooked the green.

With some effort, Gavin made his way through the crowd. Everyone seemed to be shouting or crying or both. He knew from experience it would be a while before they calmed enough to hear him assign quarters.

He ran through the castle and up to the parlor where Damaris's women usually spent their days. They were there. The two young ones were huddled together and crying. Edith looked as if she were about to be ill or to faint. Meg was attending her. Damaris was pacing like a caged animal. When she saw Gavin, she ran to him.

"I was so worried about you!" she said as she embraced him.

He allowed himself the briefest enjoyment of holding her before he said, "I want you and the women to stay in the inner rooms, well away from the windows. There's no reason yet for you to go to the keep, and I pray it will never be necessary. If you feel you must go outside, use the bawn courtyard beside the keep. The main courtyard is filled with villagers."

Damaris's face was pale and her eyes were wide, but she nodded. "Where will you be?"

"I'm going onto the parapet and see exactly how many ships are arriving. I never expected Sir William to be able to summon so many."

A cannon located immediately above the parlor roared, and he felt Damaris flinch, though she made no sound. "Don't be afraid," he told her and the other women. "Those are our defenses. That sound means they're keeping you safe. If we can sink the ships before they land, we can avoid a land battle." He didn't tell them how small the chances of that were. He kissed Damaris and said, "I have to leave. Will you be all right?"

She nodded and managed to smile. "I'll be fine. Keep yourself safe for me."

He found he could return her smile after all. "I will. Until later, my lady."

"Until later."

He was surprised to find how much he wanted her even with the scent of battle in his nose. He turned and hurried from the room.

Chapter Thirteen

Gavin hurried up the stairs and out onto the parapet. Robert was already there. "How the devil did he manage to find so many men to bring against us?" he demanded. "You saw Craigmore. It never had so many men, even before we imprisoned the ones still in Thornbeck's dungeon!"

Robert was studying the ships through a spyglass. "They're flying different coats of arms. He must have enlisted other castles to aid him."

The ships were making a wide berth of the walls containing the cannons and were heading toward the unprotected docks at the village. In the far distance Gavin could see the much smaller village fishing boats as specks on the ocean. There would be no way now to let the fishermen join their friends and families in the castle. They would have to take their chances in the village or row to the mainland.

"We've hit one!" Robert shouted. "Look!"

Gavin saw a billow of smoke rise from one of the nearest ships. Its crew was running about, but the fire was in the sails and out of their reach. As he watched, the cannoneers launched several more missiles at the prey. All of them found their marks and two pierced the wooden hull. "It's taking on water!"

As he watched, the ship shuddered and listed to the starboard. Several men slid across the deck and into the water.

"She'll go down," Robert said confidently. As another ship eased closer to pick up the survivors, the cannons opened fire on it. Soon it, too, was in trouble.

"Three have escaped." Gavin watched the remaining ships sail past the cannons' range. "Hold your fire!" he shouted to his men. "There's no point in wasting powder." He pointed at the opposite wall. "Take every second cannon to the landward side and position them there!" His men hurried to obey. Cannons weren't a good defense against men on foot, but they could do damage and they would be necessary if the Scots built a war machine to batter the walls or to catapult fire or rocks over it.

"Where's Godfrey?" Gavin asked.

"I last saw him in the courtyard trying to maintain order there. He was telling the men from the village that they'll be expected to fight beside ours on the walls. He was giving them instructions."

"Aye. We'll need every man we can find." The villagers were primarily fishermen, but Gavin knew most men had some experience in using bows and arrows.

Gavin left the parapet and searched until he found Thornbeck's steward. He had never seen Harley look ruffled, but today he was almost in a state of panic. "Andrew, have quarters been found for the villagers?"

"Aye, Sir Gavin. But we thought not to need them so soon! There's no linen on the beds or carpets on the windows. We have only rush lights in quantity!"

"Rush lights are fine enough. They aren't used to candles and won't miss them. As for the linens, the women can make their own rooms. See that linens are given to them. I want to clear the courtyard as much as possible."

"Yes, sir."

Gavin went to the main door and surveyed the milling crowd. Men, women and children were wandering about as helplessly as their pigs, goats and cattle. Gavin shouted for their attention. "I want you men who are sound of body to go to Sir Godfrey, over at the gate. You women get your children together and bring them inside. Slowly! Don't push!" He watched the women start herding the smaller children toward the steps.

"You older boys there! Gather the animals together and drive them into the pens by the stables." Gavin watched as the boys began separating the animals from the people who held to them to be sure the task would be done.

At the gate, Godfrey was assembling the men and pointing at the various places of defense on the walls. Several of the men already has been issued bows and quivers of arrows. The men stationed in the gate towers were handing out others. Order was being attained.

Gavin went back inside. The hall and screens passage were filled with crying and shouting women and children. Their eyes were wide and frightened and they stared at him almost as fearfully as they would have if he were Sir William. He made a calming motion with his hands.

When they became quiet enough to hear him, he said, "The man over there on the stairs is Andrew Harley, Thornbeck's steward. He has rooms for all of you." Gavin knew the man was probably known to all the villagers, but in their confusion they had forgotten his function at the castle. "Slowly, slowly," he shouted as the women surged toward Andrew. "The Scots haven't even landed yet. You'll be here for a while. There's no reason to rush."

Andrew had several nervous maids with him. As Gavin watched, he instructed some of the village women to follow one maid or another and for the others to wait their turn. Allowing the villagers to run unchecked through Thornbeck was not to be allowed. The maids led their charges away toward the wing of the castle that had been constructed for the purpose of sheltering the villagers in case of attack.

"Sir Gavin?"

He turned to see Gil Hobson beside him. "Aye, Gil?"

"I see my mother there with my brothers and sisters. Can I go help her get them settled?"

"Go ahead, lad." Gavin saw the fear in Gil's eyes and remembered his young page was new to service and had never seen battle preparations before. "When they've been settled in, go to Sir Godfrey and aid him with the men. You know all their names and this will be a help to him."

Gil ran to obey, and as Gavin watched, Gil embraced a thin woman while several smaller versions of Gil wrapped themselves around his legs and waist. Gil pointed the way and his mother followed him up the stairs toward their new accommodations.

By the time the Scots had anchored their ships and rowed their men to the docks in the shallower water, Gavin had the castle ready for battle. He stood on the parapet above the gates and watched the enemy march onto the green.

His practiced eye told him these were seasoned warriors. William had recruited them well. One of the men, backed by several followers, came out onto the center of the green. Robert said, "That must be Sir William."

"Aye." Gavin sized up his nemesis. There was no family resemblance to Damaris at all. William was swarthy in coloring and not above average height. His age was apparent only in the graying of his hair and a slight stiffness in his gait. "I expected him to appear older."

"Don't underestimate him," Robert said. "For all his years, he's still a viper."

William stood there for a long while, staring at the castle, then he lifted his arm and shouted. Clearly this was the signal his men had been waiting for. With a loud cry they ran forward.

"Hold your fire until they're in range," Gavin shouted to his men as he fitted an arrow to his bowstring. "Now!" He drew back his bow and sent the arrow into one of the men in the lead. The man stumbled and fell under the feet of those coming behind him.

For the rest of the afternoon Gavin and the others fired. The cannons roared and belched smoke that hid the enemy at times. When ladders were brought to scale the walls, the villagers poured boiling water onto the men who tried to climb them. When the Scots abandoned the ladders and backed out of range of the scalding water, grappling irons were tossed down from the parapets and the castle men hauled as many ladders as possible out of the Scots' reach.

When nighttime finally brought the fighting to an end, Gavin was as tired as his men. Nevertheless, he stayed on the wall, watching fires being kindled on the green as the enemy encamped for the night. Occasionally an arrow would strike the walls, but for the most part, the Scots were content to rest and tend their wounded.

"We brought down a lot of them," Robert said.

"Aye, but not enough. By morning they'll be rested and back at us. Set guards to be sure they don't try to take us in the dark." He left Robert and went down the precarious stairs that led from the parapet to the courtyard.

In the part of the castle overlooking the sea, Wat Hobson was still awake and talking to his cronies in a harsh whisper. "What are we to do, I ask you? Wait here until the bloody Scots take the castle and kill us all?"

"What else is there?" Ben asked in a tired voice. "I've been pouring hot water over the wall and wrestling with grappling hooks all afternoon. I don't feel I'm waiting idly by."

"I was working as hard as you. But why should we have to? Aren't the castle folk sworn to protect us? It seems to me we've been protecting ourselves!"

Another of the fishermen, Davie Cochran, said, "We could try to make it to the mainland. We'd be safe there."

"Leave the island?" Wat stared at Davie as if he were talking nonsense.

Trying to interject reason, Ben said, "We couldn't get to our boats. The Scots are between us and them. Besides, the castle is fastened tighter than a clam. We couldn't get out if we tried."

"I saw how the gate works," Wat said. "I was with those who secured it. There are three wheels to turn and the gates open."

"We can't go out," Ben repeated.

"It would be sure death," Davie agreed reluctantly. "By the saints, but I hate being locked anywhere!"

"We wouldn't have to be if it had been handled differently." Wat leaned closer. "We should have stayed in the village and taken our chances."

"What! And be slaughtered where we stood?" Davie glared at him.

"The Scots have no quarrel with us. It's the ones here in the castle that are their enemies. We're only poor fishermen. I wager we would have been left alone."

"I don't know about that." Davie shook his head. He had a pretty young wife. "My Mary's with child. I couldn't risk it for her sake."

Wat grunted impatiently. "You're letting that lass turn you into a milksop! The Scots wouldn't have any more quarrel with your Mary than they would with you. Why would they?"

"Mary is pretty. A man is a man."

Wat turned back to face Ben. "What about you? Has your Hettie stolen your courage?"

Ben avoided Wat's eyes but he shook his head. "Not a bit of it."

"We should have taken our chances," Wat said restlessly.

Ben tried not to sound too glad of the fact but argued, "It's too late now, at any rate. We're fastened here in the castle and it's here we'll stay until the battle is over."

Wat scowled at them both. "There's ways out of here. We could leave our women behind, if we've a mind to do it. Gil knows the castle. He could tell us where to find a small gate that we could slip through."

"And then what? The Scots have likely taken over our houses for sleeping quarters. They may have cut our boats loose or sunk them for all we know. I'm not so fond of rowing that I wouldn't mind taking a few days off." Ben stretched. "I'm going to find Hettie and go to bed."

"Aye, me, too." Davie stood as if he were glad of the excuse to leave the conversation. "Mary will likely be worried. You know how women get when they're carrying a child."

Ben grinned and nodded but Wat only frowned more deeply. "Go on, the both of you. I'll sit here by the fire for a bit." He watched them go. He didn't really think either of them was a coward, despite what he had said to them. But they were too solicitous of their wives, in Wat's opinion. He didn't let Bess determine what he was to do or not to do.

Gavin passed the wing where the villagers were quartered and automatically noted that most of them were sleeping by now. The men were hardened from fishing, but they weren't

used to hauling tubs of boiling water or shooting bows. They
would feel some sore muscles in the morning.

He went into the castle by the main door and Andrew
Harley bolted it after him. "Shall I leave it locked for the
night, Sir Gavin?" the steward asked nervously. The doors
inside the castle's wall were almost never barred.

"Aye. Sir Robert can come in by the small door."

Andrew gave one of his stiffly formal bows. "I'll give orders to admit him when he knocks. My lady Damaris says
I'm to tell you she's in the ladies' parlor."

"Thank you." Gavin went to the stairway and climbed to
the next floor. He ached from tension as well as exertion and
he wanted to see Damaris more than he wanted food or
drink.

As soon as he opened the door, she rose and came to meet
him. The other ladies stared at him as if he were suddenly a
stranger. Gavin realized it was because most of them hadn't
seen him since he had married their mistress that afternoon, nor were they accustomed to seeing him begrimed
with cannon soot and sweat. "How are you?" he asked.

"We're all right. I was worried about you. What news is
there?"

"It's calm for the night. The Scots have to rest, too." He
gazed down at her. Her eyes were worried, but she wasn't
giving in to her concern. She took his hand and squeezed it.

"Lettice," she said, "have food and ale brought to my
chamber. My husband is tired." She smiled up at Gavin.

Meg stood and put aside her needlework. The other ladies also prepared to end their evening.

"We'll need no attendants," Gavin said, never taking his
eyes from Damaris. "I've sent word to my valet already."

"But, my lady," Meg started to object, "surely you'll
need us to loosen your laces!" She sounded shocked that
Damaris might prefer for Gavin to do it.

"Not tonight, Meg," Damaris said firmly. She went to the
door and Gavin followed her out. When they were in the
corridor, Damaris said, "We've shocked poor Meg."

"I gather she's never been married."

"Nor even betrothed."

"I'm afraid she will be shocked many times in the future." He felt the small bones in her hand. Despite her height, Damaris was delicately made. "I'll be gentle with you. You're not afraid, are you?"

She averted her eyes. "Of course not. I've thought about tonight ever since this morning." She looked up at him and added, "I was so worried about you. I heard the shouts and the cannons moving to guard the gates. It was all I could do to stay with my ladies and not run to your side."

He laughed and put his hands about her. "What a warrior you'd have made!"

When they reached her chambers, Gavin looked around with interest. Damaris stayed by the door while he moved about the room. "So this is where you've slept all your life. It's not quite as I pictured it." He touched the red and gold brocaded curtains that hung on the bed's frame.

"There was no time to sew new bed linens." She looked at the curtains. "These are faded by the sun because I hate to have the windows covered unless it's rainy or cold out." Now that they were here in her chamber, she was seized by an unexpected shyness.

He looked at her. "What's going through your mind for you to look at me in that way?"

"I was thinking how large you seem in this room. I've never seen a man here before, not even Papa. You seem to fill the chamber."

He came to her and put his arms on her waist. "I think for all your brave talk, you've a bit of a maiden's shyness."

Damaris looked down. "Not that I'll ever admit to."

"Some shyness is only natural." Gavin gently touched her face. "That's why I wanted our first time to be here, alone in our chamber. Not on the grass at the Maidens."

"I didn't understand. Meg has explained a great deal to me this afternoon. She and Edith have told me what to expect." She looked up at him with some trepidation.

He wondered what they had been filling her head with. "How would either of them know what transpires on a wedding night if they've never been married?"

Damaris frowned slightly. "I never thought of that."

"Whatever they told you, my advice is to forget it. I liked it better when you were eager for me and willing to give yourself to me without question."

Damaris held him tightly and rested her cheek against his chest. Beneath his clothing, she felt the unyielding hardness of the leather vest he wore to deflect arrows. She had tried so hard not to admit even to herself that she feared for his safety. Now she had him alone for the entire night and, for these hours, at least, she could be certain of his wellbeing.

"You're trembling."

"I was so afraid tonight would never come. I kept thinking of you on the parapet with arrows flying all about and I was so afraid you'd be hit."

"Your love is my good-luck charm."

She sensed he was smiling, but she didn't lift her head to see. "Why did my uncle have to arrive today? We have enough to dread when the queen and Lord Westcott learn of our marriage."

"Are you having second thoughts? It's rather late for that."

"No. I'll never regret having married you. It's just that my life has turned upside down so suddenly. I feel as if my world is coming apart."

He put his fingers under her chin and lifted her face so he could look into her eyes. "Let's see if we can put it back together again."

He kissed her and Damaris opened her lips eagerly. As she kissed him she felt his fingers work her laces free in back. She didn't want to know how he had become so proficient at unlacing a woman's gown without looking at the fastenings. There were truths about his past that she would rather not hear.

As she felt her gown loosening, she drew back enough to pull at the hook and eye that held his jerkin closed. Men's clothing was a mystery to her, but it was a puzzle that she was eager to decipher.

Gavin slipped the jerkin off and tossed it aside. His doublet felt soft and padded beneath her fingers. The sleeves tied on at the shoulders, and the front was secured by invisible hooks and eyes from close to his neck to his waist. One by one she unfastened them.

When he was free of the doublet, Gavin pulled her gown away, leaving her in her chemise. Although the chemise reached from her neck to her wrists, and to the floor, Damaris felt naked under his gaze. She could feel her cheeks growing pink. Slowly he started unbuckling the front of his leather vest as she unlaced the sides.

The vest had been burnished to a reddish brown, and she tried to dismiss the marring streaks left on it by arrows that had come close to ending his life. She didn't want to think at this moment how precarious all their lives were.

The cool night air on her skin reminded her that she had forgotten to get her night rail from the trunk. She was so accustomed to Kate or Lettice doing that for her. "I'll get my nightgown," she said. "Your trunk isn't here yet. What will you sleep in?"

Gavin laughed softly. "Neither of us will need night-clothes. I'll keep you warm enough."

She gazed up at him. She had never in her life slept naked. As far as she knew, no one ever did. Meg and Edith rarely agreed about anything, but they were of one mind when it came to the dangers of exposure to night vapors.

"Trust me. Once you grow accustomed to it, you'll never want to sleep bundled up in clothing again." He was smiling at her reticence.

"I have a lot to learn," she admitted.

"I'm a willing teacher."

He slowly drew her chemise off her shoulders and let it fall to the floor. Damaris watched his face closely for any sign that she had fallen short of his expectations. With all the clothing and layers of tight lacings, he couldn't have known what her body would look like unclothed.

His eyes grew darker. "You're beautiful!"

She realized she was holding her breath. "Am I?" She had rarely seen anyone, even her ladies, who wasn't fully clothed. She hadn't been all that sure a man would find her body attractive and that certainly wasn't something she could ask her attendants.

"You're perfect." In one fluid motion, he bent down and picked her up as if she weighed no more than thistledown and carried her to the bed. Gently he lay her on the cool sheets. "You're even more beautiful in person than you were in my dreams."

She smiled. "You dreamed of me? Like this?"

"More times than you'll ever know." He watched her as he removed his shirt and tossed it aside.

Damaris studied his body and felt her pulses quicken. He was beautifully built. Hard muscles ridged his stomach and bulged on his arms and chest. His hips were lean and narrow, his legs muscled from years of horseback riding. She didn't find his manhood at all frightening despite the things Meg and Edith had told her that afternoon.

Slowly, as if he were afraid a quick movement would alarm her, Gavin lay beside her. His body was hot against hers and she caught her breath when their skin touched. Wonderingly she ran her hands over him, enjoying the feel of his muscles and his warmth.

Gavin knotted his fingers in her hair and kissed her again. Damaris felt her world spin and she held tightly to him. His hands were exploring her body and igniting fires everywhere they touched. When he cupped her breast in his palm, she moaned softly. Never had anything felt so good! Then he began rolling her nipple gently between his thumb and forefinger and she realized there were greater pleasures to come.

He took his time, learning her body from head to toe. Damaris felt as if she would explode from wanting him, even if she wasn't entirely certain what that meant. He was bringing sensations to life that she had never dreamed existed. She felt her body start to tremble and wondered what was to come next.

Gavin left a trail of kisses down her cheek and neck, pausing to lick the pulse that was pounding in her throat. Damaris rolled her head back on the downy pillow and gloried in the passions he was awakening.

As he moved lower, she closed her eyes and wondered if she would burst from her desire for him. His warm lips moved over her breast, and when he took her nipple into his mouth, Damaris's eyes flew open in surprise.

Slowly he laved the pouting bud with his tongue and teeth, teasing her until she moaned and arched her back to give herself more fully to him. She laced her fingers in his hair as he moved to give the same attention to her other breast.

Just when she thought this was surely the most wonderful thing one person could do to another, Gavin moved his hand over her waist and hips and touched the soft hair where her legs joined.

Heat seemed to explode within her. Damaris opened her eyes to see him watching her face. He was smiling and she could tell it gave him as much pleasure to watch her as she was experiencing from his hands and lips. She searched his eyes and saw the leashed passion there.

As he explored her most tender recesses, her breath quickened. She ran her hands over the hard wall of his chest, marveling that he could be so powerful, yet so tender in loving her. Willingly she opened her legs wider to allow him greater access to her body.

Gavin knew exactly what to do to bring her to the point of trembling eagerness. Damaris kissed him and met his tongue with her own. She loved the taste of him in her mouth. He stopped kissing her only to go back to her breast. The slow, deep motions of his fingers made her moan again and she held to him as if she would spin away into oblivion without him as her anchor.

He seemed to sense the exact moment when she was certain she could bear his deliberate teasing no longer, and he shifted his weight upward and knelt between her legs. Damaris put her hands on his hips to pull him toward her. He entered her only slightly, then paused to kiss her and to give her body time to adjust to him.

As gently as possible, he eased himself into her. Damaris felt an instant of pain, but her body was so hungry for him she paid it no heed. Gavin sensed it, however, and he stopped until she was again eager to give herself to him.

Slowly he started to move within her. Damaris had never felt anything remotely as pleasing. Her body knew what to do and she fell naturally into the rhythm he set. After a while, she moved more confidently, setting her own pace without knowing how she knew to do it.

She felt his muscles bunching and releasing beneath her hands and his kisses on her neck and face. She had become a part of him. His pleasure was her pleasure and hers was his. When even this pleasure wasn't enough, he moved deeper, more deliberately. Her body responded instantly.

At first Damaris didn't know what was happening. It was as if her body were spiraling upward toward some unknown precipice. Every move he made brought her closer to a mystery she hadn't known moments before.

Suddenly, incredibly, fireworks seemed to burst inside her. She cried out with the intensity of the ecstasy and held to him tightly. Wave after wave of pleasure roared through her and she wanted it never to stop, even as she knew she couldn't bear so much for very long.

Gavin gave a muffled cry and pressed hard into her and Damaris realized he was feeling exactly what she was experiencing. After a while, he rolled to his side, still holding her locked against him. Her hair was wrapped around them both and her leg was still curved over his hip. For a long time they held each other, reveling in the bliss of their lovemaking, letting their senses slowly adjust to the prosaic world.

Drifting in the afterglow of his loving, Damaris opened her eyes. To her surprise, he was lying there watching her. Words couldn't express the depth of love she was feeling. There was no point in even trying to speak of such a miracle. She touched his cheek tenderly, gazing deeply into his eyes. He smiled as if he knew exactly what she was feeling.

"I love you," he whispered. "If I hadn't loved you before, I would have fallen in love with you tonight."

"It was so wonderful," she murmured, tracing the line of his lips. "I never dreamed anything could be so marvelous! How could anyone fear or even dislike this?"

He smiled at her naive question. She didn't care. She was too warm and satisfied from their loving. Her body was still resounding from the pleasure he had given her.

"I love you," she whispered. "How often can we do this?"

He laughed and held her close. "My decadent little pagan. Just give me a minute to catch my breath."

She smiled at him. "I like seeing your face on my pillow." She glanced past him. "We didn't even draw the bed curtains against the night air and the windows are open."

"Are you cold?"

She shook her head and her smile widened. "Not at all. I may never be cold again." Gently she stroked her hand over the swell of his shoulder and down the arm that lay relaxed across her. She touched a long white scar. "What happened to you?"

He glanced at it. "It's from a saber cut. It's an old one."

She lifted her head enough to kiss it. "Be careful, Gavin. I don't ever want you to know pain again."

He stroked the hair back from her face and his palm dwarfed her cheek. "I'll stay safe for you. More important, I'll keep you safe."

"We're surrounded by our enemy, but I believe you. Never have I felt so protected."

Gavin gazed at her for a long time and she wondered what he was thinking. There was a sadness in his eyes that she didn't want to question. Their world was far from secure. If the Scots didn't end their happiness, Queen Elizabeth might. She closed her eyes and cuddled against his chest.

Beneath her cheek she could hear the steady thud of his heart. He felt so alive and so virile, even in repose. "I'm certain no woman has ever been this happy," she told him softly. "No one has ever been more greatly loved."

"No. I think perhaps you're right." He stroked her hair and rested his cheek against the top of her head. "Nor has any other man been so fortunate in a wife."

"A wife," she repeated, wonder in her voice. "Father Gregory spoke such simple words, but how much they've given us."

"We had our love before," he reminded her.

"I know, but now no one can separate us."

He didn't answer and she didn't ask for reassurance. For this one night they needed to pretend their happiness would last forever and that their union was truly indissoluble. Damaris held to him and let her love grow until it filled her entire being. No one would ever separate them, she told herself. Never. She wouldn't allow it. Not when she loved him so much.

Chapter Fourteen

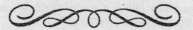

William glared up at the castle and wished he could find a way to breach its walls. "We've tried everything," he complained to Sir James.

"Aye. The men report they've had no luck at tunneling under the walls. The castle sits on solid rock."

"I know. I told you they wouldn't be able to do it." William and his men had been on the island for almost a week and they were tiring of storming the walls only to be beaten back under a rain of arrows. "It was useless to try."

James glared at him. "I had to have them try something. It's no good to send them out to be shot at every day. There's talk of them wanting to go back home."

William shook his fist. "I'll personally shoot any man who tries!" William knew he had to be firm with the men. They weren't all from Craigmore and weren't as loyal to him as he wished them to be. "We have to stick together."

"So I told them." James crossed his arms over his leather chest guard and studied the castle. "Is there no way in but this?"

"We tried every other way," William snapped. He turned to look at the village.

He had quartered his men in the houses there to shelter them from the rain and wind. Sleeping on cots and beds had placated them for a while. Trouble was coming, however. They had already consumed most of the food William had brought with them. "I'll need to have more provisions sent over." He had hoped to take the castle as quickly this time as he had before. He spent hours at a stretch wondering about the man in command of the castle and whether he had a weak point. So far one hadn't been found.

"We're staying, then?"

"Of course. I've not come this far to back down! We'll lay siege. Eventually they'll have to come out. They can't have a never-ending source of food in there. Once it's gone, they'll surrender quick enough." William hoped he was right. The Scots he had convinced to join him in the attack were fierce warriors but not given to discipline or strategies. He had no real hold over them.

James nodded thoughtfully. "That could work. It won't be fast, though. We saw them driving livestock into the gates, remember. They may be able to hold out longer than we can keep our men here."

"I don't care if it beggars me to pay for their services! I'll have Thornbeck if it's the end of me!" He glared back at the castle. "Get some men to help you and go for supplies."

James nodded and went to obey. William again went over what he remembered of Thornbeck, trying to recall anything at all that would help him break through its defenses. He knew as well as James that a siege was as boring to fighting men as it was tedious to those trapped in the castle. Could he buy their loyalty for as long as it might take? How many provisions were stored in the castle?

Gavin gave Gil a bag of coins and clapped him on the shoulder. "Godspeed, lad." His voice sounded hollow in the water room beneath Thornbeck. Several boats bobbed at their tethers in the dimness. The rush light was in a bracket up the steps and barely reached the room. It was important that none of the Scots see what was about to happen, should any of them be out on the water.

Gil nodded and touched the St. Cuthbert's bead he wore about his neck. Gavin knew he must be afraid, but he wasn't showing it.

"Do you remember the way to London?"

"Aye. I can find it again."

"That's why I decided to send you rather than someone else. I need my men on the battlements and none of the villagers have been there." He touched the bag of coins.

"There's plenty here to buy a good horse. Speed is essential."

"I understand."

"If you row straight west from the island, I don't think you can be seen by the Scots. It's a dark night. It's likely they'll never know anyone has gone."

"I'm strong. I'll be on the mainland before they can put out to catch me." The boy grinned. "I may hate fishing, but I know all there is about rowing a boat."

Gavin went to the wheel on the wall as Gil stepped into the boat he had chosen. "Are you ready?"

Gil hesitated, then nodded.

Slowly Gavin turned the wheel. It creaked but the iron gate started to rise. As soon as it was high enough for the boat to slip under, Gil pushed away and ducked low to pass onto the sea. As Gavin lowered the gate, he watched the boy lean into the oars. The light boat skimmed swiftly across the black water and soon was gone from sight. Night had fallen early that evening because a storm was building. He hoped Gil would make shore before it broke.

Gavin locked the gate in place and paused to look at it. This was the castle's weakest link, in his opinion. It could only be opened from inside the castle, but a good charge of explosives might blast a hole in the ironwork gate. Apparently Sir William didn't remember the gate existed. Gavin hoped Gil would reach court and send help in time.

He had wavered in his decision to send for reinforcements. Thornbeck was an easy castle to defend and he had enough men for the purpose. He had assumed William would use the strategies Damaris said he had employed in the past—rush the castle for a while, then give up and return to Craigmore.

That afternoon, however, he had seen a ship leave for Scotland, and he knew that had to mean that William was sending for supplies, ammunition, or both. A siege seemed likely. With all the villagers and his men in the castle, in addition to Thornbeck's normal staff and the prisoners in the dungeon, Gavin wouldn't be able to hold out long in a siege. Did William realize that?

Godfrey and Robert had suggested that one way to conserve rations was to kill the prisoners, but Gavin couldn't bring himself to do that. To take a man's life in battle in defense of one's own was one thing, but to kill a defenseless man was something else. But there was no denying that the prisoners did eat a great deal of the food he needed to last out the siege.

He went up the stairs and nodded at the guards on the door. It being the only entrance into the castle from the water gate, he had had it reinforced with metal straps, and he was confident it was as secure as it could be made. Plus, the steps curving up to it within the tower would prevent an enemy from getting a running start to batter it down, even if they managed to breach the water gate. The only forced entry could be from hacking the door literally to pieces or burning it down, the latter of which would be difficult due to dampness in the wood on the water side. After he crossed the threshold into the castle proper, the door clanged shut behind him, and he heard the satisfying sound of the iron bolt sliding into place as he walked away.

Rush torches had been placed at intervals along the walls to light his way back to the main rooms, but the passage was still thick with shadows. In the flickering illumination of the rushes, he could see that the stone walls were slick and shiny from the ever-present dampness. From somewhere nearby he heard the drip of water on rock. It reminded him of the first time he had seen Thornbeck as he entered through this same passageway. So much had happened in such a short time.

In the days since his marriage, Gavin had found a happiness he had never thought possible. Damaris was everything he had ever hoped for in a woman. She was intelligent, responsive and, best of all, she loved him. He still felt that was a miracle. Each moment he spent away from her seemed impossibly long. But along with the benefits there also came a liability. He could, and would, fight to the death for his principles or at the queen's orders, but now he had someone to worry about. If anything happened to him, what would become of Damaris?

He thought about her intended bridegroom, Neville Lord Westcott. Before he had dispatched Gil to court for reinforcements, he had considered the possibility of sending him to Westcott instead, for the journey there would have been a shorter one and the response could have been quicker. But reason held that Westcott might already be en route to Thornbeck with a mere handful of retainers, as he had no way of knowing Thornbeck was under siege, and Gil might not have been able to find him at all, much less in time for him to have gone back for his fighting men.

He wished he hadn't thought of the man. If anything happened to Gavin, Damaris would be given to Westcott, after all. The idea pierced him with pain. The thought of Westcott pawing at her filled his mind with rage and set his blood to boiling.

For that matter, Gavin wasn't all that certain that the queen wouldn't find some way to annul their marriage and give Damaris to Westcott whether Gavin was alive or not. Not only did he have to defend Thornbeck against the Scots, he might have to pit himself against Westcott as the next order of business. He didn't welcome the prospect.

He set out to find Damaris and located her in the upper parlor, where she was sewing with her ladies. When she saw him, she smiled and came to kiss him. Her skin glowed with her happiness. "How odd it seems," he said in a low voice the others couldn't hear, "for us to be so happy at such a time."

"Did Gil leave safely?"

"Yes. I have no doubts that he will reach land soon and be on his way to find the queen."

"He should know the way quite well if we continue sending him on errands there," she said with a smile. "Soon he'll know the country between here and London as well as he knows the village."

"He's a brave lad. I've never had a better page." They had drawn closer to the women and Meg smiled at his words. He remembered Damaris telling him that Meg and Gil were kin.

"I saw a ship leaving this afternoon," Meg said. "Doesn't that mean the Scots will soon go home and leave us in peace?"

Gavin shook his head. "I'm afraid not. Most likely it means Sir William is sending for more supplies." He heard a rumble of thunder and a hard rain suddenly pattered against the stones outside the window. "I believe we may be in for a siege."

"A siege?" Lettice said with a worried glance at Kate.

"If I were Sir William, that's what I'd do. He can't batter the door down, he's tried. We shot his men before they pushed the ram close enough to the door to do any damage. They had to abandon it, and the few who have tried to retrieve it for another try have been taken down, as well. He can't tunnel through solid rock, and the castle walls are too tall to scale without great difficulty. His only hope is to starve us into surrender."

"How long can we hold out?" Damaris asked. Her voice was calm, but he knew her well enough by now to know she was frightened and refusing to show it.

He reached over and covered her hands with his. "As long as necessary. I've told Gil what to say to bring the troops and supplies we need. However, we have a great many people here to feed."

"You could get rid of the prisoners," Edith surprised him by saying. She tapped her foot restlessly on the floor. "All they do is eat and sleep. We can't turn them loose or they'll aid Sir William. I say we drown them."

Gavin kept his face expressionless. "Sir Robert and Sir Godfrey suggested more or less the same thing. I told them we won't do it."

"Why not?" Edith's pale eyes met his and he saw her fear. "They're our enemies!"

"They're also men. I'll imprison them gladly. I'll give them to the queen to do with as she pleases, but I'll not kill them in cold blood." He grinned at Damaris. "I finally see the family resemblance between you and your kinswoman. You're both rather bloodthirsty, aren't you?"

Damaris frowned at him. "I've admitted I did wrong to go to Craigmore. But had I succeeded, Sir William and his men wouldn't be here now."

"You have me there." He went to a bowl of fruit on the table and picked up an apple. "We should start rationing the food," he said as he studied the fruit. "It's better to be prudent than to wish later that we had been."

"Rationing food?" Kate's eyes grew round and fearful.

"It's just a precaution so we don't run out before the queen's men arrive." Gavin tossed her the apple. "I'm not suggesting we go hungry. Just that we not waste anything."

Kate nodded but it was clear that she was still troubled. Lettice looked no happier over the prospect.

"I'll tell the cook before we go up for the night," Damaris said. "I'll see to it he prepares only what we need at each meal."

Gavin held out his hand. "Come. Walk with me on the parapet."

Damaris was willing but the other women exchanged nervous glances. "In the rain, Sir Gavin?" Edith asked as another purr of thunder sounded in the distance. "We'll catch our deaths in such weather!"

"You and the others need not come," he said. "I want to talk to my wife alone."

They went out into the corridor and Gavin took her hand. "I wish there was some simple way of talking to you without an audience. It's not much better now that we're married. We're only alone in our bedchamber."

"Mayhap we should stay there more often," she said with a teasing smile.

"Don't tempt me."

When they reached the parapet, Damaris breathed in the moist air. In the light that spilled through the doorway, she could see black puddles on the hourds and the stones were as shiny as jet. As long as they stayed close to the door they were sheltered from the rain, and Gavin stood so that his body further protected her from the elements. She looked through the slanting rain at the men who stood stoically at their posts. They were wearing oiled hides over their clothes to protect them from the storm, but she knew they must be uncomfortable. "Edith would never make a soldier," she said. "She hates getting wet."

"It's better for a few of my men to get wet than for Sir William to use the thunder to cloak a new attack. We wouldn't hear them until they were in the castle with this storm going on." A flash of lightning and a clap of thunder emphasized his words. "My men are used to being outside in all sorts of weather."

She stepped into his embrace. "It's a good thing you came to Thornbeck so I can look after you. I can tell you haven't done such a good job of it on your own if you've made a habit of being outside on nights like this."

"I've survived." He put his arms around her and held her close. "You feel so good! I've wanted to hold you all day."

"I know. I almost came in search of you just so I could hear your voice. I love you to distraction."

"I don't want you outside in the daytime. It's safe enough here at night, on this section of the wall. Sir William's archers can't see us up here. They probably couldn't hit us anyway in this wind."

Damaris caught her skirts as they billowed out into the rain. Pale blue lightning rimmed the parapet and castle walls just before deafening thunder crashed in its wake. "I love stormy nights," she said, her voice full of excitement. "Especially when there's plenty of thunder and lightning. It's like fireworks!"

"Spoken like the pagan you are." He studied her face in the next flash of lightning.

"I wish I could be at the Maidens on such a night. Papa always forbade me. He said it would be dangerous since the hill is so high and there's no cover."

"I'm glad he kept an eye on you. Otherwise you might not have survived long enough for me to meet you."

"At times I think I'm invincible." She rested her cheek on his chest but she was looking out at the storm. "It's as if I'm part of the standing stones."

"You bear no resemblance to a stone in any way. Trust me."

She held out her hand and let rain dash against it, dappling her sleeve. "It's cold."

He took her hand and kissed the rain from it. "Do you want to go inside?"

She shook her head. "I'd rather be out here with you." She tilted up her face for his kiss.

"Your lips taste of rainwater," he said as he stroked her cheek. "We can't stay here long or you'll be soaked."

She kissed him again. "I don't care as long as I'm with you. My clothes will dry if Meg hangs them in front of a fire."

"Damaris, I've been thinking."

She pulled back to study his face. "You sound as if you're about to give me bad news."

He gently drew her back to him and kissed her forehead before placing her cheek against his chest. "If aught should happen to me, what will become of you?"

"Nothing will happen to you."

"But if it should?"

Damaris was silent. "You're thinking of Lord Westcott, aren't you?"

He nodded. "If something happens to me, you're to go to court as fast as you possibly can. My father is there and he'll protect you. As my widow, you would be allowed to remain in his household. But you'd have to give up Thornbeck."

"Give up Thornbeck? Forever, you mean?"

"The queen may be determined that Westcott have this island. I can't bear the thought that he might have you, as well."

"What of my people? If he's as bad as you say, I can't abandon them to him!"

"You would have no control over him if you stayed. Promise me, Damaris. Promise me on your love for Thornbeck."

She was silent for a long while. "I know you'd never ask me to do this lightly. Yes, Gavin. If aught should happen to you," her voice trembled on the words, "I'll find your father and beg him to give me sanctuary."

He sighed in relief. He hadn't been at all sure she would agree to this promise. "Gil can take you there."

"Lord knows he should have the way memorized by then," she said with a trace of humor.

"I've written my father and told him of our marriage. Gil carries the letter with him. I know he'll see that my father receives it."

"Aye. Gil can be trusted to do as you say."

"If the worst happens, tell Gil he's to serve either Robert or Godfrey as he would serve me. Either will be good to him and train him well. His dreams of escaping a life as a fisherman mustn't be wasted."

"Stop talking like this!" Damaris held to him tightly. "Naught will happen to you!"

"Have you been gazing into a witch's ball, my little pagan?" he asked with a laugh.

"Has Meg told you about my copper bowl?" she surprised him by asking. She sounded upset.

"What copper bowl?"

"Never mind."

He wondered what she meant, but something told him he would be happier not knowing. "We have to go inside. You're getting wet."

She didn't object so he opened the door for her. She looked distracted, as if she had something weighty on her mind.

"I'm going to walk about for a bit," he said. "I want to tell my men and the villagers about the rationing so they'll expect it tomorrow." He started to lead her in the direction of the ladies' parlor.

"I think I'll go up to our chambers first and put on dry clothes. I don't need Meg or the others to help me." She smiled at him, then turned and hurried away.

He watched her for a minute; her clothing wasn't that wet. Damaris was no good at hiding things from him, and he was curious what she was up to. But he knew she couldn't find much to harm her inside the castle, and she would never try to leave it. Even if she did, that would be impossible with his men at every door. He went in search of Robert and Godfrey.

Damaris hurried up the winding stairs that were closest to her chamber. She wanted to be alone for what she had to do.

She couldn't believe she had let something so important slip her mind.

Once she was inside her bedchamber, she fetched the copper bowl and poured water into it from the pitcher on the table. She took it to the nearest window and placed it on the windowsill. Soon the water calmed and its surface reflected only the occasional flash of lightning. Damaris stilled her thoughts and gazed intently into the water.

She looked below the surface but not so deep as the bowl itself. Instead she concentrated on the water in the middle. Suddenly her nerve failed and she looked away.

What if she saw something terrible befalling Gavin? The bowl was capable of revealing such a calamity. Her mother had apparently seen the reflection of death or she wouldn't have risked taking her newborn baby to the Priestess stone. But she had, and as a result, Damaris had survived and grown healthy. The future could be changed.

Once again she peered into the water. She saw lightning reflect off its surface, then the accompanying roar of thunder caused the water to shimmer for a moment before becoming still again.

Although the water in the bowl was only inches deep, it was as if she were looking into a pool of infinite dimension. There, deep within, pictures were starting to form. She saw Thornbeck as it looked in the winter with snow falling softly all about. With no flags flying from the parapet, she couldn't tell if it was in enemy hands or not, but no firelight glowed from its dark windows.

With a frown she tried again, this time concentrating on Gavin. A moment later, she saw him in Thornbeck's courtyard, the snow gathering on his broad shoulders. He was gazing up at the castle but she couldn't understand the haunted expression on his face.

Damaris pulled away. An uneasiness was growing inside her. She had never seen anything like this in her copper bowl before. Why would she see the castle in the winter? It would be months before the first snowfall.

She tried to tell herself that this was the news she had sought. The siege couldn't possibly last that long and she had seen Gavin in the courtyard in the snow. But why hadn't

she been with him and why had he stood there just staring
up at the castle when he could be inside in the warmth? Did
it mean they would be apart and longing to be together
then? Her copper bowl always showed her the truth, but
sometimes it was couched in such oblique symbols that she
had difficulty understanding it.

She tossed the water out the window and wiped the bowl
dry with the linen towel. Gavin would still be at Thornbeck
in the winter. Surely it had meant that. Everything would be
all right if he was here. The bowl was only confusing the issue by showing him in the dead of winter. The phrase *dead
of winter* brought a frown to her brow. Wasn't winter also
a symbol of death? She shook her head to put the thought
away. He would be here. Everything else would work out if
Gavin was here.

Nevertheless, she was glad to put the copper bowl away
and leave her room. Instead of reassuring her, the bowl had
only added another uncertainty. As she walked down the
corridor she saw the flashes of light from the windows. Few
storms of this severity had struck the island in her memory.
Had this skewed her vision? She wished there was someone
she could ask.

Gavin had gone to the villagers' wing of the castle and was
meeting with them in what had once been the servants' hall.
He could tell right away that they were more nervous and
upset than they had been since the invasion first began. "I
know the storm is a bad one, but it's nothing to fear."

Wat Hobson stood and gestured toward the window.
"We've seen signs! You haven't lived on this island as long
as we have! We know bad omens when we sees them!"

Gavin wasn't superstitious, so he said, "What signs do
you think you've seen?"

"There was a black cloud shaped like a spitting cat," an
old woman said from near the back of the room. "And I
seen the army riding before the storm!"

"What army? Sir William hasn't had time to bring in
more men." He frowned at the woman.

"She means the ghost army," Wat said. "I've seen it, too.
So have others!" Several of them nodded.

"It was only clouds," Gavin said. "Nothing else. Surely you aren't afraid of clouds!" He hoped to show them how illogical that was but no one spoke. "Tell me about this ghost army."

"It only appears when someone is about to die in the castle," Wat said. "It's been seen here for as long as the castle has stood. We've all heard about it all our lives!"

"Did you see it before Lord Fleetwood was killed?" Gavin asked reasonably.

Several shook their heads and looked at one another.

"We don't see it *every* time," Wat said as if that should be obvious. "But when we do see it, it always means death!"

Gavin picked his words carefully. "There's already been death at the castle. We lost two men on the walls today and three the day we were invaded. No doubt, if the clouds mean anything, they were foretelling that."

"How could they foretell something that's already happened?" Wat demanded. "Do ye take us for fools?"

"No, I don't. Nor do I believe in superstitions such as ghost armies. If there were such a thing, I would surely have seen it myself. I was on the parapet all day. I saw clouds and a storm building. Nothing else."

"The castle folk can't ever see it," Wat scoffed. "That's part of the legend. You've become part of them now that you've gone and married our lady."

Several of the villagers nodded and murmured among themselves.

"What else have you seen?" Gavin asked. "We have clouds shaped like a cat and an army. Anything else?"

"I seen three fish jump at once in the cook's pond," the old woman spoke up again. "That's bad luck!"

Gavin knew she was referring to the man-made pond near the kitchen where the cook held live fish until they could be cooked. "The pond is full of fish. It would be odd if three didn't take it in their minds to jump at the same time. We can't count that."

"What's the use telling you?" Wat said. "You're set in your mind not to believe us whatever we say. You ain't from here and can't know our ways."

"You're right. I don't know everything about the island. But it's my home now and I'll learn your ways in time."

Wat muttered something Gavin didn't quite catch, but from the man's expression, he felt sure it hadn't been complimentary. He told himself that villager would bear watching; men like Wat were born troublemakers. It was hard to believe he was Gil's father. "Does anyone else have aught to say?" He waited.

"What of the fishermen that weren't on hand when we came into the castle?" a woman asked from the back. "My brother was one of them."

"We've had no word. I assume they've gone to the mainland. They'll be safe there." Gavin didn't point out that if the men had returned to the village they might well have been killed. The villagers were frightened enough as it was.

"What's this about rationing the food?" Wat demanded. "Are you going to starve us so those Scots in the dungeon can keep eating?"

Gavin gave him a level look that made Wat shift uneasily. "None of us is going to starve. We're only being careful with the food. We don't know how long it may have to last. You all know we can't bring in more with the Scots camped on the green and in the village."

"But what about the prisoners?"

"What would you have me do with them?" Gavin demanded. "Turn them loose so they can join the other Scots? Kill them like wild animals? Who among you could do that?" As he had expected, no one volunteered. Killing a man wasn't easy unless one was trained to do it. This wasn't a question he would have asked his own men.

"I've sent word to the queen that we're under siege. I expect her to send an army long before we run out of food. I anticipated this attack, and I've stocked the larders and bins. We have the animals you brought from the village. We won't run out of food soon." He hoped this was true. Even though the crops had been harvested and the yield had been good, the island wasn't large enough to have provided the great supply of surplus grains and dried garden foods and meats they might need.

"Starting tomorrow, Sir Robert or I will oversee the doling out of food. We'll be fair but you're not to grumble or demand more. That will only cause us all to be at odds, and we don't need that. We all have to work together."

"We could take our chances with the Scots!" Wat shouted. "Then we'd have our own houses about us and food from our own gardens!"

Gavin closed the space between himself and the troublemaker in four long strides. He grabbed Wat by the shirt and yanked him up, his feet almost clearing the floor. "I'll not tolerate talk like that!" He glared coldly into Wat's shifting eyes. "If I hear you say that again, I'll shoot you myself! Is that understood?"

Wat nodded weakly and Gavin released him. Wat slunk away.

"Does anyone else share his opinion?" He glared about the room but no one made a sound. "Let me tell you what the Scots will do to anyone who leaves this castle. They'll kill him and leave him to rot on the green. They aren't going to allow you to return to your houses! Their army is living in them! Do any of you think they'll allow you to tend your gardens and bring in your day's catch of fish and politely buy them from you as if it were an unending market? No!"

He strode to the far wall and back. "You may think I'm a stern taskmaster, but you'd fare much worse under Sir William. Don't any of you remember what happened when he took the castle? Was there a single family that didn't have a man killed or a woman debauched? I think not! And that was after he had the castle under his power! You'd fare far worse now that we're warring with him!"

He stopped in the center of the room and glared at them all. "I know some of you must agree with Wat Hobson. That's the nature of men. But I'm telling you the truth when I say your only chance of living is to stay safe here at Thornbeck. And whether you will it or not, I'm going to keep you safe. The gates are under heavy guard so you may as well resign yourselves to seeing this through. Are there any questions?"

There were none and, after a moment, Gavin turned and strode from the room. He was glad to reach the empty corridor. Robert and Godfrey needed to hear what Wat had said. They would all have to keep an eye on him. If the man hadn't had a wife and children, Gavin would have been glad to let him escape out the water gate and take his chances, as slim as they were. Men like that could cause trouble in the best disciplined situations.

Gavin hoped the siege would end soon so he could be free of the man. The more he saw of Wat, the more he understood Gil's determination to escape the life fate had dealt him.

Chapter Fifteen

For several days Damaris and her women attendants had been moving Thornbeck's valuables to the keep. She had decided to place the jewels and the silver and gold serving pieces in the attic space between the conical roof and the ceiling. The place was small and might be overlooked if the Scots managed to take the keep.

"I see no reason to do this," Meg repeated for the seventh time. "If the Scots come this far, all is lost anyway."

"We have to do something to pass the time." Damaris handed a cask of jewels to the boy she had positioned in the small opening. "Even if all is lost, I have no intention of seeing my family's treasures stolen." To the boy she said, "You're to remember where this is but tell no one. Do you understand?"

The boy, one of Gil's brothers, nodded. His eyes were wide with apprehension.

"Don't be afraid. The Scots will never think to question you." Damaris turned to Meg to take a silver ewer from her. "What of the tapestries?"

"Lettice and Kate are seeing to their removal."

The boy took the ewer and said, "We've run out of space, my lady. There's scarce room to add another spoon."

"Come down then." She held up her arms to steady the boy. Together they closed the trapdoor and she listened closely for the invisible latch to fall into place. Nodding her head that the treasures were secured, she said, "Unless someone knows exactly where to look, they would never know a door is there."

Meg gave the boy a stern look. "Remember that you're to tell no one! Especially not your parents!"

"Aye, mistress. I remember."

Damaris ruffled the lad's hair and gently pushed him toward the door. "Off with you. I will need you no more today." When he was gone, she said, "That one reminds me more of Gil than do any of the others."

Meg's brow furrowed. "You'd do better to remember who their father is and what he is. There's nothing about the man than can be trusted."

"He's your kinsman."

"Not a bit of it! I'm kin to his wife, Bess. If she hadn't have been so free and easy in her youth, she'd been able to do far better than Wat Hobson!"

"Aye, but her children are a credit to her." Damaris looked about the round room. " 'Tis a dismal place." The wooden floor was so embedded with ancient dust that it looked soft and its edges merged into the stones of the wall, which were almost the same color.

"I had hoped never to see the inside of it again," Meg commented, looking around. "I'll have men put beds in here and on the floor below. It will be safest if you stay on this floor. It's farthest from the entrance."

"If they come that far, another floor won't matter. Besides, I have no intention of sleeping here until it's necessary."

Meg frowned at her. "You have to. Sir Gavin said you're to move here today."

"I don't want to leave him and he refuses to sleep here. He says he needs to stay closer to his men. We'll stay in my chambers. You and the other women will sleep here."

"I will not! I won't stay here while you're in the castle! What if you need me?" Meg protested.

"What if the walls are somehow breached? I can run here quickly if I don't have to see to you and the others. You know how slowly Edith moves and neither Kate nor Lettice can do anything quickly. I want you all out here so I know you're safe."

"And I want you safe, too," Meg argued.

Damaris put her hand on Meg's sleeve. "I know you worry about me, but Gavin will certainly keep me safe."

Meg looked unconvinced.

"I never knew being in love could be like this," Damaris said as she went to the arrow slit that served as a window. Below she could see the usual bustle and activity in the courtyard. Opposite the window was the parapet and she could see Gavin standing there with Robert. "He's become my world, Meg. I can't think of my life without him."

"It was the same with your mother and father. I never understood it."

"Did you never fall in love?"

"Once." Meg turned away and Damaris knew she would answer no more questions. Whomever Meg had once loved had been a mystery all Damaris's life.

Nevertheless, Damaris asked, "Who was he? You never tell me anything about him. Do I know him? Did he marry someone else?"

"He was married to another and there was no hope of him ever wanting me. I never had any hope that he might." She turned away. "He's dead now."

"That's so romantic! Why do you never talk about him? If I had loved and lost, I'd probably talk about him incessantly. How long has he been dead?"

"You ask too many questions. I had hoped you'd outgrow that." Meg went to the stairs and looked down. "I think I hear Kate and Lettice coming with the tapestries."

Deciding to drop her probing, Damaris motioned for Meg to follow, and she led the way to the floor below, where they ran headlong into Kate and Lettice and the men who were carrying the tapestries for them. Because of its round shape, the keep usually had a breeze from some quarter, but the window slits were too narrow for the rooms to be terribly drafty. The tapestries had been brought here because they were valuable. Damaris showed the men where to hang them, and against the drab stone walls they shone like brilliant jewels.

"Hang the others in the upper room," Damaris instructed the men. "We'll also need beds in here. Bring as many as the rooms will accommodate."

With her eyes large and her face full of concern, Kate asked, "Will the Scots breach the walls? Have they devised a way of battering down the gate?"

Damaris gave her an encouraging smile. "No. This is only a safety measure." At times Damaris forgot how young Kate and Lettice were. "There's no need to be frightened. Sir Gavin and his men will keep us quite safe."

"Then why must we come to this awful place?" Lettice asked as she looked around. "I've always heard the keep is haunted and I don't want to sleep here."

"None of us does. And there's no such thing as ghosts," Damaris added. She had heard the same rumors. The keep reminded her unpleasantly of Craigmore Castle. "Come on. Let's finish hanging the tapestries, and it will be more cheerful."

The Hobson boy suddenly ran back into the room. "My lady, there's trouble!" His eyes were round and he was out of breath from running.

"What is it?" she asked even as she lifted her long skirts to run after him down the twisting stairs.

"Ma said I was to come and get you. It's Pa and the others. There's trouble in the making!"

Damaris found Wat and two of his cronies in the servants' hall that had been set aside to be used by the villagers while they were in the castle. When she entered, the loud talking suddenly stopped. "What's going on here?" she demanded. She saw Bess and some of the women move farther away.

Wat pointed his finger at a scowling young man. "He was making up to Davie's Mary!"

Damaris glanced at the man and over at the woman in question. She was considerably younger than Davie Cochran and one of the prettiest women in the village, but she was no flirt. "Well, Marcus? What do you have to say for yourself?"

The young man glared at Davie and Wat, then looked at the ground. "I didn't mean aught by it. I was just passing the time of day."

Damaris glanced at Mary. "Is this true?"

Mary nodded, keeping her eyes downcast.

"We didn't have none of this when we was in our own homes," Wat snarled. "Marcus wouldn't have dared to make eyes at a man's wife if she was at home where she was supposed to be!"

"It sounds to me as if it was all a misunderstanding." Damaris moved among them, soothing them with her presence and her voice. "Marcus, in the future, stay away from Mary Cochran. Wat, I don't see why you're involved in this."

"Davie's my friend! We sticks together!"

"Marcus isn't a bad sort. While we're all in the castle, people are bound to pass the time of day. It's to be expected."

"Not by me, it ain't!" Wat didn't dare speak too roughly to Damaris, but he glared at those around him. "Ben was with us. He can tell you Marcus was smiling and bobbing around like a toy on a stick. I call that making eyes."

"I wasn't doing no such thing!" Marcus shouted, and took a step closer to Wat.

Damaris put her hand on Marcus's arm. Marcus came from a family that was notorious for its quick tempers, even if he wasn't a born troublemaker like Wat. "No harm has been done. Let's forget the unpleasantness and try to get along."

"How much longer will we be caged in here?" Wat asked. "My fishing nets are rotting in the sun and my boat needs caulking. I can't afford to stay here forever!"

"You haven't any choice. It's safe within the castle walls and it's too dangerous for you to go back to the village. Surely fishing nets and a boat aren't worth risking your life." She tried to coddle him into agreement with a warm smile.

Wat frowned at Bess, who moved farther away. "My woman don't half watch the young'ns here. They're running wild and she's getting lazy from not having enough to do. It's ruining my family."

Damaris looked at Bess. The woman was young but she looked much older than her years. Her faded gown was swelling from another pregnancy, and she seemed too tired to do much of anything. "I'll have a talk with her."

Wat hadn't expected this. He frowned at Bess, then at his friends. "I can straighten her out myself." He gave a firm nod to Ben and Davie. "It's my place to keep her in line."

Damaris ignored him. She went to Bess and said quietly, "I'd like for you to come with me."

Bess darted a frightened glance at Wat, but she followed Damaris out of the hall as instructed. Two of her younger children clung to her skirts and peered fearfully up at Damaris.

When they were away from the others, Damaris said, "Bess, would you like to stay here in the castle? After the others return to the village, I mean?"

"How can I, my lady? I'm a married woman and Wat would never agree to stay." She automatically smoothed the hair of her youngest child.

Damaris was glad to see neither of the children were old enough to repeat this conversation to their father. "I wasn't suggesting that Wat stay here. I know he mistreats you and I'm offering you sanctuary."

Bess stared at her. "I could leave him, you mean?"

"You'd still be married. I can't do anything about that. But I can find work for you here. You and your children who are old enough could learn to weave or spin. The boys could be apprenticed to tradesmen here."

Tears filled Bess's eyes. "You'd do that for them? You'd see to my bairns?"

"Then you'd like to stay?"

Bess nodded vigorously. "I'd give anything to get away from him," she whispered as if she might be overheard. "He's too hard on the bairns. It's not in a little child to be quiet all the time or to work as hard as he expects the older ones to do."

"Don't mention this to him. When it's time to leave, I'll tell him you and the children are to remain here."

Bess took her hand and kissed it fervently. "Bless you, my lady! I'll tell St. Cuthbert what you've done for me!"

"Thank you. You'd better go back now or he'll be angry with you. Tell him whatever you please to keep him from being rough with you."

Bess gave Damaris one of her rare, shy smiles and picked up the youngest child. The other trotted along beside her as she went back to the hall.

Damaris hoped she had done the right thing. Her father had never interfered with the villagers' lives unless he thought someone was in danger, but Damaris had always liked Bess and her children and she couldn't stand by and see Bess and the little ones mistreated when something could be done about it. She knew Gavin would agree with her intervention.

Damaris listened in the direction of the hall and judged by the silence that the unpleasantness had died down for now. She was concerned, however, about Wat's insistence on being allowed to leave the castle. It was impossible, of course. For him to do so would endanger them all. But talk such as that could cause problems.

There was already trouble. The larders were emptying at an alarming rate; they were already down to eating the salted fish and dried peas. Two days ago Gavin had told the cook to make the rations even smaller, and there had been loud complaints, led for the most part by Wat. If Damaris had had a choice, she would have sent Wat to the Scots in short order.

She went back to continue supervising the move into the keep.

Gavin walked the parapets with Robert. Below, well out of range of the castle's arrows, the Scots were roasting a beef—upwind of the castle. As the smell of the cooking meat drifted over the walls, Gavin's stomach growled in protest.

"They know how to torment us," Robert said. "Do you suppose they realize how little food we have left?"

"They couldn't possibly know that. Maybe I made a mistake in not killing the prisoners."

Robert thought about it while they walked. "We could still release them. Let Sir William feed them for a while."

"And give him more men to send against us?" Gavin leaned on a merlon and gazed down at the cook fire.

"If this many can't get in, a few more won't make any difference. And if they're gone, we don't have to feed them."

"We barely feed them as it is. I cut their rations before I did everyone else's."

"I assumed that. They may be too weak to fight."

Gavin nodded. "Perhaps. And they've been inactive for months. They will have weakened."

"We could drop them over the wall and not have to open the gate."

Gavin gauged the height. The walls were tall but the green below was grassy. "As soon as night falls we'll do it. A few broken bones will be to our advantage. Who knows? Once Sir William has his men back, he may decide to leave us alone."

"And pigs may sprout wings," Robert said wryly.

Gavin grinned and slapped his comrade's arm. "Look on the bright side. It could happen. Especially if they take back a story of the revelry in Thornbeck."

"What revelry?"

"The one we're going to create tonight."

As soon as dark fell, Gavin gathered his men in the hall. The musicians were told to play as loudly as possible, and the tables were pushed back to allow room for dancing. Damaris gave orders that candles, not rushes, were to be lit in the hall and in the corridors between the dungeon and the main doors. Everything the prisoners were to see had to look as if Thornbeck had enough food and fuel to last indefinitely.

When the music was playing and the couples were dancing, Gavin and Robert took a band of men down to the dungeons. They unlocked the heavy gates and the prisoners slowly emerged.

They were in good condition considering they had languished in a dungeon for so long. Their beards were long and they smelled, but none were starving or dying. One said to Robert, "So you've decided to murder us, then? We all thought it would come to this." He curled his lip in a sneer of pure hatred.

Robert smiled back. "You underestimate us. We've come to release you."

The men looked at each other in amazement. None of them believed him. "What do ye take us for? Idiots?" the first man asked.

Gavin gestured and his men shoved the prisoners up the slick steps that led into the castle proper. Long before they reached the screens passage, the music and laughter were clearly audible. They were putting on a good charade. Only if one knew to listen for it, did the laughter sound forced and a bit too frantic.

The prisoners glanced from side to side as they were marched down the passage, taking note that the way was lit by candles, not only mounted in the wall sconces but in the coronas suspended from the ceiling, as well. As they passed the entrance to the hall, they could see couples in fine clothes, dancing a pavane and laughing. Godfrey came to the doorway and lounged there eating an apple.

Gavin didn't give the prisoners time to notice any more, but drove them out into the courtyard. They gulped in deep breaths of fresh air as they went toward the gate.

"Up the steps," Gavin said as they waited for him to open the gates.

"What? Up there?" The man who seemed to be their leader narrowed his eyes. "You're going to push us off the walls?" His men murmured in sudden fear.

"It's not such a long drop and there's grass below. Surely you didn't take us to be such fools as to open the gates with a Scots army on the other side." Gavin smiled but his eyes held no mirth. "Up the steps or die in the courtyard. It's up to you."

The prisoners trudged up the stairs, bracing their steps against the rough stone wall. At the top, the smell of cooking meat reached them, and Gavin felt their restlessness. If it wasn't for the chains the men still wore, they would attack regardless of their weakened state.

Without bothering to release the chains on their wrists, Gavin gestured toward the wall. "Over the side. Your dinner is waiting for you."

After a pause, they rushed at the wall and threw themselves over. Gavin heard their cries as they fell in the darkness and the soft thuds as they landed. When the last one was gone he stood beside Robert. They watched the former prisoners run toward the cook fires, some dragging the men who had been lamed in the fall.

Gavin grinned at Robert. "Let's hope they cooked plenty."

"We put on a good show for them."

The Scots around the cook fire jumped up in alarm as the first of the prisoners ran into the circle of firelight. Several raised swords and struck at the men before they recognized them.

"I never thought of letting the Scots kill their own." Gavin leaned on the crenel to watch. "That should do something to their blasted morale!"

Quickly, though, the Scots realized who the newcomers were and hurried to help them into the firelight. Soon came the distant sound of iron striking iron as they freed the prisoners from their chains.

"I hope we did the right thing in releasing them," Gavin said.

"We've bought ourselves more meals. We can hold out longer now."

Gavin glanced back toward the sea that separated them from England. "I hope Gil has reached the queen by now. We can't hold out much longer. In two days we'll have to start butchering the village animals. The horses will go next."

Robert nodded. "We'll make it."

Gavin looked at his friend through the darkness. "Robin, I have a boon to ask of you."

"Of course. Whatever it is, I'll grant it."

"If aught should happen to me, see to Damaris."

"Nothing will happen to you." Robert shifted uncomfortably. It was the worst kind of luck to speak of one's own death at a time like this.

"I know. But if something should. I've written my father about her. Take her to him. He will look after her as if she were his own daughter, for love of me. If, however, anything has happened to him, as well, will you take care of her?''

Robert stared at him. "Why do you ask this of me? Have you had a dream?" It was well-known that some men saw their own deaths in dreams and that the dreams were sometimes prophetic.

"No. I've not become a soothsayer." Gavin looked back at the fires. "It's only that I love her so dearly. The queen has chosen a husband for her and if I'm not here, she will be given to him." He glanced at Robert. "It's Neville Lord Westcott."

Robert's gasp was spontaneous. "Not Lord Westcott! Why would the queen do such a thing?"

"She can't know him as we do. She would only see him as a strong protector of Thornbeck. That's why I have to be certain that Damaris will be safe."

"Aye. I'll see to her if need be. And if your father can't take her, I'll marry her myself!"

"I don't ask you to go that far. Just be sure she's safe."

"You can count on me."

"Good. I knew I could." Gavin went down the stairs and back into the castle through the main doors. He didn't want to think of Damaris married to anyone but himself, but if he were dead, Robert would be a good choice.

He stopped in the doorway to the hall for a minute to watch the dancing. Across the room, Damaris was whirling about in the cushion dance with Godfrey. With her height and grace, she stood out from the crowd. She was laughing merrily, as if she were totally unaware of the enemy at their gate. Only a discerning eye could detect that the other ladies present were not Damaris's peers, but rather her ladies-in-waiting and some of the household staff wearing borrowed clothing. Above his head, the musicians played skillfully.

At the end of the dance, Gavin claimed Damaris and drew her onto the floor. "We've never danced together," he said as the music began.

"I didn't know if you danced or not. There's so much we don't know about each other."

He led her in the measured pace, reversed and led her back. "I was taught to dance just as my brothers and sisters were. I may be a younger son, but my father is still a baron."

"You do it very well," Damaris said with a smile, her steps carrying her away from beneath the coronas where candle wax occasionally dripped onto the floor. "And you're by far the most handsome man here."

He smiled. "You make me wish more than ever that we were at peace and that I could dance with you on a regular basis."

"We will when this is over. Are the prisoners gone?"

"Over the wall, every one. By now they're consuming the Scots' dinner."

"Good. Let their army be hungry for a while."

Gavin looked at her. She had lost weight but she never complained. He had a suspicion that she wasn't eating all she was rationed, but instead was giving it to some of the children in the castle. Her pale skin was almost translucent, and on close examination, he noticed dark circles under her eyes. He silently cursed the Scots for putting her through this.

"When it's over, I'm going to take you to court. Assuming, of course, the queen will allow me back in. I want you to meet my family. My father will adore you."

"Papa spoke of him often. Especially after I turned down your hand. I think he was trying to make me feel badly about my decision."

"Good for him."

Damaris smiled at him as they made another reverse. Her raised hand found his as naturally as if they had danced together all their lives. "I've done something that may cause a bit of trouble."

"You? I don't believe it." His words were wry. "What have you done now?"

"I've given Bess Hobson permission to stay in the castle with her children so she can be free of that lout of a husband."

"Good. I'd have done the same. Gil will be glad to hear it."

Damaris glanced at him. "See why I love you? You're the most perfect and gentle of men."

He laughed. "Tell that to the prisoners I just tossed over the wall."

"Were many injured?"

"Not enough. The first ones broke the fall of the others. They'll live to fight again, I'm sorry to say."

"Did they believe our charade, do you think?"

"I'm sure they did. You can hear the music clearly on the wall. That's why I haven't asked the musicians to stop. In fact, I think it would be a good idea for them to play every night. Let the Scots think we're having a round of parties while they sleep on the cold ground and in the village huts."

"How devious you are. I like that."

Gavin laughed as he spun her around and fell into step with her again.

A few evenings later, feeling too confined and needing some air, Damaris stepped out into the courtyard and filled her lungs with a deep breath of sea air and licked her lips to taste the salt. Overhead, the clouds ran before the wind and she wondered if yet another of the late summer storms was building. Morale in the castle was low and there was less food now than ever. Most of the animals from the village had been slaughtered, as well as the dairy cattle and sheep from the castle stock.

As she paced, she suddenly became dizzy and stumbled but caught herself on a wall close by. She hadn't been eating as much as Gavin assumed, and it was beginning to tell on her, but she couldn't bear to see the children cry from hunger. She had lost weight and was certain this was the cause of her periodic dizziness.

Gavin saw her and came to her. He put his arms around her to steady her. "You're safe for now, love. If I could get to Sir William, I'd send his black soul to hell!"

A tear coursed down her cheek as she nodded against his chest. She knew Gavin was doing all that he could. Whether it would be enough remained to be seen. As she clung to him, the sound of several children crying in the courtyard below came to her and she lifted her head. "I have to go to them." She pushed the tears from her cheeks and tried to smile up at him. She failed. "Damn Sir William and his men! May they rot in hell!"

Gavin watched her go to the children and gather the youngest girl into her arms. The others she gave hugs and smiles, lovingly touching each one and calming them. The little girl hugged Damaris as if she knew she was safe in her arms. He had never seen anyone so loyal to her people, and it was easy to see that they all loved her, as well.

Across the courtyard Wat and his two friends stood apart from the rest. Judging by their scowls, Gavin knew they were likely blaming him for their confinement in the castle. He was watching them closely these days and had considered fastening them in the now-empty dungeon to keep them from spreading sedition among the others. Damaris was against it, but Gavin would override her if necessary. He had to do all he could to protect her, his men and the castle. Even if it caused ill will among the villagers.

Chapter Sixteen

Damaris curled into Gavin's embrace and glided her hand over the bare flesh of his powerful chest and lean waist. Pale morning light was pearling the room beyond the bed curtains. Soon they would have to get up and face another day of siege.

He stroked her hair and turned his head so their eyes could meet. "I wish I could take you away from this."

"I wish we were both free of it and that my uncle was back in Scotland where he belongs." She hadn't even set her foot on the floor, yet she already felt tired. Was he this exhausted, also? She couldn't be sure just by looking at him. He always seemed so strong and confident. Except this morning.

"What are you thinking?" she asked.

"I'm wondering why the queen's men haven't arrived. Gil has had ample time to find the queen, raise an army and come back here. For that matter, Lord Westcott has also had time to arrive. Where are they?"

"I have no idea. Surely the reinforcements will arrive soon."

He stared sightlessly at the cloth medallion overhead where the bed curtains met. "Of course they will." He didn't sound as positive as he had before.

"You don't think they're coming, do you?" Dread began to grow in her middle.

"They'll come, all right. But I'm wondering if the queen is taking her time on purpose. Maybe she intends to let us suffer before rescuing us."

"Would she do that?" Damaris leaned up on her elbow to look at him.

"I don't know. She's a confusing woman, our queen. Her mind and heart are that of a man in many ways. Like her father, she has quick passions and a temper to match. I've known her to be quite vindictive. If I've angered her too greatly by marrying you without her permission, she might not be as careful of our safety."

"But this island is important to the crown!"

"Yes. And for that reason, she'll come eventually. But she may let Sir William break us before she arrives."

"That makes no sense. By then Sir William will be ensconced in Thornbeck and they'll have to rout him out."

"She'll know that our reserves of food are gone if we have to surrender. All she would have to do is lay a siege of her own. It would by necessity be over soon."

Damaris sat up and hugged her knees against her chest, taking no particular care to cover her naked body. She rested her chin on her knees as she said, "I hadn't thought of that."

Gavin brushed her hair aside and stroked the smooth skin of her back. "I didn't want to worry you. I probably shouldn't have told you at all."

She looked back at him. "Why did you?"

"Because you're my wife and I don't like to keep things from you. Not when they pertain to your own welfare."

"What can we do?"

"I've given it a lot of thought. Gil was able to slip out. It's possible that we could send another boat out the same way. One, maybe two, could row from the island unseen."

"At that rate, it would take months to get everyone out of Thornbeck!"

"It would take only one trip to transport you to safety."

Damaris stared at him in disbelief that he'd suggest such a thing. "I'll never leave without you."

"I may not give you a choice."

"No, Gavin! I refuse!"

He pulled her back into his embrace. "Don't fret so. I won't send you away until I know there's no hope. But I also won't stand by and see you starve to death." He held her tenderly and rubbed his cheek against her hair. "I couldn't bear that. Nor can I surrender, knowing you're here in the castle. Sir William would have no leniency toward you this time."

"I know."

In a voice so low Damaris could barely hear him, he said, "I heard a story once when I was a page to the knight who trained me. A castle was laid siege and the master of the castle had his wife murdered before he allowed the enemy to overtake his castle."

"How terrible!"

"He didn't, however, have time to kill his daughters. Later he was said to have wished with all his heart that he had preserved them from their fate as he had his wife."

Damaris felt vaguely sick. It was a sensation she experienced often these days. She held tightly to Gavin.

"I could never harm you. I'd die myself before I'd let anything ill befall you. Your only safety may lie in escape. It would mean leaving me and the other men behind, but I think your ladies could slip away with you. Once you were on the mainland, you could go straight to my father and he'd protect you."

"I won't leave you."

He smiled at her. "Not even to keep your women safe?"

She frowned. "You already know just how to maneuver me about so I will agree, don't you? Well, this time you're wrong. I won't leave you even for the safety of my women. They can be taken to the mainland without me."

"You're a stubborn woman." His eyes and voice were gentle with his love for her.

"I love you. If I can't be with you, I don't want to go to safety."

"And if I give you no choice?"

"I'll somehow raise my own army and return with them. And then I won't have Thornbeck's stone walls to protect me." She lay her cheek on his chest. "If boats can be taken out, why can't we send men for supplies the same way?"

"I've thought of that. We might be able to make one trip without being caught, but not two. The Scots are watching us too closely for just such a move. If a boat or two were to leave the water gate, they could probably outrace the Scots to the mainland, but they wouldn't be able to come back. I'm still amazed we were able to get Gil past them."

Her nausea was passing, and as she caressed the firm wall of his chest, she said, "I never want to be away from you. Especially not when you're in danger."

"Not even if I tell you it weakens a man to have to worry about someone other than himself in a battle?"

"You'd worry about me if I were here or away."

He sighed. "Already you know me too well."

"I had a dream last night. We were free and had gone to the Maidens. We made love among the buttercups and clover."

"Let's hope the dream was prophetic. They'll only bloom a little while longer. Thornbeck can't last until they come back again next May."

"It may be just as well. If you hold a buttercup too long, your skin feels burned. I'm not sure I want to lie naked in them."

"Ever the romantic," he said with a laugh. "I'll remember not to lay you down in the buttercups."

Damaris heard the door open and sighed. "That will be Meg and the others."

The other door opened, as well. "And that will be George," Gavin said, "come to see if I'm going to stay in bed all day." He looked at her longingly. "I'd rather be here with you than walking the parapets with Robert."

"Tonight." She kissed him lightly. "We'll be together again tonight."

The curtains parted and Gavin's valet entered, his eyes modestly averted. "I've brought your clothing, Sir Gavin. Will you arise now?"

"Yes." Gavin swung his legs over the side of the bed and sat up.

Damaris wrapped her night rail about her and left the bed from her side. Gavin would dress inside the bed curtains. She would dress in the room with the curtains shielding her nakedness from George.

"You've become a lazy one," Meg chided good-naturedly as she poured water into the washbasin for Damaris. "You used to be up before any of us."

"I don't have as much energy these days." Damaris ran the damp cloth over her body. With so many people relying on the well, she was forgoing being immersed in her bathtub. She missed soaking in the steaming water and told herself that that was the first thing she would do as soon as times returned to normal.

When she was clean, she dried herself with a linen cloth and pulled on the chemise that Meg had brought her. Kate helped her on with her kirtle, and as they laced her into it, Meg said, "You've lost more weight. This one used to fit snugly."

"We've all lost weight. I'll gain it back." Damaris never let her ladies see how worried she was. Meg knew the true state of the castle's larder but Edith and the younger ones didn't. It would only worry them.

"I've never liked to see a woman too thin," Edith commented while she chose a headpiece to go with Damaris's gown and kirtle. "My father always said it was unlucky."

"Your father said everything was unlucky," Meg chided. "I never heard of such a thing."

"Well, it only makes sense, doesn't it? A well-rounded woman has plenty to eat and is well cared for."

"It could also mean she's with child. A round belly doesn't mean luck."

Damaris was only half listening to them. As Lettice started pulling bits of her chemise sleeve through the slashings in her kirtle sleeve, she ran her other hand over her middle. Could she be with child? That would explain her queasy stomach and the dizziness that came and went.

The thought was elating and frightening, all at once. She wanted to bear Gavin's children but not during a siege when neither of them might survive. And in the back of her mind was the row of tiny graves in the chapel. Would she prove to be better at bearing healthy children than her mother had been?

"Damaris?" Meg said. "Do you not hear me?"

"What? I'm sorry. I wasn't listening."

"Do you prefer the green gown or the gold one?"

"I want neither. The day is going to be warm. I'll wear only my kirtle." Her thoughts went back to the new idea that she might be carrying Gavin's child. They had certainly made love often enough; they held each other every night, frequently more than once.

"Are you well?" Meg asked suspiciously.

"What? Yes. I'm fine. Come. We'll go to breakfast." She looked at Gavin, who was emerging from the curtains fully clad with George at his heels. She let Edith put her French hood in place and arrange the bongrace over the nape of her neck, then she put her hand in his.

She didn't want to tell him yet. He had enough to worry about as it was, and she wanted to wait until she was positive of her condition.

Gavin kissed her goodbye, and after he had left to see to his duties, she and her ladies went downstairs to eat their meager portions of bread and cheese. None of them spoke while they ate. Worry and hunger made for poor table talk and nothing else was in anyone's mind these days.

Damaris wondered if Gavin was eating breakfast. If she was voluntarily cutting her own portions, it seemed likely he was doing the same, and she never saw him at the table in the mornings. He claimed to eat after talking to the men who had been on duty all night, but she suspected he was only telling her this to keep her from worrying more than she was. He, too, was growing thinner by the day.

Damaris saved a wedge of her cheese and a portion of her bread and gave them to a little girl she found playing in the screens passage, then went to the outside door and looked out. In a few minutes her ladies joined her. The courtyard was filled with people as usual, but they seemed to move more listlessly these days.

She could hear the arrow smith at work in his shed, which was one of those built into the outer wall, and from the carpenter's workshop beside it came sounds of lumber being sawed. The latter was sad to hear, for she knew it meant he was at work building coffins. There had already been several deaths among the elderly. Their burials would have to wait until they could be taken to the churchyard in the village. In the meanwhile, they were being kept in sealed coffins in the cool vaults below Thornbeck.

Shouting from beyond the walls drew the attention of all those in the courtyard, and the people slowed their work to listen. Damaris recognized her uncle's voice. "Hallo, Thornbeck! I, Sir William Fleetwood, swear to reward anyone who will open the gates to me!"

Damaris glanced at her women. "Stay here."

She hurried across the courtyard and up the steep steps to the parapet. At the center of the green, barely out of reach of the castle's arrows, William stood with his second-in-command and several other men. They were eating meat as they stared at the castle. Damaris could smell the cooking food and knew her hungry people could, as well. Silently she cursed him, wishing she could do more.

William saw her and she lifted her chin under his stare. Again he shouted, "I have plenty to eat out here! And fresh water to spare! It can be yours for coming to get it!"

Gavin came to stand beside Damaris. "He's good at this."

"He's a devil!"

"Aye. That's what I mean."

"All you have to do is open the gate and come out!" William shouted again. He grinned as he bit into the fistful of meat, and Damaris was sure he was staring at her while he chewed.

She looked down at the courtyard. To Gavin she said, "No one will be fool enough to listen to him."

"I hope not. I don't want to have to watch for attackers inside the walls as well as outside."

"My people are loyal."

"Our people are hungry." His voice was sad. "I don't know how much longer we can hold out. The well water is sinking. Godfrey said he heard about it this morning."

"Our water? Thornbeck has never had a problem with its well."

"Too many people are using its limited supply. We're taking more water than nature can put back in a day's time." He looked at the clouds on the horizon. "I've told Godfrey to have oiled tarpaulins put on the roofs to catch rainwater. As much as it rains here, we may have enough if we're careful."

Damaris put her arms around him, regardless of who could see them. "We'll get through this. We just have to have faith and not give up."

Gavin held her briefly, then stepped back. "Talk to them, Damaris. Walk among the people and let them see you're not afraid. Tell them whatever you must to keep them loyal."

She nodded. Gavin was right. The people must continue believing in them. She went down the steps and moved among the villagers and castle folk. "Sir William speaks lies! How could he think we're so addlepated as to believe such tales? The only reward he would give us is death!"

The people watched her and some of them nodded. Damaris smiled as if she were perfectly calm and confident. "Can you imagine that he thinks we would be so foolish as to open the gates to him?" She saw Wat and Ben standing at the edge of the courtyard. As usual, Wat was scowling. Ben looked uncertain. She went to them. "Ben, you're a man of enough years to know a lie when you hear one. Have you ever heard anything so ridiculous as Sir William thinking we would believe such a promise?"

As she hoped, Ben shook his head. "Never, my lady. The man is blathering."

Wat didn't answer.

Damaris gave him a long look. "Besides, our guards have been given orders to shoot anyone who tries to open the gate, from inside or out, because of the threat to all the rest who are safe as long as the gate stays closed."

Wat glared at her but still held his tongue.

Damaris moved away, continuing her dialogue with her people, calling them by name, getting them to agree with her that Sir William must take them to be fools. In her mind, however, she was still worrying about Wat. He was a troublemaker. She wished he had been sent over the walls with the prisoners, and felt sure Gavin would be willing to do it now, were it not for the unrest it might cause among the other villagers. She doubted that but a few of them could see how potentially dangerous Wat was.

All day the message was shouted over the walls. Rewards were promised to anyone who would open the gates. Riches were promised, so was food. Of the two, food was the most tempting. Damaris knew that hungry people were less loyal than well-fed ones, but she had no way to remedy their situation. The cook's pond had long been emptied and most of the villagers' stock had been eaten. In two or three days, they would have to start slaughtering the horses.

Meanwhile, Wat was doing his own campaigning. He believed William for the simple reason that he could smell the food cooking and knew that there was no impediment in the Scots bringing food to the island. "For that matter, the sea is full of food," he told Davie and Ben and whoever else would listen. "We wouldn't go hungry if we could get to our boats."

"Do you think they left the boats unharmed? They could have sunk them," Davie said.

"Why would they do that? We're just honest fishermen. Their enemies are the castle men." Wat leaned closer. "I sneaked up onto the wall this morning and saw the village. It's not been harmed, by the looks of it."

"Our lady said our houses would likely be safe," Davie pointed out. "The Scots are using them, but they've no cause to pull them down."

"Could you see mine?" Ben asked.

"I couldn't tell for sure. My eyes aren't that good over a distance," Wat said. "We'll all have to bend our backs to the oars when we're out of this prison! I was barely able to feed my family as it was. And I don't even have my oldest boy to help me," he added with a scowl.

Davie frowned in concern. "Mary can't bring a baby into the world without a roof over its head. She needs to be in her own house at a time like this."

"Will you leave off going on about your Mary?" Wat frowned at the man. "She's not the first lass to be having a bairn! You'll soon see enough of them not to care so much about a new one to feed."

Davie tried to look as if he agreed. Ben averted his eyes.

Wat spat on the ground. "I want out of here. If I were to open the gate, would you go out with me?"

Davie and Ben exchanged a look. "I don't know," Davie said. Ben made no commitment.

"You're weak as women, the both of you! Think on it! I don't want to risk Sir Gavin's arrows only to find no one will back me."

"I have to think about it," Ben said. "You're asking us to take a great risk. You know Sir Gavin's men will shoot anyone who goes near the gate. Our lady told us so."

"Aye! He's as much our enemy as the Scots are said to be. Why should we abide by him when we would be fed, at least, if we change over?"

"I don't know," Davie repeated.

Wat grunted in disgust and spat again. "Let me know when you decide if you're men or not." He stalked away.

That night Gavin was glad to return to the chamber he shared with Damaris. His valet helped him out of his clothes inside the bed curtains and he could hear the women doing the same for Damaris in the room.

George held a bowl of water as Gavin washed the dirt from his body. The day's rain hadn't materialized after all and he felt grimy and dusty. When he was finished, he dried himself and gave the towel to George.

"Will there be anything else, Sir Gavin?"

"No, George. Thank you."

George left, keeping his eyes averted from the side of the room where Damaris was being helped into her night rail. The large bed with its drawn curtains gave her privacy from George's eyes, but the valet was well trained at being circumspect, none the less.

Gavin drew the curtains behind him and climbed into bed. In a few minutes, the curtains parted on the other side and Damaris stepped in. As usual, she was wearing a nightdress that was buttoned to her neck and reached to her ankles and wrists. However, before she climbed into bed, she unbuttoned it and stepped free of the garment.

"Meg and Edith would be scandalized if they knew how we really slept," she said as she snuggled close to him.

"I like there not being anything between our bodies." He ran his hand over her satiny skin. Even though she was slimmer than ever, she was still curvaceous and soft. Her breasts mounded against his side and her head was pillowed on his arm.

Gavin raised up on one elbow for a better look at her. She didn't braid her hair before coming to bed and it lay like a silk curtain about her, waving over the white sheet and about her pale skin. He stroked it, trailing one curling tendril over her breast. "Never has a man had such a wife."

She smiled up at him and he was almost lost in her gaze. "When you look at me like that, it's as if time no longer has meaning. I feel we could remain here like this forever."

"We would certainly make more interesting ghosts than the usual lot," she said teasingly. "I don't believe I've ever heard of a haunt doing what we're about to do."

He laughed. "Damaris, you enchant me."

Her smile softened. "I love you. All day, every day, I find myself counting the hours until we can come back to this chamber and be alone at last. If only the Scots would leave us in peace! I would take you deep into the woods and behave shamelessly."

"An enticing prospect," he said with a lifted eyebrow. "Especially since I know you mean the words."

"I've never been shameless before. I enjoy it."

He bent and kissed her, tasting the warm sweetness of her mouth. She responded by putting her arms around him and returning his kiss with growing ardor. His heart was beating faster as he pulled back to look at her again. As his hand covered her breast, he said, "I love you, Damaris."

"I know," she whispered. "I can feel it. Sometimes it's as if our minds have become one. Especially when we're like this. Haven't you noticed this?"

He nodded. "It's not like anything I've ever known before."

She smiled and lifted her head to meet his lips. Gavin had never known anyone who kissed as sensuously as Damaris. She made an art of lovemaking. Beneath his fingers her nipple grew taut and eager. Gavin lowered his head and took the succulent morsel into his mouth. Damaris sighed in ecstasy and arched her back to offer herself more fully to him.

He ran his hand over the smooth curve of her sides and hips, slipping his palm under her buttocks so he could lift her to his body. Damaris murmured in pleasure and opened her legs in invitation. Gavin was in no hurry for the completion of their lovemaking. He enjoyed giving her pleasure too much to be eager for its end.

He took his time with her, enjoying the tastes and textures of her body and hearing her sighs and murmurs of delight. He was already trembling from his effort not to plunge into her, but he was enjoying their love play as much as she was.

When her hand found him, he sucked in his breath. He was barely able to contain himself. Damaris was a quick learner and she knew exactly how to give him the same degree of pleasure that he lavished on her. "You drive me mad," he whispered in her ear as the manipulation of her fingers sent fire through his body.

"I had an excellent teacher," she replied. "Do you like this? How about this?" Her fingers shifted and created new paths of fire.

"Would you have it be over so soon?" he teased, his fingers gliding across her belly and lower to give her the same delicious torment she was delivering to him.

"No. I'd have this last forever."

With the gentlest of caresses, Gavin touched the secret bud hidden in the moist recesses of her femininity and Damaris cried out softly. With masterful strokes of his fingers, he brought her to the brink of completion, then joined his body with hers. As he did, she cried out again and held tightly to him. He could feel the hot rhythm within her that meant she had reached her first burst of ecstasy.

She rolled her head from side to side on the pillow, enjoying every second of the keen pleasure. Then she began to move beneath him.

"You're a greedy little wench," he said with a laugh as he rolled onto his back, carrying her with him.

"Yes. I'm hungry for you." Her violet eyes gazed into his and her dark fire hair tumbled about them. Not taking her eyes from his, she raised herself to a sitting position astride him and began a rocking motion, moving her body in a way that gave them both the utmost pleasure.

Gavin covered both her breasts with his hands, reveling in their warmth and fullness and the way her nipples were like pearls against his palms. Gently rolling her nipples between his fingertips and thumbs, he beaded them to greater firmness, then raised his head to capture first one, then the other between his lips. Damaris moaned with greater abandon and let her head roll back in her desire.

He ran one hand over her hips and felt the steady rhythm that was bringing them both to culmination. With a great effort of will he held back, determined to give her another pleasure before she had him. He slipped his fingers between them and almost at once Damaris cried out in release.

Gavin tumbled her over onto her side. Her slender leg curved over his hip, holding him inside her as she moved with him again. Her breath was coming fast and a fine sweat slicked her skin, making it slippery beneath his fingers. Gavin pulled her against him and let his body have free rein.

Together they moved in perfect unison, each gauging the pleasure of the other. This time when she arched against him and the hot pulsations told him she was satisfied, he let himself go, as well. He held to her as the torrid sensations burst within him. She laced her fingers in his hair and held him close as if she could never bear to release him.

For long moments they remained that way, each lost in their mutual satisfaction and love. Gavin finally rolled to his back and pillowed her head on his shoulder. Slowly their breathing steadied and slowed. He was reluctant to release the golden feeling of their lovemaking. Reality was too harsh these days.

He opened his eyes and watched her. Her lips were parted in a smile and her dark eyelashes made a lacy pattern on her pale skin. Her glorious hair was tumbled over the pillow and obscured one shoulder. Gently he brushed it away from her face and traced his finger along her hairline, down the peak in her forehead and over to the other side.

"They call this a widow's peak," he said.

"My mother had one and she was never a widow." Damaris opened her eyes and gazed up at him. "Why are you so preoccupied with death these days?"

"I'm not." He kissed her forehead, her nose, her cheek, then nuzzled in the warmth of her hair.

"Gavin, I'll not allow anything to happen to you."

He didn't answer for a long time. "Your love keeps me safe."

"You're humoring me," she accused softly.

He looked into her eyes. "Never would a husband leave a wife more reluctantly if anything should happen to me. But we can't know what will come of this siege. It grows more desperate by the hour. Do you think for a moment that Sir William would be as gallant toward me as I was toward his men?"

"I'll not let anything ill befall you." Her voice was firm and he found himself almost believing she had that power.

"Then I'll trust completely in you and our love." He wanted to ease the worry in her mind. He couldn't lie to her. He didn't want to try. She knew what position the castle was in and that disaster would beset them if Sir William was able to win the standoff. At the same time, if it gave her peace to think she could keep him safe, what harm could it do?

She relaxed into his embrace. "Good. Trust me."

He rubbed his cheek against her hair. "I do. I'll trust you forever. Just as I'll always love you."

"I love you," she echoed. Her voice was softening as she drifted into sleep.

Gavin continued to hold her. He slept little these nights. Part of him was always alert to signs that the enemy had found a way past the walls. She might believe she protected him, but he was the one who would be ready to leap into battle at the slightest unexplained sound. He eased her head into a more comfortable position on his shoulder. If love was as magic as the bards said, perhaps he was protected. He knew he couldn't bear to leave her for any reason, not even one beyond his control.

Chapter Seventeen

All the next day Damaris had the uneasy feeling that something was about to happen. When she looked up at the men standing guard on the hourds she saw the same restlessness in them. She located Gavin on the wall that overlooked the sea.

"Why haven't they come?" he demanded in frustration as she came to stand beside him. He struck the stone crenel with the flat of his hand. "Why the devil haven't the men come from the queen?"

"I don't know." She followed his gaze to the ribbon of land on the horizon that she knew to be England. The day was exceptionally clear and she could even make out the fishing village that huddled against the shoreline. The houses seemed tiny in the distance.

"I had to give orders to start killing the horses today." The words seemed to stick in his mouth. "God, I hated that! There's nothing so noble in my mind as a horse!"

"You didn't tell them to start with Woden or Merlin, did you?"

"No. The older ones will go first. Woden will be among the last. He's a trained war-horse. If we're forced to eat him, it will the most expensive meal any of us will ever consume." She could tell that speaking those words almost choked him.

Damaris reached out to touch him in comfort. "It won't come to that. Can't you feel it? Something is in the air."

"I don't feel anything."

She wasn't sure she believed him. He was looking around and sniffing the air like a hound searching for a trail. His eyes, as green as the sunlit sea, were narrowed and alert. "I never see you at the breakfast table," she said. "Do you never eat in the morning?"

"Not these days." He smiled down at her. "Don't start worrying about that. I'm all right."

"You have to keep up your strength."

"You didn't doubt my strength last night."

Damaris found herself smiling. "We aren't talking about the same sort of strength, I believe. I certainly see no weakness there."

He pulled her to him and looked into her eyes. "I do feel something in the air. It's like a storm is building, but the sky is clear." He looked back at the sea. "I've felt this before a battle at times."

Fear leaped into her throat. "Do you think Sir William is going to try something new?"

"I don't know. That's why I came up here. Most of my men are watching the green. I thought someone should check the ocean from time to time. Perhaps more ships will be arriving from Scotland." He glared back at the English coast. "Pray that I'm wrong and that we'll see English sails."

"I do. Regularly." She looked at the area where ships were most likely to sail from. The sea was empty, its surface marred only by the incessant waves that lifted the water into rolling troughs and mounds. "Meg says she's wondering if St. Cuthbert is taking a nap."

"If he is, let his sleep be troubled. We may need his protection before the day is out."

She moved restlessly to the next crenel and braced both her palms on it. "The villagers also seem to feel something is about to happen. They're milling about more today than usual."

"They're accustomed to much more activity than this. This enforced break from fishing and tending their business must be frustrating to them."

"I didn't see Wat."

Gavin didn't answer for a minute. "I wish we could rid ourselves of him. That man isn't to be trusted."

"I know. I'm glad Bess will be staying in the castle and away from him when this is over. Their children don't need such a man to pattern their behavior after. And she's growing large with yet another babe."

She ran her hand over her middle as she spoke. This morning she had been nauseated. Meg had attributed it to hunger, but Damaris was becoming more and more positive that it was caused by a happier reason. She looked over at Gavin. Now wasn't the time to tell him. Not when he was so worried about everything else.

After a while she said, "Lettice thinks she's in love."

"Oh?" He glanced at her with some of his old amusement. "Who's the man?"

"Don't laugh. It's Robert."

"Not my Robin!"

"Is it so odd? He's a handsome man and has no wife. He speaks to her often and is kind to her."

"True." Gavin thought for a minute. "Now that you mention it, he does seem to hang about the parlor more often than before. I wonder if the feeling is mutual."

"My only concern is that she's so young! She's practically a child!"

"She's fifteen, isn't she? I had sisters married at that age. It's not so young."

"Lettice will have a dowry. I'll see to that." Damaris shook her head, but she was smiling. "She came to the castle when she was a lass of thirteen. So did Kate. They're cousins, you know."

"So is almost everyone on this island."

"Her father is the boat builder and her older brothers have the forge. Her family is well-thought-of here."

"Are you matchmaking? Your efforts are wasted on me. I won't urge Robert one way or the other. He's a grown man and can make up his own mind."

"In spite of her age, if Lettice is truly in love with him, I want her to be happy. And she can hardly speak to him on her own behalf," Damaris objected. "I suppose I could speak to him, but..."

"Let's wait a while and see if the love is real enough to last. As you've said, Lettice is young."

"But as *you've* said, other women are married at that age. That's about the age I was when Papa started suggesting that I should be married."

Gavin smiled and came closer. "Love is an amazing thing. It seems to grow best under the most unlikely circumstances. A siege is hardly the place I'd have thought best suited to engender tender feelings."

"Or maybe these are the conditions that make it most likely. After all, we don't know what tomorrow may bring or if there will even be a tomorrow."

"There will always be another tomorrow. All that changes are the people who are around to view it."

Damaris nodded. "At least they have the pleasure of falling in love. That's nearly as pleasurable as love fulfilled."

"Aye. I would never have cast you in the role of matchmaker," he teased. "Not when you were so determined to remain unmarried yourself. The next thing I know, you'll be choosing Godfrey for Meg. Let me warn you, you'll be mistaken there. I've never seen a man more determined to remain a bachelor."

"And it's good that he is. Sir Godfrey isn't husband material, if you ask me. He's much too gruff."

Gavin grinned. "You're right about that."

Damaris heard a noise coming from the direction of the courtyard and she glanced back but saw no reason for concern. "Has Sir William been shouting his promises again this morning?"

"He never lets more than a few hours pass without repeating them. And he's already put a boar on the spit. Can't you smell it cooking?"

"Aye." She pressed her palm against her stomach to prevent its growling. Again the sound from the courtyard drew her attention.

Gavin was looking in that direction, also. "Is there trouble down there?"

"All was quiet when I passed through on my way here." She saw the men nearest the gate step back to watch whatever was happening below them in the enclosed area. No Scots were anywhere near the gate.

"I think I'd better go see what's happening."

Damaris followed him along the hourds and onto the stones of the thicker, newer wall. As the courtyard came into view, she saw people milling about. Wat was in their center. She couldn't hear what he was saying, but the villagers were all listening intently. Gavin walked faster.

"We can eat if we go out there," Wat was saying. He poked a finger at one of the women. "Don't tell me you can bear to hear your babies crying for food! All we have to do is go through the gate!"

Gavin shouted for Wat to stop, but he continued to talk. "There's a lot of us and not many of them on the wall today. We can have the gate open before they know what's happened."

Davie and several of the men standing by him looked at the three wheels that opened the gates. Ben rubbed the bristles on his chin thoughtfully.

Wat prodded one of the other fishermen. "What are ye? Cattle to be herded together and penned? We're men! We have the duty to feed our families!"

From within the crowd came a low growl that increased in volume until it was a shout. Damaris stopped on the wall and stared into the courtyard at familiar faces that seemed to be going mad. A movement on the green drew her attention. The Scots had heard the commotion from within and were drawing nearer.

Suddenly Wat shoved away from the others and ran for the wheels. He grabbed the first one and started hauling it around. The wooden gate behind the twin portcullis started to open.

Other men lunged at the remaining wheels and the wooden grilles started inching up. Gavin fitted an arrow into his bowstring and quickly sent it on its way—straight into Wat's back. Wat screamed and fell. Another man took his place.

Damaris couldn't believe what she was seeing. The village men were opening Thornbeck's gates to the enemy! Already the Scots were running across the green toward the gate. The archers on the walls were firing at them, but the Scots saw victory close at hand and weren't to be daunted.

Gavin grabbed Damaris's arm. "Run to the keep! Don't come out!"

She hesitated and he pulled her across the walkway and to the stairs that led to the protected bawn court. "Go!" he shouted when she still refused to move. "Get your women to safety!"

She looked down and saw Meg and the others hurrying along the walkway and through the iron gate that separated the bawn from the courtyard. Damaris hurried to do as Gavin had said.

Meg and the others were crying and in a state of panic. "I called out to the other women," Meg was saying, "but I don't think they heard me. Lettice was talking to Sir Robert when the trouble began, and he said we were to come here. Are the Scots breaking through our gates?"

"What's happening, my lady?" Lettice and Kate cried out, their words overlaying each other. "What's happened?"

"It's Wat. He's caused the villagers to storm the gates from the inside." Damaris opened the door to the keep and pushed the women inside. "Meg! Watch out for them and be sure to bolt the door behind me!"

"You're not leaving us!" Meg grabbed at Damaris's sleeve, but Damaris was already running for the steps that led up the wall.

Damaris didn't waste breath answering. She had to find Gavin and be sure he was safe.

At the top of the wall she stopped in stunned disbelief. In the short moments since she was here last, the Scots had reached the gates. Some had slid inside and were turning the wheels to admit the others. Several lay dead and some dying but more were pouring in the gates as the opening grew wider. They were hacking at anyone they saw, man and woman alike. Shrill screams of terror and pain filled the air.

Damaris caught a glimpse of Gavin's tawny hair and ran along the wall to the steps nearest him. He was fighting with a Scotsman and didn't see her. The clanging of their swords was almost lost in the noise from the battle raging in the courtyard.

She held her skirts near her body so she'd be prepared to run as soon as she knew where to go next. In the corner of her eye, she saw Sir William come through the gates, and she froze. At that same instant, her uncle looked up, saw her and started toward her. Damaris turned and ran to one of the doors that led from the parapets into the castle. She knew a safer way to reach Gavin.

She raced through the twisting corridors of the castle, and when she reached the lower floor, men were fighting in hand-to-hand struggles everywhere she looked. The stone floor was spattered with blood, and bodies lay discarded like broken toys. The smell of fear and blood was heavy in the air. Damaris was so frightened she could scarcely breathe.

From the screens passage she saw several of the castle's maids huddled in a corner of the hall. Damaris ran to them and jerked them away from the wall. "Go to the keep! Tell Meg to open the door!" The women were trembling and crying so hysterically that Damaris had to physically pull them toward the corridor. "Go! There's no time to waste!"

Although she wanted to go to Gavin's side and help him, she knew she had a duty to the castle's women. As quickly as she could, she ran through the nearly empty rooms, calling into the pantries and buttery until she had gathered as many women as she could. "Go to the keep!" she kept shouting. "You'll be safe there! Quickly!"

When she had sent the last of the women on her way, she ran back through the maze of rooms to the hall. The fighting had already spread to there, and she had to dodge from side to side to avoid injury from flailing swords and daggers.

Gavin was outside on the steps. All around him lay dead and wounded Scots, and he was wielding his battle sword tirelessly. Sweat poured down his face and matted his hair; his eyes were dark with battle lust. It frightened Damaris to see him like this, with his fury unleashed. As she watched, he drove his sword through a man, then kicked him free and tumbled him down the steps.

A man in a dark brown tunic roared as he charged at
Gavin, and Damaris gasped as she recognized Sir James
McIntyre, her uncle's second-in-command. Sir William was
right behind him. In spite of William's age, he had his sword
in one hand and his dagger in the other.

Gavin skillfully kept the castle at his back to shield him
from an attack in that direction as he parried with the two
men. Damaris knew he couldn't hold them both off indefinitely. She looked around for a weapon she could use to go
to his aid.

She picked up a discarded sword but found it was far too
heavy for her to wield. Instead, she pried a dagger from a
dead man's stiffening hand and raced toward Gavin's side.
James saw her coming, and while his attention was diverted for a moment, Gavin seized the advantage and struck
him down. He made no attempt to rise again.

As Damaris reached her husband's side, Gavin's attention riveted itself on her. He opened his mouth to shout for
her to run for safety, but just then William dashed up the
steps between them and with a wild war cry, William sank
his dagger to the hilt into Gavin's chest. Gavin staggered, his
expression incredulous, then he stumbled and fell.

Damaris plunged past him, slashing at his assailant with
the dagger in her hand. William was taken by surprise and
flinched back. His foot caught on James's lifeless arm and
he nearly fell. Damaris moved in, seizing the advantage.

William snarled and struck at her, but he was off balance
and missed his mark. She felt the blade whistle past her
cheek. While his arm was extended, she struck at him,
drawing blood. William bellowed and hacked at her. Damaris felt the blade snarl in her skirt and she jerked back,
pulling it from his hand.

William fell and scrambled wildly toward James's dagger. Damaris stabbed at him, but her full skirts hampered
her movements and she missed. Her foot hit a puddle of
blood and she fell. Gavin lay beside her. His face was pale
and his breath was raspy. "Gavin!" she screamed, realizing
suddenly that he was wounded.

Their eyes met and he raised his hand to touch her cheek.
Suddenly William was on his feet and poised to strike her

dead with James's weapon. Using the last of his strength, Gavin lurched to his feet and charged his enemy, his sword red and glinting in the sun. William had believed Gavin to be dead and the move took him by surprise. As Gavin struck his final blow, William tried to plunge the dagger into the base of Gavin's neck but his leather vest deflected it. Locked in mortal combat, they both fell down the stairs together.

Damaris screamed and stumbled after them. A glance told her William was dead. Gavin's sword had all but severed her uncle's head from his body. Gavin lay sprawled across him. She covered Gavin's body with her own and felt a faint rise and fall that showed he still breathed. Using all her strength, Damaris pulled Gavin away from the steps and against the base of the building. Shielding him with her body, she hovered over him, alternately praying and demanding that he not give up.

After what could have been an eternity or only minutes, she heard a slackening in the battle. She dared look up. Robert and Godfrey had marshaled their men and were driving the enemy back toward the gates. The Scots had seen William lying dead on the steps and were in fast retreat. As she watched, they backed the men out of the walls, killing any they could reach. The others broke and ran, many of the castle men hard on their heels. It was clear that the Scots were hoping only to escape with their lives.

"Robert!" she shouted when he passed near her. "Robert! Gavin's been hurt!"

Robert and Godfrey, along with several of their men, hurried to where she lay covering him. Damaris moved away and Gavin rolled limply onto his back. She touched his face and hands, mumbling incoherently as tears coursed down her cheeks, but he didn't respond.

Robert knelt beside him and pulled aside his jerkin to examine the wound. He looked up at Godfrey and they exchanged a worried look.

"He's not dead!" Damaris cried. "He's not! I can feel his heart beating!" She pressed her fingers against his neck and felt the irregular rhythm. "You have to help him!"

Robert covered her hand and took it away from Gavin. "He's gravely wounded, my lady. Both blows went in above his leather vest. He's lost a lot of blood."

Damaris stared at him, then struggled to free her hand. "No! He's not going to die!" She looked around wildly. "You! And you! Help me carry him!"

Robert gave Godfrey another look and Godfrey nodded as if something had been decided between them. Together they knelt beside Gavin and lifted him up. "Where will we take him? To your chamber?"

"No!" Damaris gathered her skirts and rose. "To the Maidens!"

Godfrey frowned. "My lady, you're talking madness. Let us take him up to your chamber so he may rest in his own bed."

Damaris stormed up to the large man and struck at his arm. "If you won't carry him, give him to someone else, but I will be obeyed!"

Robert looked as if his own heart were breaking as he gazed down at Gavin's pale face. "If it will ease your pain, my lady, I'll take him to the stones." To Godfrey, he said, "Help me carry him."

Damaris ignored him. "Hurry!" she said as she ran toward the gate. "Hurry!"

Robert and Godfrey, flanked by several of the men who had been close enough to hear the exchange, carried him for her. Damaris was breathing hard by the time she reached the avenue. The flanking rows of stones were like welcome faces to her after so long an absence. She paused only to be sure the men were still following, then hurried into the circle.

Some of the men hesitated, but Robert and Godfrey carried Gavin into the circle and lay him on the flat surface of the altar stone. Damaris was standing before the Priestess, staring silently up at the hole in its center.

"My lady," Robert said in a voice made husky by his concern, "let me take him back."

"Look at him," Godfrey agreed. "He needs to be in his bed. Not up here on a stone!" From the tone of his voice he obviously thought Gavin was dying.

Damaris ignored them both. As the wind whipped her skirts and tore the hood from her hair, she placed both her hands on the Priestess stone. A jolt of power shot through her and she gasped. Keeping one hand on the stone, she reached for Gavin. She put the other hand on his upper chest where the jerkin was soaked with his blood.

"I command that he be healed!" As the wind tore at her words, Damaris felt a tremble course through her. "I command that you restore him to me!"

In all the years she had come here, she had never commanded the stones. For a dreadful moment she thought it wouldn't work. Damaris closed her eyes and concentrated.

Once again the shuddering power roared through her. Despite the fear this unaccustomed feeling instilled in her, she didn't break the contact and turned all her thoughts to Gavin and their love.

She heard a gasp and felt the smallest of movements beneath her palm. Gavin's chest rose suddenly as if he had been holding his breath and was gulping in air.

Damaris opened her eyes and saw him breathing and trying feebly to move. Damaris pulled her other hand from the stone and put it over the cut on his neck and pressed as she concentrated in earnest. She refused to allow him to die.

After a while she was aware of voices around her. She swayed and almost fell. All at once she felt totally drained and exhausted. She let herself sag against the altar stone and stared down at Gavin.

His eyes were open and he was looking around, clearly confused to find himself in this place. Robert and Godfrey were hovering over him, pulling at his jerkin. "The bleeding has stopped!" Godfrey exclaimed.

"Impossible!" Robert ripped the clothing away to expose the leather chest covering. Like Gavin's clothes, it was soaked in blood. However, the two gashes above it were no longer bleeding. "How is this possible? I thought he was bleeding to death in the courtyard!"

Godfrey took a step back and stared at Damaris. "We must have been wrong about the cuts being so deep. I believe he'll live!"

Gavin was trying to sit up. Damaris eased her leg under his head to cushion it. "Be still, love. Rest," she said soothingly. "You mustn't move about so soon." She was so tired she felt as if part of her life force had flowed into him to restore what he'd lost.

"Damaris," he whispered. "What—"

"The battle is over." She lifted her head and looked at the sea. "Even now they're running back to the mainland." She helped him turn so he could look at the boats heading back to Scotland. "Sir William lies dead and you've won."

Gavin closed his eyes and lay his head back in her lap. "I'm so tired." He didn't question why he was here. He hadn't the strength.

Robert gestured to the men who were standing in a tight knot in the center of the stone ring. "Help us carry him back. Gavin lives!"

All the way to the castle, Damaris walked by Gavin and held his hand. Whether Robert and Godfrey believed the Priestess had healed Gavin didn't matter. All that was important was that he was alive and seemed likely to stay that way. She could feel life in his hand.

By the time they returned to the castle, Meg and the women had been coaxed out of the keep and were standing in the screens passage wringing their hands and crying. When they saw Damaris, they ran to her. Their hugs were almost enough to pull Damaris from her feet, as weak as she felt. When they realized the men were carrying Gavin, they hurried ahead of them to make the bedchamber ready.

Damaris had the men lay Gavin in the bed on the coverlet Meg had spread over the sheet. Kate had already run to find water to wash his wounds. Lettice and Robert were embracing by the window and holding each other in silent relief that both were still alive and unharmed. Damaris bent closer so Gavin could see her face and smiled. "You're safe now."

When she started to straighten, Gavin pulled her back. "What happened? I seem to remember being in the Maidens," he whispered, his voice still weak.

"I'll tell you all about it later. You must rest now. You have to regain your strength."

Godfrey touched her shoulder. "I've sent men to the village to get food. The Scots left in such a hurry they must have abandoned their provisions."

"Good! I need to give Gavin a meat broth. That will bring him around." She ignored her own hunger in her eagerness to help the man she loved.

Meg came to her. "I was so worried about you! When we were able to leave the keep, I looked everywhere for you!"

"Gavin was grievously wounded. I took him to the Maidens." She looked back at him; he seemed to be sleeping. "I commanded the Priestess to help him."

Meg's eyes widened. "They're saying that he was near death! That the stones brought him back to life!"

"I don't know what happened. Maybe it was because of our love for each other. Maybe Godfrey was wrong about Gavin's wounds being so severe. It doesn't matter. Gavin will recover." She didn't know why she was so positive of that. He was still deathly pale and his chest barely rose with his breathing, but she knew that somehow he was out of danger.

She went to the basin of water Kate had brought and dipped a cloth in it. "I want to wash him. Will someone help me remove his clothes?"

Robert left Lettice and went to the bed. Carefully he cut Gavin's clothing away. It was in no condition to be saved. With a gentleness Damaris had never noticed in him, Godfrey lifted Gavin so Robert could pull the ruined clothing from under him. As soon as she could, she started sponging the blood and dirt from him.

At last her tears of relief began to flow. He had several minor cuts, and bruises were starting to surface from blows the leather vest had diverted. His body looked powerful even in repose and the muscles were like pale marble under her hands. She could feel the life coursing through him, however, and knew he wouldn't stay that pale for long.

Meg brought bandages and helped Damaris bind Gavin's wounds. None of them was still bleeding, but Damaris didn't want to take any chances. Her father had once told her that infection could fly through the air, and she didn't want to risk that. Gavin needed all his strength to recover, without an infection to complicate matters.

When a bowl of hot meat broth was brought to the chamber, Damaris sat on the side of the bed and spooned it into Gavin's mouth. He awoke enough to swallow. He looked into her eyes and she smiled. He lifted his hand and covered her fingers on the spoon. There was no reason to speak. Each could see the other's love and relief at coming through such a terrible ordeal.

Damaris refused to stop feeding Gavin until the bowl was empty. Only then did she turn to the trencher Meg had brought her. The food tasted better than any she had ever put in her mouth. She closed her eyes and enjoyed the scent and taste of the food. It was such a relief to be able to eat her fill, she almost made herself sick.

Meg wanted to make her a bed beside the main one, but Damaris didn't want to be so far from Gavin. She was a bit surprised to discover it was almost dark. "Where did the day go?" she asked.

"It's more like this day has been a month long," Meg retorted. "I'll be glad to see the end of it."

"But it's been a grand day." Damaris went back to the bed and looked down at Gavin. He was sleeping soundly now, with the sheet pulled to his waist. "Gavin and the castle have both been restored to me."

"Sir Godfrey and Sir Robert are saying that he wasn't as badly hurt as they thought at first." Meg looked from Gavin to Damaris and back again. "Sir Godfrey said they thought at the time he was dying, even."

Damaris shook her head. "I don't know. I was there and I'm still not sure. He never stopped breathing, but he had lost so much blood!"

"Sir Robert thinks it wasn't all his. Otherwise, he would never have regained consciousness."

"Perhaps they're right. It doesn't matter. All I care about is that he will heal and be himself again." She looked across the room to where Edith and Kate were pouring warm water into the washbasin for her nightly bath. "I feel as if I could sleep for a week."

"And so you should." Meg turned her around as if she were still a small child and started unlacing her kirtle. "I sent George to his bed when it became obvious Sir Gavin would have no need of him tonight. We're all half-dead on our feet."

Damaris let her women undress her and she stood on the linen square to soap the dirt and blood from her body. Meg gathered up her discarded clothing. "There's no use in keeping these. I'll never be able to look at them again without seeing that dreadful battle."

Damaris shuddered and started to rinse the soap from her body. "I agree. Have them burned. They're stained beyond use."

Kate handed Damaris a linen towel. As Damaris dried herself, she said, "Where's Lettice?"

"In the corridor, talking to Sir Robert." Meg glanced toward the door that led to the series of rooms used by the women. "She fancies herself in love. He's all she talked about in the keep all day."

"I know. I've seen it myself." A deep weariness was settling into Damaris's bones. She wanted only to go to bed.

Edith started working the tangles from Damaris's hair. The task seemed to take forever. Damaris sat on the stool and buttoned her night rail, then let her hands lie in her lap. She felt as if she could fall asleep where she sat.

"Leave off. That's good enough," Meg said. "You'll worry the poor bairn to death with your brushing." She pulled on Damaris's arm. "Come, lass. Get into bed."

Damaris did as she was told. As soon as she climbed into the bed and lay back on her familiar pillow, she felt sleep creep over her. She was dimly aware of Meg covering her with a sheet and closing the curtains. Damaris half smiled to think this was the first time since her marriage that she had slept clothed. Her hand eased across the bed to touch Gavin's arm. She curled toward him and slept.

Chapter Eighteen

Gavin was still weak the next day, but by noon he refused to remain in bed a moment longer. Neither Damaris's reasoning nor Meg and George's grumbling could sway him. Complaining all the time, George helped Gavin get dressed, and when that was done, Gavin went down to the courtyard with Damaris following his every step. Once he was outside, he felt better.

"You're a stubborn man," Damaris said to him, not for the first time.

"Yes, I know." He looked around at the business of lives getting back to normal. Most of the villagers had already left the castle. Those whose houses had been badly damaged by the Scots were staying with friends or relatives or in the church. The people who lived in the castle were also doing their best to reestablish their old routines. He could hear the clank of metal striking metal in the blacksmith's shop and the softer clatter of the looms in the weaving shed. "All looks well."

"I've been at work all morning. Bess and her older daughters are in the weaving sheds. I think they'll make excellent weavers and spinners. Her sons will take longer to place. I'm going to apprentice them to workmen."

"I'll help find them places."

She smiled up at him. "You're a kind master. One would think you had been raised from birth to manage a castle."

"It's to our advantage that I was the one earmarked for a knight. A steward would have fared poorly in the fight yesterday." He reached up and touched the tender place on his upper chest. His eyes traveled to the Maidens on the distant hill. Without a word, he went out the gate and started up the ridge.

Damaris was hurrying to keep up with him. "You shouldn't walk so far! And not so quickly! By all rights you should still be in bed."

Gavin didn't answer her. He had to know if there was any truth to the half memories he retained from the afternoon before.

He reached the high ground and walked into the avenue that led to the circle. Damaris caught his hand but didn't try to hold him back. Gavin entered the circle and paused to look around. The stones stood just as they always had, silent and mysterious.

Slowly he closed the distance between himself and the taller of the stones. At the altar stone he stopped and gazed up at the Priestess. It was silhouetted against a vivid blue sky, and some of the blue seemed to have become ingrained in the rock. He recalled it had always been a slightly different color than the others.

He looked down at the flat stone by his knee. A reddish brown stain was splashed over it. Gavin readily recognized it as dried blood.

"Sir Robert and Sir Godfrey said all the blood couldn't have been yours," Damaris said. "They said most of it must have been Sir William's. You fell together."

Gavin didn't answer. He knew it was possible, but this stain had to have been made by a bleeding cut, not excess blood that had been carried on clothing. He looked back at the taller stone.

"What do you remember?" she asked hesitantly.

"I recall fighting. Sir William and his henchman came at me together. I struck down Sir James. Then I saw you were beside me and this gave Sir William the advantage."

"I'm sorry," she said contritely.

"He struck me with his dagger." Gavin put his hand on his chest. Beneath his clothing he could feel the bandages and a dull ache. "I remember being amazed that it had happened so quickly. I saw you bend over me and I think I tried to speak to you." He shook his head.

"That's all you remember?"

Gavin looked around as if the stones could supply the answer. "No. Suddenly I was in a bright place. A woman was with me." He paused and looked at Damaris. "She bore a strong resemblance to you, but it wasn't you. She never spoke to me, but I knew she was saying that I would be allowed to stay with you. That I wouldn't die. She smiled. Her eyes were so gentle. And I remember they were blue, bright blue. I remember that clearly."

Damaris nodded. "I've seen her, too. I think she's my mother. Or she may be a guardian angel. Or both."

He studied her for a moment to see if she was making fun of him. Her eyes were serious and she was waiting to see what he would say next. "All at once I was falling. I remember gasping and opening my eyes. I was here. And my chest felt as if all the demons of hell were playing there." He touched it again. "None of this makes any sense to me. Robert has told me that you insisted I be brought here."

"They must have thought I was out of my mind, but they did as I asked." Damaris went to the Priestess and gingerly put her hand on the cool stone. "I knew what I had to do. I can't explain it. Common sense would have told me to take you to our chamber until you were strong enough to move safely." Her eyes met his. "If I had, you would have died. I'm sure of it, regardless of what Robert and Godfrey believe."

Gavin shook his head in confusion. "I've fought in many battles. I know I was grievously wounded. By all rights, I should have been bedfast for days. But I was able to dress and walk up here. I can't explain what happened." He put his hand on the stone beside Damaris's. A gentle tingle ran up his wrist and forearm. "I'll never understand it. You almost convince me of the stone's magic."

Damaris covered his hand with hers. "Gavin, I've something to tell you."

Before she could say more, a trumpet sounded from the castle and Gavin looked up in apprehension. A lone ship was coming across the water, not from the angle that would have meant it was from Scotland, but rather from England.

"So. They arrive at last." Dread knotted in him. The next few hours would tell whether or not his marriage to Damaris would be allowed to stand.

Damaris looked fearfully at the ship. "It's flying the queen's colors."

He took her hand. "I won't leave you." Her fingers were cold in his and he knew she was more afraid than she was allowing him to see.

"Of course you won't. Nor will I leave you. Come. We have visitors." With more confidence than he would have thought she could summon, Damaris started back to the castle.

By the time they reached Thornbeck, boats from the ship were docking. The castle was in turmoil. Even though the ship was flying the queen's colors, memory of the Scots' invasion was still too raw for strangers to be viewed with anything but trepidation.

Damaris turned her efforts to calming her people and explaining that they were in no danger now. This, she explained, was the rescue they had requested. By the time the group of men from the English ship reached the castle, Damaris and Gavin were prepared to greet them properly in the screens passage.

She felt Gavin stiffen beside her as the men came up the steps and she glanced at him. Did he know these men? She smiled and curtsied to the man who led the delegation. "Welcome to Thornbeck."

"A pity you didn't arrive sooner." Gavin didn't smile, nor did the leader.

"I came as soon as I could." The man's cold blue eyes met Gavin's, then raked over Damaris. She wanted to move farther away but held her ground. The man was inches shorter than she was and his face was pallid with scar tissue from the pox. He looked as if he had never seen fit to smile in his life.

Gavin said, "May I present Neville Lord Westcott?"

Damaris glanced quickly from one to the other. A ball of fear settled in her middle. This was the man the queen had chosen to be her husband.

Gavin turned back to Westcott. "Word was sent that we were under siege. Why didn't you come more quickly?"

"I had other obligations. At the last minute, the queen came, as well, and that also caused delay."

"The queen? Here?" Damaris gasped.

"No, my lady. She's lodged in Bamburgh Castle. She requests your presence. And that of Sir Gavin," he added coldly. He seemed to take pleasure in adding, "Sir Gavin is to be sent straightaway to the Welsh border to quell some trouble that's been brewing there." To Damaris, he said, "I intend for us to make our wedding vows before the queen travels south. What a pity Sir Gavin won't be there to hear them."

"You didn't allow me to complete the introductions," Gavin said calmly. "This is my wife, Damaris Rutledge."

It was one of the few times Damaris had heard her married name and it sounded unfamiliar in her ears. She put her hand in Gavin's to stress the fact that she fully condoned their marriage.

Lord Westcott's eyes narrowed and an angry pulse beat visibly in his temple. Damaris tried not to shiver. "Your wife. That remains to be seen." He dismissed the issue by looking around the entry, sizing up the qualifications of the castle as if he were already considering it as his own. His men were doing the same.

Damaris glanced over her shoulder to where her women flanked her. "Meg, send someone for refreshments for our guests." To Westcott she said, "Do you prefer canary wine or alicante?" She knew these were the only wines left in the buttery.

"We've no time for the amenities. Queen Elizabeth expects us back at once."

Gavin finally smiled, but it was without mirth. "It's a good thing you didn't arrive yesterday, or she would have had to wait." He didn't explain but said to Damaris, "Are you ready to meet your queen?"

She automatically looked down at her gown and kirtle. "It's not what I would have worn, had I known."

"Our queen isn't interested in your clothing," Lord Westcott said shortly. "Come."

Damaris lifted her head. "Meg, gather together what we'll need for a stay of one night."

"Yes, my lady." Meg gave Lord Westcott a frigid look, and with Kate in tow, she hurried to do her mistress's bidding.

Damaris kept her hand in Gavin's and offered their guests no further hospitality. When Meg and Kate returned with George and two serving men carrying several trunks, Damaris said, "Now we may go." She didn't allow her fear to show as they followed the queen's men down the steps. Meg and the women, along with Robert and the men who made up Gavin's retinue, went along, as well. Godfrey was left behind and ordered by Gavin to protect the castle.

Lord Westcott made no attempt at conversation. He spent the short journey evaluating the island. Once he turned and looked back at the castle as if to ascertain some future strategy.

Damaris prayed the queen would be lenient and allow her to stay with Gavin at Thornbeck. She knew she would never allow this cold man to touch her or to call her wife—even in their short acquaintance she had seen his innate cruelty.

They boarded the ship and Damaris gazed back at the castle. If all didn't go well, this might be the last time she would see it. If the queen didn't grant Gavin the right to remain her husband, Damaris was preparing herself to give up all her claims to Thornbeck and live with him, however they might be able.

Gavin and his men were almost as stern and silent on the journey as were Lord Westcott and his retinue. Damaris didn't feel like talking, either. Meg and the other women spoke only in whispers. This was the first time Kate and Lettice had been off the island. Damaris wished it had been under happier circumstances.

The ride to Bamburgh Castle took less time than Damaris would have wished. Even so, they arrived so late there was no hope of seeing the queen and returning to Thornbeck before the following day. The castle was built on rock and looked as formidable as Thornbeck but not as inviting to the travelers. Damaris and Gavin were given separate rooms, though on the same floor.

Damaris looked up at Gavin. "What does this mean? Why aren't we to be together?"

He shook his head. "It must mean the queen has not yet recognized our marriage." He managed a smile. "No doubt all will be set straight in the morning."

Gil was there and he was grinning broadly at the sight of familiar faces. "I was afraid the worst had happened by now," he said. "Did you send the Scots back where they belong? Was there any fighting?"

Damaris put her hand on his arm. "Gil, I have to tell you. There was fighting. Your father was one of the casualties. He's to be buried in the churchyard today."

Gil blinked but showed no emotion. "And what of my mother and the little ones?"

"I've asked them to stay in the castle. They're well cared for." She saw no need to tell him that his father had died as a traitor to Thornbeck or that Gil's mother would have stayed in the castle whether his father had lived or not. If Bess wanted her son to know, she could tell him herself.

He looked relieved. "Bless you, my lady."

Gavin said, "Do you know if the queen received my letter asking her permission for me to marry Damaris?"

Gil nodded. "I was pleased to hear it, Sir Gavin."

"And the queen?"

"She was less than pleased."

Gavin nodded. "I thought so. We'll remain apart tonight, Damaris. There's nothing to be gained by flaunting our marriage. Discretion is important in such matters."

"Is my father-in-law here?" she asked Gil. "I want to meet him."

"No, his health prevented him making the journey. He was to stay at his London house until our return. He asked me many things about you, my lady. I answered them as well as I could."

She smiled at the boy. "I'm sure you did well."

Gil grinned. "I like him. He reminds me of a grandfather." He realized he was speaking of Gavin's father and he ducked his head as if he thought a reprimand might be coming.

Gavin ruffled the boy's hair. "He would be amused to know that." To Damaris, he said, "You'll meet him in time."

She knew what he meant. If they didn't return to Thornbeck, they would go to his father in London. Once there, they could decide what course to take and where they might live. She tried to look as if the thought didn't frighten her. They would have a place to live, but she wasn't at all sure she wanted to spend the rest of her life on someone else's estate, much as Edith was living at Thornbeck. As a younger son, Gavin might not have another choice. "I'm looking forward to knowing him," she said with a show of confidence.

She went to her quarters with Meg and the others. Women from Bamburgh's staff had prepared the room, and they gave the newcomers appraising looks as they left. Damaris went to a window and looked out.

"We'll be all right, won't we?" Meg asked as she stepped beside her. "I never expected any of this. Did you?"

"No. Who could have guessed the queen would take it in her mind to make one of her progresses to Northumberland at this time?"

"I hope I packed the proper gown and kirtle. We were so rushed, I hardly knew what to bring." Meg glanced back to where Kate and the others were unpacking the trunk. "I had to run find George, as well, and have him gather things for Sir Gavin and his men. Thank goodness he seemed to know what to do."

"He may be accustomed to packing quickly. Gavin's life hasn't been like ours." She looked out at the land. "You can't see the sea from here."

"No, not from here."

"I'll miss it if I'm not able to return to Thornbeck. I love the sea. It's been just outside my window all my life."

"Not return!" Meg exclaimed. The other women stopped unpacking and stared. "Not return to Thornbeck?"

"You may as well know." Damaris couldn't look at her women. She let her finger trail down the thick pane of wavy glass. "If the queen doesn't recognize my marriage to Sir Gavin, I intend to renounce my claim to Thornbeck. She can award it to Lord Westcott if she likes, but I'll refuse to be a part of it."

"Can you do that?" Lettice asked. "Would you be allowed?"

Damaris wasn't at all certain. "Yes. One way or another. So you all need to decide. If it comes to that, will you return to the castle or go with Sir Gavin and myself?"

"I'll never leave you," Meg said firmly.

Damaris touched her arm affectionately. "Don't answer too quickly. I have no idea where we'll go or how we'll live. All your families are on the island." She looked at Edith. "I can't ask you to travel and live under difficult conditions. Your joints ache in the winter and you need proper food that won't hurt your teeth." She looked at Kate. "Your mother would be so unhappy if she were never to see you again."

"I would come with you," Lettice said.

Damaris smiled sadly. "You mean you would come with Sir Robert." When the girl smiled and blushed, Damaris added, "We'll see. I, too, have much to think on." There was the matter of all the others she had left behind. They expected her to be gone one night. Not a lifetime.

The following morning she and the others were dressed early in hopes of an audience with the queen. Damaris hadn't slept well. She was already too accustomed to sharing a bed with Gavin and hadn't been able to relax without him beside her. On top of that, her sleep had been troubled with nightmares. In the dark hours before morning, it didn't seem all that farfetched that Bamburgh Castle had been the scene of the enchantment that spawned the Laidley Worm. Or that the evil sorceress was still hidden in one of the caverns beneath the castle, transformed by her evil into the guise of a speckled toad. There was something about the castle that invited such speculation.

She was glad to find Gavin and his men. "Have you heard when she will see us?" she asked. Her heart was racing and her palms felt damp and clammy. "What will we say to her?"

"We'll tell her exactly what happened. Queen Elizabeth is a reasonable woman." He looked at her tenderly. "You look as if you hardly slept."

"So do you."

"I missed you." Even though his voice was pitched low so no one could overhear them, Damaris found herself blushing.

"You should remember your wound. It will be a while before it matters if I'm in your bed or not," she retorted.

"I heal quickly." He flexed his arm. "In fact, this is healing remarkably fast."

They ate from the sideboard in one of the long rooms and joined a crowd of people in the set of rooms where the queen was granting audiences. Damaris was reminded of the times in her childhood when she and her father had journeyed to court. Bamburgh wasn't as grand as the royal palaces, but the people still glittered with fine cloths and jewels. Damaris was glad Meg had had the presence of mind to pack her best gown and kirtle.

It was almost noon before they were led into the audience chamber. Damaris wasn't shy by nature but she was taken aback by the lushness of the surroundings. When Elizabeth made a royal progress, she traveled with all the comforts of her home. The walls were covered with rich tapestries and there were even carpets on the floor, rather than hanging on the walls. Elizabeth sat in a chair as elaborately carved and gilded as any that graced the royal palaces. The queen was no less brilliant than her trappings.

She wore a white gown embroidered with gold and silver thread. The bodice was encrusted with jewels and precious stones. More jewels were scattered in the embroidery pattern on the wide skirt of her gown. Her kirtle was scarlet velvet and held more of the elaborate embroidery. Her chemise at neck and wrist was of lawn so fine as to be almost transparent. On her wrists, fingers, neck and ears were jewels of such size and brilliance as Damaris had never seen before.

Damaris's memory of court was that of a child. Now she realized the extent of the opulence. She made a deep curtsy. Beside her, Gavin bowed. When the queen nodded, she rose to her feet.

"I have received your letter," Elizabeth said as Gavin straightened. "I was not pleased."

Damaris glanced to one side and saw Lord Westcott and his men standing together, frowning at them. Seeing him so casual in the queen's presence almost unnerved Damaris.

"I ask your pardon, your majesty. On Thornbeck it's easy to forget proper protocol." Gavin smiled at the queen as if he had frequently had conversations with her.

Elizabeth didn't return his smile. She gazed at Damaris until Damaris shifted uncomfortably. "I take it this is the woman you'd have me agree that you marry." To Damaris she said, "I recall your father. He was a loyal subject."

"Aye, your majesty. He was. Papa died trying to defend Thornbeck for England." Damaris thought it couldn't hurt to remind her queen of that.

Elizabeth shifted a bit in her chair and her jewels danced in the changing light. She was just past her prime but still looked youthful. Her hair was red and curly and was combed back from her unusually high forehead. Her face bore no obvious traces of the smallpox she had endured less than a year before, and her eyes were bright. Damaris was struck by their intelligence and quickness. She thought Elizabeth would still seem every inch a queen if she were dressed in sackcloth.

"You're aware that I've chosen another man for you?" she asked Damaris.

Damaris glanced at the baron. "Yes, your majesty. But I don't prefer him."

Elizabeth seemed surprised at her answer. "How can you know that, even if it mattered? You couldn't have met him more than a day ago."

"Aye, but I already love Sir Gavin." She looked up at her husband. "I would have no one but him."

Gavin said, "There's something else you may not know as yet. Damaris and I were married over a month ago."

Elizabeth sat even straighter and she lifted her chin in a way that signified displeasure. "You're married? Already?"

"Aye, your majesty. By the chaplain at Thornbeck."

"Why did you ask my permission if you planned to take matters into your hands whether I should say yea or nay?"

"I sent another letter to tell you what I had done. I assume it never reached you. We thought it best to be married because the Scots were upon us and we knew not how it would go."

"I don't see that being married would have affected the outcome one way or another. Did you not receive my letter telling you I was sending Lord Westcott to the island?"

"We married before the letter arrived," Damaris said quickly. "It barely made it to the island before we were surrounded." This wasn't quite true, but they had known of the queen's decision for less than an hour before the ceremony. The chaplain might not remember the sequence for certain and the date set in the registry was the same as the invasion.

Elizabeth looked from one to the other as she considered. "You have displeased me a great deal, the two of you."

"I'm sorry for that," Gavin said. "That was not our intention."

"I could have the marriage annulled." Elizabeth seemed to be thinking out loud.

"Our fathers arranged the match before Papa died," Damaris said. "He wanted me to marry Gavin. I was only following his orders."

"I was under the impression that you had refused him."

Damaris fell silent. How had the queen known that? She saw now why so many English subjects viewed the queen as almost a deity. Then she recalled that Gavin's father lived at court and might have mentioned the proposed match to the queen.

"Thornbeck is a strategic island," the queen was saying, her eyes on Lord Westcott. "That's why I want one of the peerage in control of it. Sir Gavin is a brave knight but he has no title. He can't command enough men to protect the castle."

"He has the loyalty of all the men on my island," Damaris objected. Gavin tried to silence her with a stern look but she knew she had to argue her case or lose him. "They all love him and would fight to the death at his command. Many of them already have."

"What do you mean?"

"The Scots laid siege to Thornbeck and it lasted until two days ago, your highness. All the men of the castle and most of the village men fought most bravely under Sir Gavin's command."

"Until two days ago, you say? Why wasn't I told of this?" She looked back at Lord Westcott. "You led me to believe your men arrived well over a week ago to rescue Thornbeck!"

"I saw no reason to concern you," he said smoothly, casting a glare at Gavin. "The Scots have been quelled and Thornbeck hasn't been lost. As I expected, Sir Gavin was able to carry through without mishap."

"Without mishap?" Damaris exclaimed. "You saw the graves being dug in the churchyard as we passed. You couldn't have missed seeing them! Those were my people being buried and you don't consider that a mishap?" The queen's words finally sank in. "You were sent to rescue us and you didn't come!"

Gavin nudged her pointedly as he glared at Westcott with barely leashed fury. Damaris bit back the rest of what she wanted to say.

"I didn't notice the church," Westcott said silkily. "I saw no burials. I did exactly as your majesty ordered me to do. I went to Thornbeck and I ascertained there was no problem that needed my intervention. As I was instructed, I brought back Sir Gavin and Damaris Fleetwood."

"Damaris Rutledge," she corrected icily. "We told you at Thornbeck that we had married."

Westcott looked as if he would like to strike her but he kept his silence. Damaris knew she was taking a grave risk in making him her enemy. There was no guarantee that she wouldn't be sent back to Thornbeck as his wife.

"What brought about the end of the siege?" Elizabeth asked. Her bright eyes were darting from Gavin to Westcott and back again.

"One of the villagers broke under the threats and promises of the Scots' leader, and opened the gates." Gavin drew in a deep breath. "During the battle, their leader was killed, and the Scots army quickly dispersed. They retreated to Scotland as fast as they could flee."

"The leader of the Scots was my uncle, Sir William Fleetwood," Damaris added. "He was the man who murdered Papa. All these years, Sir William has been the primary threat to Thornbeck. Gavin killed him."

"I see." Elizabeth tapped one jeweled finger on the arm of her chair. "Sir Gavin, you were only doing the job I sent you to do. I see no reason in this to award you the lady of the castle."

"Your majesty, may I speak?" Robert said as he stepped forward and bowed.

"You may."

Robert looked at Gavin and Damaris. "There's more that you should hear. This wasn't merely a battle where Gavin is concerned. In the fight with Sir William, he was dealt a grievous blow. One that might have killed him."

The queen looked at Gavin with interest. "Yet he stands before me. How can this be?"

Robert shook his head. "I know not. I thought Sir Gavin was severely, perhaps mortally, wounded. Our lady Damaris ordered that we take him to a certain ring of stones that lies on a hill on the island. When we did, his bleeding stopped."

Elizabeth leaned forward, her eyes intense. "What are you saying, sir knight? That the stones somehow made him well?"

"These stones are rumored to be magic, your majesty," Damaris said hastily. "When I was born, my mother saved me from the fate of all my brothers and sisters who came and went before me by passing me through the hole in the stone. I had Gavin taken there in hopes of saving his life, and as you can see, he lived."

Robert pointed at Gavin's chest. "He was wounded here, your majesty. Twice. I saw the wounds myself. I've seen men die of less." He pointed to Gavin's chest. "I believe not in magical stones, but his bleeding did stop."

"Show me," the queen commanded.

Gavin loosened his jerkin, doublet and shirt. As he pulled the cloth aside a murmur spread around the room.

"That appears to be a less serious wound than you say," Westcott said. A cold, mirthless smile lifted his lips. "I believe they're lying, your majesty."

"Silence." Elizabeth frowned at him. To Gavin, she said, "I find your story intriguing."

"I can't explain it, your majesty, but I swear on my father's life that it happened just as Robert has said." Gavin pulled his clothing straight and started relacing it.

Robert continued. "I know it's not my place to say it, but all I know is that if any two should be together, it's these two. It's always been said that true love can do the impossible. As I've said, I believe not in these stones. But his wounds were deep and it's my opinion that he lived rather than leave his lady." He frowned as if he had realized that his last statement might leave him open to ridicule. "He was gravely wounded in your majesty's service. And his battle strategies were brilliant. No one else would have gotten us through the siege with so little loss of life."

Elizabeth seemed to be considering this. Damaris slipped her hand into Gavin's. It might not be proper protocol, but she was too frightened to be so far from him.

"It would seem I can do no less than to grant you the hand of the woman you love," Elizabeth said at last. "It appears you've earned it in your defense of my castle."

Damaris caught her breath. Was she hearing the queen correctly? In her state of worry she wasn't certain. She had one other argument that would work in their favor. After taking a deep breath, she said, "There's one other thing. The marriage has been consummated. I'm with child." She heard Gavin draw in his breath and she glanced up at him.

"You seem surprised, Sir Gavin," Elizabeth said wryly.

"I had no time to tell him until now." Damaris smiled up at Gavin. He was looking at her as if she were the most precious object he had ever seen.

Elizabeth glanced from one to the other, clearly interested in this exchange. "I'd still have the island commanded by one of my peerage, however. Kneel, Sir Gavin." She extended her hand toward him. Gavin knelt before her. "I create you baron of Thornbeck. You may rise, Gavin Lord Rutledge."

Gavin stood and put his arm around Damaris. "Thank you, your majesty. I swear to always be loyal to you and to raise my children to do the same."

"I assumed that. Otherwise, I wouldn't have granted you this honor. Leave me now before you say something to damage your cause." The corners of her lips tilted up in a hint of a smile and she waved her glittering fingers in dismissal.

Damaris made another low curtsy as Gavin and the men bowed. Now that the audience was over, she was eager to leave the royal presence. For all Elizabeth's majesty, there was an element of danger about her that Damaris found unsettling. She wasn't positive that the royal favor was a steady commodity.

As they were leaving the audience chamber, they heard the queen say, "Westcott, I'll have a word with you now regarding the discrepancy between your story and the truth." From the queen's tone of voice, Damaris felt sure that Westcott was in serious trouble and she had little sympathy for him.

When they were out of the audience chamber and past the two gathering rooms, Gavin pulled her to him. "Is it true? Are you really with child?"

Damaris nodded, her eyes bright. "That's what I was about to tell you yesterday at the Maidens. The time hasn't been right to tell such important news since then."

"That announcement alone might have been enough for Lord Westcott to refuse you. He's overwhelmingly arrogant. He wouldn't willingly agree to marry a woman who was carrying another man's child! Not even for Thornbeck. He's already turned down one proposed marriage for a similar reason, and that woman was a widow carrying the babe of her deceased husband."

"Why didn't you tell me?"

"I had no reason to know it was important." He pulled her into a window recess and drew her to him. "You're sure? You weren't just saying that for the queen's benefit?"

"No. I wouldn't do that. Or rather, I wouldn't have, since I didn't know it would rid me of Lord Westcott."

Gavin brushed her lips with his kiss. "I'll take good care of you, Damaris. Of you and the babe."

"Just continue loving me and take me back to Thornbeck. That's all I ask."

"I could never stop loving you."

By this time Robert had found them. "So now we must call you Lord Rutledge! I always did say you were born under a lucky star!" Robert laughed heartily. "And you've already started your line! Remarkable!"

"I'm still getting used to idea myself," Gavin said, giving Damaris an adoring look.

Damaris kept her arm around him. "How soon can we leave for Thornbeck?" she asked.

"I'll go find your women and tell them to pack at once, if you like." Robert glanced at Gavin, who nodded in agreement.

"I'm eager to be home," he said with a hug for Damaris. "This has turned out far better than I ever had reason to hope."

"Aye. I was afraid I'd be on my way to be married to that dreadful man by now," Damaris confessed. "It may take a while before I stop looking over my shoulder for him."

"He won't bother us. Not now. He has to answer to the queen." Gavin touched her cheek. "Robert, find the women and let's leave this place."

When they were alone, Gavin drew Damaris back into the recess and farther away from prying eyes. "I want to kiss you and hold you and keep you safe forever."

"And you will."

"Are you afraid?"

She paused. It hadn't occurred to her that he might have also worried about those tiny graves in the chapel. "No. It will go well with us. I can feel it."

"My fairy wife. Will I ever understand these feelings of yours?"

"Most likely not." She smiled up at him. "I mean it when I say I have no reason to think I will have the trouble my mother did. Meg has said she was never of strong health, not even when she first arrived at Thornbeck. I'm never sick."

"I'd rather have you than any babe." Gavin looked worried, even though he tried to keep his voice light. "I've heard of this sort of thing being handed down in families. If I had to choose, I'd pick you over an heir."

Damaris was touched by his words. She knew how terribly important an heir was to any man, especially to one who had only minutes before been made a baron. "You won't have to choose," she said confidently. "You'll see."

Gavin didn't look convinced, but he held her tight until a passing group of people made them give up their refuge. Even as they ascended the stairs to find Meg and the others, he held her hand firmly. Damaris walked lightly by his side. She was certain she would never have to fear anything again. Not with his love to protect her.

Epilogue

"What are you doing out of bed?" Gavin demanded.

"Why are you up here spying on me?" Damaris countered. She went to the cradle and bent over it. "It was most difficult getting all my women to leave me alone for a few minutes."

He came to stand beside her. Their baby lay nestled in the white linens, waving her tiny fists in protest. He felt a warm glow in the center of his heart. "Isn't she beautiful?" he asked in a soft voice. "I've never seen such a perfect baby."

"How many babies have you seen?" she teased as she picked up their daughter.

"I have nieces and nephews by the boatload. None were ever as beautiful as this one. Certainly not when they were newborns."

Damaris cradled the tiny bundle. "You don't mind that she's a girl?"

"I'm not at all disappointed." He reached out and let her grasp his finger. She blinked up at him. "She sees me." He bent closer. "Look what color her eyes are."

"All babies have oddly colored eyes."

"They're violet, like yours! Do you think they'll stay that color?"

"Mine did."

Gavin took the baby from Damaris. She was dwarfed in his arms. "I find myself becoming besotted over her, and I had never laid eyes on her two days ago." He let the baby catch his finger again. "Look how perfect her fingers are! She will be playing the dulcimer before she's a year old! And look at her fingernails! They look like those tiny shells we find on the beach."

Damaris touched the pale red hair on the infant's head. "Alison is a day old now."

"I like that name."

"You liked several others, as well," Damaris said with a laugh. "Alison Damaris Maria Matilda. The child will never learn to say all that, let alone spell it. And I do want our daughters, as well as our sons, to be taught to read and write!"

"Certainly. Then when she follows her mother's example and goes off to battle the Scots, she can leave us a note. As for her name, I only suggested she be named after her mother and grandmothers."

"She sounds as if she should be royalty."

"As far as I'm concerned, she is." He touched the baby's tiny face. "Have you ever felt anything so soft?"

"You should be glad I was able to get rid of my ladies for a while. Meg would never have let you hold Alison for so long."

"I came up here with the intent of sending them all away for a while." He looked at her. "Why did you send them away? Surely Meg doesn't keep you from Alison, as well."

"No, I had something else in mind." She avoided his eyes.

"Damaris, what were you up to? I can tell it's something I won't like."

"I'm going to take her to the Maidens."

He stared at her for a moment. "No." He saw no reason to elaborate so he smiled down at his daughter.

"Gavin, I must."

He looked back at her. "Nothing is wrong with her, is there?" A sense of dread started to build in him.

"No, no. Don't look so stricken. I only want to be certain that nothing becomes wrong." Damaris touched the baby's hand where she was gripping Gavin's finger. "I keep thinking of the tiny graves in the chapel."

"You mustn't think of that," he said gruffly. They had been in his mind, too.

"Look how much we love her already! Could you bear it if anything befell her?"

Gavin was silent for a moment. "Bring her yellow blanket. It's windy out."

They went down the back stairs in order to avoid any of Damaris's ladies who might be returning to the chamber. Gavin held the baby, and Damaris's hand. Her labor to deliver the child had been easy, but she was still to be cosseted, in his opinion. He knew there was no point in trying to persuade her to let him go on this mission alone. Nor could he, as someone had to hand the baby through the stone and someone had to be on the other side to receive her.

As he had said, the wind was strong that day. It flattened the silky May grasses along the ridge and made white froth on the waves offshore. The early blooms on the daisies and clover nodded and bobbed. "I must be addled to allow you to talk me into this," he grumbled as they went down the avenue of stones. "What if you get sick from coming up here?"

"I won't." She drew in a deep breath and turned her face to the wind. "I feel better for getting out."

They entered the circle and he felt Alison stir in his arms. "She seems to know where she is. It looks like I'll have another just like you on my hands."

Damaris smiled up at him and went to the Priestess. She paused, then placed both her palms on its hewn surface. Damaris lifted her face, closed her eyes and seemed to be drinking in strength from the stone. At times Gavin felt he had, indeed, married a fairy bride.

She opened her eyes and took the baby. For a moment she held Alison, smiling down at the tiny face. Then she glanced back at Gavin. "Go to the other side of the stone."

When he was in place, Damaris lifted Alison and handed her through the circular hole in the stone. As she did, the wind lifted and whipped her hair and the corner of the blanket free. The wind sighed through the circle and the Maidens echoed the whisper.

Gavin glanced around as he took the baby. He could well understand why the circle was called the Whispering Maidens. Only a little imagination was needed to see them leaning together in groups as if they were telling one another a secret. The Priestess stood perfectly straight, the sighing sound rising and falling with the wind. Gavin held Alison close to his chest and went back around to Damaris. "Is that all we do? Can we go back to the castle now?"

She smiled. "Almost." She put her hand on the Priestess and closed her eyes again. "I see children. Our children to come. There's a son next, and another boy after him. Then another girl."

Gavin took her hand from the stone. "Enough. I'm not sure I want to know the future."

"It's nothing to fear. I see them all strong and straight and a credit to us. We'll have a son and heir next. A boy to carry on your name and our line."

Gavin looked back down at Alison. She was falling asleep as if the wind were singing her a lullaby. "Will they all be as fey as their mother?"

Damaris shrugged. "You moved my hand away from the stone too soon. Besides, I thought you said you didn't want to know the future."

"I have no need. I can tell by the way she's fallen asleep in such a place that she's going to be exactly like you, hair, eyes and all."

She smiled at him mischievously. "The boys will be like you. At least the first two will be."

He studied her, trying to decide if she was teasing him about all this or not. At times it was difficult to tell. Her hair whipped like a flag about her face and her eyes were like jewels. "Come. I have to get both of you back to our chamber."

As she fell into step with him, he added, "And you can tell Meg that I'm coming back to my own bed tonight. Robert snores when he sleeps and talks incessantly about Lettice when he's awake."

"Meg will say it's too soon."

"I can control my animal instincts," he said in exasperation. "What does she think I am? A beast?"

"You know Meg. She's overly protective of me and now of Alison."

"We should find her a husband. She has too much time to dote on you. She'll spoil Alison shamelessly!"

"Of course she will. And so will you and I."

"That's different. We're her parents."

Damaris laughed softly. He noticed there was a spring in her step after visiting the stone. Gavin decided that was better not dwelled upon. He looked down at the sleeping face of the baby that was already a tiny replica of Damaris and knew he would love them both forever.

*   *   *   *   *

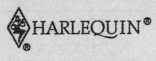

THE WEDDING GAMBLE
Muriel Jensen

Eternity, Massachusetts, was America's wedding town. Paul Bertrand knew this better than anyone—he never should have gotten soused at his friend's rowdy bachelor party. Next morning when he woke up, he found he'd somehow managed to say "I do"—to the woman he'd once jilted! And Christina Bowman had helped launch so many honeymoons, she knew just what to do on theirs!

THE WEDDING GAMBLE, available in September from American Romance, is the fourth book in Harlequin's new cross-line series, **WEDDINGS, INC.**

Be sure to look for the fifth book, **THE VENGEFUL GROOM,** by Sara Wood (Harlequin Presents #1692), coming in October.

WED4

**LOOK TO THE PAST FOR
FUTURE FUN AND EXCITEMENT!**

The past the Harlequin Historical way, that is. 1994 is going to be a
banner year for us, so here's a preview of what to expect:

* The continuation of our bigger book program, with titles such as
Across Time by Nina Beaumont, *Defy the Eagle* by Lynn Bartlett and
Unicorn Bride by Claire Delacroix.

* A 1994 March Madness promotion featuring four titles by
promising new authors Gayle Wilson, Cheryl St. John, Madris Dupree
and Emily French.

* Brand-new in-line series: DESTINY'S WOMEN by Merline Lovelace
and HIGHLANDER by Ruth Langan; and new chapters in old favorites,
such as the SPARHAWK saga by Miranda Jarrett and the WARRIOR
series by Margaret Moore.

* *Promised Brides*, an exciting brand-new anthology with stories by
Mary Jo Putney, Kristin James and Julie Tetel.

* Our perennial favorite, the Christmas anthology, this year featuring
Patricia Gardner Evans, Kathleen Eagle, Elaine Barbieri and
Margaret Moore.

**Watch for these programs and titles wherever
Harlequin Historicals are sold.**

**HARLEQUIN HISTORICALS...
A TOUCH OF MAGIC!**

HHPROMO94

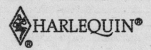

HARLEQUIN®

Don't miss these Harlequin favorites by some of our most
distinguished authors!
And now you can receive a discount by ordering two or more titles!

HT #25525	THE PERFECT HUSBAND by Kristine Rolofson	$2.99	☐
HT #25554	LOVERS' SECRETS by Glenda Sanders	$2.99	☐
HP #11577	THE STONE PRINCESS by Robyn Donald	$2.99	☐
HP #11554	SECRET ADMIRER by Susan Napier	$2.99	☐
HR #03277	THE LADY AND THE TOMCAT by Bethany Campbell	$2.99	☐
HR #03283	FOREIGN AFFAIR by Eva Rutland	$2.99	☐
HS #70529	KEEPING CHRISTMAS by Marisa Carroll	$3.39	☐
HS #70578	THE LAST BUCCANEER by Lynn Erickson	$3.50	☐
HI #22256	THRICE FAMILIAR by Caroline Burnes	$2.99	☐
HI #22238	PRESUMED GUILTY by Tess Gerritsen	$2.99	☐
HAR #16496	OH, YOU BEAUTIFUL DOLL by Judith Arnold	$3.50	☐
HAR #16510	WED AGAIN by Elda Minger	$3.50	☐
HH #28719	RACHEL by Lynda Trent	$3.99	☐
HH #28795	PIECES OF SKY by Marianne Willman	$3.99	☐

Harlequin Promotional Titles

#97122	LINGERING SHADOWS by Penny Jordan	$5.99	☐
	(limited quantities available on certain titles)		

	AMOUNT	$
DEDUCT:	10% DISCOUNT FOR 2+ BOOKS	$
	POSTAGE & HANDLING	$
	($1.00 for one book, 50¢ for each additional)	
	APPLICABLE TAXES*	$_____
	TOTAL PAYABLE	$_____
	(check or money order—please do not send cash)	

To order, complete this form and send it, along with a check or money order for the
total above, payable to Harlequin Books, to: **In the U.S.:** 3010 Walden Avenue,
P.O. Box 9047, Buffalo, NY 14269-9047; **In Canada:** P.O. Box 613, Fort Erie, Ontario,
L2A 5X3.

Name: _____

Address:_____City: _____

State/Prov.: _____Zip/Postal Code: _____

*New York residents remit applicable sales taxes.
 Canadian residents remit applicable GST and provincial taxes..

HBACK-JS